broken GROUND

ANNA PAIGE

For my amazingly supportive husband, Shaun.
Everything I know about love, I learned from you.

ALSO BY ANNA PAIGE

Broken Series:

Broken Ground

Flawlessly Broken

All the Broken Pieces

Thrill of the Chase Series:

Chasing Kade

Thrilling Ethan

Standalone titles:

Off Script

Join Anna's mailing list to remain up to date on new releases and be part of subscriber-only giveaways.

PROLOGUE

Last October

THE SOUND OF splintering wood rang in my ears as I swung the sledgehammer, feeling the familiar burn in my arms as I hefted its weight high over my head. I loved that burn, the fatigue in my muscles, sweat rolling down my back as my chest heaved. That burn was like being energized and relaxed at the same time. It was freedom. My arms continued their protest as I swung again and again, reducing the weathered lumber to a haphazard pile of jagged uneven chunks.

Using reclaimed or salvaged components for my projects meant that I usually got to indulge my destructive side before engaging my creative talents. First I destroyed, then I reinvented. Some of my finished projects could be found in million dollar homes. Several had been featured in magazines. While I took pride in that recognition, I found far more satisfaction in the creative process than in the approval of others. Knowing I could take something broken and battered, something with no apparent value, and turn it into something beautiful; that's what drove me. Thrilled me. Fighting had once given me a similar rush, my youthful temper had landed me in more fights than I

1

cared to count, but that didn't last. Even sex couldn't compare. After years of one-night stands, I decided that sex was just something to do. It was a welcome release, nothing more.

I swung the hammer one more time and left it where it fell, then dragged it over and let it rest on the floor by my feet. The radio played softly in the background, an old Buckcherry song. I inspected the disassembled pile of scrap before me, and an image began to form in my mind. I hurried over and picked up a sketch pad, and turned back to the scattered pieces on the floor as I considered the possibilities. My attention was so focused on the mental picture that I didn't realize I wasn't alone.

The soft scraping sound off to my left barely registered at first. I was accustomed to the stray cat that sometimes came in and sat in the rafters of my garage while I worked. He never got too close, being half-feral, but he was as curious as any other cat, so we just sort of co-existed. I'd leave small treats where I knew he would find them but we never interacted. I assumed he had made another appearance and thought no more of it, but a minute later I heard the sound again and the hair on the back of my neck stood on end. I looked up from my sketch pad and knew my night had just gone to shit.

Marissa stood there smirking as she leaned casually on the door frame, wearing scarcely enough clothing to cover her, much less keep her warm. She was my former assistant and most recent in a long line of indiscretions. She tried to cross one long leg over the other in what I was sure was meant to be a sultry move but actually ended up making her lurch to the side, and nearly fall out the door. I'd have laughed if I wasn't fully aware of what was coming next.

Shit. She's drunk and pissed. This isn't gonna end well.

My last assistant had relocated when her husband was promoted and transferred to the West Coast. When Marissa had shown up with an impressive resumé and glowing recommendation from her former employer, she had been hired pretty much on the spot. Work was so hectic at the time, I could ill afford not to have someone to fill the position. The only problem? She had a few other positions in mind as well, much more personal ones.

I'd studiously ignored her flirtations for weeks, surprising both myself and my business partners with my restraint. Knowing that mixing business with pleasure was always a bad idea, and an even worse idea when you are in a position of authority, I managed to circumvent her advances, keeping a respectful distance.

Okay, I'm no saint. I'm all about the quick and dirty, no-strings hook up. No slow dances, no exchanged numbers, no promises made, and everyone left satisfied. It had worked for me all these years, with very few issues. Avoiding Marissa was less about the issue of propriety and more about the fact that I'd have to work with her afterward. That was breaking my cardinal rule.

Never fuck someone you have to look in the eye every day. Ever. It just invites misunderstanding. No matter how adamant you are that you don't want strings, if you fucked someone you had to see all the time, it wouldn't be long before they looked at you and saw a goddamn marionette.

Case in point? The scantily clad, half-drunk former employee that hovered at the entrance to my shop.

I knew I was in trouble when I walked into work one morning and found her sprawled across my desk totally naked. I may not have been interested, but my dick sure was. One fucking time. One stupid slip up. And it landed me on every-body's shit list. Spencer and Brant, my best friends and business partners, were so pissed they wouldn't take my calls. Marissa, who quit her job after our ill-advised hook-up in hopes that not working for me would clear the way to our happily ever after, had now taken to harassing phone calls, emails, and text messages. Apparently, my lack of response had spurred her right toward direct confrontation.

Just fucking great. Followed my dick right off a cliff again.

Not wanting things to escalate, I gave her a disarming smile.

Her responding sneer did nothing to bolster my hopes. "Well, Clay, glad to see ruining my life hasn't stifled your creativity." She gestured around the shop. "From the looks of this place, destroying things is a habit of yours." she slurred, her face twisted into a hate-filled sneer.

I tried for an authoritative and calm tone of voice. "Marissa, you've been drinking. You aren't thinking clearly right now, so maybe we should discuss this another time." I took out my phone. "Let me call you a cab and we can talk about this later."

She snorted derisively, swaying slightly on her feet as she jabbed a finger in my direction. "I tried to talk to you but you wouldn't answer. I'm sick of being ignored, and I wasn't going to wait for you to decide when I was worth talking to. So here I am. You can't avoid me if I'm right here in front of you."

I quickly typed out a text to Spencer, hoping against hope that he might look at his phone and decide to read the damn thing. I held her eye as I put my phone back in my pocket. "Fine, no cab yet. How bout I get you a cup of coffee?" Gesturing to the small kitchen area to my left, I started to move in that direction. "I can have it ready in no time."

She threw her hands up in frustration. "I don't want any fucking coffee! I want you to tell me what I did wrong!" She staggered through the shop, working her way over to me. "You said we would never happen, but we did. I knew you'd give in. I could tell you had feelings for me by the way you looked at me, the way you made love to me." There were tears in her eyes as she reached me and took my shirt in both hands. Desperately wringing her fists into the fabric, she pleaded. "I knew you'd never agree to a relationship while I was working for you, so I quit. For you. Because I love you. There's nothing standing in our way now, so why don't you want me? Why won't you admit that you love me?" She sobbed as she looked up at me. "Are you trying to make me hate you?"

Goddamn it! I really fucked up this time.

Her shattered expression was tinged with the tiniest bit of hope. That little trace of hope was more painful to see than her tears. I did that. I was fucking stupid, and because of that, everyone around me was either hurt or disappointed or both. Yes, I was up front with her. I told her it was just sex and she agreed to it, which should have absolved me of all guilt but it didn't. I knew before I even had the condom open that it was gonna end badly. I knew I was making a mistake. That didn't stop me though, and now here I stood, watching an endless stream of tears roll down the face of the woman whose heart I just broke.

A part of me was screaming reminders of the crazy things she'd done, the threatening messages that showed a completely different woman than the one weeping before me. Her hatred had come across loud and clear over the last few weeks. And as angry as I was at some of the things she'd said, I was also relieved that she no longer professed her love. Hate was easier to deal with.

She *should* hate me.

I did.

Rather than giving a response that would only cause her more pain, I just stood there silently. She wailed and balled my shirt in her fists, and I allowed her rage at me all she wanted. It was the least I could do. Stupid impulsive mistakes were a habit of mine, some of which I'd never get to atone for. I deserved this, to witness the suffering brought on by my selfishness. I owed her at least that much, since it was the only thing I had to give.

I wasn't sure how long we stood there. Me with my back rigid and head bowed, her with her face buried in my chest, hands still twisted in my shirt as she quietly sobbed. It must have been a while, because ignoring the vibrating phone in my pocket had worried Spencer so much that he came to check on me. I could see his eyes widen as he climbed out of his truck and noticed the other vehicle parked there.

He strode into the shop, eyes flitting over the mess of my work in progress laid out on the floor before he noticed us. He stood stock still and sadly shook his head as he watched her. He gave me a sideways look that told me exactly what he thought: I was getting what I deserved. There was no sympathy for me there, rightfully so. I didn't want him to feel sorry for me. I wanted him to help her. I had no clue how to handle it, how to make it better for her, but Spencer was Mister Sensitive, and I was hoping he'd know what to do.

He nodded to me and made his way over to us. He gently placed a hand on her shoulder, a sympathetic look on his face. She lifted her head from my tear soaked shirt and met his eye. He leaned over and whispered softly in her ear. The radio playing made it impossible to make out what he was saying, which made me nervous. He was just as pissed off at me as she was. I had to hope he would help her first and take his anger out on me later. As he pulled back, she made a soft whimpering sound and looked back up at me.

Having nothing to say to make things better for her, I said the only thing that I could. "I'm so sorry. I really am."

She smiled sadly at me before she released her hold and smoothed my shirt. "Me too."

With that, she turned and made a wobbly path to the door. Looking on as she navigated the various piles of wood, metal, and tools that were strewn about, I asked Spencer, "What did you say to her?"

He also kept an eye on our departing guest as he sighed. "I told her it was time to let go, that it's not her fault, and that the part of you that she's trying to appeal to doesn't exist. You can't possibly understand how she's feeling because you've never allowed yourself to love anyone. Not even your fucking self." He turned to me with a withering look. "I also told her I'd drive her home, so get your keys; you're following us. If I don't take her home in her car, she'll have to come back to get it and I don't think that's in anyone's best interests. Prepare yourself for the return trip. You'll be in the truck alone with me for a decent chunk of time and I intend to have my say. I've fucking had it with this shit. You and I are either going to come to an understanding or we're dissolving the partnership. Brant and I will buy you out, if necessary. We're both tired of *your* dick getting *us* into trouble. We've bailed you out for years but this time you're messing with *our* company." He glared at me a moment before he turned and headed for the door.

I was halfway across the room, after fishing my keys out of my coat pocket, when he popped his head back in. "She says the keys are in her purse and she left it in here."

Shrugging at him, I looked around the room, trying to remember if I had seen it. There was so much shit around the shop that finding it would turn into a game of Where's-Fucking-Waldo. Spencer shuffled in, head down as he inspected the floor and every flat surface he could find while studiously avoiding eye contact.

Shaking my head, I made my way to him. "You keep looking, I'm gonna make sure she didn't leave it in the car because I don't remember her having it when she came in." He grunted in agreement and didn't look up.

When I stepped outside, the first thing I noticed was the sound of a car engine running. I looked over to the source of the sound; it was her Jetta. She didn't appear to be inside it, so I immediately headed to the side of the workshop, expecting to see her bent over the shrubbery, emptying the alcohol-soaked contents of her stomach.

Just as I stepped from the gravel to the grass, the revving of the Jetta's diesel engine pierced the air.

As I spun toward the sound of gravel flying, I heard Spencer yell, "Shit, Clay, look out!"

I barely managed to jump out of the way as the car bore down on me. From behind the wheel, Marissa jerked her head in my direction as I leapt to safety and the sound of twisting metal filled the air.

CHAPTER ONE

Present Day

"YOU WHAT?" SPENCER looked at me like I was stupid. I'd known when I came back to town for this morning's meeting that I'd have to tell him about my plans. He was taking it about how I'd expected.

"I offered to escort Ali to a charity function in D.C. next weekend. A gala, I believe it's called." My voice was even and reasonable.

"That's what I thought you said but I was half hoping I was hallucinating." He reached for a pen from the cup on his desk and began tapping it against the blotter. Yep, he was pissed. "I thought we had an understanding, Clay. I thought you said you'd keep your hands, and everything else, off the fucking employees."

His raised voice set my teeth on edge. He knew better than to shout at me. Rather than react, I sat stoically and waited for him to rein it in. If he didn't, this was going to end badly. I may have been a fuck-up, but I bowed down to no one.

Not even him.

After a failed attempt to stare me down, he sat back in his

chair, rubbing his hands through his perfectly styled hair, leaving it in disarray. "Alright, let's try this again. Explain to me why you thought dating your assistant was okay, particularly given the shit storm surrounding the last indiscretion. The one that was barely eight months ago, by the way."

He was getting on my nerves.

Seeing that he was slowly unwinding, I decided to engage. "It's not a date, Spence. She's a friend, that's all. You're the one who encouraged me to have a non-sexual relationship with a woman. Well, here you go. Ali is it. A friend, someone to hang out with who understands the misery of being stuck out there in Bum-Fucked-Egypt. Nothing more. Hell, you were the one who told me you weren't worried about us hooking up because she's not my type. I believe your exact words were 'too much of a good girl...' and 'out of your league...', remember? And I agree, she's not my type but that doesn't mean we can't be friends. So what's the problem all of a sudden?"

Denson, Virginia, was about as rural as it gets. Working on a project there was a close second to a colonoscopy on my list of shit to avoid. But for the last few weeks, that's exactly what I'd been doing — the project, not the colonoscopy — and the only reason I wasn't half out of my mind was Ali. Her near-constant smile and quick wit had been like a soothing balm for me.

I owed her for that.

And, despite her not being my usual type, I may have also wanted to spend as much time with her as possible, but that was neither here nor there.

Spencer watched me for a long moment before answering. "It's not that I think there's anything going on. I just don't want you put in a position that might tempt you. Let me ask you a question..." he narrowed his eyes, "Does she know who you are and your connection to this build? I mean, I would assume that you told her, given what a close friend she is."

He did not just fucking ask that.

It was my turn to glare. "No, Spence. She doesn't know and I see no need to enlighten her on the subject. As far as I'm concerned, I'm the lead designer and project manager on the build, nothing more. Period. I don't need the small town gossips stirring up shit best left in the past and, to be perfectly fucking honest, I don't need you doing it either." By the time I finished speaking, I was gritting my teeth to the point of pain.

He held his hands up as if to ward off an attack, but spoke in a level, patient voice that indicated he'd gotten the answer he was expecting. "Easy, killer. I wasn't trying to ruffle your feathers. It was just a question. I won't bring it up again but I also won't pretend that I approve of you keeping it from her. If she's as great a person as you say she is, she will understand and — more importantly — as your friend, she deserves the truth." He cut off the terse reply I was poised to deliver and shifted the conversation to business. "I'm glad you're stepping up for a friend, it's admirable. Keep in mind, however, that you'll be attending this event as a representative of the company and anything that transpires — good or bad - reflects on us. Our business reputation has to come first. Even though the Marissa thing isn't public knowledge, we can't afford another mishap like that." The word mishap came out a little forced, as if he was trying his best not to sound condemning. "The last thing we need is to appear vulnerable with vultures like Holden Shepard circling overhead."

Holden Shepard was one of the wealthiest men on the East Coast. He was shrewd, determined, and an utter jackass. He spent nearly twenty years as a notorious womanizer before 'settling down' with the first of five wives. While his personal relationships were sort of an industry joke, his business practices were deadly serious.

Holden got what Holden wanted. Period.

And if his persistent calls and inquiries were any indication, what he currently wanted was a large stake in our company.

Coastal Building and Design, or CBD, was our baby, idealized and then realized by my partners and I. The three of us — Spencer, Brant, and myself — started the business the year after we graduated college and turned it into one of the most prestigious design firms in the Northeast. We had our sights set on expansion but we'd damn well do it without Shepard or anyone else.

Just the thought of that pompous prick having any claim to our company set my teeth on edge. "He's not getting a damn thing, so let him keep wasting his time. He'll fade away eventually. He considers his time too valuable to waste much of it on a dead end. And I have no intention of doing anything to sully the company's reputation or break our agreement, so stop worrying."

After Marissa tried to turn me into roadkill, Spencer had threatened to dissolve the partnership. The only way to set his mind at ease was to agree to sign a contract that could be used to force me out of the company should I do anything 'detrimental to the company name', such as screwing the employees, which in turn, would cause my partners to lose their shit. It was basically a bastardized shareholder's agreement that we'd jokingly nicknamed the 'Clay Clause'.

Spencer watched me for a beat before reaching out and hitting the intercom button. When his assistant's voice came through the speakers, he instructed her to step into his office and bring my assistant with her. My Richmond assistant was nothing at all like Ali. Whereas Ali was closer to my own age, Charlotte was mid-fifties and had a maternal way about her, much the same as Spencer's assistant. The two of them ran the office efficiently and still found time to lecture us about our diets, often bringing in lunches for us as a way to assure our proper nutrition.

He looked at me and gave a sarcastic grin. "I'm trusting you on this but it's going to cost you." There was a knock at the door and he grinned like the Cheshire cat. "If you're going to look presentable while taking Cinderella to the ball, you'll need all the help you can get." He pointed at our assistants and winked. "Nothing better to get you all scrubbed and polished than these two mother-hens."

They stepped forth in a flurry, with a matching set of grins, already chattering about tuxedos and how handsome I'd be with a touch of purple in my lapel to bring out my eyes.

Fuck.

I scowled over at a grinning Spencer.

That son of a bitch was enjoying this.

Truth was, since Spencer handled all of the social obligations associated with the company, I didn't have a tux and I had no idea about proper 'gala etiquette', so I just had to grin and bear it for now. Spencer was going to pay for this shit, though.

Oh yes, he was.

Judging by the look of amusement on his face, I'd need to find my happy place, and soon.

Despite my earlier protests, my mind immediately went to Ali. As it had since the moment she stepped into my life.

Six weeks earlier...
Denson, Virginia

THE LANE LEADING to the property was overgrown, the low-hanging limbs scratching the top of my truck. The screeches of the branches reminded me of a horror film, calling forth visions of claws scraping over bare metal and working wonders on my already frayed nerves.

To someone seeing the place for the first time, the lane would probably be beautiful. Wisteria-laden branches formed a canopy of sorts that was highlighted by fragrant honeysuckle. I remembered that smell, used to love it. Now it's a sickly sweet reminder of the past, remembered pain wafting through the truck's windows on the breeze.

This is bullshit. I should have just refused the job.

What would Gran have done if I had? She was eighty freaking years old and weighed less than a hundred pounds.

I gave Spencer pure hell when he told me he'd double-booked jobs just to get her off his back.

We had never done simultaneous jobs. Ever. Brant and I always worked together on builds, and Spencer's creative scheduling meant we'd be working separately. I was not happy with the situation and made sure he knew it.

His excuse?

"It's Gran, Clay. How would you have handled it? You would have done the same thing I did and we both know it. Gran always gets her way."

Much as I'd wanted to argue, I couldn't. He was right.

She was determined and there was no reasoning with her.

I'd even tried to call her to reason with her, convince her to use another company or reconsider the project altogether. That had gone about as well as one would expect.

She'd chided me for asking how she was doing, claiming the tone of my voice when I asked made her feel like I expected to hear stories of arthritic joints and liver spots when she was perfectly fine. Her oft-used mantra was 'any day spent on this side of the dirt is a good damn day'.

Before I could even begin my gentle prodding she'd cut me off saying she was on her way out to the beach with her friends. My whole body had shuddered when she said, "We're going to soak up some sun and try not to get sand in our wrinkles. I can't be late because it's my turn to bring the booze and Edna gets pissy if she has to wait. Last week at poker night, we ran out of vodka and she raided Betty's cabinets. The dumbass drank two bottles of vanilla extract before she realized it was the non-alcoholic imitation stuff." She clicked her tongue ruefully.

I was still cringing when she made a kissing sound and hung up.

Typical Gran, strategically avoiding the issue.

Which landed me smack in the middle of my own personal hell.

Denson.

Without even the consolation of having my regular build crew or partner to soften the overwhelming sense of isolation.

Brant was off to Charleston to handle an enormous project on his own, taking our usual crews with him. The plan was to check in with one another often, reserving time for at least one strategy session a week using whatever means necessary whether it be Facetime, Skype, or — gasp — an actual fucking phone call. Aside from needing to keep appraised of each other's progress, we also had to put in time designing upcoming jobs, which would probably end up being a never ending string of emails and file shares until we both signed off on them.

It was going to be a long ass summer.

I grunted in annoyance at the mere thought of it, a death grip on the steering wheel.

Dammit, I'd rather be any-fucking-where else than here.

I finally emerged from the lane onto the freshly cleared driveway, keeping my eyes trained on anything except the dilapidated house to my right. Not the best strategy given that I was left to stare at the lake path, which occupied the far left corner of the property's back yard.

Screwed either way.

I parked alongside the house, keeping it in my peripheral vision as I absently flipped off the air conditioning. I had a sudden chill, goosebumps crawling across my flesh.

I sat there for a beat, forcing myself to shift into business mode so I could look at the place with objectivity.

The past is gone. The damage is done. Focus forward.

When I was moderately sure I could manage, I climbed from my truck and turned an assessing eye on my surroundings. The house had never been completed, twenty years of decay causing it to look haggard and spectral. The porch sloped precariously toward sagging stairs, the weathered roof sloping in the same direction and looking about as welcoming as the wide open jaws of a great white shark.

If there was anything to be recovered from that house, I'd be surprised. But I'd leave it to the salvage crew to decide. I wasn't about to set foot in that place.

I shuffled around the property for a while, checking out the side yard and large field that was once horse pasture. Anything to avoid that lake path.

I checked my watch and frowned. The assistant Spencer hired was supposed to be meeting me here to walk the property and give me the keys to the rental house I'd be staying in for the duration of the build. She wasn't due for half an hour, which gave me no excuse not to finish my inspection before her arrival.

Dammit.

According to Spencer, he'd met her when seeking recommendations for contractors in the area. With our usual crews working in Charleston for the summer with Brant, we were in need of qualified crews for the Denson job. Spencer had decided to inquire with the local property manager and see who they used for maintenance and renovations.

Instead of the realtor who owned the place, he'd found Alison Walker who was filling in while the owner was tending to a sick spouse. She offered to help research the local contractors and Spencer was so impressed with her findings that he offered her the job as part-time assistant on the project.

Apparently, the realty office was slow and she was going out of her mind sitting around there all day so she agreed to split her time between there and the build. I was just relieved he found someone on such short notice.

Though I hadn't met her, Spencer assured me that she would be a more than adequate assistant. She was grossly over-qualified for the job according to her résumé. Though she was currently in Denson temping at the realty office, her actual job was as CMO for a major D.C. marketing firm. The title itself was enough to land her the menial position as my assistant, no references required.

Pair that with the fact that she'd taken a leave of absence to come to the boonies and help out a friend... Spencer was beyond impressed, as was I.

A creaking sound off to my right startled me out of my musings; the sound of a house in its death throes.

I blew out a breath and forced one foot in front of the other until I was at the far left corner of the yard, pushing myself to get the unpleasantness over with before she arrived and found me dawdling there like a chickenshit.

I looked toward the lake path, and just as I anticipated, the memory of my grandmother's last trip here overwhelmed my mind, fighting past the carefully erected barricade that had held it back for so many years.

The most gut-wrenching thing I'd ever witnessed played out before my eyes as if I'd stepped back in time. I could see Gran there on the path, walking back from the lake with a small box of mementos tucked under her thin arm and tears streaming down her face. She'd said goodbye to her daughter, not at that stuffy funeral, or a graveside where the grounds crews were standing idly by waiting to throw dirt on the polished coffin. No, she said goodbye in the place my mother, Rebecca, had loved most. The lake. Gran said she could feel her there that day.

Twenty years later, I could still feel her.

She could be seen in everything; from the buttery yellow

petals that lined the path — having fallen from the wildflowers that flanked the walkway on both sides — to the broken cracked earth beneath the aged house.

The sun peeked out from behind a fluffy cumulus cloud and I could feel its warmth on my back, chasing away the chill that had been plaguing me since my arrival. The smell of the honeysuckle growing in huge thatches in the wood line was more pungent than any I'd ever encountered. I could almost taste the tiny droplets of nectar on my tongue, something I hadn't tasted since I was a child. It was a fleeting moment of comfort, gone in an instant and replaced by the bitter twang of regret.

It was my fault. Gran lost her daughter and I lost my mother. All of it... my fault.

She'd been gone nearly twenty years.

Because of me.

Get out of your head, Clay. There's nothing to be gained.

Irritated with myself for losing focus, I swallowed the lump in my throat and strode down the path with heavy steps, as if marching off to war.

I'd barely made it into the clearing when my steps faltered.

The lake was just as I remembered it, large and still with the mountains flanking it on three sides, the lush sentinels reflected in the cool water. The pier showed its age but still stood straight and proud.

Everything was as it had been twenty years ago when Gran made her final trip here.

Except one thing.

The mere sight of that one huge difference was enough to steal the breath from my lungs and cause my chest to tighten painfully.

There at the edge of the water between me and the pier was an enormous willow tree. It had to be at least forty feet tall, with long sweeping branches that nearly touched the ground. It was full and lush.

And impossible.

I just stood there gawking at the damn tree, blinking like a mole as if it were an apparition that would eventually dissolve into thin air.

My heart pounded in my suddenly tight chest and I could hear the rush of blood in my ears.

There's no fucking way.

The last time I was here — the last time anyone was here, for that matter — the tree had been a sapling. A dying sapling that had been split in two, kicked, stomped, and tossed aside like garbage by an asshole kid with emotional problems.

Me.

That day all those years ago, Gran had insisted on bringing several of us with her to the property. She swore she might need help carrying whatever belongings had been left behind, but we all knew she just didn't want to be alone, so we trailed behind her with stoic expressions and counted down the minutes until we could leave.

The entire property had been so cloaked in sadness and despair that none of us could find our voice. We wouldn't have known what to say anyway. Our ages ranged from twelve — like myself — to fourteen. All boys. All clueless as to how to comfort her.

Me being her grandson, the other boys had expected me to know what to do.

All I had to offer was guilt and anger, which I had taken out on the tiny tree my mother and I had planted by the lake.

When Gran found the battered sapling, she'd emitted a choked sob that I could still recall to this day.

It was heartbreaking.

And the sapling had ultimately been left behind, all hope of its survival wiped away by the vicious assault. Gran never said a word about it again. She didn't even act angry, just sad.

That had been the worst of it.

That twelve-year-old version of me had wanted desperately to help, to try to fix it but I didn't know how. I couldn't take it back. All I had known was my own pain. I wasn't equipped to handle everything that had happened.

Looking at the enormous willow twenty years later, I still felt ill-equipped and overwhelmed.

I took a few tentative steps in that direction and stopped. The wind had jostled the low-hanging branches, revealing the scarred trunk. It was split into two distinct segments that resembled the letter y. One half of the tree hung out over the water, the other seemed to be reaching toward the tree line.

I released the breath I hadn't realized I'd been holding and started to edge closer, studying every nuance, every branch.

"Excuse me. Mr. McGavran?"

Startled, I spun toward the melodic voice.

And froze.

The voice belonged to a woman who stood several yards away, just a few steps into the clearing. Her long dark hair hung loose around her shoulders and stirred slightly in the breeze. Though I couldn't be sure from this distance, I'd have guessed she was a good six inches shorter than my six-foot frame. Her face was partially obscured by the large dark sunglasses she wore, a necessary accessory given the glare of the sun on the lake. Their size and shape reminded me of something Audrey Hepburn wore in a photo I'd once seen. She wore a tailored, feminine shirt and capris with wedge sandals that made her legs look amazing.

Shit. I'm checking her out.

Not a good idea.

She stepped forward with a smile and held out her slender hand. "Sorry to startle you. I'm a little early, I know." She quickly surveyed the area as she closed the distance between us. "I'm Alison Walker, your new assistant. Ali for short."

I returned her smile and slipped her soft hand into my

rough one, marveling at the ripple of awareness her touch evoked. "No apology necessary, Ali. It's nice to finally meet you. Please, call me Clay. I'm not much for formality." I released her hand, letting my fingers skim her palm as she pulled away and marveled at the tiny shudder I saw roll through her shoulders.

Interesting.

Fuck. Stop doing that, stupid. So she's hot; it's not like you've never seen a damn woman before.

"Nice to meet you, Clay. I'm informal myself, so that'll work out well for the both of us. After years in an uptight D.C. office full of stuffed shirts and dry humor, the laid back way of life around here has been a welcome change. Well, mostly. Sometimes I do miss the noise of the city," she admitted.

As if to punctuate her statement, the wind died down and everything was eerily still.

I slid my hands into my pockets and slowly swept my gaze across the area, smiling at the coincidence.

Ali was smiling, too. "See what I mean?"

I nodded in the direction of the house. "Trust me, before the summer is over, you'll be sick to death of construction noise. Saws, drills, hammers, the diesel engines in all that heavy equipment... you'll be hearing it in your sleep."

"Sounds like heaven. Bring it on," she chuckled.

"You may regret saying that," I warned. "I'd invest in a good set of ear plugs if I were you."

She chuckled and handed me a stack of papers from her purse, along with a set of keys. "Your accommodations are ready. I know you don't check in until the weekend, but the place wasn't rented to anyone and is open this week so I went ahead and snagged the key for you." Her expression went from informal and easy to business in an instant. It was kind of hot. She cleared her throat and nodded to the papers in my hand. "The lease is up the first week of September but can be extended, if necessary. And all the amenities Spencer suggested are included; both indoor and outdoor pools, two floors in addition to the basement where the pool is located, etcetera. The only thing it doesn't have is separate living rooms and kitchens for each floor, but Spencer indicated those requests weren't deal breakers. All the other info is in the paperwork. If there's any problem, give me a call. My cell number is on the front of the first page."

I thanked her and half-heartedly skimmed the pages before folding them and placing them in my back pocket, slipping the keys in the front.

Satisfied that I had no questions, she gestured to the willow, slipping back into the easy, relaxed version of herself in the span of a heartbeat. "I don't think I've ever seen a weeping willow of that size before. The way the limbs almost touch the ground is spectacular. I wonder how old it is."

"Twenty years." I answered automatically, realizing too late that I was opening a conversation I didn't want to have. I still hadn't fully recovered from the shock of discovering it, though, and the idea of sharing the tree's origins was appealing. "I'm actually surprised to find it here. When it was a sapling, it was severely damaged and no one thought it would survive. It was kicked and stomped repeatedly by a hateful little jackass who then decided to use it as a wishbone and basically ripped it in half before leaving it on the ground to rot." It was surprisingly freeing to talk about it, even if Ali had no idea I was talking about myself.

She cocked her head at me quizzically as if to ask how I knew.

I dismissed the look with a simple, "I know the owner. Some asshole kid — excuse my language — stomped it and kicked it, then split it in two when it was just a sapling. The owner thought it died."

"I can see the resilience in its stance, it's proud, regal; a survivor." She nodded to herself and studied the tree for a moment before sweeping her gaze across the lake, a soft smile on her face. "I can't wait to set up my easel. This place is gorgeous and that tree is going to be a great focal point."

"Easel?"

"Didn't Spencer mention anything to you about me doing some painting on weekends or non-work days?"

After a moment of confusion, I laughed when I realized what happened. "He did mention something but wasn't clear enough, apparently. I thought you were going to be donning a roller on occasion to help out with the interior."

She giggled softly, the sound of it was far too pleasing to my ear. "I'm not that kind of painter, usually, but I'm not opposed to helping out."

"I'm sure that won't be necessary but thank you for the offer." I considered a moment and told her, "Most weekends will be quiet around here, you can paint then. I'll be here a lot myself working on various projects, so you won't be out here totally alone. That's probably best given the possibility of bear activity."

"You really think bears are going to be coming around with all the construction noise?" She sounded doubtful. I couldn't read her expression because of the sunglasses.

I nodded emphatically. "Oh yeah. Remember, there won't be much noise on days the crews aren't here, so that's when it's most likely they would come around. They're curious by nature and for the last twenty years, they've had the run of the property. It's a very real concern. So much so that we are using reinforced shatterproof glass in all the first floor windows and doors. No one wants Yogi bear busting in on dinner, you know what I mean?"

Her smile was beautiful, full soft lips that had curved upward as I spoke. "I can see why that would be a problem. I hear they have really shitty table manners."

I laughed involuntarily at her joke and the language. She was going to fit right in, I could tell.

I gave her a quick walking tour of the property, or at least the few acres that were cleared and of interest to us. There were over two hundred acres total, with all but ten being wooded. There were several small creeks and ponds way in back and an underground spring that fed the lake.

Ali continued to marvel at the beauty of the place and I found myself envying her lack of familiarity with the property. She could look at it and see it for what it was, not what it represented.

I saw half a house standing tribute to half a life.

She saw possibility for rebirth.

I saw pain and loss.

She saw hope and beauty.

Maybe, with a lot of time and a little luck, I could find a way to see things through her eyes.

WE WERE WALKING back to where we'd parked when she asked a question that gave me pause.

"So, this place belongs to Spencer's family?"

I stopped walking and furrowed my brow, causing my sunglasses to shift higher on my nose. "No. Why would you think that?"

"When he and I talked, he kept referring to the property owner as Gran, I just assumed it was his grandmother." She mirrored my expression, her brows scrunching up behind the rims of her dark glasses.

Ah, now I get it.

I chuckled and resumed walking, giving her as much of the truth as I was comfortable sharing. "Everyone calls her that. Well, everyone below retirement age anyway. She used to be our hometown's favorite source for childcare. Most of the kids spent time in her care, at one time or another. She called all of us her 'babies' and we all called her Gran, at her request. Over the years, as we all grew up, we still called her that and eventually, so did everyone else. Even Vanessa, her daughter, usually refers to her as Gran. Trust me, you'll see her around here this summer and she'll expect you to call her that, too. Might as well resign yourself to it now."

Ali laughed softly and matched my unhurried pace. "So you and Spencer grew up together?"

"I'm not sure we're all that grown up but we've known each other since we were ten. Actually, we met at Gran's when he moved to our neighborhood and became one of her babies, too."

"That sounds like me and Talia. She's my best friend since we were eight. We're basically inseparable. She even came with me to help out for the summer, dividing her time between D.C. and Denson. She owns a restaurant in the city so she stays in our apartment in D.C. half the week. She's there from Thursday afternoon until Sunday afternoon to handle the weekend rush, then comes back here to help out at the diner the rest of the week. We have a small apartment here in Denson to eliminate the need for constant commuting."

"Diner?"

We drew closer to our vehicles but I stopped in the shade given off by the sagging porch, hesitant to end our time together.

She stepped into the shade beside me and nodded. "Yeah. My friend and his wife own two small businesses in the area. The realty office, which is where I met Spencer, and the cutest little retro diner two blocks over. My ailing friend, Teach, runs the diner, and his wife, Marilee, runs the office."

She reached down to pluck up a buttercup, a wistful expression on her face. "Teach was my favorite college professor.

English Lit. Technically, the course wasn't necessary for my degree but I took it anyway because my inner book nerd wouldn't allow anything else." She absently fidgeted with her necklace, a book-shaped locket that caught the light and set her cheeks aglow from the reflection. The letter A was engraved in the golden cover. "Anyway, we bonded over our mutual love of all things book related and kept in close contact over the years. He's sort of like an adopted grandfather, much like Gran probably is to you."

I nodded in agreement but said nothing, content to enjoy the melodic sound of her voice.

"When Marilee called to tell me about Teach's stroke, she was a wreck. On top of her worry for Teach, she had to find a way to keep both businesses going in their absence. I told her I had it covered and to focus on Teach, not the diner or the office."

I couldn't help but be impressed with her. "So, you took a leave of absence from a lucrative position in the city to come here to the middle of nowhere and help out a friend? Damn, we should all have friends like that."

"No. We should all *be* friends like that." She corrected absently. "And don't nominate me for sainthood just yet. My motives aren't entirely altruistic. I needed the break."

She reached up and removed her sunglasses, using the corner of her top to polish away a smudge. When she lifted her eyes to mine, I was stunned silent.

Her eyes were a brilliant, fluid green that seemed unnaturally clear, startlingly so.

And familiar.

A wave of déjà vu rolled over me, washing away the question that had been poised on my tongue. All I saw was that familiar green. I frantically searched my memory for the source of the feeling but came up empty. After a moment, I removed my

sunglasses, as if it would somehow help me make the connection. It didn't.

I knew this woman from somewhere.

But for the life of me I could not recall where.

And why was she looking at me like she recognized me, too?

Ali's gaze locked on mine for a moment that seemed to
stretch into infinity. Her eyes widened slightly as she took in a
slow uneven breath, my sudden hyper-awareness of her was
almost enough to allow me to count every molecule of air she
drew in.

It was an odd sensation to stand there that way, speechless
and unbalanced, unable to recall those eyes, that face, but
knowing she'd crossed my path before.

For the first time since my arrival at the property, my
surroundings had no impact whatsoever on me.

I was too busy reeling from the impact of her eyes on mine.

She managed to recover first, slipping her glasses back on
and saying exactly what I was thinking, "Why do I feel like I
know you from somewhere?"

Finding my voice took a couple of tries, the barren desert
that was once my mouth thwarting my attempts. When I
finally pushed past it, I shrugged. "I thought the same thing but
I have no idea where we would have met. Maybe I just have one
of those faces."

"No. That's the problem. Your face isn't one I'd be likely to
forget." Her cheeks flamed red, and she stammered a bit, obviously wishing she hadn't said that. It was rather adorable.
"What I meant was that I didn't recognize your face, per se.
There was just something about you that gave me the feeling of
déjà vu. I felt it even before you took off the glasses." She
leaned forward slightly, studying me. "Is your hair naturally
blond or is it lighter right now because you spend so much time
outside?" I could almost hear the wheels turning in her mind,

imagining it darker or shorter or longer... anything to help jog her memory.

I absently ran a hand over my hair, its length perfect for looking messy and not much else. "Nope, natural blond here, although it does get lighter in the summer months. It's usually what most people refer to as dirty blond, which sounds kind of unhygienic."

She laughed softly.

It was on the tip of my tongue to ask if she'd spent much time in the bars around Richmond, but I bit it back. She wasn't one of my conquests. Of that, I was sure. "Maybe it will come to us after we've spent some time together. We have the whole summer to figure it out." She nodded in agreement, and I gave her my most charming smile, thinking that there was an awful lot we could discover about each other over the next couple of months. For instance, was she a screamer? A moaner? Hmm...

Stop screwing around, stupid, before you end up losing your company.

No. Fucking. The. Employees.

I needed to get out of there before I fantasized myself into a hard-on.

"Well," I told her, "I need to get going. I have a few things to take care of back in Richmond before this weekend but I should be back Saturday night, if you want to get a little painting done on Sunday before the work starts next week." Much as I wanted to get away right that moment, I also wanted to see her again as soon as possible.

Not a good sign.

Her natural expression seemed to be a soft smile. At the mention of getting to paint, it widened into an excited grin. "I'd love that. I have to go berry picking for the restaurant that morning but I can be here after lunch. Talia and I have had to add a second trip to pick strawberries each week because her desserts sell out so fast."

"I thought you said she wouldn't be back until that afternoon, are you going alone?"

"Yeah but I don't mind. The owners encourage a bit of sampling and I get to soak up some sun before the heat gets too unbearable. Plus, my Jeep barely has enough room for the flats of berries, so no one else would fit."

I pointed toward our vehicles. "My truck is a crew cab. Between the floorboard, back seats, and bed, you could haul enough berries to feed an army." Shit. Why did I say that?

She tilted her head, her perpetual smile joined by a quizzical look half-hidden by her shades. "So, is that an invitation to borrow your truck or an offer to help pick?"

I chuckled lightly. "Well, I suppose it's an offer to help since I'm the only one who drives my truck. Don't feel like you have to accept, though, if you'd rather go alone."

Her smile slipped a little but her voice was laced with excitement. "No, I appreciate the offer. I spend plenty of time alone as it is. If you really don't mind, I'd be happy to have the help. The strawberry patch isn't too far and it won't take very long with the both of us picking."

"I don't mind at all. Actually, I'm looking forward to it." I didn't really care about the activity — I was looking forward to spending time with her.

Yeah, this was bad.

CHAPTER TWO

Richmond
Friday Night

I MADE MY WAY past the substantial line outside the club on my way to the VIP entrance, taking in a deep lungful of the warm night air. I needed this, needed a few hours to unwind and shake off some of the stifling tension that had been dragging me under these last few weeks. There was a potent mixture of expensive bottled fragrance mixing with just the slightest hint of desperation wafting off of the crowd impatiently waiting to gain entry.

I strode through the doorway, nodding to the bouncer who gave a curt tip of his head and returned to glaring at the throng.

If any of them knew him, really knew him as I did, they'd stop their bitching before things got ugly. He'd only remain stoic for so long.

Trying not to get jostled by all the people on the dance floor, I slid through gaps in the thrashing bodies and gave apologetic smiles as I accidentally bumped a few people. Eventually, the VIP section came into sight. We always met here at Haven — the hottest club in town and a favorite of ours because we helped design it — to celebrate the completion of a job. We'd tied up all the loose ends on the Windemere job that week and would kick off the next week with new projects.

I was an hour late for our celebratory meeting, but it couldn't be helped. Well, I probably could have rushed through my afternoon with Nicole but I was having a little pre-celebration, celebration, and she was down for anything.

Nicole had been my friend with benefits for the last several months; a willing outlet for my sexual energies with no romantic entanglements to worry about. It was a perfect arrangement. No man in his right fucking mind would have walked away from her before he'd had his fill. That day or any day. The guys would understand.

Unless I told them the truth. Which would never happen.

The truth was while I was balls-deep in Nicole, all I was thinking of was Ali.

Ali. A woman I'd only met a couple of days before. The stranger with familiar green eyes. Yeah, they probably wouldn't understand my fascination. Shit, I didn't understand it myself, but I couldn't get her out of my mind.

I'd given it a shot, several shots, with Nicole that afternoon to try to get Ali out of my head. I'd discovered that a body under me wouldn't do a damn bit of good unless it was Ali's.

I was fairly sure Nicole and I had just had our last hook-up. It just wasn't working now that my mind was on another woman. I'd actually left more frustrated than when I started. She'd felt it, too. The time had come to call it a loss and go our separate ways. No harm. No foul.

Spotting my partners in the far corner service area, I started in that direction as a hand snaked around from behind me and landed on my ribcage. A pair of unnaturally firm breasts pressed into my back. "Babe, I haven't seen those amber eyes in forever. It's been way too long." The familiar voice was enough to make my balls shrivel.

Fuck. Just what I need.

I took a steadying breath and turned, a fake smile plastered on my face. "Jessica, how are you?" I politely asked as I took a step back to separate myself. I wasn't at all interested in how she was doing as I looked toward Spencer and Brant in desperation, hoping that one of them would bail me out. Dammit, they were too busy talking to even realize I was there. I was on my own.

So much for wingmen.

She leaned into me and began running her hand up and down my chest, her long acrylic nails leaving little marks on the fabric of my shirt, working their way lower with each pass. She was talking, but all I could focus on was getting the hell away from her. Our casual hook-ups had ended over a year ago, but she always forgot that after a few drinks.

We'd had fun for a while, but it fizzled out quickly, at least on my end. Her propensity for calling me 'amber eyes' was just one of the things that had eventually turned me off. Having my eyes described as 'amber' or 'amber and jade' drove me crazy. It was bad enough having to call them hazel. Always reminded me of the damn wiry-haired witch in the old Bugs Bunny cartoons.

There was nothing more effective at deflating an erection than naming a part, any part, of a man's anatomy after a woman. It was just one of those things.

I interrupted her whiny reply, which included something about being terribly bored and wishing I'd call her sometime, when I apologetically said, "Work is keeping me super busy. I'm actually here for a business meeting, and I'm already late. Have a good night. Hope you find what you're looking for." I flashed a smile and backed away before she had a chance to latch on again. Feeling like someone was staring daggers into my back, which I knew damn well she was, I hurried over to the booth that was already stocked with my favorite Kentucky Bourbon.

I stalked straight over to the glasses, and after dropping in one of the clubs signature spherical ice chunks, poured myself several fingers. Wordlessly, I raised my glass in the direction of my confused friends and downed the entire thing before refilling and sinking miserably into the plush leather booth.

"Hard day, amber eyes?" Spencer joked, indicating that he'd seen Jessica accost me. He was goading me; he knew the nickname was one of the main reasons I broke things off with her. He slowly sipped his Scotch and looked at me expectantly, a sly smile on his face.

"Yeah, Clay, you never drink that fast." Brant added and focused on his nearly empty snifter of Brandy, blissfully unaware of the Jessica sighting.

He and Spencer could have passed for brothers. Both were the same height and build, roughly two or three inches shorter than me, both had dark hair. The only difference was their eyes. Brant's were a light, icy blue while Spencer's were so dark brown they looked black.

Those dark eyes paired with Spencer's dark hair made him look intimidating unless he was smiling, which he often did. I'd actually watched the security guard at our bank keeping a wary eye on him as if he gave off some kind of dangerous vibe.

I found that fucking hilarious, particularly since he was the kind-hearted one of our group.

I cut my eyes at Spencer. "So, you saw Jessica waiting to pounce and you didn't warn me? Thanks, bro."

"I didn't see her until it was too late. Sorry." He glanced over to where she stood talking to some poor bastard who had the bad fortune to stumble within reach. "She get her claws into anything important?"

"Nah. I'm used to fending her off. I just hate being cornered like that." I shrugged, eager to move on.

Spencer was shaking his head at me when the server made an appearance, taking particular interest in whether he needed anything or not. She was obviously new since the staff here was well aware that flirting with him was a waste of time. To my knowledge, he hadn't so much as looked at a damn woman since his divorce. Bitch took half his shit and all his testosterone, apparently. He smiled politely at the server and turned back to our conversation without ever noticing her interest.

Poor bastard.

She was kind of hot.

Brant looked over at me with a knowing expression and a shake of his head. He saw it, too. "So, how many calls have you gotten from Shepard this week?" He rolled his eyes. "It was a record week for me with three calls, Spence got two, and we're running out of ways to tactfully express our disinterest in his offers."

I couldn't help the scowl on my face. "None. Unless Caroline has been brushing him off and not mentioning it, I haven't gotten any calls from him this week or any other week." I couldn't decide whether to be grateful or offended.

Spencer laughed. "He probably did enough homework to know you'd be the first of us to tell him to go fuck himself."

"Sure would." I sipped my bourbon and shook my head. "I'm still trying to figure out why neither of you have done it yet."

Brant shrugged and returned his attention to his glass while Spencer jumped right in with an answer. "Simple. He's a snake. The best way to get rid of a snake is to wait for it to get bored and slither away. If you engage it, poke at the damn thing, you risk getting bitten. We may have a damn good thing going but we've got nowhere near the clout he does. If we piss him off, he could refocus his efforts on ruining us just for the hell of it. He doesn't have many friends but he does have deep pockets and a mean streak. Let's just bide our time until he loses interest."

"I'd rather hand him his balls on a silver platter but that's just me." I joked. "Probably why I'm not allowed to handle that side of things, huh?"

Brant laughed into his glass and Spencer nodded emphatically before changing the subject. "Did you get a chance to meet the new assistant while you were in Denson?"

It took me a minute to decide on a response. I didn't want to sound too affected one way or the other. "I did. I gave her a quick tour of the property and she brought by the rental agreement for the cabin. She seems competent enough."

Brant chimed in. "I looked at her résumé the other day. She's so overqualified for this job it's pathetic. CMO of a marketing firm slumming it as Clay's assistant? That's like Muhammad Ali in a slap fight." He looked at Spencer with something akin to awe. "How the hell did you manage that?"

Spencer laughed and shrugged his shoulders. "Boredom is a great motivator. It's not like there's much going on in Denson. She was pretty stoked at the idea of having something new to do."

Brant turned to me with a smirk. "He begged." Spencer huffed indignantly and leaned forward to refill his drink, ignoring the accusation as Brant continued. "That's the only logical explanation for someone who is that smart and accomplished to want to take a bullshit job like that. I bet he cried a little, too." He chuckled and looked over at me for support.

"Oh yeah. I bet he crawled into that realty office on his hands and knees, pleading with her to take the job because we couldn't find anyone else in that shithole town to do it."

"Fuck. You. Both." Spencer didn't sound quite as bored as he wanted to. His shoulders were bunching in that tell-tale way they did when he was getting annoyed.

"Aww, come on, Spence. Don't be like that." Brant managed to barely hold back his laughter, but it was obvious in his voice.

He pointed at Brant, hand and voice both steady. "So she's well-educated and doing a small time job. Can't imagine how anyone would find satisfaction in that. Right?"

The remark was a thinly veiled reference to Brant's own

level of intelligence. The bastard had an IQ near 180, had graduated high school at fifteen, and was smarter than every professor who taught him in college. He was a fucking genius, no doubt about it.

"Point taken. Yes, I work with my hands for a living despite what was expected of me and I love every minute of it. Maybe she is the same. No judgement. I was just fucking with you."

Spencer's face fell a bit when he realized how Brant had taken the comment. Brant wasn't known to joke around often and had truly meant no offense. Something about being as smart as he was also left him ill-equipped in social situations. It was that trait in particular that had been the foundation of our friendship. Being so much younger than everyone else in college, he'd stayed to himself and tried to focus on his courses. For the most part, he was invisible.

Then, in our third year, Spencer and I were paired with him for a huge project. We'd sneaked into the lecture hall late, hiding at the back so we could nurse our hangovers in relative obscurity, and ended up sitting beside Brant. When we were assigned in groups of three according to our seating, Brant became our third.

We learned more from working with him on that assignment than we learned in the entire rest of the course. He was fucking brilliant.

When some of the frat guys started hassling him a few months later, Spencer and I stepped in. He was younger, smarter, and quiet by nature, which made him a prime target. I was still in my barroom brawler phase so it worked out well for everyone. Except maybe the frat brothers who got their asses handed to them.

From that day on, it was the three of us. We spent the next year planning a business, and the year after graduation we made it happen. That one for all and all for one shit wasn't just something you read somewhere. It was something we were and are.

Brothers.

Spencer reached toward the small table that held our drinks — along with an assortment of garnishes that no man in his right mind would add to booze this good — and flicked a lemon slice at Brant, laughing to break the tension. "Suck it, asshole."

Brant calmly placed the fruit in his mouth and bit down, making a disgusting slurping sound before flipping Spencer the bird.

I cleared my throat and waited for their attention. "We came here to celebrate, boys. I say it's time we get to it." I raised my glass, the ice orb clicking against the side. "To another job well done." They raised their glasses in salute and we took a deep drink to commemorate the occasion.

Spencer added, "To the next job. Well, jobs. May they go just as smoothly as the last."

The pleasant burn of my aged bourbon was somehow tempered by the thought of the upcoming project. Oh, the build would go great despite my intense desire to avoid it. Our work was never anything short of spectacular. That wasn't my vanity talking. It was a fact.

This time, though, no matter the budget, the cost would be a lot higher.

Maybe higher than even I could have predicted.

SUNDAY MORNING FOUND me and Ali out picking berries before the dew had even evaporated, tasting a few along the way and chatting agreeably. There was no awkwardness, no wary distance. We just fell into step with one another like it was the most natural thing in the world.

It was disturbingly exhilarating.

It took three trips to get all the berries in the truck. We settled into a companionable silence as we carried the last batch toward the parking area, each enjoying the morning sun before the heat settled in and made the day miserably hot. As we stood at the rear doors and loaded the berries in the back seat of my rig, Ali reached down and plucked up a handful. Occupied as I was with strapping the flats of fruit in on my side, I was startled when an enormous, blood-red berry was suddenly right in my face, held there by small, delicate fingers. I glanced up at Ali. She grinned at me playfully and held it up for me to taste, almost daring me to eat from her hand.

Challenge accepted.

Not taking my eyes off hers, I wrapped my lips around the plump flesh, slowly biting down and savoring every sun-warmed drop of juice. Her hand shook almost imperceptibly, and I watched with satisfaction as a shudder rippled over her. Still not breaking eye contact, I retrieved a berry from the flat in front of me, holding it to her lips. When she started to drop the hand that she had used to feed me, I took it in my free hand and repositioned it so that I could capture the last bit of fruit.

Watching her intently, I nibbled and sucked the last of the strawberry she'd offered, patiently waiting for her to take a bite. I allowed her hand to drop from my lips but held her wrist in my grip, not wanting her to take it back just yet. She watched me, transfixed for a moment before slowly parting her lips and placing them around my offering. Moving slowly, obviously enjoying both the berry and the moment, she sank her teeth in, her lips nearly brushing the tips of my fingers. The soft sucking sound she made as she captured the juice that threatened to spill over her lips nearly broke my resolve.

Fuck. I wanted to be the one licking that sweet juice from her lips.

I was so close to acting on it that my tongue made an involuntary pass across my lower lip, mirroring her movements and making her eyes widen as she watched me. I could practically taste the sweetness of her lips, the warmth of her skin. What had started out as a playful gesture had turned into a wildly erotic moment, one that I knew held the power to break me, as did she.

My internal struggle raged on. Every cell in my body screamed for me to take this woman, the throbbing erection that strained against my jeans leading the damn charge. My pulse buzzed in my ears as my grip on her wrist tightened fractionally, preparing to pull her in and claim her mouth. I'd half convinced myself that one taste was all I needed, just one fleeting trespass over the line before retreating to a safe distance.

Yeah, right. She eats a goddamn strawberry in front of you and you're ready to jump her right on the spot. You're a pinnacle of self-control. So, what happens when you see her with a banana, fucknut?

It was with the sheer force of will that I managed to release my hold on her. As my fingers released her and skimmed over the skin of her wrist, I saw a flicker of disappointment in her expression followed quickly by a look of relief. She dropped her eyes and the air around me cooled, as if her gaze had been a blanket that was suddenly ripped away, leaving me cold and exposed.

We drove to the diner in relative silence.

WHEN WE DROPPED the berries off at the diner, Ali insisted on treating me to breakfast as payment for my assistance.

As we walked into the diner and out of the heat, I noted the sign on the door that boasted the best fresh strawberry pie in Virginia. Glancing around, I was surprised by the interior. Either someone had paid out the ass for a beautiful retro makeover or this place was the genuine article. The real soda fountain, Wurlitzer jukebox playing softly in the far corner, leather booths, and chromed counter-stools could have been done by most designers and made to look appropriate. There was something about the feel of this place, though.

The lighting, the obviously one-of-a-kind pieces, they made me think it was the real deal. It had a feeling of history, so overwhelming that it was hard to look away, as if ghosts of patrons past were welcoming you to their favorite hangout.

The mouth-watering smells from the kitchen elicited an immediate response from my stomach. The smoky scents coming from the grill mingled together in the air in such a way that after one whiff, I was instantly ravenous.

Ali let me scope the place out for a bit before indicating a table at the back. We took our seats amid the sounds of forks clattering and coffee spoons clicking against ceramic cups.

Our waitress came by and brought us coffee, leaving menus strictly for my benefit since Ali basically helped manage the place. I told the kindly older woman — whose name was Fay according to her nametag — to take her time getting back to us, since I had no idea what I wanted.

Well, I knew but what I had in mind was most definitely not on the menu.

After a few minutes, the silence between us was beginning to get uncomfortable. Deciding to break the ice a bit, I turned to Ali. "I noticed the size of your book collection earlier. That bookshelf is packed. Did you bring them all here from D.C.?"

Ali and Talia's Denson domicile was a small apartment over a dry cleaning business that looked to have been closed down for quite some time. When I'd picked her up that morning, I'd briefly stepped into the apartment and noticed that the only personal touches — at least in the area I'd seen — were several canvases stacked against one wall and a huge collection of books. They were stacked tightly on a book shelf, on the coffee table, everywhere. I'd known instantly whose they were.

She visibly relaxed for the first time since what happened at the strawberry farm. "No, I didn't bring any of them from home. I've collected them all these last few weeks." She smiled softly as she spoke, a far-away look in her eye, her body there with me in the diner, but her mind wandering in some distant place. "There's a used book store two streets over from the office. I stumbled across it a few days after I came to town. Mismatched shelves from floor to ceiling and the smell of dusty old pages, it's my favorite place to spend time when Talia is in D.C.. I sneak over there during my lunch hour and dig through the stacks sometimes. There's a sitting area in the back where I'll sit and read while I nibble on a sandwich. I eat lunch at the diner when Talia is here but the noise in there keeps me from enjoying a book, too much distraction. While she's away, I have lunch with the books."

"Why not just bring them back to the office to read? It's pretty quiet there most of the time, right?"

She hesitated, her brow pinching in thought. "For some reason the quiet in that bookstore is different from the quiet everywhere else. Most of the time silence is the absence of something and it feels lonely. But in there, the silence seems to be caused by the presence of something, something extra that only exists in that room. Like all those books are a barrier to the noise, even the noise in your own head, holding the world at bay so you can enjoy their stories in peace."

I'd never been one to read for pleasure, never found the joy in it that so many people did, but hearing her talk about it and how it felt in that store made me wonder. Lately, I needed a little help with the noise in my head. Maybe it was worth looking into.

She studied me for a moment with a curious expression, absently fiddling with her locket. "Enough about my bookish tendencies. What do you do for fun? Any hobbies?"

Since I was trying to avoid any more sexually charged moments, talking about my *favorite* hobby was out of the question. "I'm not sure I'd call it a hobby, exactly, but I do spend a lot of time working on custom design elements using salvaged materials. Furnishings, structural pieces, decorative pieces, whatever my mind will churn out." I shrugged. "Primarily, CBD builds houses. Some of our projects have been featured on *MTV Cribs* and some would have looked great in *Gone with the Wind*, just depends on what the client is looking for. I like designing the homes from the ground up, alternating ideas with Brant and trying to one-up each other with our creativity, but I still spend most of my non-working hours in my workshop making pieces that incorporate salvaged materials. No blueprints, no straight lines, just a sketch pad and a few tools."

Ali's soft smile returned as she asked, "So, is the work you do outside of the company's projects totally separate or do you build things to go in the houses, too?"

"Some of our clients request personalized pieces but I do the majority of the designs with no particular buyer in mind." I scrolled through photos on my phone, handing it to her and motioning for her to scroll through the album. "That first pic is a massive chandelier that went in one of the houses. I used old copper pipe and stained glass the client salvaged from his grandfather's estate. Several of the items in that album were sold at auction, pieces made out of old car parts and reclaimed wood. You'd be surprised at the amount of interest they get."

Ali took her time inspecting the photos, her soft smile radiant when she handed back the phone. "As excited as I am to find out you're an artist too, I'm kind of intimidated now. Those pieces are phenomenal."

I waved her off. "Don't even try it. I saw the paintings in your living room this morning. You're a pretty kick-ass artist yourself. I didn't mean to snoop but I couldn't look away, they were so beautiful."

A blush crept up her neck, slow like a heated caress. She cleared her throat and muttered her thanks, embarrassed by the praise. Instead of talking about her art, she turned the conversation back to me. "So, I guess being out here means you won't be getting much artwork done, huh?"

"I'll probably tinker a bit on my days off. Nothing major. I should probably take the time off to recharge anyway. There's a chance I'll need to be at full creative capacity in a few months."

She perked up at the insinuation, leaning forward in anticipation. "For what? A work thing or an art thing?"

I couldn't help smiling at her enthusiasm. "It's definitely an art thing. Recently, I was offered a contract to build several dozen pieces for a large theme park. They're devoting a whole section to the park to a set of rides built around a post-apocalyptic rise-of-the-machines kind of thing, and they want me to build decorative elements. Mostly sculptures, figures made of twisted metal that look like they are coming to life and scaling the buildings or, in some cases, they might be the buildings themselves come to life. They're already gathering supplies, but I'm still debating whether or not to accept the contract."

She looked impressed. "Do you use salvaged materials as a 'green' statement?"

Our server stopped by to take our orders before scurrying off to the kitchen. I wasn't even sure what I'd asked for, my focus was solely on my companion.

I picked absently at the pink packets of artificial sweetener from the small tray on the table. "No, nothing as politically correct as that." Pausing, I considered how to best explain it. "I like using materials — whether it's an old wooden chair or a rusted out car — that no one would think of as valuable. I like taking something weathered or broken and turning it into something of worth. I've been doing it in one form or another since I was a kid, long before the perilous state of the environment was ever realized."

Her obvious interest made me keep going. "It was a talent born of necessity, really. I broke something of Gran's when I was barely thirteen, something really important that her husband had given her. I couldn't fix it, which I hated, so I took the pieces and made it into something else. That way it wasn't really gone. Just different. After that, I discovered that I liked building things out of old broken pieces. Been doing it ever since."

"I'd love to see your artwork in person sometime. Do you plan to do any special pieces for the house you're building here?" She sounded excited at the prospect. For some reason, it pleased me that she was interested in my work. I'd never cared what people thought before but, as I was discovering, Ali was different. I wanted to share things with her because she was so willing to share with me. Well, I'd share some things, but certainly not everything.

Some things weren't meant to be said out loud. To speak of them gave them substance and made them real.

Did I plan to do a piece for Gran's build? I'd already started on something, but I wasn't sure it would ever leave my shop. "I'm not sure yet. Still brainstorming ideas." I felt like an asshole as soon as the lie left my lips. "Gran hasn't asked for anything particular so anything I made would be my own concept. Trust me, if she wanted something made, she'd have told me by now. That woman is not afraid to speak up." I smiled at the truth of that statement.

Ali laughed. "She sounds like a lot of fun." I glanced over at her, sarcastically raising one brow until she continued. "Seriously, any little old lady that can make you and Spencer shake in your work boots is worth knowing."

"You'll see for yourself at some point." I smiled at the thought. She had no idea what she was in for with Gran.

After our meals had been eaten and our coffee cups were empty, we decided to put in a few hours at the property.

Ali worked at the lake and I worked in the old barn at the back of the property, trying to turn it into a suitable workshop to house my personal projects, just in case I should decide to bring them here.

Neither of us infringed on the other while we worked — artistic courtesy — and just as the sun was on its downward arc below the mountaintops, Ali emerged from the lake path with her supplies neatly gathered beneath her arm, her canvas and easel casually held in her other hand as if she did this all the time.

I rushed forward to help her load her things and stood by her Jeep while she situated herself behind the wheel.

It was a little surprising when she invited me to have dinner with her and Talia, whom I'd never met, but I was so enamored with her that I gave an immediate and resounding 'yes'.

Anything to stay close to her.

CHAPTER THREE

THE DAY JUST kept getting better and better.

I was introduced to Talia, who was in full-on chef mode when we arrived. She wiped her hands on her floral apron and gave me a mega-watt smile that was genuine and welcoming. Ali laughed at her and muttered to me that her friend loved feeding people, so my attendance was a happy surprise.

Talia was a few inches taller than Ali, with long blond hair and whiskey-brown eyes. She had a dancer's body, willowy and flawless. Everything about her screamed model, not chef.

And, while her beauty was obvious to me, I didn't feel the first stirring of attraction. It was kind of jarring to look at a woman that stunning and not get a twinge of arousal. For a split second, I wondered if my dick had lapsed into a coma.

A moment later Ali giggled at something Talia said, and I had my answer.

Her singsong voice sent a jolt straight to my cock.

Nope. All systems 'go'. As long as it was Ali.

I had to force myself to focus on where I was and not what I was feeling. Soon I was swept away in the conversation and the food. Talia prepared an amazing meal. I could see why she had a restaurant. She told me that she had tried to incorporate some of her dishes at the diner, but the locals didn't seem to take well to change. With the exception of her desserts, they loved those.

Watching Ali and Talia interact was interesting. They acted more like family than best friends. From what I gleaned during the conversation over dinner, Talia had sworn off dating for the foreseeable future.

And so had Ali.

When Talia joked about me being the only man to grace their tiny Denson apartment in all these weeks, I quirked a brow at her statement.

She wryly assured me that she and Ali were just friends. They weren't switching teams, just taking a much needed break from the game. Ali chuckled and agreed with the analogy. Neither of them looked the least bit worse off for not having a man in their lives, either.

While I was watching *them*, Talia watched *me*. She was subtle about it, but I caught her on more than one occasion. It didn't feel like attraction, or even suspicion was her motivation. She just seemed to be studying me, especially when Ali and I were talking. It would have been unnerving if she wasn't such a pleasant person otherwise. She laughed and joked, seemingly comfortable with my presence.

When they asked about my background, I gave my standard answer, letting it roll off my tongue the way I'd done countless times before. "I grew up in a small town halfway between Fredericksburg and Richmond. No siblings. Met Spencer when I was ten and became fast friends. We attended college together; I was on the swim team, and he was on the Dean's list, which is a fitting analogy for the two of us. I like anything that gets my blood pumping — running, swimming, whatever — and he's all business; planning, studying, networking. That combination worked out well for us in the long run. After graduation,

Spencer and I started CBD with our friend Brant and have been working to the exclusion of nearly everything else ever since. Brant and I are always on site working up a sweat and Spencer is behind the scenes keeping it all together."

They asked a few more questions, and I answered as vaguely as possible until they seemed to realize just how much I hated to talk about myself and switched topics.

After that, we talked about inconsequential things and drank wine late into the evening. By the time I was ready to leave, even Talia felt like an old friend. It was nice, so much so that the girls insisted that we repeat the gathering every Sunday. I wholeheartedly accepted the invitation.

And so it went for the next couple of weeks.

Working at the property on Saturdays while Ali painted became the highlight of my week; dinner with her and Talia on Sundays running a close second. The food, the conversation, and especially the company were all spectacular.

Ali handled the job site beautifully in my absence on those rare days I needed to go back to Richmond for meetings. She juggled the schedule like a pro and made sure the contractors had all their materials, and everyone was happy. Much to Spencer's relief, she also took quickly to his anal-retentive way of handling all the bookkeeping associated with a build of this size. With Spencer tied up doing all the administrative work for Brant's build in Charleston and handling the office in Richmond, she was a godsend. He never would have been able to keep all that shit coordinated on his own.

For her part, Ali couldn't be happier. She swore she enjoyed the work she was doing for us. It wasn't hard work, not for her, but it was busy work and that was something to be valued when you were stuck in a one-horse town like Denson. It made the days go by so much faster.

Construction of the house had begun. The foundation had been poured, encasing the basement structure. Soon framing would start. I was excited to be making progress but checking each item off the list just reminded me that my time with Ali was limited. I dreaded the day we finished the house.

The irony was not lost on me.

I'd started out my time in Denson counting the days until the job was done so I could get the hell out of there, now the idea of leaving brought with it a profound sadness.

~

BY THE FIRST week of June, the heat had set in to stay. Up until that point, the mountain air would cool things down in the evening but that luxury was over. For the most part, Ali seemed to take the soaring temperatures in stride. She claimed that she was used to it, having grown up in the south. It amazed me that she didn't even seem to perspire. Once in a while there was a thin sheen on her neck or the exposed portion of her chest but that was it. I'd wondered on several occasions what it would take to get her drenched with sweat.

I had several scenarios on my list.

Despite my mounting attraction, our friendship had taken the forefront. Which was why I knew something was wrong the moment I laid eyes on her that Friday afternoon.

I'd taken a conference call at the cabin that morning, getting to the property after lunch. The crews were hard at work, nail guns popping, drills and saws whirring, the sound ricocheting rhythmically. Making my way to the back of the partially framed structure, I spotted Ali in the distance. She had her back to the house, arms folded over her chest as if she were cold, which was not her normal posture. She never appeared as closed off as she did at that moment, and I found it odd.

When she heard my approach on the gravel, she turned. Something was definitely off. She gave me a thin smile, starting in my direction. "I didn't expect you so soon. How did the conference call go?"

"Fine. Boring as usual." I waited for her to reach me. "Everything alright here?" If someone had given her trouble... My fists clenched at the thought. I'd hate to kick someone off the site, but for her I would.

She looked over at the house, crewmen busily working in various areas. "The guys are doing a great job. Everyone is progressing on schedule, and there haven't been any issues." Her expression told me her mind was a hundred miles from this place.

With the noise reaching a crescendo, I gave up hope of having a conversation at our current position. I leaned over and spoke close to her ear, making sure she could hear me. "Let's take a walk. I want to check the pier again."

The breeze picked up, and her hair brushed against my cheek. Her scent invaded my senses, hints of peach and vanilla making me pull back to stave off the urge to bury my face in her dark locks. When I looked down, there were goosebumps on her exposed arms. We both were affected, it seemed.

Rather than wait for her to respond, I started off toward the path. I couldn't hear her steps over the construction noise, but I could feel her there behind me. I always seemed hyper-aware of her presence. We reached the lake and, finally able to hear myself think, I turned to her. "So, what's going on? And don't tell me nothing because I can see it on your face." Though my words were gruff, my voice was soft. Whatever was going on, I was worried about her. Her ever-present smile was something I'd come to depend on these last few weeks, and I didn't like it being gone.

She didn't answer right away. If Spencer had hesitated like that, I'd have handed him his ass, but she was different. Her pause wasn't for dramatic effect, it was something else. I couldn't let it drop, whatever it was. "Is it the diner? Or Lauren? She giving you shit again?"

I'd learned not long after meeting Ali that Lauren, one of the waitresses at the diner, was Teach's niece. She also went to college with Ali and Talia and had some sort of grudge against Ali that no one knew the source of. She worked fine with Talia but lived to make Ali miserable. It was made all the worse when I'd run to the diner to pick up lunch one afternoon, and Lauren had all but thrown herself at me. She'd studied me with her icy blue eyes like she was tracking prey. Her glossy black hair had brushed my shoulder when she leaned close to tell me what time she got off, her tone insinuating that she'd like me to get her off shortly afterward. I politely refused her attempts and was rewarded with a scornful look that morphed into something akin to rage when Ali had come in and sidled up next to me at the counter. Needless to say, Lauren wasn't a fan of either of us.

Ali sighed and walked over to the willow, taking a seat and leaning against the damaged trunk. "Lauren is always a problem, I'm almost used to it. And the only trouble I ever have at the diner *is* Lauren. She's getting bolder lately, breaking things and purposely screwing up orders, as usual, but now she's doing little shit to make me look incompetent. Messing with the register so that my books will be off, not actually stealing, just making it look like the money is coming up short. Things like that. She's not a real threat, though, she's just a pest. I wish she would realize that Teach had a reason for not asking her to run the diner and whatever it was, it had nothing to do with me and everything to do with her."

"So if it isn't her that has you upset, and it isn't the diner, what is it?" If Lauren's attempts at sabotage weren't the worst thing going on, I was afraid to know what was.

She stared out at the lake. The sun was shimmering on the

water and sending ripples of light across her face. "I got a call from GFS this morning." She stated blandly.

My heart sank at the mention of her D.C. employer. What if they wanted her to come back? Would she go now and leave me here alone for the rest of the summer? Shit. Despite my panic, I managed a steady voice. "Oh yeah? What did they say?"

Her arms crossed again, fists balled up on either side of her torso. "They informed me that I was expected to attend the upcoming gala the company is hosting. I was the head of the committee who arranged the partnership with the charity, and I'm required to be there."

I wasn't sure I understood her distress. "I take it you don't want to go." More of a question than a statement but it was pretty obvious from her reaction.

She blew out a breath. "I don't know. Outreach Hospice, the charity being benefitted, has been a passion of mine for years. It's not that I don't believe in the cause. I do, more than I can even express, but everyone in my department will be in attendance. Including my ex, Keith." She virtually spat the name, and I got an icy cold feeling on the back of my neck that told me I wasn't going to like what she said next.

Ali blew out a big breath and met my eye. "Remember when I told you my reasons for being here weren't entirely altruistic? That I needed a break?"

I nodded and tried to understand the look of shame in her eyes. What could she have possibly done?

"My leave of absence, the one everyone thinks I took to come help my sick friend? The leave of absence came first, two weeks before Teach had his stroke. It was also involuntary and unwarranted."

"Why involuntary?" I wasn't sure if I even wanted to know.

She stood and walked over to the pier, placing her hands on the railing as if she needed the support. "Remember, you asked." I kept quiet, and she went on. "When I finished college and imme-diately got hired on at GFS, the biggest marketing company in the Northeast, I was ecstatic. It was a crappy low-level job, but I knew I'd earn my way to a better position. What made it the most exciting was that my college boyfriend, Keith, had been hired on as well. We had these big plans for the future, both of us ambitious and dedicated. We enjoyed working together for the first few years, even though we were technically in different departments." She paused for a moment to rub her hands over her arms as if she were chilled. "Then the CMO position was posted and everything changed. We were both recommended by our department heads and, at first, it was a joke between us. We even planned a vacation to celebrate the promotion, no matter which of us got it."

"As the date of the announcement approached, his attitude changed, became hostile and mocking. The people in the office even treated me differently. I couldn't understand it. He and I had our problems, but he hadn't ever been outright mean to me. I just couldn't figure it out."

I felt myself tensing at the thought of him mistreating her but said nothing. It wasn't as if I'd have known what to say anyway.

"When the announcement came, I was elated. I had worked my ass off from day one, sometimes seventy hours a week, and I felt I deserved it. Keith didn't see it that way. There was a huge argument, and we ended up parting ways soon after." She stopped for a minute, looking far away. "I thought it was over, that his hateful attitude wasn't my problem anymore. But I was wrong. He spread rumors about our break up, made me out to be some kind of corporate shrew, swore most of the work I'd turned in was stolen from him, told co-workers that I'd aborted his baby against his wishes because it didn't fit into my career plans. That one was my favorite. He played it off like he was devastated. There was never any baby. We barely even looked at each other the last year we were together between work and social obligations." There was something in her voice that went beyond mere anger.

"Jesus. How did you respond?"

"I didn't. I decided people were going to believe what they wanted, and nothing I could say would change that. To vehemently deny a rumor just lends it credibility in the eyes of gossips. I kept my mouth shut and figured it didn't matter what they thought. It was just bullshit rumors."

Somehow I knew it was more than that. "Did the rumors stop?"

"Eventually. It was like he just gave up his stupid vendetta. For a while, I was perfectly happy in my new position at work and with my newfound freedom from Keith. Talia and I were sharing an apartment, just like we planned when we were little girls. It was perfect. But you know what they say…"

"Let me guess, 'All good things must come to an end'?"

"Well, I was going to say 'life's a bitch', but yours works too. I came into my office after lunch one afternoon to find all three of the partners standing over my desk, scowling at something on my computer screen. The screen I distinctly remember turning off before I left."

"What was on the screen?" She definitely had my attention. A feeling of dread had slowly crept in and took up residence in my gut.

"One of the secretaries called the partners after she says she came in to put something on my desk and noticed an open email on my screen, one that divulged confidential information about our client list and contracts. It was addressed to one of GFS's competitors."

"That son of a bitch," I muttered, instantly pissed the fuck off. That pretty much explained her suspension. Calling it administrative leave didn't change what it was. It was an accusation, plain and simple.

She was quiet for a while, looking out over the water with

an unreadable expression. She was probably upset even thinking about it. When she spoke, I was proved wrong. "You automatically knew it wasn't me." She said thickly, almost in a whisper as she put a hand on my arm to turn me toward her. "You barely know me. How do you know I'm not lying, trying to blame Keith as punishment?"

"Because that's not who you are," I said simply, knowing I was right.

Letting go of my arm, she shifted, dropping her head and looking at the ground. "You can't possibly know that. Even the people closest to me had their doubts... wondered if I was guilty." Her voice cracked.

I stepped closer, placing a hand under her chin and lifting it so that she met my eye, my body mere inches from hers. "Then they're the ones who don't know you." I pointed at her chest. "No one with as big a heart as yours would lower themselves to revenge. You've got too much backbone to rely on scheming to make a point." I dropped my hand but held her gaze. "Sneak attacks are for fucking cowards, Ali. You're not a coward."

"Thank you for that," she said quietly as she backed away and stepped into the grass, making her way over to the willow.

"So, it's not the gala you want to avoid, it's him." I asserted. "Understandable."

"It's not just him. It's all of them. It's the partners, whose only reason for not firing me outright is fear of my stepfather, who I'd never even tell about the situation much less ask for help. They think I'm some pitiful wretch who needs to be saved by my mother's rich, powerful knight in Prada armor."

During one of our Sunday dinners, I'd learned that Ali's mother had left her and her father when Ali was barely a teenager. The woman was more interested in money than family, and she knew her blue-collar husband and small town life weren't about to land her where she wanted to be. She'd eventually remarried, repeatedly, and was currently on husband number four. Ali said she didn't even bother to get to know them anymore because they had a short shelf life.

I laughed my ass off when she told me she'd taken to calling them all "Benjamins" because all her mother saw when she looked at them was hundred-dollar bills. Ali didn't want their money or use their connections because she wanted to make it on her own.

I admired the hell out of that.

From the way she described her father, I'd say she was more like him. Grounded, generous, content, and kind-hearted. My favorite story of hers was the one where she admitted her dad's version of 'hunting' involved a camera rather than a gun. It was his odd hunting practice that inspired Ali to paint. She started out using his wildlife photos as her inspiration.

I installed wildlife cameras all over the property the week after hearing that story.

I wondered if her father would have rethought his 'no guns' policy if he'd been privy to Keith's machinations, which I was sure he wasn't.

Ali was starting to pace as she listed all the reasons she didn't want to attend the gala.

"And it's all those bastards who bought into Keith's lies, who think I'm guilty, that I'm some monster who stomped him into the ground on my way to the top." She scoffed. "Imagine how much fun I'll have all night hearing the whispers as I pass by."

"Who gives a damn what they think, Ali? You know who you are. If they can't see how amazing you are, fuck them."

She looked at me and laughed. "You don't understand. I'm not afraid of them, I'm not afraid of Keith either. I'm afraid of my reaction to the whole situation. I've fantasized about bashing Keith's face in for almost a year now, and I know he's going to try to goad me into causing a scene, it's how he operates. If I can't keep my cool, I'm definitely out of a job. Never mind that I will have embarrassed the charity I've worked so hard to support. The children at Outreach Hospice deserve better than to have me ruin their benefit." She shook her head. "That's what I'm afraid of."

From the look on her face as she described kicking Keith's ass, I had no doubt she meant it. So she had a fiery temper? Good. One more item on the list of things that turned me on about her. "Are you taking Talia with you? Maybe she can diffuse the situation."

This time, Ali's laugh was genuine and loud. "Talia? She'd be the one to throw the first punch. No way can I take her along, we'd end up in handcuffs for sure." She wiped her eyes, having laughed so hard they started to water. "I needed that laugh, though. Thanks."

"How about if I take you?" She looked shocked at my offer, but there was no way she was as surprised as me. I hadn't meant to say it. The idea popped into my mind and then shot right out of my mouth. Fuck.

I may not have meant to say it, but the idea instantly struck me as a good one.

She sputtered a bit before finding her voice. "You?" She shook her head. "I couldn't ask you to do that. This is my drama. I appreciate the offer, but I didn't tell you about it so you'd try to fix things. I'll be fine. I just needed to vent."

Shit. I forgot she was so stubborn. I'd need a different approach. "I wasn't offering to fix anything, slugger. I just thought that you could use some moral support. It also wouldn't hurt to bring along a potential contributor as your date. Maybe your bosses would see it as ambitious."

She raised her brow. "Potential contributor?"

"Yeah. Spencer, Brant, and I have been looking into new opportunities to support. We have funds earmarked for it but haven't settled on anything yet. With the year half over, we need to find a charity soon." I tried to be nonchalant, but she was having none of it. Before I knew it, she had jumped up and launched herself into my arms.

She squeezed so tightly I was afraid she'd break a fucking rib but I was enjoying every second. "Thank you so much! I can't believe you'd do that for me." She let go and stepped back. "You don't even know anything about the charity. Are you sure you don't want to gather some info first?"

She'd used the words 'children' and 'hospice' when discussing the charity... hell no, I didn't need to hear any more. I was in.

"I don't see the need, but you might want to put together something for Spencer to look over. Not that he would rescind the offer, but it would assuage his OCD tendencies to have all the specifics on paper."

She was practically jumping up and down. "Lucky for him, I'm obsessed with details." Her smile was radiant. I had done that. I'd put someone else's problems first, taking her from desolate to elated in the span of one conversation. I'd wanted to help her and I did. Not because there was anything in it for me, not because I was attracted to her, but because she was someone I cared about, and I didn't like seeing her upset.

Looked like I was capable of being a good friend after all.

CHAPTER FOUR

D.C.
Present Day
The Evening of the Gala

I STEPPED OUT of the limo in front of the address Ali had given me. The apartment she shared with Talia was in a middle-class area of D.C., surrounded by small businesses that looked both new and trendy. Coffee shops, tiny art galleries, and bookstores peppered the storefronts across the street. It was the perfect location for Ali. Like the whole block had been built to suit her.

Tugging slightly at my collar, I made my way to the entrance. The doorman stood sentry and didn't smile as I approached. "May I buzz you in, sir?" He sounded so bored I nearly yawned in sympathy. For someone his age, which I guessed to be early twenties, standing there all day probably wasn't the most stimulating of jobs.

"Yes, please. Apartment 7B."

He moved at the pace of a sloth on fucking tranquilizers, taking his time locating the correct button, which I could see from five feet away. I reconsidered my earlier assessment, maybe he wasn't bored. It looked like he was fucking stoned. I bet he could find 7B if he was standing in front of a vending machine with a case of the munchies.

Just as I was about to step around him and hit the button myself, he found the damn thing and pressed. A moment later, as I confirmed my suspicion with a good look at his bloodshot eyes, Ali's voice crackled through the speaker. "Yes?"

Stony the Sloth cleared his throat. "Ma'am, you have a guest." He looked at me. "Your name, sir?"

"Clay McGavran," I told him in a clipped tone.

He passed the information on to Ali, and she asked that I come on up.

She buzzed to unlock the door, and Stony shuffled over to hold it open. The idea that he was in charge of keeping unwanted guests out pissed me off. He couldn't fend off a couple of girl scouts in his condition.

Though he'd welcome the cookies, I was sure.

When I exited the elevator on seven, I was surprised to see only two doors. Their apartment accounted for half the floor. Not bad. Square footage was a premium in D.C., and they looked to have plenty. Hell, the ceilings in the hallway were easily nine feet high, as would be the ceilings inside. I couldn't imagine going from an apartment that size to that tiny place above the old dry cleaner in Denson.

The door to 7B opened as I approached, and Ali stuck her head out into the hallway. "Hey, sorry I'm running a little behind. Come on in." She disappeared back inside.

I stepped into the spacious apartment and closed the door behind me. Yep, high ceilings and an open floor plan with lots of room. The furnishings were modern and attractive, mostly muted colors with a few bright accents. Everything was spotlessly clean and organized, including the two mammoth bookcases that sat on either side of the television. The TV was probably large, but it was dwarfed by the dark cherry pieces flanking it.

I smiled as I took in the apartment, seeing little hints of her everywhere. Spying a large bureau covered in framed photos, I couldn't help myself. I walked over and examined the pictures, most of which were probably of family. Ali with an older man whose hair and eyes matched her own, Ali and Talia at their college graduation, Talia and a middle-aged couple who I assumed to be her parents, though neither had her golden blond hair. Two little girls probably less than ten years old playing at the beach, one dark-haired and one blond. The two of them really had been close all their lives. Farther back, nearly hidden behind the other frames was a picture of Talia standing in the kitchen behind a beautiful blond moppet who couldn't have been more than two or three. They were making cookies, from the looks of the counter in front of them, smiling and sticking their tongues out for the camera.

I heard Ali enter the room behind me, her heels clicking on the hard floor. I turned, photo still in hand, with the intention of asking about the little girl.

As soon as I saw Ali, the question flew right out of my mind. I blindly sat the frame back on the table, only half aware of where I placed it. When my eyes fell on her again, I was instantly mesmerized. She was stunning. Absolutely fucking gorgeous. So much so that my mouth dried up and I lost the ability to speak. I just stood there like a jackass, gawking at the most beautiful creature I'd ever laid eyes on.

Her dress was a dark charcoal gray that shimmered in the light. The thin straps left her smooth shoulders exposed, and the fabric hugged her figure down to mid-thigh where it loosely fell to the floor, with a deep split up one side. She'd traded her usual locket for a diamond bar necklace. The vertical pendant nestled into her cleavage, pleasantly accentuating the full swell of her breasts.

Fuck the gala, I was content to just stand there all night and stare.

She cleared her throat and smiled when I met her gaze. "You look quite handsome, Mr. McGavran." She nodded to my tux, which was feeling a bit snug in the crotch area all of a sudden.

With much effort, I managed to corral enough saliva to allow speech. "You... um," *Shit, get it together.* "You're breathtaking." There, that was better. Not nearly enough to describe her but it would have to do.

Her cheeks reddened. "Thank you. I'd take credit for it, but it was all Talia's doing. She's the one with all the fashion sense. I'm more of a jeans and t-shirts kind of girl." She grinned. "It drives her crazy, too. She hated having to go to work tonight because she was worried I'd try to sneak out of here in flats. I had to send her a pic of me wearing the heels so she'd relax."

I chuckled. "Well, as long as we're confessing, I'm in no way responsible for this either." I indicated my appearance. "Spencer sicced the office staff on me, the bastard. Next thing I knew, some old guy was running a measuring tape up my thigh and asking whether I dress left or right while my assistant watched. I felt a little violated, to be honest."

Ali thought that was hysterical.

I plastered an affronted look on my face. "I guess it could have been worse. At least Gran and Vanessa didn't get their hands on me. They both tried, though. Caroline, my Richmond assistant, is a friend of Gran's, and she spilled the beans about tonight. It was pandemonium for a while there, trying to fend them all off. Sometimes I think Vanessa is just as bad as Gran, maybe worse since she's still young enough to chase me down if I try to run." They were the mother-daughter tag team from hell, so Spencer sort of bailed me out by having the assistants handle things.

Ali's laughter hadn't slowed one bit, and that was my objective. I planned to keep the tension at bay and Keith if necessary, though she wouldn't want me to step in.

A damsel in distress she was not.

Once she calmed down and ran to check that her make-up hadn't smudged, she plucked a small clutch purse from the coffee table and motioned toward the door. "You ready for this, Mr. McGavran?" She teased.

"I was born ready, Miss Walker." I winked at her and offered my arm, escorting her to the elevator.

The event was being held at one of the largest and most popular convention centers in D.C., according to Ali, whose word I would take since I had no idea about such things.

I stepped from the limo and turned to offer a hand to her as she exited, her eyes locked on the brightly lit entrance at the top of the stairs. I released her arm to close the door, signaling to the driver that he could park.

As I turned back to her, I saw the tension in her stance and in the rigid angle of her jaw. She was nervous but doing all she could to appear unaffected. When she turned to me, her smile was practiced, functional, and it didn't reach her eyes. Before she could take a step in the direction of the building, I reached for her hand, pulling her a step closer so only she would hear my words. "You'll do great, slugger. And I'll be right by your side all night. Have as much faith in yourself as I have in you, okay?"

Her green eyes searched my face for something though I didn't know what. Then she shifted her hand in mine and laced our fingers together the way one would with a lover. I gave her hand a gentle squeeze before lifting it to brush the back briefly with my lips. Something passed between us, some new strand added to whatever tether had been pulling us together all these weeks.

Without another word, and with much more confidence, we

approached the entrance. Ali with her shoulders back and head held high, and me with her tiny hand tingling in mine.

THE ROOM WAS enormous and so elegantly decorated that I was half afraid to touch anything. It made me slightly uncomfortable. I kept checking my hands to be sure there was no dirt on them. I had to keep reminding myself that I belonged there. I may have ended my days with dirt under my fingernails and sweat down my back, but I still matched the incomes of half the people there. I just wasn't one to show it. It seemed crass, somehow.

We made our way around the room slowly, having to stop and plaster on interested expressions and fake smiles every few feet when Ali was stopped by some acquaintance. Each time we excused ourselves, she muttered, "Keith's minion," letting me know just how duplicitous most of her colleagues were.

Or just how smooth Keith was.

Last week, Brant called to tell me about a strange email he'd gotten. Apparently, he'd received anonymous tip about Ali's suspension from GFS. Spencer hadn't mentioned getting the email, so I assumed it was only sent to Brant.

And I'd bet my left nut that Keith was the source.

We finished our initial lap around the room and were headed to the bar for a much needed drink when she stiffened, going completely rigid against the hand I'd placed at her back. I looked down at her, poised to ask what was wrong.

The hatred I saw on her face was jarring. She breathed slowly, deliberately through flared nostrils, teeth clamped together as her jaw worked, and her eyes, god her eyes were the brightest most penetrating shade of green I'd ever seen. They practically glowed, and not in a good way. I didn't need to raise my head to know who she had just seen.

Keith had arrived.

After a moment, I shifted the hand at the small of her back to grasp her around the waist. I pulled her against my side and whispered, "You can do this, slugger. Just pretend he's not even here. It's just you and me out having the time of our lives. Alright?"

She didn't look at me but nodded affirmatively.

"C'mon then, let's get that drink." I nudged her to get her going, and she moved confidently across the floor.

We stood at the bar, sipping our top-shelf drinks and quietly watching the flurry of activity around us. The room was filled with servers scurrying about, fetching drinks for those too important to do so for themselves. Forced smiles and meaningless chit-chat abounded. It was fascinating to watch clusters of people form and then, as they one by one departed, those remaining appeared to be gossiping about whomever had just left. Round after round of condescending remarks and sideways glances. No wonder Spencer was such a people-watcher. This shit was hilarious.

When one of the partners stopped over to chat with Ali, I introduced myself and told him that I'd been recruited by Ali to donate to the cause. I also mentioned that several of my business associates were donating as well, something I'd not told Ali beforehand.

She was shocked at the news. She'd have been even more shocked if she saw the size of the donations. I preferred to keep that figure to myself, though. I wasn't interested in gratitude, I just wanted to contribute to a respectable cause. I'd taken a peek at the information packet Ali sent Spencer. The charity being honored was incredibly worthy.

Her boss, Mr. Glenn as he was introduced, shook my hand and then turned to commend Ali on a job well done. She thanked him for his words and he soon excused himself to mingle. The moment he was gone, she turned to me. "You never told me you'd secured donations from other companies. That was such an amazing gesture, thank you."

I shrugged, uncomfortable with the praise. "Spencer did most of the work after you sent over the background information. All I did was suggest a few names."

She leaned over and placed a chaste kiss on my cheek. "Either way, thank you. And thank Spencer for me, too. I'd do it myself but who knows when I'll see him again."

I told her I would give him her thanks and turned to have our drinks refilled. When I turned back to her a minute later, she was staring icily into the face of her ex. I turned to glare at the piece of worthless shit that had tried to ruin her life.

And it clicked.

In the span of a single heartbeat, I knew why Ali seemed so familiar the day we first met.

And I wished like fuck I'd never remembered.

~

Fredericksburg
Early last year...

I STALKED THROUGH the halls of the hospital, the astringent smell stinging my sinuses. My phone grasped tightly in my hand, I raised it to again check the room number Spencer had messaged me. Looking up at the placards outside each room as I passed, I got more and more frustrated.

Why the fuck are the halls arranged like a honeycomb. What sadistic bastard designed this shit?

I got to the hallway that should have housed room 318 but after 317, there was a fucking storage closet. I was about to fucking break something. Where the hell was she? I pulled up my contact list and scrolled through, looking for Vanessa's number as I stomped down the hall. She worked in this maze, maybe she could help.

I turned yet another corner and, thank God, ran smack into Spencer. He looked at me as if I was a two-year-old. "Would you quit playing in the halls and get your ass in here. She's asking for you."

He turned, and I followed him to the room, still two corridors away.

When I crossed the threshold, I stopped.

She looked so small, pale, fragile. She wasn't supposed to look like that. She was supposed to be up running around like she was 18 instead of nearly 80, burning up the streets and calling us constantly to tell us about her crazy adventures. The woman in that bed looked nothing like her. Tubes and monitors were dripping and beeping. It wasn't right.

Her eyes opened as Spencer took a seat by the impersonal motorized bed. When she saw me, she smiled, a thin toothless smile that did nothing to ease my nerves. They'd taken her teeth? What the fuck for? I'd never seen her without them, not ever. It seemed like such an indignity to have them taken from her.

The longer I stood there, the more pissed off I got. At the hospital for treating her like an old lady, at Spencer for not telling me sooner that she had been sick, and mostly at her for coming so close to doing the one thing she promised she'd never do.

She motioned me over, but I stayed by the door.

"You said it was just a cold." I accused.

She sighed and pursed her lips. "I thought it was. It's not like I wanted to get pneumonia, Clay. It just happened."

"You've had it for weeks, and it never occurred to you to get checked out? You lied when you talked to us on the phone. Said you'd just had a physical and you were fine. You told me Vanessa had checked you out herself. Surely your daughter the nurse would have known you were sick, right?" I glared at her and shook my head. "She didn't know because you never saw her, dammit. It was a lie, Gran." I paced by the foot of the bed, needing to keep moving or I'd throw something. "Are you giving up on us? On me?" I hadn't meant for my voice to sound so damn small, but she promised.

"No, honey. I'm not giving up on anything. I'm just a stubborn old

fool who thought a little Vapo Rub was the cure for everything. I'll be out of here tomorrow and good as new in a few days." She looked over at Spencer and winked. "I have to be. I've got concert tickets for next weekend, and it's someone else's turn to spring for the beer."

He laughed and squeezed her hand, but I wasn't to be moved. I was fucking pissed, and no amount of joking was going to fix it. "That's just great, you two laugh it up. Real funny sitting here staring at your IV and catheter bags hanging from the bed. Fucking hilarious." I stepped over to the door. "I'll check on you tomorrow. I need some air."

I walked out and closed the door behind me.

As if I wasn't pissed enough, now I had to find my fucking way out of this place.

When I finally located an elevator, I selected the first floor and waited to see where the fuck it would spit me out. I hadn't been this angry in a long damn time. I needed to get away from the smell of antiseptic and into some place that smelled of booze and cigarette smoke.

The elevator doors opened, and I stepped out into another bland hallway. Fuck. Weren't there signs around here somewhere to tell you where to go? I looked both ways, neither looking like the way out. Randomly choosing a direction, I ground my teeth and hoped for the best.

Soon I came up on a set of double doors marked 'Emergency' and knew salvation was in sight. There had to be an exit through there.

I pushed the metal plate that opened the automatic doors and stepped aside as an orderly pushed through with a gurney. I turned to peer at the elderly woman he was transporting, and my heart sank again. Gran had probably looked like that as they wheeled her to her room.

It was with a profound sadness that I turned and stepped into the emergency room and nearly knocked over the poor woman who had been walking by.

She had her head down, long mahogany hair framing her face and obscuring it from view. I reached out to steady her, and she gasped. I looked on in horror as my hand unfurled from around her badly bruised upper arm. Shit! "Oh God, I'm so sorry Miss. I wasn't paying attention to where I was going. Are you alright?"

She didn't lift her head, didn't speak, just nodded and scurried off in the direction of the exit. Since I was headed that way myself, I kept an eye on her as she crossed the room. She limped slightly and nearly stumbled over someone's bag on the way out. Hanging her head like she was, it was a wonder she didn't run into the damn wall.

Something about her set off warning bells in the back of my mind.

She slipped out the doors as a young couple with an infant carrier was coming in. I stood back and let them through, but my mind was still focused on the dark-haired woman with the bruises. As soon as I was able, I darted through the door and scanned the area for her. I had nearly given up when I realized she was standing on the curb, several rows across the parking lot talking to a man.

From where I stood, I couldn't make out what they were saying but she seemed to be trying to move away from him. I watched for a moment longer, not wanting to intrude without reason, and nearly jumped out of my skin when she yelled "Get the fuck away from me," right in his face.

I was halfway to them when I saw his hand dart out and lock onto her wrist, keeping her from walking away. The last ten feet or so were a blur of movement I didn't really see. All I saw was his face as he snarled at her. The next thing I knew, I had the little bastard by his shirt collar, pinned against someone's SUV. He was wide-eyed and stunned at first, but that didn't last long. "What the hell are you doing, asshole? I'm trying to talk to my girlfriend, and you swoop in like a lunatic." He struggled against me, unable to get a satisfying grip. "Get the fuck off me before I call the cops, hero!"

I leaned into his face and sneered. "Good idea. Let's call so I can tell them about the bruises all over the woman you were just manhandling. That'll work out really well for you, you fucking pussy."

I slammed his head against the glass to emphasize my point. He glanced at something over my shoulder, and I turned to follow his gaze, secure in the knowledge that he couldn't go anywhere.

The woman was several spaces over, standing beside the open driver's door of a Jeep, peering at us over the hood. I still couldn't make out her face, but there was a flash of green as she turned and climbed into the car, speeding out of the parking lot a moment later.

After I was sure she had made it safely out of there, even waiting for the traffic light to change from yellow to red just in case, I dropped the little prick and watched with glee as he crumpled to the ground, gasping for air. I leaned down close, looking him right in the eye. "If you want to see tomorrow, you'll keep away from her. I've got access to her information, and I might just use that number she gave to check on her. I'd hate to find out you didn't listen. Understand, you little cocksucker?" I didn't have access, Aunt Vanessa would never give out confidential information, but I was convincing enough that he looked persuaded.

He nodded his head vigorously and tried to scoot back out of my reach.

Given my mood, he was lucky I didn't bash his skull in. As I climbed into my truck to leave, the woman's bruised arms flashed in my mind. Yeah, he was lucky I didn't fuck him up. If he ever crossed my path again, I still might.

~

AS I SNAPPED back to the present, I stood there watching him. The look of recognition on his face was quickly followed by fear. It took him a minute to get his shit together, and it was one of the best minutes of my whole fucking life.

The worthless piece of shit remembered me.

Good.

Ali stood ramrod straight beside me. She was unaware of the tension between me and Keith because she was fighting her hatred for him. As much as I wanted to torment the little bastard, I had to keep it together for her. She was the one with something to lose here tonight.

Her voice was laced with undisguised disdain as she asked him, "What do you want, Keith?"

He was at least six inches shorter than me, but his shorter frame didn't mean he was weak. He had the build of someone who routinely lifted weights, something he hadn't had when I pinned him against that car all those months ago.

Over-compensating for the humiliation perhaps? No matter. I could still take him. And I intended to, but not tonight. Not this way.

He pointedly ignored me and smirked at her. "Shouldn't you be reserving your spot on the unemployment line? Traitor."

I instantly understood her concern about being at the gala. I wanted to throat punch that little bastard myself.

She gave him a bored expression, making me proud. "Shouldn't you be off somewhere shopping for hair plugs?" When he barely fought the urge to touch his hair, actually raising his hand to check before catching himself, I nearly lost it. Being half a foot taller than him, I could see that his hair was indeed thinning. Ali chuckled. "Unlike you, I have no reason to worry. Can't prove something that didn't happen." She turned and lifted her glass. "If you don't mind, the smell of cowardice is quite pungent, and it's rolling off of you in waves. Perhaps there's some sort of deodorizing spray you could use next time." She pinned him with narrowed eyes as she lowered her voice, "Until then, fuck off."

He looked affronted but after his eyes darted to me, he bit back his reply.

Good idea, fucker.

When he slinked away with beet red ears and a childish scowl, I couldn't help laughing. She really did know how to handle him. But I wasn't done with him yet. Far from it.

I peered over at her, at the look of satisfaction and relief on her face, and I knew I couldn't tell her what I'd remembered. She would be mortified. She had way too much pride to take it well, and I was way too invested to give her a reason to push me away. No matter what, she couldn't know that I knew.

She met my eye and tapped my glass with hers in celebration, but all I kept seeing were those damn bruises.

After Ali had dispatched of Keith, she seemed to relax and enjoy the evening. She even managed to keep her composure during the presentations, which was not an easy feat.

I had damn-near cried and I was a hardass.

When they brought out some of the families who the charity sponsored, you could have heard a pin drop. As the parents stood and tearily spoke of their last days with their children, of the gift of being able to have that time with their babies without worrying about the financial repercussions of missing work, it tore my heart out.

Without charities like Outreach Hospice, parents would have to choose. Go to work so you could feed your family and pay for your child's medications or stay home with them and watch them suffer without. No one should have to make such choices when they're already in so much pain.

One of the last speeches was to honor the donors to the charity and included the level of sponsorship each had provided though they didn't mention exact figures.

I couldn't help watching Ali as the last of the speeches ended. She stood and clapped, as we all did, but her hands were trembling, and her whole body shook. This charity meant something more to her, something deeply personal.

The possible reasons for that frightened me.

After the formalities were over, Mr. Glenn approached us again, all smiles. He offered his hand, and I shook it. "I can't thank you enough, Mr. McGavran. Your donation and those of your associates were the largest of the evening. I want you to know that your generosity is much appreciated." I said nothing, just shook his hand firmly and released him.

He turned to Ali and gave her a warm smile. "Alison, I must

say that I'm impressed with your gumption. You've handled yourself well throughout everything. It's a sign of true class and dedication, and it didn't go unnoticed." He shook her hand as well. "I'll be in touch soon. Enjoy your leave of absence, I suspect it won't last much longer."

She smiled and thanked him, looking encouraged. When he left us once again, I asked if she wanted to stay a while longer. She grabbed me by the hand and pulled me onto the dance floor by way of reply.

Several drinks and dances later, Ali started winding down. She excused herself to powder her nose before leaving. I headed off to retrieve my jacket, having checked it when it became cumbersome on the dance floor. The evening replayed in my mind as I waited for the attendant to produce my garment. The feel of her in my arms, the squeals of delight when I dipped her and spun her across the floor. It was like being drunk without touching a drop. She did that to me just by being close. It was addictive.

And dangerous.

Once I had my jacket, I tipped the attendant and made my way back to the ballroom to wait for her.

When over ten minutes had passed without her return, I decided to go look for her. Keith and his date had been noticeably absent for the last hour or so, and something in my gut told me he hadn't retreated that easily.

A few minutes later, after pacing the hallway that led to the restrooms, I decided to check the quiet hallways at the far end of the building. I was just about to turn a corner when I heard her voice. "Whatever it is you think you know about me, you don't. So back off."

The reply was a woman's voice, high-pitched and haughty. "Keith told me all about you, didn't you, babe?"

When I heard his smug voice my fists clenched. "Not much to tell, I mean, look at her." He laughed. "Playing dress up and trotting out your boyfriend's checkbook won't make them believe you. You've been marked, sweetheart. Even if you keep your job, they'll never forget. Never. Not even daddy's money can erase it."

"He's not my dad, and I would be careful if I were you, Keith. I'd hate to spill your little secret to your obviously uninformed friend here." Ali was pissed but still in control. I wasn't sure what to do. Did I step into the middle of it and risk pissing her off, or stand there and let them shred her which was pissing me off?

I couldn't fucking win.

"What secret? What's she talking about?" That voice was like nails on a goddamn chalkboard.

He scoffed. "Nothing, she's just trying to deflect attention, hoping that her bullshit will distract you. Ignore her."

Ali wasn't backing down. "Fine. Believe him if you want, you'll find out soon enough. Certain... *shortcomings* are difficult to hide."

"Shut up. Who'd take the word of a frigid bitch like you?" Keith growled. Apparently, he hit his mark because he said, "See? Look at her dropping her head like a damn dog, she's ashamed because she knows it's true. Does the hero in there know he's got himself a cold fish? Guess he's in for a surprise, huh?" He snickered. "I've got to give you credit for making sure he stroked that check before he found out."

I barely heard her when she muttered, "Go to hell, Keith."

That was it. I was done listening to this shit.

I stepped around the corner and took in the scene before me. The hallway looked like a service corridor, none of the high-end art pieces adorning the walls, no exotic plants on silk draped tables, just a few unmarked doors and windows that overlooked the courtyard. Three people stood in the empty hallway, but only two heads swiveled in my direction.

Ali didn't look up, but I could tell from the shift in her

posture that she knew I was there. Standing way too close for my liking, Keith and his date backed away from her as soon as they registered my presence. I walked over to stand at her side and turned to face them. "There a problem here?" No response. "Maybe things in the ballroom got stuffy, and you were looking for someplace to get some fresh air." I shifted my gaze back and forth between them, nodding. "I couldn't agree more. That sounds like an excellent idea. How bout we step outside?" I pinned him with a stare, voice deadly serious. "You want to step outside with me, Keith?"

He and his date both seemed a lot less cocky than they had been a minute ago. Must have been something I said.

I stared him down, enjoying the random twitch in his jaw. He was pissed, but he'd never have enough balls to challenge me. Cowards like him rely on their ability to exploit weaknesses, and I didn't have one. Not where he was concerned.

His date, however, seemed to have some balls. She eyed Ali and said, "You boys do what you like, Ali and I can stay here and finish our conversation."

When Ali lifted her chin and met the woman's eye, there was no hesitation. "Absolutely."

Keith shifted on his feet, pulling at his collar and looking nervous as hell. "No, baby," he said to his companion, "We should probably be leaving now. It's getting late."

I couldn't tell if he was more afraid of me taking him outside, or the idea of Ali spending time with his date. Either way, it was pathetic. Such a fucking coward.

His date gave him an incredulous look and turned to leave, obviously getting a good whiff of his cowardice. When she slipped between me and Ali, she bumped Ali's shoulder. Hard.

Fuck. Not a good idea.

Ali's hand shot out and snared the woman by the arm, snatching her back as she stepped close enough that barely an inch separated their faces. The woman struggled to free herself, but Ali held firm. "I'd advise you to watch where you're going. You wouldn't want to get yourself hurt." Her eyes were narrowed, teeth bared. "Either tread a little more carefully, or Needle Dick over there," she pointed at Keith, "will have to carry you to the car. Understand?"

She released the wide-eyed woman, giving her a shove in Keith's direction. Ali and I watched her as she stumbled over to him, and they stood looking at each other, neither seeming to know what to do.

Ali turned to me for the first time since my arrival, a tight smile on her face. "I'm ready when you are." She glanced down at her empty hands. "Well, as soon as I grab my purse. I must have left it on the table."

I nodded, not taking my eyes off of Keith. "You go ahead. I'll be right there." His eyes widened, knowing I wasn't finished with him yet. "Actually, meet me at the bar, one last drink and we'll head out."

I could feel her eyes on me. I knew she didn't want me fighting her battles, and she was probably pissed that I wanted to stay behind. She didn't argue, though. "Alright. Don't take too long or I'll drink yours too." She turned and made her way back to the ballroom, her heels clicking on the expensive marble flooring.

When I could no longer hear her footfalls, I closed the distance between Keith and myself. His date muttered something about meeting him at the car and scurried away, rubbing her upper arm. That left us all alone in the deserted corridor. I could see his pulse in his neck, the vein bulging rhythmically under a fine sheen of sweat. He couldn't quite look me in the eye, choosing instead to look slightly to my left.

Pussy.

He was so pathetic it almost sucked all the fun out of it. *Almost.* I wouldn't make him piss himself tonight, though he looked to be on the cusp of it already. No, I had only one point to make and then he could scamper off to make amends with his escort.

I decided I'd made him sweat long enough. The stench of him had become repulsive. I leaned in, bringing my face so close he had no choice but to meet my eye. "Don't worry. I'm not in the mood to get blood on my shoes tonight. I just thought you should know that you're wrong about Ali. She is far from frigid." I smiled as his eyes widened in surprise. "I made her come twice in the limo on the way here, so I'm pretty sure whatever problems you guys had in the sack had nothing to do with her." I leaned back and regarded him with a thoughtful expression, arms crossed over my chest as I studied him. "If I had to guess, I'd say it was operator error. You just don't know how to fuck."

His face turned scarlet, and he dropped his eyes, saying nothing.

"Yep, that's what I thought. Dropped your head like a damn dog, so it must be true." I waved him off dismissively. "Have a good night, Keith. Please pass my sympathies along to your date. It sounds like she's the one who's in for a disappointment."

I walked away without a backward glance, leaving him to tend his bruised ego.

CHAPTER FIVE

A SHORT TIME later the two of us were riding in silence back to her apartment, the limo's plush interior providing little comfort. When I'd joined Ali at the bar, she'd said nothing just sipped her drink for a few minutes before draining it and giving me a pointed look, as if to say 'take me the hell home'.

I couldn't be sure if she was angry with me, or still seething from the run-in with her ex. Either way, I wanted to fix things between us before parting company for the night. If she thought I overstepped, I wanted her to tell me, take it all out on me if that's what she needed. Sitting there in the seat across from mine, she looked like she was about to explode, and not in a fun way.

She'd been staring out the heavily tinted windows for several minutes, her clutch held tightly in her hands. The slight furrow of her brow and tensing of her jaw was more alluring than it should have been. I decided I'd wasted enough time letting her work the shit out in her head. It was time for her to talk to me. Hopefully, she wouldn't bite my head off.

I cleared my throat, careful not to be too loud. She stiffened but didn't turn. Frustrated, I started talking anyway. "I know the night wasn't exactly perfect, but I'm still honored to have been your date. You're probably angry at me for what I did earlier and I'd like to tell you I'm sorry... but I'm not." That got her attention. She looked over at me with narrowed eyes and crossed her arms over her chest. It wasn't easy continuing my thought with her cleavage pushed up like that. *Shit. Focus.* I lifted my eyes to hers, realizing she had seen my inadvertent inspection. "I'm not going to apologize for taking him down a notch, he desperately needed it. Hell, he needs much more than that but I toned it down out of respect for the venue."

She nodded almost imperceptibly but still looked angry. "I appreciate that you didn't mop the floor with him. Shame I didn't have as much restraint." She shook her head. "I knew I'd end up letting my temper get the better of me. Dammit."

"Wait, so you're not mad at me?"

"Pfft... you weren't the one who couldn't keep their hands to themselves."

I was so relieved that I almost laughed. I smiled at her and shook my head. "She had that coming. She slammed into you because she thought you could be intimidated. When she realized she failed, she backed down. Typical bully MO. I thought it was hilarious." She quirked a brow at me, looking slightly amused. I threw my hands up, looking sheepish. "Hey, I can't help it. All guys are hard-wired to enjoy girl fights. It's in our DNA."

She laughed for the first time since leaving the Gala. It was music to my ears, but it didn't last long. She looked at me for a moment, a new worry in her eyes. She shifted in her seat and dropped her gaze before saying, "I'm sorry you had to hear all the horrible things Keith and I said to each other. Between that and my temper, I can't imagine what you must think of me now."

There was sadness in the way she said the last sentence, as if something important between us had been tarnished by the events of the evening. I hated that look. I hated that the bastard who put it there wasn't worthy of her.

More than anything, I hated that he had made her believe she was broken.

I slid forward in my seat, resting on the very edge, and reached for her hand. She unfurled her arms, taking her time as she watched me in confusion. When she placed her right hand in mine, I squeezed it reassuringly. "You want to know what I think of you?" She tried to turn away, but I reached up with my free hand and slid my fingers along her chin, turning her back to face me.

It hurt my heart when she flinched involuntarily at the unexpected touch. Keith had done that to her, the son of a bitch.

I pretended I didn't notice her reaction, keeping my hand there and lightly stroking her jawline with the backs of my curled fingers. "I think you're amazing. I think you're strong. I think you're intelligent and hard-working and loyal and beautiful." My gaze flicked to her lips before refocusing on her eyes. "Like I told you before, those people don't know you. Not even him." Her eyes clouded at the reference to her ex. "I think he's the one that knows you the least, Ali. If, in all the time you were together, he didn't see what I saw the first time we met, he's even dumber than he looks." A tear rolled down her cheek, and I whisked it away with my thumb. "You're the warmest person I know."

She took a deep breath, blinking several times to clear away the tears. She squeezed my hand as she said, "Thank you. I know he's just an asshole, and I shouldn't let him get to me." Her voice fell to a whisper. "But he knows exactly where my weaknesses are, and he never lets me forget."

I knew exactly what 'weakness' she was referring to, and I had a strong suspicion that they were both wrong. I'd seen it in her eyes, the heat of desire, the hunger. All she lacked was someone to bring it to its peak and then send her tumbling over the edge. Both Keith's demeanor and Ali's apt nickname for him were clear indications that he just wasn't equipped to handle the job. Instead of trying to learn what she craved, he convinced her she was broken.

I started to speak but wasn't sure what to say. I didn't want to make her uncomfortable by discussing his allegations openly, but I wanted desperately to argue with her, to tell her not to buy into his bullshit. I debated it in my mind for a moment, trying to figure out what to say to convince her and then wondering if she'd even want me to say anything.

The decision was made for me a moment later when the driver announced that we had arrived at Ali's building.

She smiled at me as she released my right hand and glanced at the hand that was still stroking her jawline. "I guess this is it. Thank you for escorting me and for standing up for me, even though you knew it might tick me off." She nuzzled my hand for a moment, sending a jolt of heat straight to my cock. Lifting her head and waiting for me to retract my hand, she brightened. "And most of all, thank you so much for what you did for Outreach Hospice. You have no idea how grateful I am."

When she moved to exit the limo, I stopped her. "Wait a second." I climbed out and held the door open, offering my hand to help her slip out. She took my hand and stepped from the car, righting herself on the sidewalk and mumbling her thanks as if she thought I was just going to climb back in and drive away. There was no way I was doing any such thing. Instead, I nodded to the entrance. "Please allow me to see you to your door, Miss Walker."

She looked momentarily perplexed by the request but

smiled and nodded, threading a hand through my proffered arm and grasping my bicep.

There was a different doorman this time, one that appeared to be more sober than the last, who smiled fondly at Ali, telling her he'd missed her the last few weeks. She pretended to scowl at the older gentleman and told him he was just missing the coffee and snacks she usually brought down for him. He chuckled but told her that the treats were only part of it as he held the door for us.

I could tell she was still upset as we waited for the elevator. Her eyes were once again downcast, and there was a crease between her brows that I had come to recognize. She was still bothered by Keith's accusations and even more so because I had overheard them, which had to have been mortifying for her. Knowing I had very little time left, I tried to conjure the words necessary to fix the situation but continually came up blank.

Nothing.

Nada.

We stood in silence as the elevator climbed to her floor. When the doors opened, I motioned for her to exit ahead of me. As I followed her to her door, I struggled for something to say. Anything. I glanced over that the other apartment, grasping for a source of conversation. "I imagine it's nice only having one neighbor. My last apartment, I had three and one of them liked to have his band over to practice at all hours. Drove me crazy." I hadn't thought about that crappy apartment in ages. I was desperate for something to say.

She looked over at the closed door of 7A and nodded, reaching into her bag for her keys. "Yeah. They're pretty quiet. They're an older couple who don't get out much. Sometimes I go over to check on them and ask if I can pick up something for them at the market. She's always baking things and bringing them over. They're sweet." She mumbled 'aha' and pulled a small keyring from her purse.

She turned to face me, poised to say her goodbyes, when her clutch slipped from her fingers and fell to the floor. It landed at her feet, its shining metallic color matching her heels. She groaned in frustration and started to retrieve it, but I held out a hand to stop her, signaling that I'd get it.

As I knelt down in front of her and reached for the bag, her breath caught. I glanced up and realized I was eye-level with the deep slit in her dress. The creamy flesh of her thigh peeked out from behind the silky gray curtain of her gown. Crouching there, I was so close I could smell the scent of whatever lotion she had used, one that made her skin shimmer in the light and beg to be touched. Whatever it was, it was making my mouth water.

I turned my face toward the opening, knowing she could feel my breath on her exposed skin. When goosebumps formed a moment later, I knew I had her attention. It wasn't intentional, at least not at first, but there was no doubt that she was aroused. I heard her breathing turn shallow as I leaned closer and picked up the purse, making sure to exhale on the way down, skimming my breath down her entire thigh and calf. She shivered as I slowly stood, our bodies mere inches apart.

I offered her the shiny bag and, when her fingers deliberately brushed over mine as she accepted it, it was my turn to shiver. Her eyes were hooded with obvious desire. Her erect nipples strained against the thin fabric of her gown.

Frigid, my ass.

As if sensing that I'd been thinking of Keith's accusation, her whole demeanor changed, her expression crestfallen. She shook herself and stepped over to unlock the door.

When she had it open, she turned to tell me good night. The look on her face was almost more than I could bear. She looked ashamed and dejected as if she truly fucking believed she was broken. "I'm sorry, Clay. I really can't do this." She smiled sadly. "I don't want to humiliate myself any further, so I'll just say goodnight, and I'll see you at work on Monday. Okay?"

She didn't wait for my answer, didn't look me in the eye, just closed the door with a soft click.

The look on her face as she shut that door would haunt me forever. It was a good damn thing I didn't know where Keith lived. I'd have tracked him down and broken his worthless fucking neck. But that wouldn't fix this, no amount of payback would change her mind, convince her she wasn't broken.

Revenge wouldn't help, but I knew damn well what would. I'd told Keith Ali had come for me twice tonight. Time to turn that lie into truth.

I took a deep breath and knocked on the door.

I'd been steeling myself for damnation all along... time to jump into the flames.

～

ALI OPENED THE door, her brows drawn together in confusion. "Clay? I thought..."

I didn't give her time to finish. I stepped over the threshold and placed my hands on both sides her face, tilting her head back so she would look me in the eye. There were streaks of moisture on her cheeks, proof that she'd been crying. I wiped them away with my thumbs and held her there. My tone garnered no argument as I spoke. "Alison, you are not frigid." She tried to look away, a defense mechanism I'd come to recognize. I leaned down into her line of sight. "How can you not see that? Out there in the hallway just now, are you telling me you felt nothing? That you weren't turned on?" She met my eye, and a blush crept into her cheeks. I nodded. "I thought so."

She gasped when my mouth crashed into hers, my kiss firm

but slow. She responded instantly, her lips parting and inviting me in. I took my time slowly exploring her mouth, nibbling her lower lip, grazing her tongue with mine in slow, soft strokes. She pressed herself closer, groaning into my mouth and I responded by pressing my body into hers as I kicked the door closed behind me.

The sound of the door slamming caused her to jerk her head back, her lips swollen and pink as she studied me. Her gaze flicked to my mouth, and I knew she wanted more, but I wasn't going to kiss her again until I made my point. I left one hand cupping her face and lowered the other to her hip. When I brushed my fingers across her abdomen, her muscles fluttered involuntarily, making her shudder.

I leaned in so close that I could feel the heat from her lips, but I didn't make contact. Her eyes had drifted shut in anticipation of my kiss. When I didn't follow through, she opened them slightly, and I waited for her to look at me fully before speaking. "What about now? Are you thinking about what it would be like? The two of us together? Because I am, and it wouldn't be the first time." I brought my hand up to caress her breast through her gown paying special attention to the hardened nipple, brushing my thumb back and forth. "How do you like it, Ali? Do you want my mouth here? Sucking and licking until you're ready to explode? Swirling my tongue around that tight nipple while you're pulling my hair and grinding yourself against me?"

She threw her head back and moaned as I rolled the nub between my fingers, my mouth moving down her exposed neck. I took my time as I trailed my tongue over the sensitive flesh, stopping frequently to employ my lips, alternating suction and soft exhalations that caused her to shiver.

I'd wanted to do this for weeks, spent countless hours imagining just how she'd taste... and now I was starved for her. If I didn't go slowly, that thin thread of control would snap, and I'd take it farther than I should.

The feel of her skin on my tongue was addictive, consuming. My entire body was attuned to it, in the same way an addict must feel at the precise moment he gets his fix.

It was euphoric skimming her flesh with my mouth, hearing her fast, shallow breaths as I explored.

When I reached the dip between her neck and collarbone, I flicked my tongue across the crevice over and over, doing exactly what I planned to do when I made my way to her sweet pussy. A little preview so she'd know just how fucking serious I was about making her come.

Her chest heaved under my mouth, her hands on the back of my neck pulling me into her. Soft whimpers escaped as she panted, causing my cock to swell painfully against the constraint of my slacks. Shit. Those little noises she was making turned me on more fiercely than anything I'd ever heard in my life. It was such an honest, pure sound. Nothing forced or attention seeking about it. She wasn't playing a part or doing what she thought was expected. It was genuine enjoyment, and it made me want to rip the expensive dress from her body and bury myself inside her just to see what those moans felt like from the inside.

Her whole body shook with desire, she tossed her head from side to side as she fought to hold herself upright, her legs trembling beneath her. She needed to brace herself against something, fast.

I returned my attention to her mouth as I spun us around and backed her up against the door. She leaned back against it and sighed into my mouth. Satisfied that she wasn't going to fall, she took control of the kiss, gently sucking my tongue before nipping at my lip and starting over. Jesus, this woman could kiss better than most women fucked.

While she drove me absolutely crazy with her mouth, I slid

my hand up her outer thigh, tracing the slit in her gown and caressed the warm skin with my fingertips. I barely held back a smile when she shifted to press her core against my leg. She probably hadn't even been aware of it, she was just that responsive.

Not one to disappoint, I pressed my thigh into her, the heat of her body easily felt through the layers of fabric between us. She shuddered and sucked my lower lip. Hard.

Fuck. Who was supposed to be coming, me or her? I had to focus, or I would forget the point of this.

I pulled my leg back, the loss of heat immediate. She whimpered in frustration, which was just as sexy as the whimpers of pleasure. Hmm... teasing her might be fun.

Next time.

No, there was only tonight. There would be no next time. I'd prove to her that she wasn't broken, and that would be the end of it. But I'd damn well enjoy tonight. Watching her come would be better than any orgasm I'd ever fucking had.

I slipped my hand into the opening in the gown and moved it to make space so I could continue my exploration and rub her through what felt like silk panties. I kept my attention away from her clit, knowing that was exactly where she wanted me but enjoying myself too much to rush things. I skimmed the back of my hand across her mound, realizing that she was waxed completely bare beneath the thin fabric, causing a low growl of appreciation to rumble deep in my throat.

I moved my other hand to the back of her neck, gripping the hair at her nape and softly tugged until she pulled her mouth away from mine and met my eye. "Do you feel that?" I zeroed in on her clit with my fingers, her panties already so damp I could feel her arousal on my fingers. "You're drenched. You're dripping wet and ready for me." Her hooded eyes rolled back as I ran two fingers up her slit, pressing firmly over her clit and circling it over and over. When she looked at me again, I pressed a quick kiss to her lips and held her eye. "Tonight isn't about me, though. This," I licked her lower lip, "is about you. Everything tonight is for you, to show you just how fucking perfect you are." I pressed my forehead against hers, my voice dropping to a whisper. "Did you hear me, Alison? You're absolutely perfect, and I'm about to prove it."

She tried to nod, but I shook my head and raised a brow in question. I needed to hear her say it, no misunderstanding, no mixed signals. Eventually, she found her voice, low and raspy with desire. "Yes, please don't stop."

That was all I needed to hear.

I pushed the slip of fabric aside and plunged two fingers into her dripping pussy, the tightness surprising me. Christ, she was snug. My dick twitched in my pants, protesting its captivity. Ignoring it, I withdrew my fingers and brought them to my lips. Ali's eyes widened as she watched me lick them clean, groaning in pleasure as I lapped up her sweet juices before plunging them back inside her. I worked her with my hand, thumb poised over her swollen clit as I thrust into her again and again.

It wasn't long before I felt her walls tighten around my fingers, her body tensing as the orgasm built inside her. I pressed my lips to the spot just above her collarbone, knowing it was particularly sensitive. I flicked my tongue over it as I dipped my fingers into her and used my thumb to rub slow circles over her throbbing clit.

She leaned her cheek against the top of my head and gasped as the orgasm ripped through her. She threw her head back, and I snapped mine up so I could watch, not about to miss one second. Her expression was a mixture of shock and rapture, as I knew it would be. Her pussy milked my fingers as I continued to stroke her, pushing against the sweet spot just behind her pubic bone and making her cry out as she came. I wrapped my free arm around her waist and held her up, seeing that her legs were starting to give out as she rode my hand, gasping and calling my name. My cock pulsed, and I thought I might come right there.

She called out again, and I had to bite my fucking lip to distract myself, the sound of my name tumbling from her swollen lips was enough to make my balls tighten and my dick throb with need. She was about to make me come without even touching me. I was dumbfounded by my reaction and more aroused than I'd ever been.

A minute later she breathed a contented sigh and straightened. I removed the arm supporting her taking my time to be sure she was alright to stand on her own but left my fingers deep inside her. I brushed my thumb over her clit, careful not to apply too much pressure to the sensitive nub and she closed her eyes, a contented smile on her face.

I leaned in and took her mouth in a slow, deep kiss. When I pulled back, I took a moment to just look at her. She was so damn beautiful she actually glowed. She sighed again and opened her eyes, smile widening when she met my gaze. She looked as if she wanted to say something but couldn't find the words.

How cute, she thought it was over.

Not even close.

I slowly withdrew my fingers and slipped them back into her, going as deep as possible. Once. Twice. Three times. After the third time, when her eyes had once again filled with arousal, I pulled out completely and brought my drenched hand up in front of her. She glanced at my slick fingers and stilled, obviously waiting for me to taste them as I had before. When I turned my hand to face her and held my fingers to her lips, her eyes widened but she licked her lips in anticipation. I nodded for her to open her mouth. "Here, beautiful. See for yourself how sweet you taste. Trust me, there's plenty for the both of us."

She reached up and grasped my wrist, bringing my hand to

her lips and taking my index and middle fingers into her mouth. She licked and sucked until I thought I'd lose my fucking mind. She pulled back until just the tips of my fingers remained then bobbed her head and took them both fully into her hot mouth. My cock throbbed in my pants as I watched her, imagining her on her knees before me, taking all of me into her mouth, swallowing furiously as I shot my load down her throat.

Fuck. Me.

I removed my fingers from her mouth, and her lips turned down in disappointment that I'd taken away her toy. Stepping so close that my erection pressed deep into her belly, I ran my hand over her thigh. "I'm glad to see you're still eager to play because I'm not done with you yet. I still haven't gotten my fill of that sweet pussy."

She pressed herself into me, her lips nearly touching mine as she spoke. "Take what you want, Clay. I can't wait any longer."

Oh, God. Don't say that.

If I took what I wanted, I'd be breaking my promise to Spencer, and I swore I wouldn't do that. Although I probably couldn't pick him out of a lineup right now if my life depended on it. Regardless, I swore I wouldn't fuck the employees, and I wasn't. I was just going to make her come a few times. Not the same thing.

Just keep telling yourself that, dumbass.

Ali pressed her lips to mine and resumed sucking on my tongue. I thrust in and out, fucking her mouth and kneading her breasts in my hands as she ground herself against me. I broke our kiss and moved slowly down her body, kissing my way to her breasts, her abdomen, her hip. The silky feel of her gown under my lips was surprisingly arousing. When I got to her left thigh, I ran my hand up the slit in her dress and pushed it up to her hip as I ran my tongue over her bare skin. Ali took the length of the dress in her hand and held it to the side, clearing my path.

I pushed her panties to one side and exhaled at the beauty of her.

I pressed my lips to her smooth mound and snaked my tongue out to run it quickly through her slit. She trembled and leaned against the door giving it a hard bump, placing her hands on my shoulders to balance herself. I glanced up as I ran my tongue over my lips, letting out a soft moan of appreciation as I savored her. She was the sweetest thing I'd ever tasted. I put both palms on her inner thighs and pushed, forcing her to open for me. I exhaled slowly, blowing cool air over her hot flesh.

Completely smooth and glistening wet, she was perfect. I pressed my face into her, exploring her folds with my tongue, dipping into her hot channel and circling her clit. I couldn't help nibbling her soft, bare, skin, which elicited an encouraging response from her. Each time I nipped her with my teeth she pressed herself into me, mewling and panting.

I moved over and brazenly bit her inner thigh, careful not to break the skin but using much more force than I had on her more delicate flesh. She writhed against me, gasping, and I knew there would be a mark. The idea of her finding it in the morning sent a jolt of pleasure to my cock. She would see the imprint in the mirror and remember my mouth on her, devouring her pussy like I was starving for it and just how good it felt to come all over my hand, my face. She'd relive it all over again in an instant because I had marked her, claimed her. Another deep growl ripped through my chest.

Tired of fighting the scrap of silk covering her, I clamped my teeth down on the thin band at her hip and pulled it apart with both hands. She sucked in a breath as I moved to the other side, repeating the action before tossing the ruined garment over my shoulder. Even without the panties in the way, craning my neck limited my access to her and her legs were beginning to shake. Not wanting to stop to find a comfortable spot, I wound my arms around her thighs from underneath and stood, sliding her up the door and bringing her legs over my shoulders.

Thank fuck for high ceilings.

I looked up from between her legs and saw the surprise on her face morph into raw hunger. She had her hands behind her, grasping at the tiny ledge at the top of the doorframe for balance. I winked at her and placed both hands on her ass, angling her lower body away from the door and holding her up in front of me before diving face-first into her pussy.

I licked and sucked at her clit then moved to thrust my tongue into her opening, feeling her clench appreciatively around me every time. Looked like someone had good muscle control. Testing my theory, I pushed my tongue into her as far as I could and groaned when she milked it. She was toying with me, and it was starting to test my resolve.

I decided it was time to show her who was in charge. I pulled my tongue from inside her and swirled it over her clit in hard circles, faster and faster. One of her hands threaded through my hair, pulling my face deeper into her pussy. I pulled my right hand around, managing to continue to support her body and still impale her with my thumb.

She tightened around me, thighs clamping down on either side of my head, pussy squeezing the thumb I'd buried inside her. I licked faster, harder, dipping down to flick the sensitive tip of her clit. The harder she squeezed, the faster I licked, sucked, and plunged my thumb into her. Round and round we went for several minutes. So long that I was a hairs-breadth from sliding her down the doorframe and onto my rock hard cock.

Just as I began to seriously consider breaking my promise, she stiffened and screamed. A string of obscenities fell from her lips, making me smile as I sucked her clit, letting her ride out her orgasm completely before I licked her clean.

When the last ripples of pleasure had gone, I let her slide

slowly down the door and stood before her, my hands resting lightly on her hips.

Feet planted firmly on the floor, she rose on her tiptoes and kissed me, tasting herself on my lips with a satisfied sigh.

I jumped when her fingers trailed over the bulge in my pants. She smiled into my mouth as she wrapped her hand around my cock and squeezed me through the fabric. Pulling back, she looked at me with a lascivious grin. "Looks like it's my turn." She ran her fingers up my length and licked her lips.

Oh, fuck. I hadn't planned on this. Hadn't thought that far ahead. I'd been so focused on her, on making her come just to prove she could, that it genuinely never occurred to me that she'd want to return the favor. Shit.

I claimed her mouth again, giving myself time to come up with something to say. She wound herself around my body like a cat, making coherent thought damn near impossible. I cupped her face with both hands, deepening the kiss and letting out an involuntary growl when she bit my lip. Fuuuck. I wanted inside her so bad. Maybe I should let her do what she wanted. She obviously intended to wrap those pouty lips around my cock. If what I'd done to her didn't count as sex, that shouldn't either, right?

Somewhere deep down I knew it was bullshit, but in my highly aroused state it sounded perfectly rational.

When she pulled back and began running her tongue down my neck, I didn't stop her. I didn't stop her when she circled her thumb over the head of my cock through my slacks. I didn't stop her when she unfastened my belt or when she unbuttoned my pants. I said nothing when she freed my throbbing erection, her eyes widening as she noted my size. She looked somewhat intimidated as she prepared herself to pleasure me.

Still, I said nothing.

But when she took me in hand and slid me all the way to the back of her throat in one swift move, I couldn't stay silent anymore. I growled, I moaned, I panted like a fucking teenager getting blown for the first time. I shook as I fisted my hands in her hair, clenching my jaw to keep from screaming as she bobbed up and down, taking every inch of me time and time again.

When she took my balls in her hands, caressing, pulling, fondling, I damn near lost it. She flicked the sensitive spot just below the head of my cock with her tongue, lapping at it. She leaned back and met my eye as she rubbed my tip across her lips, teasing me to the point of torture before taking me in her mouth and trying to swallow me whole.

She toyed with me for what seemed like hours, keeping me on the brink of exploding but never pushing me over the edge. Finally, she looked up at me with pleading in her eyes. "Come for me, please. I want to taste you like you tasted me." With that, she slammed my cock to the back of her throat and held it there.

I was gone.

A wave of heat rushed over me, pooling in my groin. My balls tightened. My cock pulsed. I shuddered and gasped, fisting her hair and pushing deep as I came. I spurted hot into her hungry mouth and she never missed a beat, her throat working around the head of my cock as she swallowed everything I gave her with a series of moans that vibrated through my whole fucking body.

When I'd emptied myself, I pulled back, afraid I'd choked her in my enthusiasm. She grasped my ass and pulled me forward, pushing my dick back into her as she sucked and licked me clean.

She stroked me softly with one hand as she released me from her mouth inch by inch and rose to her feet, planting a searing kiss on my lips.

She pulled back and playfully kissed my nose as she released me and began righting my clothes. Once she finished, she laid her palms on my still heaving chest and grinned. "No way was I letting you leave here unsatisfied. Not after that." She grasped my arm and tugged me further into the apartment. Her legs were still wobbly, forcing her to lean against me as we crossed to the kitchen. "I don't know about you, but I could use a drink."

CHAPTER SIX

WE STOOD IN THE spacious kitchen, choosing to lean our backs against the counter rather than have a seat at the center island as we sipped twenty-year-old scotch and caught our breath. Our sides touched as we took turns sighing into the comfortable silence.

After a while, I raised my glass to inspect the amber liquid. "This is excellent scotch. Lots of depth."

Ali glanced over at me and smiled as she nodded. "Talia's restaurant carries it, and her distributors adore her, so they send her an extra bottle once a quarter as a gift." She laughed softly, cheeks still flushed from our tryst. "Funny thing is Talia hates the stuff. She rarely drinks anything other than wine."

I chuckled. "It's a nice gesture, nonetheless. One I'm sure means a great deal to her, even if we're the ones truly benefiting."

Ali nodded and tapped my glass with hers. "To free booze." She turned to me, lip curving into a seductive smile as she held her glass up. "And to being mistaken. I've never had so much fun being proved wrong."

I clinked my glass to hers and took a deep drink, warmth

spreading in my chest as I kissed her lightly on the lips. "I'll drink to that."

Eventually, we finished our drinks and moved to the living room where we both plopped down on the couch, exhausted from the long evening. Ali slipped the straps off her heels, and they clattered to the floor as she rubbed her instep and sighed. "I swear, I'll never understand how some women wear those things every day. My feet are killing me."

I patted the empty cushion between us and motioned for her to give me her feet. She looked a bit surprised but complied, taking her time stretching her gorgeous legs across the couch. The same legs that had just been wrapped around my head as she rode my face.

Fuck, I could still taste her.

Keeping my focus off the impossibly high split in her gown, I took her slender feet in my hands and scooted under them so that the one I wasn't massaging would rest in my lap. I took her right foot in both hands and kneaded my thumbs up her instep, working my way to the ball of her foot, and back down to her heel. Her low moan of approval made my cock jump and begin to press against my fly again.

Shit.

I clenched my jaw as I listened to the soft sounds she emitted each time I pressed and stroked her tired feet. Not the same sounds she made when she came, but they were still arousing as fuck. I switched to her left foot and her right leg fell to the side, giving me a clear view all the way up her inner thigh. My mouth watered at the sight and my cock twitched in protest, having not had the pleasure of sinking into her tight pussy yet.

Yet?

Nope, it was done. Point made, theory proven. It was time to close the book on this and get the fuck out of there before I took it too far.

Yeah, because I hadn't already done that.

I finished with the massage and set her foot back onto my lap. Her eyes were closed and for a moment I thought she had fallen asleep. I placed my hand on the top of her foot and rubbed lightly, causing her to open her eyes. When she shifted to sit up a bit, a gap in her gown revealed the swell of her breast.

Twitch.

I focused on her face, trying desperately to ignore my erection. "It's getting late, and you look... tired. I should go so you can rest." I smiled knowingly. "I'm betting you sleep like a log tonight."

She blushed but held my eye. "I have a feeling you're right." She swung her legs off my lap, inadvertently brushing my cock as she did. "Let me walk you to the door." She stood and reached back for my hand with a sated smile.

I slipped my hand in hers and followed her to the door. She placed her hand on the knob and turned, eyes widening when I bent down and retrieved her shredded panties. I held up the scrap of ruined silk and grinned as I slipped them into my pocket. "Don't want Talia to come in and stumble over these. Literally."

She was still blushing but there was heat in her eyes as she nodded in agreement. "Wouldn't want that to happen." She blinked and cleared her throat, the heat disappearing. "Clay, I know this was only tonight, that it has to be that way. Neither of us can afford any complications right now, and I don't want you to worry that I'll try to make it into something it's not."

I should have been thrilled that she knew the score, that we couldn't go any further than this, but her words felt like a punch in the gut. I couldn't take the time to examine my reaction right then, though. Unsure what I wanted to say, I just stood there.

Ali rushed to fill the silence, trying to reassure me. "It's alright, Clay. Honestly. What happened here tonight," she placed one hand flat against the door, right where I'd held her body as I devoured her, "was incredible. You showed me a part of myself I never knew existed. You did things no man has ever done and made me feel like a woman for the first time in my life. I won't ask for more than that." She stepped over and placed her hands on either side of my face. "Even if I live to be a hundred, I'll never forget this night. Or the man I shared it with." She pulled me in and kissed me, her mouth soft, her movements slow and deliberate.

It was a goodbye of sorts and, when I left there a few moments later, there was a feeling of heaviness in my chest that I knew would be with me for a long time.

I WOKE UP the next morning thinking of Ali. Not that it was a huge surprise. I'd gone to sleep thinking about her, too. I had to go back to Denson, the inspector would be by the next morning, and I needed to be there. I wanted to offer to give Ali a ride back, but I knew she planned to go with Talia.

The two of them had worked it out specifically for that reason. Talia hadn't returned to D.C. on Thursday like she usually did. She waited for Ali to finish up at the realty office on Friday, and then they ran to the berry patch and paid a lot more money for pre-picked berries so that they could leave as early as possible, Talia driving them home to D.C. to prepare for the Gala.

I couldn't ask Ali to go back with me after they had gone to all that trouble. Could I? I debated the idea as I showered, shaved, and ran a brush through my unruly hair. By the time I was dressed, I'd convinced myself to leave her alone. Then after I finished packing up my things, I'd decided it wouldn't hurt to ask.

Two hours in the truck together would give us plenty of time to sort things out.

I had no fucking clue what we needed to sort out, only that it was important that we talked. Maybe I didn't like the idea that she assumed it was easy for me to walk away. Maybe I wanted her to know that I hadn't used the situation to get what I wanted from her. Whatever the reason, I wanted her with me today. It was important.

I blew out a breath as I placed the call.

When she answered, the sound of her voice made my heart gallop in my chest. She sounded chipper as always. "Good morning, Clay."

I smiled despite my tension. "Good morning to you. Did you sleep well?"

There was humor in her voice as she said, "Better than I ever have. How about you?"

Oh, I had a hard-on most of the night and couldn't stop thinking about you screaming my name while I buried my face in your hot, tight pussy. "Like a rock." *Close enough.*

She chuckled, and I could hear her spoon clinking against her coffee cup as she stirred in what was sure to be a mountain of creamer. "You still at the hotel?"

I'd booked a room in D.C. rather than try to drive back to Richmond after the Gala. Good damn thing, too. "Yeah, just getting ready to check out. Thought I'd call before I left to see if you'd like to ride back with me." The offer hung in the air for a moment and I kind of wished I could reach out and snatch it back.

She paused, the sound of her sipping her coffee filling the dead air in the line. "Can you hang on just a second? I need to check with Talia."

"Sure. Take your time." I felt like a shit for asking when I knew she'd planned to go with Talia, but I couldn't help myself.

I could make out faint voices on the other end but couldn't

catch what was being said. After a minute, Ali came back on the line. "That would work out well, actually. I'm still getting my things together, running way behind. Talia's head was about to explode because she's in a rush to get dinner started." She laughed. "Her pot roast takes all day, but it's so worth it."

I was suddenly smiling from ear to ear. "Perfect. She can go on ahead, and I'll be over to pick you up in about an hour. Is that enough time?" She told me she'd be ready by then. "I'll even bring breakfast. Craving anything specific?"

I sure as hell was.

She told me to surprise her, which sent my mind straight into the gutter again. I told her I'd see her soon and ended the call thinking she'd looked plenty surprised when I'd coaxed that first orgasm out of her. Stunned was probably a better description. I kept seeing it in my mind over and over, her writhing against me, shaking, panting, fucking glowing.

Shit. I was getting hard again.

Good thing I had a little extra time before I picked her up. I needed a cold shower. Or a warm hand... I'd decide on the way to the bathroom.

ALI PROBABLY WOULD have met me in front of her building had I bothered to call when I arrived. Since I wasn't sure how much stuff she would be carrying, I decided to do the gentlemanly thing and walk her down. I stood quietly while Stony the red-eyed doorman buzzed Ali's apartment. He looked a bit more lucid this morning, but I remained unimpressed.

When I repeated my name so that he could announce me, there was a dim flicker of recognition. After Ali had confirmed that I was welcome, he nodded to me and said, "You were here last night, right?" I told him I was and went to step through the door as he mumbled. "I thought so. Double shift yesterday had me pretty worn out, but I knew your face was familiar." I just grunted noncommittally, fighting back an eye-roll.

Sure. It was the hours that were fucking with his memory.

I couldn't help stewing a bit on the way to Ali's apartment. I still felt that having that guy manning the door felt like a serious safety issue. Do what you want on your own time, not my business. But when you're watching the door for someone important to me, be on your fucking toes.

It pained me to admit it, especially to myself, but Ali was becoming very important to me. Not just because of what had happened between us, although I'd be a fool to believe my attraction to her wasn't part of it. More than wanting to bang her like a screen door, I also wanted to protect her. That was the scariest part, I think. I looked at her and saw someone grounded and confident, someone who could stand on her own. So why did I feel so damn compelled to save her, protect her? Why did I want so badly to follow a step behind, arms at the ready in case she should fall?

She didn't need saving and she damn sure didn't want it. She hadn't once asked me to save her from anything, so this wasn't a reaction to something she'd been putting out there. It was an instinct, plain and fucking simple. This was me, wanting to break all my rules for her. I wanted her to count on me, to know I had her back no matter what.

And it was freaking me the fuck out.

I'd spent the last twenty years cultivating my charming but aloof persona, making damn sure everyone around me knew that I didn't want personal attachments. The only people close to me had been the ones who were around before things had gone so bad, before my choices cost someone their life. Spencer, Gran, Vanessa, they all knew, but they stuck around, dug their heels in and refused to leave even when they had every right to run screaming from the train wreck that was my life.

Would Ali do the same? What if she found out? Would she stick around or...?

Didn't matter, she'd never know. I couldn't risk telling her. Not now. I couldn't give her a reason to leave because I was afraid that was exactly what she'd do. And, more than anything, I didn't want to let her go.

She may not have needed me to save her but having her in my life was saving me.

~

AFTER I INSISTED on carrying Ali's things to the truck, despite her assurances that she could handle it, we made our way downstairs. Stony held the door, and I motioned for Ali to go first, then bristled when he took his time inspecting Ali's cleavage as she exited the building. Her V-neck t-shirt wasn't particularly revealing, but there was still plenty for him to appreciate. She had on khaki shorts that showed off her toned legs and wedge sandals. Casual and fun, just like her.

When I walked out behind her, Stony had moved to watch her retreating form, perfect ass slightly swaying as she walked. I cleared my throat, and his head whipped around. He knew he'd been caught. I didn't say a word, but the hostile stare I gave him caused him to swallow uncomfortably and drop his gaze to the ground as he muttered, "Have a good day, sir."

I had to force myself to relax as I approached the parking lot behind Ali, not wanting to explain my sour expression.

We loaded her things in the back seat with mine and hopped into the cab of my truck, the aroma of hot coffee and warm donuts greeting us as we did. Ali grinned as she sipped her coffee, looking impressed. "This is delicious. You got it just right." She placed it in the cup holder and reached for the paper bag between us. She giggled when she rummaged through it and found the ones with strawberry icing. "You know, Talia makes amazing strawberry donuts. I'll have to get her to make you some."

"That sounds great. I've been craving strawberries a lot lately." Ever since we shared that moment at the berry patch.

She must have known what I was referring to because she blushed. "Yeah. Me too."

We spent the next few minutes in silence while we ate our sugary breakfast. I nearly ran off the fucking road when she began licking the icing off her fingers. One by one, she placed them in her mouth, licking and sucking them clean. Fuck. Me.

Eyes on the road, McGavran.

Finished with her breakfast, and her fingers, thank God, Ali turned in the seat and tucked one leg under the other. She was facing me, and one glance at her told me she wanted to talk. Despite my original desire to do just that, I found myself dreading whatever was about to come out of her mouth. There was a good chance that she was regretting what happened between us. If so, I was about to get the 'I just want us to be friends' speech for the first time in my life. I could deal with being nothing more than friends, it would be much less complicated that way, but the thought that she might regret our encounter fucking gutted me.

We stopped at a red light, the truck's cab silent. I took a deep breath and met her eye, afraid of what I might find there. She was smiling. Genuinely smiling as if she'd never been happier. Thank fuck. She placed her elbow on the center console and rested her chin on her hand, studying me. "Something occurred to me this morning."

Oh shit. "What's that?" I wasn't sure I wanted to know.

A horn blared behind me and I returned my eyes to the road as I rolled through the intersection. I could still feel her gaze on me. "I never found out what was said after I left you alone with Keith last night. I think you owe me some details."

Damn. I'd forgotten all about that. "I guess I do." She was

going to be pissed, but I had to tell the truth. "I told him that he was wrong about everything but especially about you being cold." I'd never use the term 'frigid' in her presence again.

"And?" She knew there was more.

"And I told him that he just didn't know how to fuck because I'd already made you come twice on the way to the gala."

She jerked upright, shocked. Her body was twisted toward me, and I could feel her staring. I may have flinched slightly. She was about to rip my head off, and I brought it on myself. I should never have said anything to him. She didn't need me defending her.

When her howl of laughter ripped through the cab, I instinctively stomped the brake, panicked at the sudden noise. It took me a second to grasp what was happening, Ali was bent forward in the seat, clutching her stomach as she laughed hysterically into the floorboard. I checked my mirrors — relieved that no one had been behind us because we surely would have gotten rear-ended — and pushed 'resume' on the cruise control.

I couldn't help laughing as I watched her. She sat back and wiped her eyes though more tears streamed down her face a second later. We both laughed for several minutes, her out of apparent amusement, and me in relief that she hadn't been angry. She got herself together enough to speak and looked at me. "It wasn't exactly a lie, more of a prediction." Then she cracked up again.

Though she was obviously alright with what I'd done, I had to say something. "I'm sorry if I overstepped, but I couldn't help it. The hateful little prick had it coming."

Her laughter peaked all over again. She sputtered out, "Little prick is exactly right." before she doubled over again.

It took some time before she finally calmed down and, when she did, I asked something that definitely crossed the line and was likely to piss her off, but the curiosity was killing me. "Had you ever orgasmed before last night?"

She sucked in a breath, blushing all the way down her neck but holding my eye. Not wanting to run us into a ditch, I turned my eyes forward. Her voice was surprisingly steady when she replied. "Yes, just never with a partner."

Oh, holy fuck, I was picturing her pleasuring herself, and it made me instantly hard. I was dying to ask for more details. With her hand? A toy? Both? I would have loved to see that show. My God.

She snickered at my reaction, my desire probably obvious on my face. "I get to ask you a question now, right? I mean, it's only fair." I nodded hesitantly, and she sat looking at me for a moment. I could feel the heat of her stare on the side of my face. "How old were you your first time?"

"Thirteen." Her soft gasp told me she thought it was too young and, although I agreed, I didn't regret it. "I was stupid and in a hurry for something I didn't even fully understand." That was the truth, sadly. I didn't want to focus on that. I was more interested in my next question for Ali. "Is Keith the only lover you've had?" If she'd only been with him, and he had no clue what he was doing, it made sense that she'd never come with anyone before.

"No. My high school boyfriend and I..." she trailed off. "But it was only a couple times and hardly lasted a minute each time. He was seventeen, after all, and just as inexperienced as I was but he was sweet, and he truly cared about me." Her voice was laced with sadness when she went on. "It may not have been the best sex ever, but at least he was a good guy. If I'd waited, if I'd given that first time to Keith, it would have been the biggest mistake of my life." She touched the hand I'd rested on the console. "The only real first I had left, he didn't get. I gave that to you."

I flipped my hand over, palm side up, and she threaded her

fingers through mine. "I'm more honored than you'll ever know, Ali."

She leaned over the console and rested her head on my shoulder "Even though we're just friends, can we still have this sometimes?"

Not sure what she was talking about, I squeezed her hand. "This what?"

She squeezed back and nuzzled my shoulder. "Just being close like this. Nothing sexual has to happen. I know that was a one-time thing, that it has to be that way because we work together, but I'd really miss being close to you. It's comforting, safe. You know?"

I did know. I'd never been a snuggler, but with her I craved it. Her touch, her warmth, I needed the contact as much as she did, maybe more so. "I'd miss it too, Ali." I stroked her thumb with mine. "There's nothing wrong with comforting a friend, so there's no reason to stop." Of course, I knew that every touch, every hug, every caress was just pushing us closer to crossing the line, but I didn't give a damn right then. Not with her body pressed against me, and her hand in mine. It was where I wanted to be, and I wasn't going to pretend otherwise.

At least not today.

CHAPTER SEVEN

Denson

WHEN WE WERE about a mile from Ali's place, I leaned my cheek down onto her head and whispered, "Almost there, sleeping beauty." She stirred but didn't sit up, so I tried again. "Ali? We're back in Denson. We'll be at your apartment in a minute." She made a sound that was eerily like a growl. It was kind of sexy.

She groused a bit longer before sitting up, blinking rapidly into the early afternoon sun. "Wow. I can't believe I fell asleep." She turned to me. "You should have woken me."

I just smiled and shook my head. "No way. You were tired. Besides, even unconscious, you're better company than Spencer."

She chuckled as she adjusted her wrinkled clothes. I turned into the parking lot beside her apartment, and the smile fell from her lips. She stared out her window and placed one hand on the door. Confused, I parked the truck and leaned over to follow her gaze.

Talia stood on the landing by the door to the apartment, phone in hand and white as a damn sheet. She paced and gestured with her hands as she spoke to whoever was on the other end, looking distraught.

Ali turned to me with wide eyes. "Something's wrong."

We both jumped out of the truck and raced up the stairs to Talia. Ali got there first and, when Talia saw her, her face crumpled. She hung up on whoever she had been talking to and pulled Ali into a fierce hug. Ali turned them so that she was looking at me over Talia's shoulder. Her expression was scared and confused.

I stood there like a damn idiot, not knowing what to do or what was wrong. When Talia pulled out of the embrace and raised a shaking hand to point into the apartment, I was immediately alarmed. She sniffed and wiped her eyes. "God, Ali. I can't believe this." Her shoulders shook, and I thought she was going to break down. I was relieved when she managed to continue, though a cold feeling of dread was worming its way through my stomach. "It's all ruined. Every painting, every book, every scrap of clothing, all of it."

Ali looked like she might shake her friend. "What the hell are you talking about? What happened?"

Talia pointed again and this time I stepped over to the door, barely squeezing by them. What little I could see from the threshold was enough to chill me to the bone. It was like a damn tornado had hit. Talia finally found her voice. "Someone broke in and destroyed everything in sight. I didn't make it through the whole apartment, but there was black paint splattered everywhere. All the books are in the living room floor, and they're all torn apart and covered in paint. There are broken dishes everywhere. I could see your shredded canvases all down the hallway and there are cut up bits of clothes everywhere." Her voice climbed an octave with each sentence.

Ali gasped. I turned to find her peeking around me into the apartment. She looked around at the devastation and her lower lip trembled. Once. Then she looked up at me with anger in her eyes. "Somebody just fucked up. Colossally." She turned back to Talia. "Did you call the police?"

"Yes. They'll be here soon. Since it's," she used air quotes, "just a vandalism, they didn't seem to be in too big a hurry."

Standing out there sweating our asses off wasn't going to help the situation. I gathered the girls, and we headed back to the truck. At least we could wait for the police in the air-conditioning.

Ali sat in the back with Talia, comforting her friend between angry glances at the apartment. I watched them in my mirror, offering whatever small encouragement I could, but I felt useless. I couldn't do a damn thing to fix what had happened, and it pissed me off. They were both shaken, even if Ali was putting up a good front. I'd seen her lip tremble, and I'd watched her hands shake as she ushered Talia to the truck.

When the police arrived, I stayed with the girls as they inspected the apartment. I walked with them down the hall and heard Ali fight back a sob as she stepped over the remnants of her paintings. We discovered that Talia's room was relatively untouched with the exception of some broken picture frames, all of which held snapshots of her with Ali from what I'd seen.

It quickly became apparent that whoever had done this only targeted one of them. Ali. The more we saw, the madder I got. Some fucking body was going to pay for this. I'd make sure of it. Whoever the coward was, their ass was mine.

After what seemed like hours of pointless questions, the responding officers suggested a hotel, given that the apartment looked like a landfill. I watched the look that passed between Ali and Talia, both of them angry and afraid. No way were they going to a damn hotel. Not that this town had one anyway. There was a motel a few blocks away, but that shit was not happening. I stepped up and shook the officer's hand. "That won't be necessary. The ladies are coming with me."

He nodded and handed Ali a card. "This is the number of a

clean-up crew. It might take a few days, but they can get this place spic-n-span. If you think of anything that we should know, discover anything is missing, give us a call." He offered a sympathetic smile and nodded for his partner to follow him out.

I turned to Ali. "If there's anything left of your clothes and personal items, you can pack them up and bring them with. If not, we'll just buy everything you need." She just stood there, staring. I ignored that for the moment and addressed Talia. "You seem to be in good shape as far as clothes and stuff, but the same offer applies to you." I looked between them both, trying to be as comforting as possible. "If you don't want to touch a damn thing in this place, we'll get in the truck right now and go. I'd completely understand if you didn't want to take a single thing with you." I met each of their gazes.

Talia sniffed, tears welling up again as she stepped over to me and pulled me into a hug. I patted her softly on the back and whispered reassurances as her tears dripped onto my shirt. She released me and walked down the hall to her room.

When I turned back to Ali, I expected to have a fight on my hands. I knew she wouldn't like the idea of me stepping in and taking charge, but I couldn't just ship them off to a crappy motel and walk away. That was not fucking happening.

So, if she wanted to argue, fine by me.

She wasn't looking at me, though. She was watching Talia retreat down the hall, listening to the quiet sniffles echo through the decimated apartment. When she finally met my gaze, she looked at me adoringly for a moment and launched herself into my arms. Unlike my embrace with Talia, this one was desperate, urgent. My arms tightened around Ali until I thought I might break her. Her whole body pressed against me as if she wanted to be as close as humanly possible. I lifted her until her feet were off the floor and her legs wrapped around my hips. We stood there like that for several minutes, listening to the shuffling sounds coming from Talia's room as she packed.

I carried Ali over and gently lowered her so that she sat on the dining room table, first making sure that there was no debris present that could cut her. I leaned down and placed my palms on either side of her, the surface of the table cool to the touch as I searched her face. "Do you want to bring anything with you? I can help you pack if you don't want to go back there alone."

She shook her head, her sad expression making my chest tighten. "No. It's all tainted somehow. Even the stuff that could be saved wouldn't be the same." She looked up at me, pleading for understanding. "Does that sound stupid?"

I kissed her forehead and rubbed a hand over her head to smooth her tussled hair. "Not at all. I'd feel the same way if it were me." I reached out and took her hand, tugging gently. I needed to get them both the hell out of here. There was nothing keeping them here tonight. They may very well decide never to return at all. And that was fine by me. "Come on. Let's check on Talia and get the hell out of here. You both have the things you brought back from D.C. for now, and we can get whatever else you need later. That's why God made online shopping."

She tried to smile. I could tell she really wanted to hide behind her usual chipper demeanor, but all she could manage was a nod and a shuddering breath. I pulled her to my side and held on as tight as I could, wishing like hell I could do more.

BY THE TIME we got to my cabin, both women had visibly calmed. Neither of them was at one hundred percent, but I knew that was going to take some time. Knowing someone was in their space, touching their things, destroying irreplaceable items, it had to feel like a colossal violation. Once they had some time to bounce back, we needed to have a serious talk about finding whoever was responsible. Tonight, though, I just wanted them safe.

I insisted they park their cars under the large carport — which would have been a two bay attached garage if it only had doors — and helped them with their meager possessions.

I'd decided to give them the first floor, as I'd planned to do for Spencer, should the need for his presence arise.

Shit. Spencer. I needed to let him know what was going on. I had to go back to Richmond in a couple of days for yet another meeting with prospective clients. It would wait until then. I was in no mood to hear his mouth, and it had been a long day.

We entered the first floor, and I walked them through the space, which was only half the size of the second floor because of the carport.

Ali insisted that Talia take the larger bedroom with the en suite, and Talia was too drained to argue. They each placed their things in their respective rooms and followed me to the second floor for the rest of the tour, deciding to check out the indoor pool and game room in the basement later.

The second floor consisted of two bedrooms, one of which I'd converted into a makeshift office; the living room; a small eat-in kitchen; a balcony overlooking both the backyard pool and the mountains beyond.

It was decorated tastefully, with comfortable, plush furnishings and understated artwork that bowed to the natural beauty of the location.

I turned to offer something to eat or drink, the words dying on my lips as I watched Ali embracing her friend, whose shoulders were shaking.

They needed some time alone to sort through shit.

I quietly signaled to Ali and motioned toward the back yard, mouthing the words 'going for a swim'.

She gave me an appreciative nod and shuffled Talia over to the couch to sit down.

I changed into my trunks and silently placed two bottles of water on the coffee table in front of the girls on my way out to swim a few laps.

I needed to burn off some energy. I was still wired from the events of the day. The thought of someone doing that to Ali, destroying her things so viciously had me so enraged that there was no way I'd be able to sleep that night unless I was so exhausted that I collapsed.

The afternoon sky was thick with clouds, keeping out the worst of the heat. I sliced through the water, doing lap after lap until my lungs burned. I flipped over onto my back and floated long enough to catch my breath then went right back to it, repeating the cycle as often as necessary.

Somewhere around my fifth breather, as I floated there and stared at the fast-moving cloud formation over the cabin, a few droplets of water splashed my face. I looked over to find Ali sitting on the pool's edge, feet dangling in the water. I smiled and waved her in but she stayed put, content to just watch. I resumed floating but navigated myself closer to where she sat. When I bumped one of her legs with my foot, I decided I had floated long enough.

I lifted myself out of the water and sat down as close to her as I could get without dripping on her. She reached behind her and retrieved a large fluffy towel, handing it to me with a nod. I dried myself and waited for her to speak, knowing she sought me out for a reason.

She stared up at the sky for a while before speaking. "I can't thank you enough for everything you've done for us today. I'm not sure what I would have done without you." She truly meant it, I knew that, but she also hated having to take my help.

I slid over and bumped her shoulder playfully. "You're not fooling me, slugger. You would have told me to mind my own damn business if it hadn't been for Talia. You agreed to stay here because you're worried about her. Tell me I'm wrong."

She didn't say a thing to deny the accuracy of what I'd said. Her hand dipped down into the water, and she smirked as she splashed me in retaliation, obviously not liking how well I could read her. I dabbed my face with the corner of the towel and shook my head in amusement. As soon as she looked away, I whipped one of my feet across the water, splashing her back.

She laughingly called a truce, and I offered her a corner of my towel to dry her face. She graciously accepted, scooting closer to my side and placing her hand in mine. "I hope you don't think I'm ungrateful or anything. I really do appreciate you looking out for us. I just hate feeling helpless. That's exactly what it felt like today, looking at the damage and knowing there was nothing I could do about it." She looked at me wryly. "I'd think it's safe to say that whoever did it was not a fan of mine. At all. That's the worst part. Talia suffered because I pissed someone off and they didn't have enough balls to confront me directly."

I hadn't been planning to bring it up until the next morning at the earliest, but Ali was ready to talk today. "I've been thinking about that. The 'no balls' part makes me immediately think of Keith. Problem is, we know exactly where he was last night. There's a slim chance that he could have made it here and done that before morning. And there's no way it could have happened in the daylight hours because, even though the cleaner's is closed, there are adjacent businesses that open early. Someone would have seen or heard something."

She nodded. "Yeah. The people around here don't miss much. If nothing else, a small town has the added benefit of neighbors looking out for each other."

"Agreed. So, after I crossed Keith off the list, I immediately thought of Lauren." I knew Ali's mind had gone there too. "You mentioned her purposely causing trouble at the diner, breaking things, messing with the register. Is it possible that she would have upped her game and trashed your apartment?"

I could see the muscle working in her jaw. Just thinking about Lauren had her angry. "I wouldn't put it past her. She knew I was leaving Friday night because I posted the schedule early, and she threw a fit because I had her working all weekend. I'd definitely put her at the top of the list." She straightened suddenly, brows shooting up in surprise. "Actually, that's the extent of the list. Keith and Lauren." She seemed deflated by the thought. "You'd think that I'd have pissed off more people than that. It's kind of sad, really. They say that the true mark of success is having a horde of haters."

I gave her hand a squeeze and chuckled just as I had an epiphany of my own. "Shit."

She frowned. "What?"

"I forgot that you left here on Friday." From the look she was giving me, she didn't make the connection. "That means Keith technically isn't cleared. The break in could have happened either night. Talia said the door was closed, and there was no sign of trouble until she walked into the apartment, so no one would have noticed anything amiss unless they went inside."

She looked skeptical, head tilted to the side, face drawn into a scowl. "Yeah, but we didn't piss him off until the gala last night. What reason could he have had to break in on Friday? I mean, he's a dick, but he hasn't tried to contact me all this time, why would he do it the night before he knew he was going to see me?"

"Maybe he liked knowing what was waiting for you when you got back. It might have given him a feeling of superiority to look you in the eye knowing you hadn't discovered what he'd done yet." I shrugged. "Then again, I could just want it to be him so I can finally stomp his ass."

She laughed. "Finally? You've only met him once." Damn.

She didn't remember running into me last year. I had to be more careful if I wanted it to stay that way. She was stressed enough as it was without adding that memory to the mix. "Imagine dealing with him for years." She hooked a thumb at her chest. "If anyone gets to kick the shit out of him, it's going to be me." I smiled at her tenacity. There was no doubt she meant it. I'd hate to be that son of a bitch if she found out he was behind this. She leaned against my side, her warmth causing goosebumps to break out over my chilled flesh. "Much as I'd like to blame Keith, my money's on Lauren. She's had a problem with me since college, she resents my being asked to run things for Teach and Marilee instead of her, and she looks like she could spit nails every time she sees you and me together."

I had to agree. "Yeah. I'm pretty sure I pissed her off by turning her down, so seeing me spending time with someone she dislikes probably makes it even worse." I turned to look at her and thought I caught a hint of surprise in her expression. I guess I hadn't mentioned Lauren's not so subtle offer, which she'd only missed witnessing by a few minutes. I briefly filled her in before adding, "Sorry if my presence added another layer of anger toward you."

Ali laughed and laid her head on my shoulder. "Your presence has been the one thing making this place tolerable these last few weeks. If she doesn't like us spending time together, tough shit. She can add it to the list of topics for her next whiners anonymous meeting." She swore more when she was stressed. I hated that she was dealing with so much, but I had to admit the cussing was kind of hot.

A couple of hours and a few beers later, Ali was almost back to her amazing lighthearted self. Once I'd gotten changed, and she'd unpacked her things, we took our beers and settled on the second-floor balcony. From there we wouldn't disturb Talia, who had decided to lie down for a while. Ali tipped the long neck to her lips and then used it to point toward the pool. "I'm assuming you still swim a lot since you wanted both indoor and outdoor pools."

"I try to swim as often as possible. After doing it so much in college, it became part of my routine. I don't always have time if I'm tied up with a big job or doing a lot of work in my shop, though. I have a pool at my new house but I kind of miss my old apartment. The building had an enormous pool on the roof and something about being up there above the city all alone was calming. I used to do a hundred laps every morning, weather permitting. That's why I opted for the indoor pool here. No excuse not to get my laps in if the weather is a factor." Actually, I mostly wanted it so I could swim naked without worrying about nosy neighbors, not that there was another house close enough for that to matter. "I also swam most evenings when I lived there, not so much at the new house."

"I like the idea of swimming in the evening. Way up there on the roof like that, I bet you could float there on your back and see every star in the sky." There was that wistful inflection I liked so much.

Too bad she was wrong.

"Actually, the stars are hard to see because the lights of the city drown them out. Every so often I could pick out a few, though."

She looked deflated. Taking a long draw on her beer, she muttered, "I hadn't considered that. It was a nice thought anyway."

Shit. Should have kept my mouth shut.

I rushed to say something, anything to bring back that smile. "It's not a rooftop view, but I'm willing to bet you could see a million stars from this pool."

She stood and walked over to the railing, lifting her eyes to the wide-open sky. "I think you're right. I guess being out in the middle of nowhere has a few perks after all."

"You're welcome to find out. I'll even cook us dinner while we wait for the stars to make their appearance." I wasn't sure where that had come from, hadn't planned it, but I genuinely liked the idea.

"You cook?" She sounded both impressed and shocked.

I leveled my stare at her. "Of course. Why is that surprising?"

She laughed. "You're the one who once mentioned Hungry Man dinners and said you usually eat cereal bars for breakfast. I assumed you weren't into cooking."

"Oh. Well, I'll have you know that I'm fairly proficient in the kitchen." *And a fucking genius in the bedroom.*

I really needed to find a way to stop thinking shit like that. It was a one-time event.

An *epic* event, but still.

"Gran used to lecture all us boys on knowing how to care for ourselves. We had to help around the house, do laundry, and assist in the kitchen. We all hated it, but she said knowing how to do those things would save us a lot of grief later on." Yep, that did it. Mentioning Gran = No more innuendo.

Ali looked amused. "What grief was she saving you from?"

I took a long swallow of my beer, draining the last of it and setting the empty bottle on the floor by my feet, the patio's expensive indoor/outdoor carpeting softening the sound. "She told us that we'd have more time to find the right woman if we knew all that stuff. She figured most guys ended up in bad relationships because they scooped up the first available woman for fear of starving to death or running out of clean underwear."

Her laughter rang out, echoing into the distance.

TALIA DECLINED DINNER and drifted back to sleep, the stress of the day exhausting her.

The sun had been set for half an hour though there was still fading light coming from behind the mountains. We decided to wait a while to go out to the pool, letting our dinner digest. The clouds disappeared hours before and the heat of the day had finally dwindled to a tolerable level, so I decided to cook outside where we could enjoy the scenery. Grilled salmon flavored with lemon and dill, which I served alongside fresh grilled vegetables.

Ali cleaned her plate, leaving me feeling oddly proud.

Grabbing a couple of fluffy white towels from the linen closet, I padded out onto the patio. Ali had gone on ahead and was sitting on the patio chaise waiting for me, her silhouette taking on an air of mystery in the fading light. Since most of her things had been shredded in the break-in, she had to either borrow a suit from Talia or swim in regular clothes.

She opted for a two-piece suit that made her curves look fucking amazing. The damn thing looked like it was made for her, despite it belonging to someone else. I'd barely managed not to stand there gaping with slack-jawed adoration when she stepped out wearing it.

Good damn thing that water's cold.

I let her go on ahead so I could gather my wits and figure out how to forcibly redirect my blood flow away from my cock. Not an easy task when she was bounding down the incline toward the pool, mind-blowingly beautiful in every conceivable way as she disappeared into the darkness.

"Hey, don't forget to kill the porch light." She called, laughing when her request echoed back at her, getting fainter with each repetition. I shifted the towels under one arm and grabbed two of the plush floating pillows from the storage room before dousing the light. I could barely see Ali's outline before I switched it off, and I couldn't see my hand in front of my face after. As I slowly stumbled in the direction of the pool, there was a small flash of light in the distance.

Ali held the lit match to something that sat on the table between the lounge chairs. A moment later the distinct flickering of a candle flame became the beacon toward which I moved. As I neared the seating area, several more candles joined the first. "That better?" she asked, the light dancing over her face,

"Much, thank you. I thought I was going to break my neck trying to find the pool." I joked.

"Definitely no city lights to obscure our view." She observed teasingly as she made her way to each of the small tables to light candles. By the time she was done, there was just enough light for us to see the outline of the pool but not so much that it would be bothersome.

I laid the towels on the chaise she had just vacated and shuffled over to the shallow end. Ali joined me, and I handed her one of the pillows, which resembled neck rolls and were the perfect size to hold our heads slightly out of the water so we could converse. We stepped in slowly, adjusting to the cool temperature before moving deeper. She sucked in a sharp breath when the water reached her thighs, a sound that struck me as staggeringly erotic. It was the sound I'd imagined her making as I thrust into her fully for the first time, a scenario I had replayed in my mind countless times. I was suddenly thankful for the darkness. It helped shield her body from my notice. That was probably for the best as I was sure she would drive me to distraction. The lack of illumination also concealed the burgeoning erection that her gasp had inspired.

I'd only waded in up to my knees trying to keep pace with Ali, but that plan was out the fucking window. I sucked in a breath and dove toward the deep end, the frigid temperatures at the deepest point would hopefully help my situation. I needed a quick dose of ball-shriveling cold water.

∾

WITH DARKNESS ENVELOPING us, we silently floated through the water on our backs staring up at a sky full of stars. The only sound was the slight lapping of the water and the intermittent rustling of leaves in the soft breeze. We occasionally brushed past each other, fleeting touches of warmth to fight off the chill.

As the moon rose higher in the sky, the events of the past few days replayed in my mind: the gala, Keith, remembering that night at the hospital, the sound of Ali panting my name, the taste of her on my tongue, the look of despair when she saw what was left of her things. All of it pulled me in different ways.

I wanted to protect her, avenge her, fuck her, hold her.

And I also wanted to get the hell away from her.

In my thirty-three years, I'd hurt far more people than I cared to remember. I'd hurt her too if given the chance. It was inevitable, ingrained in my very soul. I was never going to be the man she deserved. I'd realized that long ago.

As she floated past, and her fingertips threaded through mine pulling me into her side, I realized something even more devastating.

I couldn't give her up.

CHAPTER EIGHT

THE SMELLS OF coffee and bacon greeted me when I awoke the next morning. Smiling, I rolled out of bed and stretched my sore muscles, briefly wondering how damn many laps I'd done the day before. Apparently it hadn't been enough because I'd tossed and turned all night. The stresses of the day and my proximity to Ali had kept my mind churning all night.

Before I could even finish dressing, my phone rang.

Spencer.

Fucking awesome.

It was like the guy had radar, he always knew when I wanted to avoid him.

I slid my thumb over the screen and brought the phone to my ear, giving my usual greeting. "Good morning, fucker."

"Yeah, good morning, manwhore." His voice was strained, not a good sign. "Sorry to start off your day with bad news but we've got a problem."

I pinned the phone between my ear and shoulder, reaching for a shirt to pull on now that I had guests to think about. Spencer's tone had me nervous already. "Whatever it is, we can figure it out. What's going on?"

He blew out a breath. "You're not gonna like it."

Oh for fuck's sake! "Would you just spit it the fuck out please? I hate when you do that."

"Fine, asshole. I just got a letter from an attorney's office." I could hear pages shuffling in the background. "According to this, Marissa Barnett is bringing a civil suit against the company. It alleges here that she was sexually harassed and wrongfully terminated when she thwarted unwanted advances. She's suing for three million." He spat out the last sentence with such vehemence that I was stunned silent.

What the fuck? Speaking as quietly as possible with my blood boiling in my ears, I shot back, "Everything she's saying happened is a goddamn lie. You know she pursued me, she's the one that threw herself at me. Fuck, Spence, I walked in and found her draped across my desk naked." I was fuming now. Realizing I might be overheard despite my attempts to lower my voice, I stepped from my bedroom into the en-suite and closed the door, pacing. "That crazy bitch can't say we fired her. She fucking quit. And she turned in a letter of resignation. It's in her file!" My voice shook with rage.

"Actually, the file is missing. No one knows where it went." He sounded more puzzled than pissed.

"I'm sorry, what? How the fuck did that happen? No one has keys to those cabinets except us and our..." I stopped pacing and flicked a glance at myself in the mirror.

"Assistants?" Spencer finished for me. "Yeah, I thought of that too. She turned in her keys when she left, but there's still the possibility that she made a copy. I wouldn't have even considered the prospect if there hadn't been some recent issues with files being moved." The ominous tone in his voice made my skin crawl.

"What recent issues?" I wasn't sure I wanted to know.

"My assistant mentioned a couple months ago that she thought she needed to go over our filing system with Caroline. When I asked why, she said she had been finding files in odd places, stuffed all the way in back rather than in their proper place." Caroline had almost thirty damn years of experience, so I doubted that she was to blame. "And it's happened several times since, the most recent instance was no more than a month ago when the employee files were strewn all over the damn place, totally out of sequence and some were even in the wrong cabinet altogether. None of our office staff was responsible, I'm sure of that."

"Motherfucker!" I gritted. "That's probably when she took her file."

"I have someone here now, changing out all the locks on the cabinets, entry doors, and offices. If she's planning a return trip, she's SOL."

"Okay, so where does all this leave us? She can't get away with this shit."

Spencer's voice turned steely cold. "Don't worry. She was so focused on you the whole time she was here that I was never on her radar. But I'm about to be."

I leaned against the counter and barely resisted the urge to punch something. "This is all my fault. Fuck!" The sound echoed off the walls, and I forcibly lowered my voice. "You warned me. You knew I was going to be the one to ruin us, and you were right. I'm sorry, brother. Sorrier than you'll ever know. Does Brant know yet?"

"No, and I'm not telling him. We're not defeated yet, Clay. Don't forget who you're talking to. Let me see what I can come up with. If I strike out, then we can tell Brant. Alright?" I mumbled my agreement. "This isn't all your fault, man. I saw the way she was coming on to you, I knew in my gut that she needed to be reassigned or let go, but I did nothing. I'm just as at fault as you. The only innocent one here is Brant. Let's put the brakes on her bullshit and send her packing."

"Gladly. Give me a few hours and I can be back in Richmond for a strategy session."

"No, you stay right where you are for now. I need to do some digging, so we can come up with a game plan. In the meantime, don't answer if she calls, don't reply to messages, do not engage her in any way." He puffed out a frustrated breath. "Lay low and keep out of trouble. I can only handle one catastrophe at a time, okay?"

Just perfect.

If I'd thought he'd take my new living arrangements hard before, I could only imagine what he'd say now.

Fuck. Me.

No matter what, I couldn't ask Ali and Talia to leave. Spencer better be able to make peace with that when he did find out. They needed me, and I wasn't letting my screw ups interfere with keeping them safe.

His radar must have kicked in again because he said, "So, now that I've ruined your morning, tell me about the gala. How'd it go? Did you turn into a pumpkin at midnight?"

He was trying for levity and missing by a mile, but I appreciated the effort.

"It was fine. Dropped a big fat check and shook a bunch of sweaty diamond encrusted hands that had never done a hard day's work in their lives."

"And Ali?"

Ali? She tastes like honey and could suck a bowling ball through a garden hose... No, wait, can't tell him about that.

Focus, Clay.

"She did fine. Her bosses seemed to have missed her." They were also encouraging about her future and gave the impression that she might just have a job to go back to, but I wasn't telling him that. He didn't know the truth about Ali's work situation, and I saw no need to tell him. It had no bearing on her job with us.

Just like I wasn't going to tell him I remembered how she and I had met. I wouldn't be sharing that story with anyone. She'd already been forced to live through it, that was enough. Repeating it, saying the words would give it new life somehow and I didn't want that, for her sake.

Spencer blew out a breath, sounding relieved. "Good. I'm glad you offered to be there for her, but I have to admit that I was worried about the ramifications. No need for the company name to be linked with any more scandal than it already is."

He was right, not that I would have let that stop me. It wasn't who my date was that had been the problem it had been what I remembered. The only thing that had kept me from beating the shit out of Keith was my respect for Ali, nothing more. Just more proof that I was selfish. "You act like you thought she and I were going to level D.C. or something. It was a charity dinner." Might as well get it all out on the table, well, most of it anyway. "But there was some trouble."

"Shit. What now?"

I loved the way he managed to make three words sound like an impeachment of my character. "Nothing at the gala. There was an issue when we got back here. When the girls got back to their apartment, it had been broken into and vandalized. Shit was shredded all over the place."

"Oh God. Are they both okay? Any idea who did it? Is there anything we can do to help?" He was sincerely concerned, panicked even, and I realized that I'd been snapping at him a lot lately for no good reason. He wasn't the one being an asshole, I was. I took everything he said the wrong way because I resented the deal he'd forced me into. The contract. Gran's house. My personal life. All of it. And he was right on all accounts. Fuck. I really was a shitty friend. He deserved better than that after all I'd put him through over the years.

"They're fine. Just shaken up. We have a couple of people in mind as possibilities but aren't sure of anything." I sat on the edge of the tub and braced myself for his reaction. "As far as helping, we kind of already are."

His voice was cautious, slow as he asked, "How exactly are *we* helping?"

"Well, they couldn't stay in the apartment, obviously, and I wasn't about to let them stay in the one crappy motel this town has to offer, so I brought them back here and gave them the first floor." I sat there cringing as I waited for his reply, hearing nothing but the soft hiss of the open line.

After a lengthy pause, he sighed. "Probably a good idea."

"I'm sorry... what?" No bitching? No accusing? No jumping up and down like a pissed off cartoon character?

"I said it was a good idea. I saw that motel, I wouldn't have wanted them there either, and they'll be safe at the cabin with you. At least until they find out who's responsible for the break in. Let me know if I can help with anything." After a long pause he continued, "So, what time is your meeting with the building inspector today?"

Wait a goddamn minute. He wasn't going to say anything else? Not even a not so gentle reminder about our deal? No lectures or pointed comments? He'd just finished telling me about the lawsuit and he's okay with me moving my new assistant in with me? "Around ten. You're not going to say anything about Ali and Talia staying here?"

"What else should I say?" Why did he sound amused?

"I don't know. I kind of expected a warning of some sort, something reminiscent of your infamous 'don't fuck the employees' speech." It came out with more of an edge than I'd intended. Dammit. Snapping at him for *not* lecturing me? I really had lost my mind.

He thought it was funny. Laughing, he asked, "If we'd decided to send one of our Richmond-based assistants to Denson for the project, chances are they would have had their own floor of the rental cabin, right?" I muttered an agreement, knowing how close we'd come to doing just that. Both our assistants had family obligations that made it difficult to travel, though. "Something like that is not unusual for long business trips. And why would I bitch at you for doing something honorable for a friend? A year ago, it would have never occurred to you to step in. You would have been in full-on 'not my circus, not my monkeys' mode, never giving it a second thought. You really are being a friend to Ali." The humor left his voice when he said, "Not to be a condescending ass, but I'm proud of you."

Much as I wanted to bust his balls for talking like a girl, I couldn't. I was surprisingly touched by the compliment. I'd never tell him that, though, it would just encourage the behavior. "Not necessarily condescending, but ass sounds about right."

~

HAVING GIVEN SPENCER my word that I'd keep him informed about the break-in, I ended the call and fired off a quick text to Brant apologizing for missing our customary Sunday night strategy session. He replied almost immediately, as he usually did, dismissing my apology as unnecessary and suggesting we try for a mid-week reschedule.

That was Brant, laid back and adaptable. Thank fuck for that.

I replied in the affirmative, silencing my phone and slipping it into my pocket as I emerged from my room. Ali and Talia were in the kitchen, leaning against the counter and sipping coffee as strips of bacon sizzled and hissed away on the stove. Seeing them there, I couldn't help thinking of standing the same way with Ali in their D.C. apartment, the taste of good scotch and Ali's juices mingling on my tongue.

Ali cleared her throat, vying for my attention. I realized I'd been standing there in a daze. At least she'd snapped me out of it before I sprung a boner right in front of them having my little daydream. Shit. I needed to learn to focus. It was difficult with her so close. "Good morning, Clay. Coffee?" Her smile was warm and genuine.

"Good morning, ladies." I glanced at Talia, who nodded and stared into her mug. Not a morning person. Dually noted. I smiled at Ali. "Yes, please. Coffee sounds great."

While Ali and I sipped our coffee and made small talk, Talia went about making breakfast. She wasn't talkative in the morning, but she could still cook her ass off, half-asleep or not.

We finished breakfast, and I insisted on helping Ali with the dishes while Talia showered and got ready for work. She washed, I dried. Neither of us made any move to use the dishwasher, preferring to stand side-by-side and work together. When we were alone, Ali said, "She's not a morning person on a good day but today she's worse than usual. I don't think she slept much."

"It's understandable. Give her some time, she'll bounce back."

She finished the last of the dishes and turned to me as I dried. "Should she be going to work today? Lauren could have been the one to trash our apartment and Talia will be working with her all morning."

"She's never shown signs of hostility toward Talia, has she?" Ali shook her head, no. "Then Talia should be fine, but I understand why you're worried." There were faint dark circles under her eyes. She'd probably been up all night, too. "I have an idea. I don't have to meet the inspector until ten, and none of the contractors are coming in until after lunch to give time for the inspection, so I have a couple free hours this morning. Why don't we go down to the diner and talk to Lauren?"

She pursed her lips, debating. "I doubt it will go well, but it's worth a try." Glancing toward the stairs, she leaned closer to me. "Just you and I, though. No need to put Talia at odds with her. So far, it's just me she hates." The corner of her mouth curled into a small smile. "And possibly you."

"Yeah, I suspect she doesn't take rejection well."

We laughed it off, but we both knew there was a very real possibility that things could escalate beyond property damage. If Lauren was behind this, she needed serious help.

WHEN WE WALKED into the diner an hour later, a full hour before Talia was due to arrive, Ali's whole body tensed at seeing Lauren behind the counter. I stood behind Ali, having held the door so she could enter first. My hand rested lightly on the small of her back and her muscles were tight as piano wire.

She wasn't afraid. If I was reading her body language right, she was fucking pissed.

She hadn't been afraid to begin with, not for herself. She'd been afraid for Talia and, now that Talia wasn't around, Ali was spoiling for a fight. It was an instantaneous transformation. She'd been fine on the way there, smiled when I held the door, but seeing Lauren seemed to have snapped something inside her. She was seething, fists clenched, jaw flexing.

I rubbed slow circles on her back and leaned down to speak into her ear. "Remember, she's no different than Keith. They get off on forcing you to react. Don't let her win."

She relaxed a bit, releasing her jaw and taking a deep breath. She looked up at me with a tight smile. "Thanks. I needed that."

I continued to caress her back while keeping my attention focused on Lauren. She had her back to us, writing something on her ticket pad. When she finished, she tore the slip off, slid it into the window, and turned. She locked eyes with Ali, and her eyes widened briefly before shifting to me with a look of distaste.

Ali shifted and pointed at the parking lot as she addressed her. "Lauren, I need a word with you. Outside."

Every eye in the place was instantly on Lauren. She glanced around at the curious customers and smirked before shrugging and making her way from behind the counter. "Anything you say, *boss*."

Snotty bitch.

I gently tugged Ali back a step to allow Lauren to pass by and out the door. I had a feeling that if Lauren tried pulling the same shit Keith's date tried, there'd be a lot worse fallout this time around.

I followed them outside, surprised by the sudden appearance of storm clouds. It wasn't raining yet, but it looked to be just a matter of time. The threatening gray clouds were moving quickly, seeming to mirror Ali's mood.

She wasted no time getting to the point. "Someone broke into Talia's and my apartment while we were gone over the weekend. You know anything about that?"

Lauren gave her a bored look. "I'm not a thief. Besides, I doubt you have anything I'd want." Her gaze flicked to me briefly. "I have much better taste than you."

"Quit looking at him, Lauren. He turned you down, get the fuck over it." There was that dirty mouth again. "And I didn't say anything was taken. Someone trashed the place. Destroyed clothes, dishes, books, even my paintings. But nothing was taken. I find that odd. Don't you?"

Lauren scoffed. "Hardly. They were probably trying to do you a favor. You dress like a preschool teacher, you always have your nose in a damn book, and your paintings probably suck. Take it as an opportunity to start over."

"Why didn't you mention any of Talia's things?" I shot back.

She looked at me with a startled expression. "What?"

"You didn't say anything about Talia's ruined stuff."

She wrinkled her nose in confusion and sputtered. "I don't

know. Maybe because she's not in my face accusing me of doing something I didn't do."

Ali took a step closer, her fists clenching again. "Or maybe it's because you knew only my stuff was damaged."

I glanced back at all the curious faces watching through the diner's front windows and hooked one finger through Ali's back belt loop, reminding her not to take it too far.

Lauren tapped her foot and crossed her arms, doing her best to look bored but failing. "I wasn't even here this weekend, so your bullshit finger-pointing is a waste of time."

Ali cocked her head to the side, genuinely confused. "You were scheduled to work the dinner shift all weekend. How could you have not been here?"

Rolling her eyes, Lauren reached into her pocket and pulled out her phone. "I switched with Fay. She worked for me over the weekend, and I'll pull two doubles this week to cover her." She scrolled through her phone for a minute and then stepped forward to hold it up in front of Ali. There on the screen was a picture of a very drunk Lauren hanging all over some bartender. She turned and scrolled again. This time the pic was of her and the bartender outside the bar, smoking something I was pretty sure wasn't a tobacco product. "See? Look at the date." She pointed to the banner across the top of the picture. "This one was Saturday night and the first one," she scrolled back to it, "was taken Friday. You can check it out, look up the name of the bar, whatever. It's in Virginia Beach, and I was there both nights with my... friend." She looked up at me and smirked. "Can't find anything that hot around here."

She started to slip her phone back into her pocket, but I stopped her. "If you don't mind, send the pics to Ali's cell. I want to check out the bar." I smiled pleasantly. "I'm just not comfortable taking your word for it, and I barely got a look at the name when you showed us the pic. You said we could check it out, right?" I half expected her to refuse, which would have told me everything I needed to know.

She narrowed her eyes at me. "Sure, I have nothing to hide." Her thumbs flew across the screen. "Am I done here or do you want to accuse me of something else?"

Ali checked her phone as two incoming message alerts sounded. "Nah. We're good for now. If I think of anything else, you'll be the first to know."

Lauren stomped off in a huff and Ali turned to me, eyes still on her phone. "I'm forwarding these to you, right?"

"Yep."

"Smooth move not having her send them to you. She wouldn't have my number either if it hadn't been necessary for work."

I chuckled. "Believe it or not, this isn't my first run-in with her kind of crazy."

Then it hit me.

What if this wasn't about Ali? What if it was about me? It never occurred to me that my ongoing problems with Marissa could follow me here, but I couldn't rule out the possibility. Marissa had even broken into the office to steal her files and do God only knew what else.

She could have found out where I was by looking at the project schedule then pulled the files that contained Gran's property address. She probably had the cabin address for that matter. Hell, she could have pulled Ali's file, too. She could have been following me or having me followed this whole time, which would have put Ali in her sights.

Maybe I was being paranoid, but I couldn't take any chances. The crazy bitch tried to ram a Volkswagen up my ass. If she was capable of that, she was capable of anything.

I needed to call Spencer back.

I dropped Ali at the realty office with a promise to pick her up at noon so we could have lunch and drive to the job site together, assuming the rain hadn't set in. I headed back to the cabin, calling my investigator friend on the way. He owed me a favor, and it was time to collect.

Last winter, he'd been in a bind to get some damage repaired before his wife found it and cut his balls off. She swore she was going to kick his ass out if he broke one more window with his homemade potato gun, so when he shot a fucking sweet potato straight through a wall, he was desperate to avoid castration. I did the work fast and free, too amused by his terror to charge the guy. It was cheap entertainment.

I'd left him a message that morning after finding out about the lawsuit, deciding to be proactive about the situation instead of waiting for Spencer, but the guy hadn't answered.

It was starting to get on my nerves.

I left a terse message and then called Spencer.

He was just as disturbed by the idea of Marissa's possible involvement as me. He promised to check with the assistants and see if Ali's file was one of the ones that had been strewn around the office. I also gave him some background on Lauren and Keith, having gotten their last names from Ali. I even forwarded Lauren's alibi pictures in hopes that he could either verify or discredit them. Spencer was adept at all things technical, so I had no doubt that he would deliver.

He suggested I stay put for the rest of the week to keep an eye on things, and I didn't argue. I'd been dreading leaving the girls alone, even for a day. I knew he was making a big sacrifice by telling me to stay. He would be on his own for the big meeting that week, not to mention all the digging he was doing on my behalf but he was putting the girl's safety first. You couldn't help being impressed by the guy. He was a class act.

He promised he'd call as soon as he had any information and hung up, eager to start his reconnaissance.

I arrived at the cabin and sat in the driveway while I made a quick call to confirm my appointment with the inspector. All systems were go. A quick dash inside to grab my paperwork and I'd head to Gran's property to meet him.

There was nothing else I could do at that point anyway.

THE CABIN WAS still and quiet when I walked in. I called out to Talia and got no response though her car was in the driveway. A little prickle of fear crept up my spine, making my pulse quicken. Instead of climbing the stairs to my room, I turned and began a slow walk through the first floor. The only sound was the low whistle of cooled air blowing through the vents, chilling my exposed forearms as I made my way across the eerily quiet space. I checked the living room and adjoining patio, noting that the rain had finally started. I had just made it inside before the sky opened up. Heavy sheets poured down on the yard beyond the patio, the fat droplets making the pool's surface look like it was at a rolling boil.

No Talia among the downpour, not that I'd expected to find her dancing in the rain after the way her weekend ended.

I made my way toward the bedrooms, calling her name along the way. When I got to the first door, it was cracked open a few inches. I placed my palm on the cool wood and pushed it open inch by inch, revealing a neatly made bed and a duffel bag I recognized as Ali's.

The other door was closed. I had to force a swallow as I moved toward it, mentally kicking myself for leaving her here alone so soon after the break-in. I knocked softly and called out Talia's name, pitching my voice so that I didn't startle her. My deep voice was a curse sometimes. There was still no reply. I knew the room had a private bath and cringed at the idea of bursting in on her in the shower, but her lack of response was starting to worry me.

I took a deep breath and turned the knob, hoping like hell I didn't catch her half-naked.

When I inched the door open, I spotted Talia lying on the bed. She was on top of the covers fully dressed, thank fuck, and blissfully asleep. She lay on her side, facing the door and holding a small throw pillow across her chest. She looked so peaceful that I hated to wake her but I knew she was due at work in a few minutes. Not wanting to scare the shit out of her, I stood by the open door and softly called her name until she stirred. She peeked at me and smiled, then bolted upright. "Oh my God. I fell asleep. Am I late for work? Shit. What time is it?"

I held my hands up in front of me, motioning for her to calm down. "It's okay. You're not late, but you should probably leave soon if you need to be there by nine thirty."

She breathed out a deep sigh, her shoulders dropping a good three inches as she relaxed. Realizing she still held the pillow, she turned to place it on the bed behind her and dropped the other item she'd been holding; a picture. It slid under the nightstand, and I walked over to retrieve it. I squatted down and felt around under the table until I found it and pulled it out.

She didn't know what I was doing until I held the crumpled picture out for her to take. I glanced down at it and stopped on an exhalation that left me almost dizzy. My lungs felt like all the air had just been forcibly squeezed out of them. She snapped the picture from my outstretched hand and muttered her thanks, unable to meet my eye.

The picture was of Talia and Ali. And the adorable blond toddler who I remembered from the picture in their D.C. apartment. The picture that I now realized had been in a memorial frame. The gut-wrenching image of embossed angel wings flitted through my mind as I remembered reaching for that frame just a few days ago. Feeling suddenly off balance, I dropped one knee to the floor. Moments later, as I battled the wave of dizziness, I placed the other knee down as well.

In the photo I'd handed Talia, she and Ali crouched on either side of the little girl, kissing her cheeks as she giggled. As soon as I saw the picture, I knew. I understood Talia's maternal nature, wanting to cook for and look after the people she cared about. I understood Ali's connection to the children's hospice charity, her emotional reaction to the parent's stories at the gala.

When Talia tucked the photo under her pillow and met my gaze, it was all right there in front of me. There had only been one or two things damaged in Talia's room, and that picture was one of them. Her reaction to the break-in, all that anguish had really been about that picture and what it represented to her.

As a mother.

She gave me a teary smile when she realized I'd made the connection. "It's the only one I brought with me. The only piece of her I have here." She studied me with a sad smile. "Still hurts every time I look at her little face, but I keep her picture close because I know one day I'll be able to look at it and remember without losing my breath."

My voice was thick when I managed to speak, the desperate need to make things right surging forward in an all-encompassing wave. "I can have it fixed, reprinted, re-framed, whatever you need. Just say the word and I'll take care of it." I would have. I'd have driven to D.C. right that instant to get the original. Anything to ease the pain in her eyes and the ache in my chest.

She smiled softly, the slightest quiver in her chin as she pulled the photo from its hiding place. "Thank you, Clay. I appreciate the offer. Ali tried to give me her locket to comfort me, but I turned her down too." She looked up at me and realized from my expression that I didn't understand the significance. "The book locket she wears has a little picture of my daughter and a dried flower that she gave Ali right before she passed away. A buttercup. Ali rarely takes it off other than to shower. I had to practically beg her to take it off for the gala. She still carried it with her, though, I'm sure."

Talia smoothed the covers with one hand, smiling at Ali's subterfuge. "I'll be okay with the torn picture for now. I'll be back home in a few days, and I can have one printed. All my pictures of her have been moved to disks that I keep in a small safe in my apartment." She ran a trembling finger over the image of her lost daughter. "Ali made me take all of the pictures off my computer. Not to be cruel but to save me from the hell I'd built for myself after I lost Amelia."

Her head snapped up, and her smile was more genuine as she explained, "That's her name. Amelia. Ali called her Millie sometimes when they played together. Anyway, after I lost her I locked myself in the apartment for weeks on end, watching a slideshow of the images on my computer, the photos looping over and over again until I thought I'd just shatter into a million pieces. I didn't talk to anyone, didn't go out, only ate when Ali forced her way in and refused to leave until I'd eaten. Sometimes she fed me like a child, wiping my face and talking softly like a mother does. After a while, she said she'd seen enough. She forced me back into the land of the living, one grudging step at a time, starting with the removal of the photos until I could handle seeing them again."

"I can't even fathom what you must have gone through, Talia, but I'm so glad Ali stepped in." My eyes burned as I realized that Ali had loved and lost that little girl, too. I was flooded with the overwhelming urge to gather them both to my chest, to hold and protect them both. "She loves you, anyone can see that, and she's stubborn as hell so there's no way she was going to let you slip away from her. That girl is a fighter, just like you."

Talia dabbed her eyes with a tissue from the nightstand and

chuckled. "Stubborn doesn't even begin to cover it, but I suspect you'll be finding that out for yourself soon enough."

The thought of Ali grieving was becoming a hard knot in my chest, an ache that I knew wouldn't be assuaged until I could hold her in my arms, even if only for a moment. "How long ago...?" I nodded vaguely toward the picture.

"Almost four years..." She stopped mid-reply and looked thoughtful for a moment. "About the same amount of time I had her with me. She was a couple of months shy of her fourth birthday when the cancer took her." Her eyes took on that distant, glazed look of someone whose mind was miles away. "It's odd to think that I've only been without her for four years. It's like her little life only lasted a few short moments, but the loss of her seems to have spanned my entire lifetime. Strange how pain alters our perception of time." She blinked over at me for a moment, the expression on her face forcing me to fight back tears.

Neither of us spoke for a while, both looking at the crumpled photo. When I could find my voice, I caught her eye and held it, wanting so much to make this better. For her. For Ali. For me. "I used to carry around a picture waiting for that day, the day that it wouldn't hurt to look at it." I didn't know where the admission came from. I hadn't intended to say anything but it just spilled out in a small voice I almost didn't recognize as my own.

"What happened to it?" Talia's voice was soft, filled with compassion.

"I gave up on it, packed it away and buried it in the back of the closet. I wasn't as strong as you. I let the pain win." It came out as a whisper, the words barely able to push past the lump in my throat. My chest ached so deeply, that I found myself absently rubbing at it, as if to alleviate the pain.

She returned her gaze to the picture. "I'm not sure how strong I am. If it weren't for Ali, I'd have given up too." She tucked it back under the pillow and turned to me. "But I'm still fighting, still making progress even if it's just a little. Moving forward is moving forward, whether you sprint or crawl." That last part seemed more for me than for her. She blinked back her tears and stood, switching gears and changing the subject. "I better find my keys and get a move on. I'm going to be late."

Still kneeling in front of the nightstand, I forced a smile and spoke around the lump in my throat. "I think you'll be alright. After all, you do know the manager."

She placed a hand on my shoulder as she walked by, pausing. "I think we'll all be alright, Clay. We've made it this far, haven't we?" She patted my back and continued out of the room, not waiting for a response.

CHAPTER NINE

THE RAIN WAS still falling when I picked Ali up from the office. When she got in the truck, she was soaking wet but she looked over at me and smiled as she fastened her seatbelt. "Glad I decided against wearing the white shirt today."

My eyes immediately fell to her chest. Damn. I tossed her a disappointed look. "Maybe *you're* glad..."

She giggled and changed the subject as a blush crept up her slim neck. "I'm not in the mood for lunch at the diner. I've seen enough of that place today. I thought maybe it was time for a change of venue. What do you think? Is there somewhere else you might like to eat?"

I quirked a brow at her and let my gaze roam the length of her body, saying nothing. I was being indecent, but she started it. Not the most mature argument, but still valid. Watching her face heat, I wondered if she was remembering the other night. Did she clench inside at the memory of my tongue stroking, tasting, and exploring her? Did images of that night flash through her mind at random times like they did mine?

Still blushing like hell, she offered a suggestion. "How about making something at the cabin? We can pick up some groceries, and I'll make us lunch."

I laughed at the way she fidgeted in the seat, clenching her thighs together. Looked like someone had taken a stroll down memory lane and ended up turned on. I knew the feeling well. "I thought you let Talia do all the cooking."

She smiled. "I do, but that doesn't mean I can't cook. I just let her do it because it's something she enjoys. She's happiest when she's flitting around the kitchen, and I'm happiest when she's happy. It's just how things are for us."

I knew from the beginning that they had a special bond, something stronger than the average friendship. After my discovery in Talia's room that morning, I understood part of the reason why. They had dealt with their grief together and forged a bond that was deeper than anything I'd ever experienced. Grief was a make-or-break kind of situation. Some people, like Ali and Talia, made it out stronger on the other side while others never recovered. I truly envied the former, those who fought their way through.

Particularly because I was one of the latter.

"I think that's a great idea." Taking her still-damp hand, I said, "We better get a move on before Talia finishes her shift and reclaims the kitchen." She nodded, and we drove toward the nearest grocery store, a flood of unwelcome memories washing through my mind.

ALI BANISHED ME from the kitchen while she worked on lunch with instructions to prepare the patio table so we could dine Al Fresco. The rain still strummed a steady beat on the roof overhead but there was no wind, so we would remain dry as we ate. I cleared the table of everything except a small vase, empty since the day I'd arrived.

I made a quick trip down to the flowerbed and filled it with fresh lilies, getting drenched in the process. The yellow, orange, and peach colored blooms were fragrant and beautiful with raindrops still beading on the petals. I was running my fingers through my hair, shaking off the water when Ali stepped out behind me. I turned to her with an apologetic grin, knowing I'd gotten her with the spray. "Sorry about that. It's really pouring out there."

"How did you get so wet?" She looked around. "The porch is covered."

I stepped aside and indicated the fresh flowers on the table. When I looked from the vase back to Ali, her eyes welled with tears. I opened my mouth to speak but had no idea what to say, so I just stepped over and folded her into my arms. I'd been needing that all morning and apparently she needed it, too. She kept her head turned toward the vase, her tears silent. "Thank you. You're being incredible about all this." After a moment, she pulled away and mumbled something about checking on the food, head down as she retreated back into the house.

Not wanting to push her, I stayed there on the patio and stared out into the distance. The mountains were partially obscured from view, their peaks shrouded by the low clouds currently spilling their contents over the valley. Once the storm passed, they would be back, beautiful and magnificent as ever. I hoped the same could be said for Ali. I hoped she could come back from this. That whatever or whoever was trying to bring her down wouldn't succeed. She was so much stronger than that, stronger than me. She truly was awe-inspiring. I wouldn't let anyone or anything take that away. Not from her.

Ali pushed the sliding door behind me open a bit farther, squeezing through with an armload of plates. I reached out and took everything I could, careful not to make her drop anything. "You should have called me in to help you."

She just smiled. "I used to waitress, too. I can carry four plates and the glasses to match with no problem."

Frustrating ass woman. Has to do everything on her own. "Just because you *can* doesn't mean you have to. I don't mind helping." I placed the plates and bowls on the table.

She waved me off. "Fine. You can help with the rest. Stubborn."

Pot, meet Kettle.

~

WE'D BEEN EATING for several minutes when Ali startled me by saying, "I'm not usually a crier. Just thought I should let you know that." She bit off a chunk of bread and chewed, a thoughtful look on her face. "Of course, you probably couldn't tell by the number of times you've seen me cry these last few weeks." The crinkle in her forehead was a clear indication that she was adding it up in her head.

"Don't do that."

She looked confused. "Don't do what? Cry?"

"No. Don't scour every moment we've spent together to do the math. Whether it was once or a hundred times, it makes no difference. Not to me."

She frowned and looked at her plate. "It matters to me."

"Why? Because you worry about what I think? It doesn't matter what I think. It doesn't matter what anyone thinks. You know who you are and that's what matters. Besides, you should know by now that I think you're fucking amazing. A few tears aren't going to change that." I reached out and ran my fingers across her hand. "Every moment with you, from that first day by the willow to this very second, has been perfect. Don't you dare regret any of it because I sure as hell don't."

She looked up, a slow smile spreading across her gorgeous lips. "Thank you for that. You're right. I regret nothing about our time together." Her fingers threaded through mine while the other hand raised her glass to her lips. She sipped her tea, finally relaxing a bit. I found myself relaxing, too.

When she lowered the glass, a small drop lingered on her lower lip, just a tiny bead that had escaped her notice. Acting totally on instinct — and clearly not thinking — I leaned across the table and pressed my lips to hers, whisking it away with my tongue. The sugary tea wasn't nearly as sweet as the lips I'd cleared it from.

Startled, she stiffened for a second before melting into the kiss, her mouth opening slightly to allow me access. With a soft groan, I placed a hand on the back of her neck and pulled her closer. Having the taste of her on my tongue again electrified every cell in my body. I'd been thinking of this, wanting it, craving it for the last two days. My hardening cock pressed painfully into the table as I stretched across it to reach her, but I wasn't about to pull back.

Her palm pressed to my chest directly over my heart before sliding up toward my neck, leaving searing heat in its wake. She dug her fingers into the back of my neck, massaging, kneading as she worked her way higher. An involuntary growl rippled through my chest when she reached back to tug the unruly strands at my nape. Encouraged by the sound, she tugged harder, pulling my whole head back as she nipped my lower lip.

Jesus. If I got any harder, I'd drill a hole in the damn table. No tools necessary.

Ali slid her hand to cup my jaw and pressed hard into me. I couldn't take it anymore. I had to be closer. It was all I could do to refrain from throwing the table and its contents into the damn yard. I managed to shift myself around it, though, without breaking contact with her lips. She twisted her chair to face me as I crouched at her side. I placed both hands at her hips, and she held my face in both of hers. The kiss went on for ages, each of us dominating for a while before relinquishing control to the other.

I nearly lost my balance when she leaned forward, sliding off the chair and onto my lap. Once we were situated there on the floor, I sat back on my heels and she straddled my lap, grinding herself onto me. The kisses became urgent, frenzied as she reached for the buttons on my shirt. I couldn't decide if I wanted fewer buttons so we could move forward faster, or more buttons so the kisses would go on longer.

No matter what, I knew I was about to cross a line I couldn't go back from. And I wanted it more than anything. I wanted her, wanted this, but would I feel that way afterward? Would I feel like an asshole for allowing it to go this far? I knew Ali wanted it. The way she was grinding herself into me left no question about her intentions. But what if this was just a band-aid for her? A way to feel good in the midst of a shitty situation? A way to take control of her life when so many things had happened that were beyond her control. Her work situation, Teach's illness, Keith, the break in, all of it must have been weighing on her.

Not that I minded being used under normal circumstances, but it was different with her. I didn't want her to look at me with regret in her eyes. I didn't want to ruin this, whatever it was, by taking it too far.

It wasn't about Spencer this time or keeping my promise to him, it wasn't even about the lawsuit. I didn't care about breaking contracts or losing the company. I didn't care about me. I only cared about her.

Shit. I really did care about her. I must if I was sitting there with her tongue in my mouth still thinking about what was truly best for her. My dick throbbed in protest of my decision, but I ignored it.

It was the first time in my life that it had occurred to me

that sex couldn't fix everything. Liberating and depressing at the same time.

When Ali finished with the last button and began pushing the shirt over my shoulders, I stopped her. "Wait a minute. We need to come up for air before things go further than we mean them to." I rubbed my hands up and down her arms, praying she wouldn't be angry.

She dropped her hands from my shoulders, placing them palms down on her thighs. Her shoulders slumped, and she breathed out a sigh before leaning her forehead to mine. "I guess I got carried away."

My heart still pounded in my chest, and my dick still strained against my zipper, but I knew I was right to stop it. "I started this. I wasn't thinking." I shrugged and looked at her swollen mouth. "Your lips are just so damn..." I groaned, frustrated at not finding the right word to describe it.

She blushed and lifted her weight off of me, struggling to keep her balance as if her knees were weak. "Thanks. You've got some great ones yourself." She offered a hand to help me up, which was hilarious since she was wobbling like a newborn calf. Not about to say that out loud, I just accepted the proffered hand and used it as little as possible as I stood. She retook her seat and polished off the rest of her tea as I slid back into the chair across from her. Setting the glass back down, she looked at me. "Is it too early to switch to wine? I could use a drink."

I looked out at the heavy rain and shrugged, trying to ignore the buzz in my ears from my still-racing heart. "It's not like we have to go to Gran's property this afternoon. Can't exactly work in this downpour and it's five o'clock somewhere, right?"

Ali went to get the wine. I stayed behind and tried to calm myself down. The sharp ache in my groin was my cock's way of punishing me for having a conscience. It was no fucking picnic, but it would fade soon and I'd walk away knowing that I did the right thing. For once.

If I'd thought for one minute that Ali was acting on genuine desire, I'd be balls-deep in her right now and to hell with the consequences. But that's not what was driving her. She was angry and feeling helpless, looking for a way to prove she was still the one calling the shots in her life, and I was a means to an end. She just didn't realize it at the time. I didn't want that. Not with her.

If I was going to flush my company and friendships down the toilet, it wouldn't be to help her prove a point. It would be because I chose it, and her, over everything else. And that wasn't a choice to be made lightly. I'd pushed this as far as I was willing to go. For now.

Ali returned with two glasses and a bottle of red wine. She filled them and placed one in front of me. After taking her seat, she took a long swallow and sighed. I sampled the wine and understood her reaction. It was delicious, and I'd never been all that crazy about red wine. I sat the glass down and realized she was watching me, an intent look on her face as if she was puzzling something out.

I glanced around uncomfortably. "What?"

Her eyes never left my face. "I was just thinking that Spencer is wrong about you."

Since when did she and Spencer talk? I hated the sharp stab of jealousy that pierced my chest at the thought of the two of them talking, laughing, and apparently discussing me. Trying to keep the irritation out of my voice, I casually lifted my glass and asked, "Wrong about what?"

"I was just thinking if you were a true manwhore, you wouldn't have stopped things."

I nearly choked to death on my fucking wine. I barely managed to swallow it, gasping and sputtering. "What? What the hell has he been saying to you?" Once I was sure I wasn't going to swallow my tongue or have a heart attack, I was pretty pissed off. How dare that bastard talk behind my back like that.

And he said it to Ali; the one woman whose opinion mattered to me.

She was wide-eyed as she watched me fight to regain my composure. "He didn't say anything. I've heard him call you that about a dozen times on the phone." Seeing that I was still confused, she tried again. "When we're at Gran's property, you always turn your call volume all the way up to hear over the equipment, right?" I nodded. "So, when Spencer calls, it's hard not to hear his greeting when I'm standing a foot away from you. He usually starts out with 'Hey, manwhore'."

Shit. She was right. Why had it never occurred to me that she could hear that? I usually excused myself to take phone calls but she probably still heard the beginning of the conversations. Fuck. Me.

"Like I said, I think he's wrong." She didn't look at me this time, probably afraid she had upset me with her admission.

I didn't want her to think I was mad at her, so I went with, "He is. The nickname is highly inaccurate. I've never charged for it in my life." I deadpanned.

Her head jerked up, and I met her gaze with a playful smile. She beamed at me, obviously relieved, and raised her glass toward me. "If you did, I have no doubt you'd be worth every penny."

I clinked my glass to hers and winked. "Might even be more lucrative than building and design. Then again," I mused, "I've heard that trying to make money doing something you're passionate about takes the fun out of it. Wouldn't want that, now would I?" I smirked.

"Definitely not." She chuckled as she sipped her wine, but I could tell she was curious about the origins of the nickname.

I had no idea how to even begin explaining my past to her and was kind of shocked that I even wanted to try. Maybe it was because whatever she'd made up in her head might be even worse than the truth, if that was possible. I'd never been ashamed of my sexual escapades until that moment. Something in the depths of her emerald eyes made me wish I could take it all back. Every hookup, every anonymous encounter, and every touch I hadn't given to her felt like a shameful betrayal. It was irrational, and I didn't understand it, but I wanted it all to disappear. As I considered all that had happened over the years, all I'd done, I felt suddenly unclean, unworthy.

I drained the remainder of my wine and reached for the bottle. Ali nodded when I arched a brow at her and I began to fill her glass, eyes on the task instead of her as I began. "Spencer's called me a manwhore for years. It started out as a joke but, given my track record with women, it sort of stuck." Done with her glass, I sat back and got to work on my own. "I don't think he means anything by it most of the time but some days he says it with just enough emphasis to make it clear that it's more of a judgment than a joke. He doesn't really approve of my choices in regards to women. I guess I've made a mess of my personal life, and he gets tired of seeing me screw up over and over." I watched the raindrops dance across the surface of the pool, not sure how to continue this conversation.

"It's not his place to approve or disapprove, and he doesn't know what he's talking about anyway. You know who you are. That's all that matters." I smiled as she turned my words back on me. "And I don't care if you've humped your way from Maine to Florida, you're not a whore. You're my friend, and I won't listen to anyone bad-mouthing my friend. That includes you." She leaned forward and tugged my chin toward her. "Understand?"

The sincerity and compassion in her eyes almost broke me. She meant what she said. I wasn't damaged in her eyes; I wasn't tainted by my past. I realized I loved her at that moment. Loved the way she looked at me without judgment, the way she saw the good in me even when I didn't. I loved everything about her.

Holy fuck. I loved her.

I absolutely fucking adored a woman who I'd been lying to from the moment we met.

No matter how I spun it in my mind, I knew I'd lose her in the end. The momentary elation of realizing my feelings was crushed beneath the impending doom of my past. I may have admitted to being a slut, but there was still one secret I couldn't bring myself to tell her. One admission that was too horrible to make. I'd spent twenty years burying it in the back of my mind, and I didn't think I could unearth it for anyone. Not even Ali.

She still held my chin in her hand, watching me. I knew I'd never get to tell her how I felt. To do so would be selfish on my part. Love and honesty went hand-in-hand, and I couldn't offer one without the other. It would just end up hurting her. I couldn't do that. She deserved better.

I smiled softly, hoping she didn't see the worry in my face or the adoration. "Understood, Miss Walker."

Her answering smile was radiant, and it made the tightness in my chest even worse.

I had to keep my feelings to myself. If I couldn't do that, I'd have to love her enough to let her go.

WEDNESDAY EVENING, I excused myself to my temporary office to get some work done while the girls watched a movie in the living room. They finally seemed to be settled in, really settled in a way that let them put their feet on the coffee table and raid the refrigerator without feeling like an intruder. They looked comfortable relaxing on the couch and laughing together at the comedy they were watching.

It was nice having them there, the sounds of their laughter and chatter in the mornings, the smell of Talia's expensive

Italian roast and thick cut bacon. It made the cabin feel alive for the first time since my arrival.

Despite the circumstances surrounding their stay, I was glad they were there.

I sat at the small desk in the spare bedroom that I'd converted into my office and opened my email, scrolling absently through my inbox while I pulled out my phone to call Brant.

He answered on the second ring, sounding excited. "Bout damn time you got back to work, slacker," he said by way of greeting. "I thought I was going to have to send a search party after you."

I laughed at his teasing. "Just letting you have a few extra days to come up with something worth building. Consider it a favor. You need all the help you can get."

We didn't usually banter so much but then again, we didn't usually have to work on independent projects either. The ball-busting was mostly relief at having time to work on something as a team again.

Once we'd sufficiently given each other hell, we got down to work and made a surprising amount of progress in the little time we had. We were laying out the blueprints for a job we were set to start in the fall and methodically going over the client's specifications to see how much wiggle room we had for upgrades and modifications.

It was a process that we went through with every project, tossing out ideas and using each other as soundboards for new concepts.

We reached a stopping point and agreed to pick it back up over the weekend. I'd long ago heard Ali and Talia head off to bed and was just about to hang up when Brant asked about the gala. I gave him the rundown, minus the mind-blowing activities at Ali's apartment afterward.

There was laughter in his voice when he asked, "So, is it true that Spence called in the office help to get you fitted for a tux?"

I inwardly groaned at the memory. When Brant's soft laughter became more pronounced, I realized the groan wasn't inward at all. "Ha ha, very funny. You know damn well he did."

"Talk about throwing a guy to the cheek-pinching, blue-haired wolves..." There was a loud thump and a few seconds of static before Brant's voice came back on the line. "Sorry, was laughing so hard I dropped the damn phone."

He didn't sound the least bit sorry.

"That's okay, fucker. Laugh it up. Spencer definitely won this round, but payback's a bitch."

WHEN THURSDAY CAME, I was nervous. Ali and I had spent the majority of the week together, whether at home or work, but Talia had been a sort of buffer. Knowing she was there, or would be there after her shift ended, had kept me from a repeat of what happened on the patio. It hadn't been easy to keep my distance. More than once I had looked at the clock and done the math to see how long I had until Talia got back from work, thinking of all the carnal ways Ali and I could be passing the available time. I'd also spent a good deal of the week just watching her, noticing little mannerisms that I found adorable. Like the way she talked with her hands when she was excited or the way she leaned subtly toward me no matter where we were, something she seemed unaware of.

Ali had been more herself as the week wore on. By Thursday morning, her perpetual smile had returned, much to my relief.

She finished her cup of coffee that morning and darted back downstairs to gather her things for a shower. I went to the sink to rinse our cups and was surprised when Talia sidled up next to me and began speaking. "You know, I've noticed something." She wasn't much for conversation in the morning, so it had to be important. I raised a questioning brow. "Ali seems like her old self around you."

"I don't think it's me. She just needed a few days to bounce back after the break-in."

Talia shook her head. "No. I don't mean since the thing at the apartment. She's been different ever since you showed up here. I haven't seen her smile so much since we first started college. She's been so damn chipper that I've seriously considered slapping her once or twice." She gave a lopsided grin that indicated she'd do no such thing. "Tell me you haven't noticed the grin she's always got plastered on her face."

I wrinkled my brow in confusion. "She's been that way ever since I met her. I assumed that was just her usual demeanor."

Talia's smile disappeared. She leaned toward me, our shoulders touching as she confided. "Not even close. She's had a crappy few years, I guess we both have, and it affected her. I was starting to think it was my fault, that maybe she had become jaded like me because we spent so much time together." She turned, gripping my shoulder in the process so that we faced each other. There was something like gratitude in her eyes. "When she met you, it was like watching the clock roll back. She was the Ali I remembered from our first days of college. She was happy, eager, optimistic, and something even more important... hopeful. I thought that girl was gone forever, lost somewhere with the girl I once was, but you brought her back."

I started to protest, tell her it wasn't anything I'd done, but she cut me off with a wave of her hand. "I don't know what's going on between you two and I don't need to know. Whatever you are to each other, I'm grateful for it. I was convinced that she'd given up after Keith." Her eyes darkened briefly at the mention of his name. "Her trusting you the way she does, that's huge for her. You must be something special." She blinked rapidly as if fighting back tears.

God, I felt like the biggest piece of shit on earth. "I haven't done anything to deserve all this praise. If Ali is happy, it's because she's fought hard for it. She doesn't need her happiness handed to her, especially by the likes of me. I'm nothing special, honestly."

Talia remained unconvinced. "Fine, then. Be stubborn. I'm used to it, having spent the majority of my life as Ali's best friend. I won't thank you for her happiness. But I will thank you for the other morning." She smiled sadly. "You didn't push me to talk about anything, and you didn't mention it to Ali. I appreciate that." She smiled when I gave her a questioning look. "Oh, if you'd said anything to her, I'd know. She would have checked to make sure I was okay. I think my mothering instincts have rubbed off on her." She paused, and I watched a myriad of emotions cross her features. "I'm glad you didn't mention it to her. With all that's happened, she's stressed enough. But, that's probably why you kept it to yourself, isn't it? You were looking out for our girl, not wanting to worry her unnecessarily."

The way she said 'our girl' was deliberate. She knew there was something between her friend and me. And the knowing way she was looking at me made me wonder if she'd guessed at the depth of my feelings for Ali.

"I like that you want to protect her. She'd probably be pissed if she heard me say that, but it's true. Ali likes to do things on her own, even when it's not the best idea." The sound of the downstairs bathroom door opening brought the conversation to a halt.

Ali's voice rang out as if she were standing near the bottom of the stairs. "Hey Talia, that piece of mechanically challenged shit you call a blow dryer won't turn on again. Will you please come do whatever voodoo is required to get it going? Maybe you should bring jumper cables because I think it's truly dead this time."

Talia stepped over to the doorway at the top of the stairs, raising her voice to be heard. "Mellow your mammaries, woman. It's fine. You just don't have the right touch. I'll be there in a sec."

"Oh, I'll touch it alright. I'll throw the frigging thing out the window. Uncooperative hunk of junk." Ali's voice faded out as she walked away, heavy steps indicating she was still fuming. A moment later, her bedroom door closed with a bit too much force.

I couldn't hold back a chuckle of amusement. I didn't even see her face during the exchange, but Ali was definitely the most adorable pissed-off person ever.

Talia winked and started toward the stairs, off to jump start the appliance in question. "I'm leaving after my shift, so it's up to you to keep our girl happy while I'm gone."

My mind didn't automatically go to all the ways I could keep Ali happy, as it normally would. One phrase kept repeating again and again in my head, causing my chest to tighten.

Our girl.

WHEN I PICKED Ali up at the office that afternoon, she was beaming. She climbed into the truck and practically vibrated in the seat from excitement. I suppressed a laugh at her adorable behavior and asked what had her so wired. "Marilee called a little while ago. Teach will be coming home in a week, as long as he keeps progressing at the rate he has been."

I forced myself to keep smiling, but all I felt was panic. "That's great. They've been away for quite a while. I'm sure they're both ready to be out of that place and back home."

She nodded happily. "I can't wait to see him. He's refused visits the entire time he's been gone, even from Talia and I, which stung a little. He didn't want to feel like he was on display." Her smile fell a bit. "Marilee said he had partial paralysis on one side in the beginning, and he didn't want anyone seeing him like that. We couldn't go against his wishes, so next week will be the first time I'll have seen him since before his stroke."

I didn't want to sound like I wasn't happy for her friend, but I had to ask. "So, what does that mean for you? Will you leave once he's back?" God, I sounded pathetic.

She straightened in her seat and looked at me, the smile frozen on her face as her brows rose. You could have heard a pin drop as I held my breath and waited for her answer. I almost wanted to reach out and pull the question back, afraid of what she might tell me.

Before she could respond, my phone rang through the speakers in my truck, scaring the shit out of both of us. She smiled and put a hand to her chest, her heart probably hammering like mine. Cursing, I fumbled with the controls on the steering wheel and snatched up my phone so I could take the call in privacy mode. "Hey, Spencer. What's up?" I thumbed the volume button on the side of the phone, subtly turning it down.

"Hey, manwhore. I have an update for you. What do you want first, the good news or the not so good news?"

Glancing over at Ali, I saw the worry on her face. I gave her a reassuring smile and told Spencer, "Good news."

I heard him fumbling through papers for a minute before he replied. "I had someone look into Marissa's recent activities, and I have confirmation that she was here in Richmond all weekend. It wasn't her."

I breathed out a sigh of relief as the weight of that possibility was lifted from my shoulders, inwardly cursing that I still hadn't heard from my own investigator. "You're absolutely sure?"

"Positive. I'm looking at her credit card statements, and I even have security footage to prove it was her making the charges."

"Do I even want to know how you got all that?" I probably didn't.

He scoffed. "Like I'd tell you, anyway. A man has to keep some things to himself." I knew that mantra all too well. "Suffice it to say Marissa is a non-issue. Now, for the bad news…" I heard typing in the background, but he didn't immediately elaborate.

I bristled. "You're doing it again, shithead. Just spit it out." My tone had Ali's total attention. Since Marissa had already been addressed, I thought it was time to bring Ali into the conversation. "You know what, hang on and let me put this back on speaker. Ali's here, and she should know what's going on."

He agreed and waited for me to make the switch back to Bluetooth. "You both there?" Ali answered for us, and he said a quick hello. "Okay, here's the deal. When I ran an image search for the two pics Lauren sent you, I found out they were originally posted online in December of last year. They were on two of her social media accounts until recently. It appears that they were removed some time Monday after she sent them to you to prove her whereabouts. She probably thought no one could find them once they were deleted. She's also 'checked-in' at a lot of places recently that I know she couldn't have been. According to her profile, she lives in Colorado and half her pictures are tagged as being taken on the West Coast. It's bizarre." He addressed Ali. "I'm going to assume you don't follow her on social media, otherwise you would have seen it."

The look of disgust on Ali's face was comical. "Um, no. I actually deactivated or deleted all my accounts a couple of years ago. Even if I hadn't, there's no way I'd follow her." Once the distasteful thought passed, she asked, "So, we know where she wasn't. How do we find out where she was? Her lying doesn't prove her guilt, just that she's not to be trusted. Believe me, I already knew that."

Spencer blew out a breath, sounding frustrated. "I can't find anything to track her with. She doesn't have any credit cards that I've found, and there's been no activity on her debit card in the last week. That fact in and of itself makes me suspicious. No one uses cash anymore, at least not exclusively."

Ali shrugged despondently, not that he could see it. "So we can't prove anything as far as she's concerned. What about Keith?"

"Keith's card was used Friday, but I haven't been able to get visual confirmation. The charge was made by phone to book a hotel room but I can't access the check-in time. So, I've called in a favor and am waiting for the footage from the entire night to be sent over. It may take until tomorrow. I'll let you know as soon as I hear something one way or the other."

Ali's good mood was shot but she smiled as she talked to Spencer, thanking him for all his help. I nearly laughed out loud when he told her she was in good hands with me. The blush that crept up her neck told me her mind had gone to the same place as mine.

We ended the call with Spencer and I asked where she wanted to go for lunch. Lauren wasn't coming in until later, so we opted for the diner. I was pretty sure Ali wanted to see Talia one more time before she went back to D.C. so she could fill her in on what we'd found out so far.

And I'd be sure to let her know she didn't have to worry about Ali.

I'd take good care of our girl in her absence.

CHAPTER TEN

THAT NIGHT ALI and I prepared dinner together. After the huge lunch Talia had insisted on serving us, we decided on salad for dinner to balance things out. She washed the vegetables and handed them off to me for chopping. We said little as we moved around the kitchen together like it was second nature.

Once we'd prepared our meal, we ended up in the living room, sitting cross-legged on the floor between the large couch and coffee table. I scrolled through the channels for something to watch while Ali poured two beers into frozen mugs. We settled on an old comedy and ended up laughing our way through dinner. It was just what we needed.

After clearing away our mess, we lounged on the couch, Ali leaning against me as she sipped her beer. She turned to me suddenly as if something had just occurred to her, one leg tucked under her and one on the floor as she sat sideways on the couch. "I never got to answer you earlier when you asked about my plans after Teach and Marilee get back."

Unsure whether I wanted the answer, I nodded.

She squinted slightly, studying me. "You assumed I'd leave once they were back, didn't you?"

Looking away, I shrugged. "I thought you'd be ready to get back home, back to your life once they didn't need you to run things here anymore."

"Just because he's well enough to come home doesn't mean he's up to taking over the diner. And Marilee might not be able to go back to work yet, either. It depends on how self-sufficient Teach is, whether or not he'll need to be looked after. They might still need me."

"Even if they don't, I do." Shit. I hadn't meant to say that out loud. My eyes snapped to hers.

She could have taken my remark to mean that I still needed her help with the project, but that's not what I meant. And the look on her face told me she understood me exactly. Her smile was absolutely radiant as her gaze flitted from my eyes to my lips to my jaw, taking in every feature in obvious delight. "You need me, Clay?"

"More than my next breath," I whispered.

Well, shit. Way to play it cool, stupid. Cat's out of the bag now.

Her eyes widened, and she blindly reached out to set her beer on the coffee table, not taking her eyes off mine. She left the mug wobbling on the table's surface and reached out with both hands, placing them on either side of my face as she leaned in. When our lips were mere millimeters apart, she said, "Show me." Her mouth dipped to mine for a brief kiss and pulled back. "Make me feel how much you need me. Please, Clay."

Oh, goddamn.

She begged.

Fucking begged me to take her.

In an instant, those two words were the focus of my entire world.

Please, Clay.

She wouldn't need to ask twice.

Her eyes widened with excitement as I closed the distance

between us and playfully nipped her plump bottom lip. That little taste wasn't nearly enough so I delved deeper, sweeping my tongue over the spot I'd just grazed with my teeth, reveling in the sweetness of her.

She made a soft mewling sound, urging me on until I couldn't take it anymore. I needed her closer.

I turned and pulled her into my lap so that she straddled me. With my cock lined up perfectly, I gripped her thighs and held tight as I thrust hard against her, making her gasp. A satisfied growl tore through my chest. I reached a hand out and gripped the hair at her nape, remembering how she'd done the same to me days earlier on the patio. I pulled her down to eye-level as I warned, "Alison, you're going to be feeling this for days."

She held my gaze as her tongue darted out to graze my lip, teasing, goading me into action. "Good."

Game. On.

DESPITE DOING MY best to pace myself, it wasn't long before Ali's top went sailing across the room. She ran her hands through my hair, alternating between soft caresses and sharp tugs while I focused on her ample breasts. The bra she wore was mostly lace and left very little to the imagination. I pulled her forward just enough so I could reach her slender neck, working my way from just below her jaw to the soft flesh at the tops of her breasts. My fingers trailed just under the edge of the cups, not quite delving all the way in, teasing her, toying with her until she began to whimper my name.

I skimmed a finger down to her navel while the other hand reached for the clasp at her back. With a quick twist, I snapped the bra open. Ali leaned back and slipped the straps from her shoulders, smiling wickedly as she removed the lacy barrier. She dropped it to the floor and straightened herself before me, inviting me to look my fill.

I loved her confidence and that she was comfortable with me, so fucking sexy.

Rather than focusing solely on her full, perky breasts I pulled her down and claimed her mouth. Not only did I need to pace myself, I also needed her to know this wasn't like last time. This wasn't me needing her body, this was me needing *her*. When she was breathless from our kisses, I pulled back and held her eye as I brought my lips to her chest. I suckled, nibbled, and tongued one breast while working the other with my hand. The harder I sucked on her tight nipples, the more she trembled. She was so responsive I had to see if I could get her off like that.

I took my time, making her squirm and shiver paying attention to see that she was on the brink, then stopping to reclaim her mouth. After nearly half an hour, I hit pay dirt. I was preparing to move from one breast to the other, giving one last hard pull on her nipple when I accidentally dragged my teeth across the sensitive skin, hard. Afraid I'd hurt her, I pulled back, but the apology died on my lips when she threw her head back and cried out. "Yes!"

Oh, so it was like that, was it? Good to know.

I resumed my place at her breast, sucking and pulling, using my teeth, and she went wild. She bucked so hard I thought she'd fall to the floor, whimpering and panting as I worked her with my mouth. She pulled at my hips, begging me to grind into her and I complied happily, never releasing her nipple as she pressed herself against me and cried out. The orgasm ripped through her, and I nearly came with her as her shuddering body rubbed against my cock. I dug my fingers into her backside and held on for dear life as she rode out the rest of her orgasm, her nipple between my teeth and my name falling from her lips.

When the last tremor had passed, she sat watching me, her

rapid breathing beginning to even out as I soothed her tender flesh with slow, soft kisses, tempering the sting. I pressed my lips to the valley between her breasts and worked my way back to her mouth, delighted to see the raw desire in her gaze. Kissing the corner of her mouth, I smiled. "That's one."

BY THE TIME I carried her to my bedroom, I'd managed to pull another orgasm out of her without delving below her waist, only losing my shirt in the process. My little experiment had been quite a success, but my balls were starting to ache and I was afraid I'd do irreparable damage if I didn't get inside her soon.

I crawled onto the king size bed and lay her right in the middle getting my fill of looking at her silky hair fanning across my pillow as she sank into the soft mattress. With a quick kiss to her already swollen lips, I moved to the edge of the bed to retrieve a condom from the nightstand, they were kept there more out of habit than anticipation. I turned back to her and slipped it under the pillow, stopping for a moment to admire her gorgeous body. She unclasped her locket, handing it to me to place on the nightstand before resuming her position against the pillows. She hadn't even attempted to remove the rest of her clothes, which I appreciated. I wanted the pleasure of stripping her bare, revealing her body inch by inch so I could savor it.

She sat up as I made my way to her, both of us up on our knees. I brushed a lock of hair away from her face, revealing a seductive smile. I almost said it then, seeing the desire, the adoration in her eyes. I almost told her I loved her but couldn't form the words. I couldn't profess my love for her with my lies still between us, coiled like a viper waiting to poison any future we might have had.

She laid her hand on my chest as her hooded gaze traveled appreciatively over my body. I wondered if she could feel the gallop of my heart under her fingers. I covered her hand with mine and brought it to my lips, kissing her fingertips one by one and nuzzling her palm before pulling her to me for a long slow kiss.

I was a little surprised — and a lot turned on — when Ali put her hands on my shoulders and shoved me onto my back. She grinned wickedly as she reached for the button on my jeans, making short work of getting them open. She tugged them slowly down, taking my boxer briefs with them, and dropped them unceremoniously to the floor. Swinging one leg over my knees, she straddled my legs and began trailing kisses over my stomach, her long dark hair tickling my sides.

When she took me in her mouth a moment later, running her tongue on the underside of my cock and pulling me deep, I had to grit my teeth to hold back a string of swears. Holy fuck, her mouth was hot. My whole body felt like it was on fire. I actually shook with need as my mind flooded with everything I wanted to do to her, with her. Then she began lightly pulling on my sac and every thought in my head vanished. She took me deep and tugged my balls, over and over until I thought I'd black out. I reached down and tried to stop her before it was too late but she just looked up at me and moaned as she gave her head a little shake.

She held my eye and took me deep, working me with her tongue as she pushed me over the edge. We maintained eye contact the entire time I emptied myself into her, coming harder and longer than I ever had in my life. It just kept going and going and she kept taking me deep into her throat until the very end.

When she was satisfied that I'd finished, she pulled back and gave the head of my cock a quick lick before moving to lie down beside me. "That's one." She announced with a smile as she laid her arm across my heaving chest.

I smirked at her use of my earlier words. "And a damn good one at that."

She sat up on her elbow and looked down at me with a wink. "Just trying to even things up."

"Oh, no. Not happening." She scowled adorably at my remark, and I laughed. "Not that I don't like where your mind is going but, if I don't get inside you soon, I may go out of my mind." She squealed when I seized her by the waist and flipped her onto her back, those damn jeans of hers the final barrier between us as I pressed my entire body into hers. I could feel the heat of her sweet bare pussy through her clothes as I sucked on her plump lower lip and fumbled with the button on her jeans. The damn thing wasn't cooperating, and I was rock hard again, dying to feel her around me.

I sat up with an annoyed grunt and wrenched the button open with enough force to damn near rip it off. Ali's responding giggle managed to curb my frustration, and I calmly removed her jeans and panties, my attention fixed on her smooth skin as I balled up the offending garments and tossed them across the room. She giggled again as the sound of them hitting the far wall tickled at my awareness but I was solely focused on her. My gaze traveled the length of her body from the girly pink of her toenails to the mouthwatering apex of her thighs to her full, rounded breasts and finally to the deep green pools of her desire-filled eyes.

How the fuck could anyone raise a hand to this exquisite creature? How could that bastard have marred her porcelain skin with bruises? White-hot rage shot through me at the mere idea of what he'd done to her. Shaking off the image of her from the night we met, I forced myself to focus on the woman she was now, the woman looking at me like I was the center of her universe.

Every inch of her was perfect. And mine. If not forever, then at least for tonight. And I was going to make every second count. I wanted to touch, love, and claim every part of her. Even her heart. A pang of sadness threatened to overcome me, knowing that her heart was something I should never have but I pushed the thought away. None of that mattered tonight. Not my past or her future, not broken promises or unfulfilled destinies. Even the lies didn't matter as long as my body could show her the truth. Nothing mattered except what we were to each other tonight. A woman who had no idea how amazing she was and a man hell-bent on showing her.

No matter what happened after this there would never be any regret, not from me. She'd awakened a part of me I'd thought was long dead and tonight I'd lay it at her feet as I worshiped her body, offering it for her to take forever. I wanted her to have it because, although she'd never know, it would always belong to her.

My heart.

Ali watched intently as I skimmed my hand up her outer thigh, reveling in the softness of her skin. With a soft pleading moan, she rolled toward the edge of the bed, her gorgeous ass exposed to me as she snatched up the condom from beneath the pillow. Resuming her spot on her back, she held her arms out and curled her fingers, beckoning me to her. When I stayed where I was, hesitant to give up my magnificent view of her body, she dropped her arms and began opening the condom.

I liked that she was taking charge and making her desire known so I stayed right where I was. Once she'd freed the condom from the wrapper, she sat up in front of me and rolled it on, a sexy as fuck smirk on her face as my breath quickened in response. She stroked my cock lightly and took my hand as she lay back, pulling me with her.

I braced myself on my arms as I positioned myself over her, shifting to one side so I could caress her face with the hand not supporting my weight. She was so fucking wet when I nestled myself against her, it took all my willpower to go slowly. I wanted so badly to thrust into her, just bury myself in her to the hilt, but I needed to take my time. Not only had it been a long time since she'd last had sex but, if her nickname for her ex was at all accurate, she wasn't used to sleeping with someone of my size. The last thing I wanted to do was hurt her. I'd go easy for now, get her used to having me inside her, and then make love to her so thoroughly that there'd be no question how I felt. I'd show her I loved her the first time around.

I'd mark her as mine the second.

And third.

I watched her face as I slowly pressed inside her, looking for any indication of discomfort. All I saw there was desire, hunger, and contentment. This was exactly where she wanted to be, and it was the greatest compliment I'd ever received. She wanted this, wanted me as much as I wanted her. I pushed a little farther in and pulled back, working my way into her an inch at a time. She was unbelievably tight, causing little moans of pleasure to escape my throat with each thrust. When I was just over halfway in, her eyes widened, and I brushed her lips with mine. "Are you alright?"

She pulled my mouth back to hers and thrust her hips up, taking me all the way in. Jesus fucking Christ, she felt so good. Between searing kisses she sighed and muttered, "Never better."

I pushed into her grinding myself in as far as I could go and stopped. Though it was a good idea to allow her a moment to get accustomed to the invasion, my real motivation was for myself. I just wanted to feel her for a minute, commit this moment to memory. The feel of her chest against mine, her hands in my hair, her pussy squeezing me almost painfully tight, it was overwhelming. It wasn't just another hookup.

It was my first time with the woman I loved.

There was a hitch in my chest as I began to move inside her, I felt her everywhere. Only she and I existed. Her hands ran up and down my body as I thrust into her, increasing my pace a little each time. She panted and moaned, pulling my hips, my hair. Urged on by her responses, I plunged harder and harder into her, my orgasm building low in my stomach.

Ali lifted her legs and wrapped them around my waist, locking her ankles behind me. The angle of entry was so fucking good that way I knew I wouldn't last long. Jaw clenched, muscles rigid, cock throbbing I pounded into her over and over, fucking loving the sounds of pleasure she was making. Her legs tightened around me, and the walls of her pussy gripped me so hard I could barely move inside her as she came. Spasms rocked her entire body as she clenched around my cock, practically milking the orgasm from me. I pounded deep as I found my release, threading my arms under her, cupping her shoulders and pulling her body down onto my cock as she sank her teeth into my bare shoulder. The little stab of pain made my dick jerk even harder, and I moved a hand to the back of her head in encouragement.

Fuck yes. Mark me.

When the last tremor had gone, I tried to shift my weight off to the side to avoid crushing her but she locked her arms around me and held me in place. Her legs finally dropped from around my waist, a contented sigh escaping her as she traced my ribs with her fingertips. "You called me Alison."

I lifted my head and frowned, fighting off the post-coital haze. "What?"

She smiled as she ran her fingers through my hair. "You usually call me Ali but when we... um..." Her face reddened as she struggled for the right words. So damned attractive. "You only call me that when you're in the heat of the moment. You did it that night after the gala, too."

I honestly hadn't realized. "It isn't a conscious thing." I

shrugged and shifted myself lower, slipping out of her and nuzzling her neck.

She chuckled, the sound vibrating her chest, making her breasts jiggle in an extremely pleasant way. I scooted lower so I could palm one while using the other as a pillow. Her fingers swept through my hair, pushing a few sweat-dampened strands back off my forehead. "At least now I'll be able to tell how turned on you are by how you say my name."

"Particularly if I'm moaning it and tearing off your clothes."

Her laughter, hearing it through the wall of her chest, echoed all the way through to my soul. It was my favorite sound in the whole damn world, aside from those moments when *she* was the one moaning.

As much as I hated to do it, and to Ali's great displeasure, I lifted myself off of the bed to head to the bathroom.

I reentered the bedroom just as Ali was shifting onto her side to face me, wincing as she did. I took a seat on the edge of the bed and reached for her hand. "Everything okay?"

She beamed at me, practically glowing. "Everything is absolutely perfect."

I cocked my head to one side and pointedly swept my gaze below her waist, my tone serious. "You looked like you were uncomfortable just now. If I hurt you, you need to tell me, so I know to be more careful." Despite my earlier promise, the idea of causing her pain actually made my stomach clench.

Pulling her hand from mine, she let it fall to my lap and began lazily stroking me. "You must be aware of your size, right? I just need to get used to you, that's all." Her hand gripped more firmly, and she watched with rapt attention as I stiffened in her palm. "I like that I can still feel where you've been. I like that I can still taste you on my tongue and the way my skin tingles everywhere your kisses have been."

I rubbed a hand over my jaw, noticing the stubble there for the first time. I grinned down at her. "Guess I need a shave."

She kept her pace, long slow strokes up and down my shaft. "Not at all. I like the stubble." A pause. "Particularly between my thighs." When I reminded her that my stubble hadn't had the pleasure of being between her legs yet, she seductively quirked a brow, surprising me with her bravery. "Sounds like it's time for round two."

"It's not good form to make a lady ask twice," I told her as I bounded back onto the bed, grinning lasciviously and wiggling my brows as I openly appraised her magnificent body.

She giggled happily at my antics, folding me into her arms. It wasn't long before her laughter was replaced by soft moans and the sound of my name. First as a whisper, then as a growl, and finally as an invocation.

WAKING UP WITH Ali beside me felt like the most natural thing in the world. I'd fallen asleep with her draped across my body, and neither of us had moved all night. I lay there for long minutes just listening to the sound of her breathing, feeling her breath dance across my chest with every exhale. I wanted to touch her, hug her closer to me, run my hands over her smooth curves, but I didn't have the heart to wake her. She'd been sated but exhausted after our second encounter, which had lasted hours as I'd licked, sucked, and fingered her to orgasm several more times before allowing myself inside her again.

I couldn't speak for her, but it was the single most erotic experience of my life. I'd never be able to look at her again without getting an erection, assuming the goddamn thing ever went down in the first place. Even now it was straining against the thin sheet that covered us, and it had nothing to do with morning wood. It was her, being near her, the feel of her next to me.

Making up my mind, I slowly shifted from under her and

froze when she muttered my name in her sleep before turning to snuggle into the pillow I'd just vacated. Even in her slumber, she was with me. It was a small thing that made me immensely happy. I tiptoed around the room gathering some clothes and my wallet, careful not to wake her.

I dressed quickly in the living room and snapped up my keys, heading for the door and praying I found a store open this early. On a whim, I scrawled out a quick note and left it on the counter for Ali to find if she woke before I got back. A goofy 'I-just-got-laid' grin on my face, I headed into town for provisions.

Thankfully, I was able to find what I needed in short order and returned within the hour. The cabin was quiet when I entered, and I was pleased that Ali was still resting. I shuffled through the kitchen cabinets, remembering that I'd seen a serving tray somewhere. With a minimum amount of noise, I managed to find it.

I arranged the breakfast I'd picked up on the tray and carried it to the bedroom, sitting it precariously on the small nightstand. I smiled as Ali shifted in the bed, turning toward me in her sleep. Even when unconscious, she was drawn to me.

Leaning across the bed, I placed a kiss at the corner of her mouth and whispered her name. She stirred, but her eyes remained closed. I tried again, kissing her forehead this time. "Ali?"

She peeked at me and smiled, snaking her arm around my neck and pulling me down next to her with a contented sigh. "What are you doing out of bed so early?" She snuggled against me, throwing one leg over mine. "I thought you'd sleep all day after all that exertion."

I laughed and pulled her hand to my chest, covering it with my own. "What kind of man would I be if I wore you out like that and didn't feed you?"

She lifted her eyes to mine and inhaled deeply, groaning in pleasure. "Do I smell coffee?" I nodded. "And bacon?" I nodded again, smiling as she frowned a bit. "How did I manage to sleep through you cooking bacon? That stuff usually works better than an alarm clock."

I chuckled. "I never said I cooked it." I hugged her to me. "I'm far too exhausted to cook so I ran out and picked something up."

She sat up, giggling and rubbing her hands together. "Good call, Mr. McGavran. I'm starved, but I really don't want to get out of this bed."

I placed the tray on the bed between us. We sat cross-legged and devoured our breakfast like neither of us had eaten in a week. I couldn't help smiling at the way she moaned with pleasure when she bit into the crispy strips of bacon. Noticing my attention, she shrugged. "Got to keep my strength up, you know."

Yes, you do.

I nodded and reached across the tray to lightly brush her nipple through the thin sheet.

Her gaze traveled the length of my body, and she grinned. "I think I've had enough food for now. I'm going to jump in the shower while you finish up." She leaned across the tray on her hands and knees, placing a searing kiss on my lips.

Seeing her in that position gave me all sorts of ideas for later. "Go ahead, I'll be done in a minute. I'll clear all this out and meet you in there." I told her with a wink.

Judging by her mischievous smile and the sway of her hips as she made her way to my shower, she was more than willing to share the hot water.

A FEW MINUTES LATER, I stepped into the steamy bathroom. Ali's silhouette was visible through the frosted glass door and I just stood there for a while admiring her. She had her head thrown back, letting the water run down her body. When she noticed me there she cracked open the door, and held out her hand in welcome. Before I knew it, my clothes were littered all over the bathroom, and I was stepping into the shower, my hand in hers as she pulled me in.

Her hair was slicked back and dripping, her body glistening under the spray. She held my shoulders and turned us so that the water cascaded down my back. "Don't want you catching a chill." She smiled, running her hands over my chest and watching the water trail down my skin.

I reached over and lifted the bar of soap. Looking at her for permission, I smiled when she nodded, and I began running the bar over her slick body. When I had enough lather to work with, I abandoned the soap and used my hands to wash her, careful not to be too rough with the tender flesh between her legs. Then I rinsed her body, spinning her back under the showerhead and watching the bubbles sluice off her skin.

She gasped and braced herself with one hand on the wall when I knelt down and threw one of her legs over my shoulder, opening her to me. I looked up and grinned at the look of shock on her face. She hadn't been expecting that. "I've washed you and rinsed you, now it's time to lick you dry."

She glanced at the still-running shower head over her shoulder. "But the water is still on."

I placed a kiss on her smooth mound and met her eye. "Exactly."

We stayed in the shower until the hot water ran out then ran half-shivering to the bedroom and dove back under the covers where, despite knowing we would be late for work, we went through two more condoms. Good thing I always kept plenty on hand.

Knowing she must be sore, I slipped on my boxers and went into the bathroom, returning with a small cloth I'd soaked in cool water. Ali sighed softly when I placed it against her tender folds. I trailed light kisses across her abdomen and pulled the covers with me as I took my place beside her on the pillows. "Does that feel better?" I asked, leaning over to kiss the crook of her neck.

"Mmm... perfect. Thank you." She practically purred.

We lay there quietly, our slow, even breaths the only sound.

Sometime later I was startled awake by a sharp rapping on the front door. I turned to look at the clock on the dresser. It was nearly ten. We were both incredibly late for work, but no one would be hunting us down, especially without calling first. Shit. I'd left my phone in the truck when I went out earlier. Maybe someone *had* been trying to reach me. I threw back the covers as Ali jumped out of bed and began scooping up her wrinkled clothes from the floor, muttering 'shit' over and over like a teenager caught by her parents. I wanted to laugh at how frantic she looked, but I was too irritated that someone had the nerve to interrupt our morning.

She scanned the room frantically, clutching her clothes to her bare chest. "Where the hell is my locket?"

I walked over and put a hand on her arm, stifling a grin. "Ali, relax. It was on the nightstand, remember?" I handed it to her and planted a slow kiss to her pursed lips. "I'll get rid of our uninvited guest, whoever it is. Okay?"

She nodded and began sorting through her clothes, dropping everything on the floor when the banging started up again. She gave up carrying everything and started digging for each garment in the pile. Watching her hastily pull on her lace panties really ruined my morning. I didn't want her dressed yet, dammit.

Whoever was here better have a damn good reason for showing up unannounced.

I pulled on some jeans and an old tee shirt, walked out into the living room and waited for Ali to get herself together. She stood in my bedroom doorway, running my brush through her tangled hair and frowning. "Do I look like I've been having sex all morning?"

The banging resumed, causing her to jump like a guilty teenager.

How could I not laugh at that? She was annoyed by my reaction and threw the brush at me as she rushed over to the stairs, heading for her room, I assumed. "It's not funny. I fell asleep with wet hair that you'd been pulling and fisting in your hands for an hour. I probably look like one of those damn troll dolls. Whoever it is, stall them."

I couldn't contain the bark of laughter that followed that statement. If she thought for one minute that looking like she'd just been made love to for hours on end wasn't the sexiest thing in the world, she was crazy. I loved every damn one of those tangles and had worked hard to put them there. She was fucking beautiful. Period.

When I heard her bedroom door shut, I hurried down the stairs and threw open the door, expecting an overzealous salesman or religious group passing out fliers. No matter what I thought I'd find, it damn sure wasn't what I got.

Standing there on the porch were Spencer, Gran, Vanessa, and Vanessa's eight-year-old son Daniel.

What the fuck?

Spencer seemed to take charge of the herd stepping up and pointedly waiting for me to move so they could enter, my dumbstruck expression apparently not giving him much pause. "Why the hell aren't you at the job site? It's freaking ten o'clock."

Irritated at his tone, I bit out, "I overslept. Did you go to the property and realize I wasn't there then decide to come here and harass me?"

Gran shuffled by, patting my arm as she passed. "Don't be silly. He called one of the crew leaders and asked if you were there. You should have just answered your phone."

Vanessa scoffed at her. "Mama, don't snap at him. He was obviously tired. Maybe he was sleeping so hard that he didn't hear it." She kissed my cheek in a motherly way and turned to Daniel. "Come on, baby, get inside so Clay can close the door and stop letting out all the cool air."

Daniel scuttled by, holding up his hand for a quick high-five. He had gotten so much taller since I'd seen him last. He definitely didn't look like a baby anymore, despite his mother's pet name for him. I closed the door and caught up with them as they reached the doorway to the first-floor. I brushed past them and pointed at the stairs. "This way. The first floor is being used by some guests, so I keep to the top floor."

I frowned at Spencer as I took the lead. The fucker knew I'd given the bottom floor to Ali and Talia. Why would he have been taking everyone there? Probably so I'd have to explain my odd living situation. Asshole. The firm set of his jaw was a clear indication that he was pissed about something, and I was pretty sure he'd be telling me what it was, sooner rather than later.

Everyone walked around oohing and aahing at the view, the pool, and the expensive interior of the cabin. Well, everyone but Spencer. He stopped by my bedroom door, cocking his head and watching me. Fuck, had I left a condom wrapper on the floor?

The look on his face made it clear that he knew.

And he was not fucking happy.

CHAPTER ELEVEN

FOR A SPLIT SECOND, I felt a twinge of remorse. I had, after all, broken a promise to him — and that damn contract — when I slept with Ali, but then the look on his face started pissing me off. He was looking at me like this was just my latest man-whoring mistake, and that couldn't be farther from the truth. There had been no mistake. Ali wasn't a mistake. How I felt about her wasn't a mistake and just the idea of him lumping my night with her in with all the meaningless sex I'd had over the years nearly sent me into a fucking rage.

Vanessa glanced between Spence and I then turned to the others. "Let's go down and check out the yard. Maybe we can bring our suits on our next visit so we can go for a swim."

Daniel ran over to me, excited. "Can we, Uncle Clay? Can we swim in your pool if my mom remembers my trunks next time?"

Despite the anger radiating off me, I had to smile at Daniel's nickname for me. I wasn't his uncle, but I liked that he said it with pride, as if he'd staked his claim to something valuable. I ruffled his light blond hair. "You sure can, buddy. There are tons of cool floats and a diving board and everything." I tried to sound excited, but I could feel Spencer's eyes boring into me. "Why don't you take your mom and Gran outside to have a look around. Uncle Spencer and I will be down in a minute." It was on the tip of my tongue to tell him about the indoor pool and game room in the basement but I decided getting them all out of the house was more important just then.

He nodded deeply and latched onto Vanessa's hand, practically dragging her out of the room and shouting for Gran to follow. Gran took her time, watching Spencer and me closely as she crossed to the stairs behind her daughter and grandson. She turned back at the last moment and frowned. "I don't know what's going on here, but I didn't come all the way out here to break up a frigging fight. Say your piece, then bring your butts down here so we can go check on the house." She narrowed her eyes at us. "Understand?"

Spencer and I muttered a 'yes, ma'am' and watched her disappear down the stairway.

Shaking my head at the fact that she could still punk us down, I turned to Spencer. "Alright, let's hear it. What'd I do to piss you off this time?" I barely managed to avoid looking into my bedroom, still considering the possibility that he'd seen an errant wrapper. I hadn't heard a sound from the first floor, so I figured Ali was holed up in her room waiting for the visitors to leave.

Spencer held up a hand and started counting off my offenses. "One — where the fuck is your phone? I was starting to think something bad happened to you, never mind that Gran was sitting there muttering about calling hospitals to see if you'd been in a goddamn accident. Considering we were passing right by the stretch of road where Rebecca died, it was a tense situation to say the least."

I flinched at the reference, but he kept right on, either not noticing or not caring. "Two — the day is half over, and you're still in fucking bed?" He glanced at my room and scowled at me.

"And don't even try to tell me you were alone." He put a hand up to silence my reply. "But we'll get to that later."

When that third finger sprang up and he looked at me, there was a shift in his expression that told me I wasn't going to like what he was about to say. "And then there's number three. I've been busting my balls trying to come up with a tactful way to get us out of this mess with Marissa but I'm coming up short. I've done everything I possibly could to avoid having to do this, but it's all we've got. I came to tell you in person before I did anything."

Goddamn, I didn't want to ask this next question. Something about the way he'd spoken made my balls shrivel, and a cold sweat break out on the back of my neck. "What's all we've got, Spence? What the fuck are you talking about?"

He shook his head and jammed his hands in his pockets, looking anywhere but at me. "There's video footage of you and her at the office."

"What?" I couldn't have heard him right. "What the hell are you talking about? That shit happened months ago. How could there have been a video all this time without me knowing?"

The look of guilt on his face felt like a kick to the gut. He still didn't meet my eye when he said, "I could tell something had happened between the two of you when I saw you together that following Monday. You looked kind of sick to your stomach, and she was acting way too friendly, touching your arm, leaning too close. I saw how you reacted to it. You didn't just push her away like you usually did, you looked ashamed every time she was in the same room with you." He finally looked me in the eye. "You had been with Brant and I all weekend, so I went over the security tapes from the previous Friday and found exactly what I was looking for."

I felt fucking sick at the thought that he'd watched me with Marissa and enraged that he'd checked up on me like that. My anger dimmed when I realized the enormity of what he was saying. "So, aside from the fact that you spied on me and lied about it for months, you also kept a copy of the video. For what purpose? There's free porn all over the goddamn internet. Why did you need footage of me screwing someone?"

His face reddened, either from shame or anger, I couldn't be sure which. "I never watched all the way through. Despite what you think, you fucking jackass, I wasn't trying to invade your privacy. I was trying to protect you from exactly what ended up happening. She got pissed because you didn't want her, and all hell broke loose."

"If you kept the video to protect me, then why am I just hearing about it now?"

He threw his hands up. "Because I thought I had it under control. When Marissa tried to turn you into a street pizza, it scared the shit out of her. I swore there would be no charges filed if she sought counseling and stayed the hell away from you."

"I know that, Spence. What the hell does that have to do with the video?"

"Before she gave in and agreed to therapy, she insinuated that she could say she was sexually harassed. She was still drunk and talking out of her ass, but it pissed me off, so I told her about the footage. I told her that the first ten minutes or so were particularly interesting since it was clear who was pursuing whom." He looked at me steadily. "You could be clearly seen shaking your head no and trying to turn her down, even pushing her clothes at her before she resorted to every dirty — and I do mean dirty — trick in the book to get you to fuck her. She knew I was right about the video, that she'd never be able to make charges stick when I had her on tape, so she backed off."

Something wasn't clicking. "So, if she knows about the video, why is she suing now?"

His fists balled at his sides, and he gritted his teeth. "Because she did more than take her file out of the office when she broke in. She got into my hard drive and sent herself a copy of the video."

My vision was swimming and tinged in red. "She what!"

"Now she says that if we fight the lawsuit, she'll post it online, after a few creative edits to make it look like she was fighting you off."

I froze. "Fighting me off? That would never work. Even the best photoshop jobs get called out online. People aren't stupid. I'd never force myself on anyone. Ever. We could discredit it in a second."

He shook his head miserably. "The damage would already be done by then. People remember the headlines not the retractions. No one will care that it was false they'll only remember that you were accused. I can counter with the real footage, but then we lose twice. Our best bet is to release the video first, beat her to the punch. Of course, that means no matter what you'll either be a fucking predator or a letch. If we don't fight back... if the lawsuit goes to court..."

I straightened, speaking with conviction. "I'll deal with it. Let her take me to court. I'll settle it and insist on a nondisclosure agreement. If it gets leaked anyway, which I wouldn't doubt because she's just that vindictive, I'll sign my shares of the company over to you. I won't drag you and Brant down with me." I nodded decisively, my mind made up.

Then Spencer said the words that changed everything.

"You're not the one she's after. She's accusing me."

THE ROOM SPUN when I realized what Spencer said. There was no way I'd heard him right, I had to be hallucinating or something. He'd never gotten within two feet of that crazy bitch. I stood there shaking my head, hoping to eject the words he'd just said from my brain. "No, no, no. She named me, the lawsuit is about me. You said so."

He gave me a sad smile. "No. I said she was suing the company. I never specified which of us she accused because I thought I could fix it and didn't want you to freak out."

Jesus fucking Christ, I couldn't breathe. I'd done this to him. I put him in the line of fire when I didn't have the sense to walk away from Marissa's advances. I'd ruined him just like I ruined everything. Son of a fucking bitch! I bent over and grasped my stomach, feeling bile rise in my throat. There was no going back from this. No way to save the friendship that we'd both been counting on since we were kids.

His voice was icily cold when he said, "And how lovely it was to come here to tell you all this and find out you're fucking another employee, clearly not giving a damn about anyone but yourself. I thought you were doing so well, thought you'd finally started to grow the fuck up. I'm fighting to save both our asses, and you're screwing the help. Again." He bent down in the doorway of my room and scooped up a thin gold chain with a book-shaped locket that we both knew belonged to Ali. He'd seen her wearing it when they met, after all, and it was very distinctive. Especially with her initial engraved in the front.

Shit.

He stepped into my space, leaning close to my ear as I tried not to lose the contents of my stomach. "Was she worth it, Clay? Were either of them worth your career? Or mine? How about my reputation? I know you don't have much of one, not a good one anyway, but mine fucking mattered to me. I don't deserve to have my life flushed down the shitter because you have to fuck every woman in your path."

He stepped back, and I lifted my head to look at him. This was it. This was how our friendship would end. "I'm so sorry, Spencer. It was a mistake, a terrible mistake that I wish like fuck I could take back." My mind flashed back to the day I'd ruined everything, the morning I'd given into Marissa's advances and taken her right there on my three thousand dollar desk. I could feel the bile in my throat. "I was stupid and careless and weak. I knew better than to touch the employees but I gave in anyway. I fucked a woman who meant absolutely nothing to me, and now I'm going to lose my company and the best friend I ever had. Over a whore who threw herself at me and my inability to turn her down. I'll fix this. I swear I'll find a way. I'll do whatever it takes to make this right."

As I righted myself and waited for his answer, the look of disgust on his face like a knife to my fucking heart, I heard a creak behind me. I spun on my heel and locked eyes with Ali, my entire body going cold. There were tears in her eyes as her gaze shifted between me and Spencer, her face contorted as if in physical pain. I started forward, wanting to explain myself, fully aware of what she'd just heard and how it must have sounded but she backed away. "Don't. Just don't." She turned and ran down the stairs, the sound of her sobs wrenching my heart until I thought it would burst.

I started after her, desperately calling her name when Spencer gripped my arm and spun me around, seething. He stood so close spittle peppered my face as he yelled. "You see?" He held tight and pointed in the direction Ali had gone, her necklace swinging from his fingers. "Are you fucking happy? Why did you have to pick her? Huh? You couldn't stand it could you? She was so far out of your league that you just couldn't rest until you'd proven what a stud you were and made her your whore."

I did something then that I hadn't done in twenty fucking years. I reared back and punched my best friend right in the face. I hit him with such force that I could hear the blood splatter onto the hardwood floor when I made contact, following through with my whole body. I was dimly aware of a shooting pain through my hand and fleetingly wondered if I'd broken it before deciding I didn't give a shit.

He stumbled back with a stunned expression, and I snatched the gold chain from his hand as he went down on one knee, blood pouring from his nose. Instead of feeling remorse for hurting him yet again, I drew back and prepared to take another swing, everything inside me screaming *she is not a whore!*

The only thing that stopped me from following through with the second blow was the sharp sound of Ali's Jeep spinning rocks as she sped out of the driveway and away from me. Fuck, I had to get to her. She had to know I'd never even think those things about her much less say them. I looked down at my stunned and bleeding friend, taking hold of his shirt collar and getting in his face, unmoved by the anger and betrayal in his eyes. "Don't you ever call her a whore again. Ever. Do you understand me? She's not just some one-night stand. I fucking love her and, best friend or not, I'll break your neck if you ever disrespect her again." I walked out then, pausing to throw a dishtowel at his chest before going in search of the love of my life.

The idea of her driving around upset scared the shit out of me. She'd been crying when she left, her heart ripped open because she thought I'd used her. She didn't need to be behind the wheel. I knew firsthand what could happen. I kept a white-knuckled grip on the wheel as memories of a time I'd long tried to forget flashed unbidden into my mind.

We're so sorry. There was nothing we could do.

The impact was just too much.

She's gone.

That one sentence kept playing over and over in my mind. *She's gone.*

I wouldn't survive it. Not this time.

It would be my fault.

Again.

~

I WAS STARTING TO panic. I'd tried the realty office, her apartment, the diner. I drove in circles until I found the bookstore she mentioned hoping she'd sought solace among the stacks.

Her Jeep was nowhere to be found, so I didn't bother going inside.

A call to Talia had gotten me nothing but a stern "What fucking part of 'keep our girl happy' did you not understand?" and a grudging promise to text me if she heard from Ali.

It was close to noon, and the sun blazed high in the sky. The summer heat pressed down on the blacktop as I drove aimlessly through Denson, looking for any sign of her navy blue Jeep. When I'd exhausted every possibility, checked every place she and I had been or even mentioned, my despair began to overwhelm me.

She'd probably gone back to D.C., to get as far away from me as she could get.

My eyes burned and my hands shook. I almost laughed at the irony of worrying about her driving when I could barely see the road through the angry tears welling in my eyes. I was angry at myself for doing exactly what I'd been trying for twenty fucking years not to do.

Care.

When I cared about someone, I doomed them. My love was a curse, and I'd known that.

I knew I'd end up hurting her, and I had.

Why the fuck hadn't I stayed away?

Not wanting to go back to the cabin and look into the faces of the four other people I'd hurt today with my careless actions, I drove toward the one place I'd desperately tried to avoid my entire adult life; the one place where my demons always waited. Because finally letting them catch up to me and pull me under was an agony far preferable to the one I was feeling right then.

~

I WAS THANKFUL for the hour when I realized the crew would be gone to lunch by the time I got to my destination. My truck shimmied over the uneven path to Gran's property. The driveway had yet to be paved, we would do that after all the commercial vehicles where done making trips, so the terrain was a little bumpy but nothing that couldn't be handled by our trucks.

Or Ali's Jeep.

I coasted to a stop beside her navy blue ride, stunned that she would choose this place as her refuge and elated that she was okay. I jumped from my truck and didn't even look around, anxious to see her and scared shitless because I had no idea if I could win her back. I knew exactly where to find her. Her presence there pulled me like a tether, and I started off down the narrow path that led to the lake. The ground was a little soggy from the recent rains, but I remained surefooted as I hurried toward the clearing, my heart pounding in my chest.

Coming to the clearing, I scanned the water's edge and spotted her huddled under the willow, her knees drawn to her chest with her arms wrapped tightly around them. Her head was down, and her shoulders shook with the force of her tears. She seemed unaware of my arrival, so I stood there for a moment, trying to come up with the right words to explain. I'd been looking for her for more than an hour, which meant she'd been crying for a considerable amount of time, with no indication that she was stopping any time soon.

I wanted to rush to her, hold her, make it better any way I could, but I forced myself to stay there and watch what I'd done to her, the pain I'd caused. Even though I hadn't been talking about her, to hear me say that of anyone must have lessened me in her eyes. I'd sounded like a callous ass.

The wind stirred the branches that surrounded her like a canopy, and she raised her head. When she spotted me, her face crumpled, and she tried to wave me away. Not about to let her get rid of me so easily, I strode over and pushed my way through the sweeping branches. I took a seat beside her, mimicking her position by pulling my knees to my chest.

I reached for her hand and she snatched it back as if burned by my touch. "Whores don't hold hands, Clay." Her voice was raw and ragged, a stark contrast to her usual melodious tone.

I sighed and withdrew my hand, propping it on my knee as I watched her. "What you heard back there..."

"What I heard was you telling your friend that I meant nothing to you. That I threw myself at you like some pathetic slut." She spat. "Do you think I wanted this?" She pointed from herself to me. "I swore I'd never let this happen again. I knew better than to trust anyone again, but apparently I didn't learn my fucking lesson the first time. At least I found out early this time, so I guess I should thank you for that. If I hadn't overheard the two of you talking, I might have wasted a lot of time thinking I mattered to you." She sniffed but blinked back the tears in her eyes, too angry to sink back into her misery.

I patiently shook my head. "No, Ali. What you heard was me reacting to the news that a woman I slept with over six months ago is suing the company to punish me because I didn't want a relationship with her. Nothing about that conversation, nothing I said back there, had anything to do with what is happening with us."

She looked doubtful. "You expect me to believe that? I heard you say the word: employee. Despite being wrong about what I was to you personally, there is no mistaking our professional connection. I am, in fact, an employee."

"So was she." I told her, my voice barely a whisper as I realized I'd have to tell her everything. Well, everything about my history with women, and particularly my history with Marissa. She just looked at me, and I knew there were a million scenarios in her mind. Rather than let her assume I made a habit of sleeping with my employees, I decided it was time to fill her in.

I began slowly, telling her that I hadn't been in a relationship since high school, touching briefly on my propensity for one-night stands, cringing when I saw the flicker of hurt in her eyes. Then I told her about Marissa. I started with her pursuit of me after being hired and how I'd fucked up by giving in. I didn't leave anything out, I told her about the harassing calls, the disturbing emails, and the failed attempt to run me down. She quietly asked a few questions but otherwise sat and listened as I laid out all the reasons I wasn't good enough for her, all the while hoping she'd want me anyway.

She didn't seem particularly angry, just curious. Until I told her that I'd been worried that Marissa had been responsible for the break-in. She glared at me as I explained how I'd had it checked out and there was no way it had been Marissa. I knew what she was thinking, and she was right. I should have told her. When I admitted I was an asshole for keeping that from her, she simply nodded in agreement.

I recounted Spencer's warning and the promise I'd made to him, laid out the terms of the contract we'd all signed. Told her how angry he was when he realized she and I were involved. She dropped her eyes then, and I reached out to touch her cheek — thankful when she didn't pull away. When she met my eye, I told her, "It's not your fault he thinks I broke my promise. And it's not mine either. He's wrong for being angry." My voice fell to a whisper. "I never promised not to fall in love." Tears welled in her eyes, threatening to spill over as she shifted closer and took my hand.

She deserved better than what I'd just done. I'd been weak

enough to tell her how I felt, to saddle her with my affection when I knew how it would end.

My love was a fucking curse, why didn't she see that?

Blinking rapidly to clear my suddenly blurry vision, I released her hand and stood, stepping to the water's edge as I told her, "You're everything I never thought I wanted. I made avoiding emotional attachment into a damn art form. It's no wonder Spencer thought..."

She spoke at my back. "Thought what?"

"He thought I'd made you into one of my whores." My jaw clenched, and I remembered the sickening crack of my fist making contact with his face. "But I didn't change you. It was you who changed me. You changed everything for me. Everything about me. When he said that, when he assumed that's what you were to me, I was so pissed, I couldn't see straight."

She stepped up behind me, tugging my sleeve until I turned to face her. "What did I tell you before? He doesn't know you like he thinks he does."

I tipped my head back and stared up at the sky, the sun peeking from behind a puffy cumulus cloud, the sudden brightness causing me to squint. "I'm pretty sure he figured that out when I decked him."

Ali's gasp sounded pained. "Oh, God. You didn't."

"I did. He assumed you meant nothing to me and when he said I'd made you my whore, I fucking lost it. It just happened, I remember looking at him and not caring that I'd made him bleed, maybe broke his nose." I looked at her, the enormity of what I'd done making my throat constrict. "How could I do that? After I'd just found out my stupidity may have ruined his life, how could I have the balls to hit him? Why wouldn't he assume the worst of me? It's not like I haven't been a fuck up all my life, and he's had a ringside seat for all of it. He should have been the one kicking my ass." Only I could take a bad situation and make it a hundred times worse in a matter of seconds.

"You're shaking," she murmured as she ran a hand down my arm.

"I'm fucking pissed. I didn't want any of this." I ran a hand through my hair, willing myself to calm down.

"You're angry because you don't want to love me?"

The hurt in her voice only compounded my anger. I spun around and faced her. "I'm angry because I *shouldn't* love you. All my love will bring you is pain. Look at how much I've hurt you already. I knew I was falling for you, and I was too goddamn selfish to walk away. And I knew telling you how I felt was only going to make it worse, but I fucking told you anyway." I placed my hands on her shoulders. "Because I wasn't thinking about you. I was thinking about me. It's who I am. I'm a selfish prick who continually hurts the people he cares about. Don't believe me?" I raised a brow and nodded toward the path. "Go ask Spencer just how toxic I am. Maybe he can fill you in when he stops fucking bleeding all over the floor."

I released her and stepped away, turning my back to her and staring out over the glassy surface of the lake.

The shove at my back was so unexpected I nearly fell in. I stumbled a moment and spun, expecting to find Spencer there, ready to take my head off.

But it was still just me and Ali.

She'd shoved the hell out of me.

What the...?

I looked down into her gorgeous face and found a look of defiance. She stood on her tiptoes poking me in the chest. "I thought you might need a quick dip to cool off. You're obviously not thinking straight because what you just said is utter bullshit. You don't get to decide whether you're good for me or not, you arrogant ass. I do. And I happen to think we're amazing together. I think you're amazing. You're also still my friend, and I've already warned you about talking shit about my friend." She took a deep breath and continued. "Love is pain, hasn't anyone ever told you that? The only ones in this life with the power to truly hurt you are the ones you truly love. Everyone knows that." She shook her head as if exasperated. "You and I are fine unless you're telling me it's over. Are you?"

"Not a chance." I bleated out without hesitation.

I leaned down to meet her lips with mine and she put her hand between us, effectively halting me. "Whoa, boy. I didn't finish. You and I are fine but what happened with you and Spencer? That's bullshit, Clay, and you know it."

Ali grasped my hand, cringing when she saw that my knuckles were bruised and crusted with Spencer's blood. I'd been so intent on finding her, I hadn't realized. She blinked slowly, as if the sight disturbed her. "Please don't ever do that again. Not for me and certainly not to him." She held my hand up so I could see my raw knuckles. "We're going to find Spencer and fix this mess. These marks on your hand are going to be the only evidence of this horrible damn day. You're going to work this out with your friend. Then, when it's all over, we are going to go back to the cabin and get shit-faced drunk because this is going in the record books as the shittiest week ever. We clear, Mr. McGavran?" She tugged me along behind her.

This woman continued to amaze me. "Yes, ma'am."

CHAPTER TWELVE

I CHECKED MY watch as we started back toward the path. "We need to hustle. The crews will be back any minute."

Ali came to a stop, looking guilty. "Actually, I sent them home for the day." She glanced around worriedly. "I um, wasn't in the mood for spectators when I got here, so I told the crew leaders that I was shutting everything down for the day." The corner of her mouth turned up slightly. "Everyone cleared out in five minutes flat. I guess none of them wanted anything to do with an agitated, crying woman."

I chuckled at the remark, but my chest tightened knowing how humiliated she must have been. I grasped her hand and brought it to my lips. "I'm sorry to have put you through that."

She leaned into my side and let me wrap an arm around her. "I'm sorry I didn't let you explain. I shouldn't have jumped to conclusions."

We reached the end of the path and turned toward the driveway, stopping in our tracks when we spotted Spencer's truck there beside mine. Ali pulled away and frowned, as we both scanned the area.

Out of nowhere, Daniel came running from the front of the

house, laughing as he bounded over to us. "Hey, Uncle Clay." He held his hand out for his customary high-five and watched Ali from the corner of his eye, looking suddenly shy.

I turned to Ali. "Ali, this is Daniel." Looking back to the blushing boy, I said, "Daniel, this is my friend Ali."

He peeked up at her from under his lashes and held out a shaky hand. Ali met my eye and grinned. She had a fan. She took his hand in hers and crouched down to his level. "It's very nice to meet you, Daniel." She glanced around. "What do you think of this place? Pretty cool, huh?"

He beamed up at her. "Yeah, Gran told me there's a lake where I can go swimming, and I forgot to ask but I bet there are fish there too. I hope there are. I like to fish."

She smiled at him and nodded. "So do I."

He looked mystified by that. "You like to fish?" He glanced at me like he wasn't sure. "Do you bait your own hooks? My mom doesn't like to touch worms. Dad says worms shouldn't bother her since she's a nurse and spends half her time wiping people's asses."

"Daniel!" Vanessa's voice rang out across the yard, causing him to spin around in fear. Thankfully he had his back to us as Ali and I cracked up at his statement. He waited as his mom approached, his posture that of a man standing before a firing squad. She pointed at him as she descended the small incline. "What did I tell you about using grown-up words?" I could tell she was fighting for composure as she stepped around him and offered her hand to Ali.

"Excuse my son; it's not entirely his fault. His father is a bad influence." She swept Ali with an appraising look. "I'm Vanessa, daughter of Gran and mother of potty-mouth." She dropped Ali's hand and glared at Daniel as she lit a cigarette.

Ali smiled at her politely. "Ah yes, the nurse." She gave the cigarette a pointed look and laughed.

Vanessa glanced at me wryly. "You've obviously spent a lot of time with Clay. He's been on my case for years to quit and loves to point out the irony of a nurse puffing on a cancer stick." She smiled at Ali. "One of these days, I might even listen."

I frowned as I looked around. "Where are Gran and shithead... er... Spencer." I looked at Daniel and cringed, mouthing 'sorry' at Vanessa.

She looked between Ali and I. "They're having a little chat..." There was a loaded pause then, "probably about the house or something."

"Uncle Clay, did you know Uncle Spencer ran into the door at your cabin?" Daniel announced. My eyes flashed to Vanessa. "He had blood all over his shirt from his nose, so Gran made him take one of yours. It bled for a long time but now it just looks puffy."

Vanessa placed a hand on his shoulder. "Come on, buddy. Let's go check out the lake. We can see if we spot any fish swimming around in there." She held my eye as she ushered him away, giving me a sad smile. She knew how close Spencer and I have always been. Was she disappointed in me? I knew I was.

Just as Vanessa and Daniel turned to walk away, it occurred to me that she didn't know about the tree.

Shit!

I spun on my heel and called out to Vanessa, not wanting her to discover the tree the way I had. My mom had been her sister and I couldn't let her go to the lake without preparing her for what she'd find.

Gripping Ali's hand, I walked over to them and dropped my voice, not knowing how she would react. "Before you go down to the lake, there's something I should tell you about."

"You mean Rebecca's willow?" She took in my stunned expression with a lopsided grin. "Gran told me about it months ago."

"She what? How did she know about it?"

Vanessa told Daniel to go on ahead but to stay away from

the water until she got there, watching him hurry down the path she smiled and turned to me. "Gran found it back in January. She and her cronies were bored one afternoon and decided to scour Google Earth looking for nude beaches." She grinned at Ali, who was chuckling. "They thought they'd be able to see some naked hotties if they looked long enough. Typical Gran. Anyway, after a while they gave up, and she started looking at places she'd been, locations that stood out in her memory." She shrugged and tipped her head toward the lake. "Eventually, curiosity got the better of her and looked this place up on the map. That's when she found the tree. She told me it was enormous and beautiful. Said it was time to bring this place back to life. That's around the time she started talking about building the house."

I couldn't believe she never told me about the tree.

She just sent me out here without any warning.

I'd have been pissed off about it if it weren't for the mess I'd made of things today. I couldn't really call her out for not telling me when I'd done something far worse.

Vanessa excused herself to check on Daniel, leaving me to clean up my mess.

After she had vanished down the lake path, Ali and I climbed the hill toward the house. Construction was coming along nicely though there was still a long way to go. The weather forecast wasn't good, heavy rain expected pretty much all damn week next week thanks to a slow-moving tropical depression creeping up the coast, so that was sure to bring things to a crawl. While bad weather sucked for the project, the idea of having lazy afternoons at the cabin with Ali sounded like heaven.

We heard voices off in the distance and watched as Spencer and Gran made their way to his truck talking quietly amongst themselves, their backs to Ali and me. Spencer hopped into the back of his truck and opened the large toolbox, meeting my eye over the diamond-plate lid. He glared at me stonily as I approached; Ali was clinging to my arm as I went. His nose was horribly swollen, and his upper lip matched its purplish tint.

Fuck.

He didn't speak to me as I stopped beside the truck. I'd purposely chosen the opposite side from Gran in hopes that I could avoid her for a few more moments. His expression shifted to a pleasant smile as he looked over at Ali. "Hey there, Ali. Nice to see you again." He looked guilty as he said, "I'm sorry for the scene you walked in on earlier. I want you to know that none of that was about you."

I couldn't help wondering if he'd said that to keep himself from looking like an asshole or if he was trying to defend me. Not that he owed me a damn thing after how I'd acted. I waited to see if Ali snipped at him over his earlier comment, but she just smiled up at him sweetly. "I know. Clay and I talked everything out." She looked at him and back at me, her voice pleasant, but her expression stern. "Now it's time for you two to talk." She stood on her tiptoes and peeked over the truck bed at Gran before turning to me. "I'm going to go introduce myself, maybe take a walk with Gran and you guys are going to make this right." When Spencer looked like he wanted to argue, she cleared her throat and interrupted him. "Please come down here so I can talk to you without getting a crick in my neck."

He jumped down and put his hands in his pockets, avoiding her stern expression and reminding me of Daniel when Vanessa caught him cussing. I barely fought back a smile.

He was wearing my favorite shirt. He could have taken any shirt in the closet, but he went straight for the one he knew I liked the most. The jackass.

That shirt was the softest most comfortable thing I owned, and I'd been picturing it on Ali for weeks now, just the shirt – nothing else. Dammit. Seeing him wearing it ruined the whole fucking fantasy.

Ali looked between us and using that take-charge tone in her voice that always got me hard she continued. "Look, I realize that men are emotionally constipated, but you two need to get it together and work this out. So you're both pissed off..." She caught Spencer glaring my way and pinned him with a withering stare, "All I can tell you is get the hell over it and act like grown-ups. Friendships like yours are worth fighting for, so you better damn well do it."

I couldn't hold back my smile any more when Spencer cowered slightly under her gaze, eyes hilariously flashing to the door of his truck as if he was contemplating a quick get-away.

She turned that look on me, and I kind of wanted to tell Spence to leave the door open for me if he decided to make a run for it. Ali rose on her tiptoes and briefly kissed my lips saying soft enough so only she and I could hear, "And do it without any more bloodshed, okay?" She winked at me and rounded the truck, taking an incredulous Gran by the hand and escorting her to the far side of the house as she introduced herself. A minute later, I heard the sound of Gran's laughter and couldn't help smiling.

Spencer watched them disappear around the front of the house with a blank expression. He turned back to me and furrowed his brow. "Shit. I think I might love her too."

Just like that, we were smiling, and I knew there was a chance I could fix things. I felt like I could breathe again for the first time since hearing the knock at my door this morning. "Careful, I'm pretty protective of her in case you haven't noticed."

He cocked his head and gave me a 'no shit' look, reaching into the bed to close the toolbox. "Ya think?" He flipped a thumb toward the house. "You sure you want the two of them hanging out? You never know what Gran might say."

Only Spencer would still be worried about the guy who just punched him out. "I'm not stressing it. Gran is wide open, but she knows what she can and cannot discuss when it comes to my personal business." I gave him a tentative smile. "But thanks for being concerned. I wouldn't blame you if you hated my guts after everything that's happened."

He blew out a breath. "Honestly? I wanted to crack your skull for a while there, mostly while the blood was pouring down my face. But after I calmed down, I realized what you'd said." He studied me. "You meant it, didn't you? You really do love her." I nodded, holding his gaze. "That's what I thought. Holy shit. I never thought I'd see the day." He considered a moment. "Okay, here's the deal. That was your freebie; your one get-out-of-an-ass-kicking-free card. Don't ever take another fucking swing at me unless you're prepared to get your teeth kicked in, friendship be damned. Comprendé?"

"Understood." I knew damn well that he didn't mean it, but I let him make his point. I owed him that much. He looked like hammered shit, his face swelling more by the minute. Eating a little crow was the least I could do.

How did I end up surrounded by so many extraordinary people? Ali, Gran, Spencer, Talia... all of them so amazing that I couldn't fathom what any of them saw in me. I didn't deserve any of them but I damn sure wouldn't let them go. I smiled at my friend and held out my hand.

He slapped it away, pulled me in for a hug, and chuckled. "And you're not getting your fucking shirt back."

ALI AND GRAN rejoined us a short while later, laughing and chatting like old friends. They both studied us as they approached, and I whispered to Spencer, "Why do I feel the urge to run and hide?"

He chuckled. "No idea, but so do I if it's any consolation."

Gran saw the two of us smiling, she playfully poked Ali's

arm. "Damn. Nice work, young lady. Couldn't have done it better myself."

Ali bumped her shoulder. "These boys just need a little nudge every now and then. I'm sure we can keep them in line between the two of us."

Spencer leaned in and whispered, "Run, dude, run."

Ali stepped into my arms, and I pulled her close as I told him, "Not this time, Spence. Not this time."

An hour or so later, we all stood in the gravel driveway chatting and enjoying the way Daniel mooned over Ali. Spencer grudgingly mentioned needing to get on the road and Gran jerked her head toward me, snapping her fingers. "I just remembered. There's a box in the back of the truck that I wanted to drop off." She glanced over at Spencer. "He was trying to get it for me when you came over and interrupted." She winked to let me know she was teasing. "I should probably explain what I want done with it all, while I'm at it." She seemed hesitant to continue.

Ali picked up on her meaning and offered, "I'll take it. I need to go to the basement and grab some of my art supplies anyway. I can put it down there until Clay gets a chance to go through it."

Daniel's face lit up when Ali reached for his hand and asked if he could help. He was smiling ear to ear as she followed Spencer to the truck to get the box.

Watching them, Vanessa turned to Gran and frowned. "I didn't know you brought anything."

Gran waved her off. "Spencer put it in the truck while you were getting Daniel ready. It's no big mystery, just some of Rebecca's things. Sketches of things she wanted to do to decorate the house, some antique door knobs she collected, nothing all that interesting." Turning to me, she said, "She had big plans for this place, some of them probably won't work, but I thought you might want to go through her papers and see if any of it can be done. I haven't looked through all of it, so I'll leave the decision to you." She touched my cheek. "I trust you to know the right thing to do."

Her expression said the words were meant for more than what was in the box. She knew I hadn't been honest with Ali, and she was saying she expected better than that from me.

I nodded and opened my mouth to ask what she thought of Ali when Spencer shouted from the driveway. "Hey, dickhead. Your phone is ringing."

Cursing under my breath, I jogged over to my truck and told Spencer, "Better answer it. Look how things turned out the last time I missed a call." He flipped me off as I looked at my phone. Blake. He was one of the crew leaders doing construction here in Denson. I frowned, why was he calling me? Ali sent them all home hours ago. "Hello."

"Hey, Clay. I um," he sputtered, "I wanted to call and check on Miss Ali." His discomfort was palpable, and I smiled at the thoughtfulness of his calling.

"She's just fine now. Thanks for checking in on her. I'm sure she'll appreciate it." He was one of the best workers on the project and a super nice guy. I wasn't surprised that he took the time to make sure she was alright.

He sounded relieved. "Oh, good. I didn't want to argue with her, but I hated leaving with her in such a state."

"No, you did the right thing."

Spencer gave me a questioning look, and I shook my head, giving a quick thumbs-up to let him know everything was alright.

"Well, it didn't feel like it at the time but I learned long ago not to mess with a pissed off woman." I smiled, nodding in agreement even though he couldn't see it. "I thought I should at least make sure she was okay. Also, I'm willing to step in for a few days if you guys need a break. I'm not sure what's going on, but I'm more than willing to run the site if that's what you need."

I had no doubt that he could handle it. I had considered asking him to take over if the Marissa thing required me to go to Richmond for a few days. "Thank you, Blake. I really appreciate that. I think we're alright for now, but I'd like to reserve the right to call in that favor at a later date."

"You got it. Just say the word."

I hoped not to need him, but it was nice to have options. Maybe I'd bring him in to supervise so I could whisk Ali away for a few days. Hmm...

I ended the call, mind still on the possibility of escaping with Ali.

Spencer waved a hand in front of my face, amused. "Damn, you have it bad. You should see the stupid grin on your face. I've been talking to you for five minutes, and you haven't blinked." He shook his head. "As I was saying, I'm still getting calls from that jackass, Holden Shepard. Have you gotten a call from him yet?"

"No, and it's in his best interests to keep it that way. We are not for sale. Period."

"I agree, but something has lit a fire under him, and I'm starting to wonder if word of the lawsuit has been leaked and he's looking to snap up the company cheap because he thinks we may fold." His tone of voice indicated concern but no judgment, which I appreciated.

"Where would he have heard that?"

Spencer just shrugged and rolled his eyes. "You know how he loves to swoop in and snatch up vulnerable companies. He's made a career of turning floundering businesses into Fortune 500 material."

"We're already Fortune 500 material. Fuck him." I was getting pissed.

"I agree. I was just giving you a heads-up so you wouldn't be surprised if he calls. He's getting pushier by the day."

I gave an answering grunt and let it drop. I kind of hoped he did call. There was a lot I'd like to say to that fucking vulture, and all I needed was an opening.

"Don't stress Shepard. We have enough going on, and he's just a nuisance anyway. He's never getting his hands on this company." He jerked a thumb toward the truck. "I'm taking Gran and Vanessa home then I'm going to check in with a few of my sources to try and find a way to avoid using the video... as soon as I get rid of this fucking headache." He touched the bridge of his nose, and I feigned like I was going to punch him again. He showed me both fists, smiling. "Careful, manwhore. You already used up your free shot."

"What did I tell you two about fighting?"

I turned at the sound of Ali's voice, grin widening as I watched her approach. She shook her head at me as she stepped into my arms. "Haven't we had enough drama for one day? Anything that still needs settling can be dealt with over drinks. Several drinks."

Spencer met my eye over her shoulder, grinning. "I could use a drink or two, myself. Too bad I have to drive everyone home."

Ali chuckled. "There's plenty of room at the cabin if everyone wants to stay." She looked up at me, her eyes full of humor at my less than enthusiastic expression. "I don't think Gran will want to, though. She mentioned that she and her friends were meeting up later for karaoke at some biker bar."

When Spencer and I groaned in unison at her antics, Ali laughed even harder. "You'd never believe some of the songs on her set list."

I wasn't all that worried about Gran, but I felt kind of sorry for those bikers.

Poor bastards.

~

SPENCER AND COMPANY left for home a little while later, after Daniel forced Ali to walk the entire property with him, holding onto her hand like a toddler while he beamed up at her in adoration. He was already smitten but, when Ali showed him the bank of vending machines we'd tucked into one of the old tack rooms, he went head over heels for her. She bought him a snack and asked about school, making him blush when she asked if he had any girlfriends back home.

He fell harder and harder for my green-eyed girl as the afternoon wore on, and so did I. She was amazing with Daniel, which I loved, but the way she fell right into step with Gran and Vanessa, it was like she was already part of the family. I wasn't sure if it was thrilling or terrifying to watch them all embrace her as one of us.

They each embraced her in the literal sense as they prepared to leave, chattering about getting together for dinner and, in Daniel's case, practically melting into the driveway when she gave him a peck on the cheek. Spencer slapped me on the back on his way to the truck, wisely not rubbing it in that Ali had pecked his cheek too. I wasn't concerned, I knew who she was leaving here with, but Daniel cut his eyes at Spencer like he hadn't appreciated sharing Ali's affections.

I had the strangest feeling, standing there watching them. There was a warmth in my chest that had nothing to do with the temperature. Seeing the connection, the bond already forming between them, gave me the most profound feeling of contentment that I'd ever experienced.

It felt almost like... home.

Ali came over and wrapped her arm around my waist, watching our unexpected visitors drive away. "You have a great pseudo-family there. I can tell they all adore you."

"They didn't even look in my direction, Miss Popularity. I

think it's safe to say you were a hit." I squeezed her shoulder and started walking across the yard to the lake path. "And Gran isn't easily impressed."

She laughed, a fond expression on her face. "She wasn't at all what I expected. An Avenged Sevenfold ringtone, a filthy mouth, and a fresh tattoo? She's cooler than I am."

I stopped. "What tattoo? Gran got a tattoo? Of what? Where?" I cringed at the possibilities. "You know what? Don't tell me. I have a feeling I don't ever want to know."

Ali wrapped both arms around my middle as she stood beside me laughing her ass off. Shaking my head, I kept one arm draped around her shoulder and gripped the arm she had wrapped around my stomach with the other. We did an odd snuggle-shuffle all the way down the path, neither of us wanting to let go even though it was throwing us off balance. When we came to the clearing, Ali sighed happily. "It's finally quiet. No work going on, no noisy tools, just the sound of the trees. I should have brought my easel down here for a while. I haven't been here to paint in nearly two weeks since the gala interfered last weekend."

"I need to get back to my project too, now that the pressure is off. Spencer knows about us, and he's good with it, we're close to figuring out the Marissa thing, and it feels like things might actually be okay for a while. Even that rich old buzzard trying to get his hands on shares of the company doesn't seem as bothersome right now."

"There's someone trying to buy up shares? Why?"

I shrugged, snuggling her closer to my side. "No idea. One thing about Holden Shepard, he does whatever he wants, and there's usually only one motivation. Money."

Ali tensed against my side, turning to face me and breaking my grip on her waist. "Did you say Holden Shepard?"

"Yeah, why? You heard of him?"

"Holden Shepard is my stepfather."

~

IT WAS A DAY FOR revelations, apparently, and none of them welcome.

I stared into Ali's emerald eyes and searched for any indication that she was joking. "You can't be serious."

"As a heart attack." She held my eye, her expression unreadable. "I guess you guys don't look too closely at your applicant's emergency contact forms. His name is on there right alongside my mother's name. It's not like I wanted to list them but you guys wanted five contacts, and they live close enough to qualify, even if I never see them."

I let that sink in for a minute, letting the ramifications play out in my mind.

"I just want you to know that I had no idea what he was up to, I don't talk to him. Hell, I barely speak to my mother." She looked stricken all of a sudden. "Oh my God, you probably think I'm working with him, spying or something. It would stand to reason given my history at GFS and what they are accusing me of."

I placed both hands on her shoulders, waiting for her to look at me. "I never even considered it. If anything, I thought that you might be a victim in this because of your association with me."

"How?"

"Even if you don't associate yourself with Holden and your mother, your names are linked. If all hell breaks loose because of the video of me with Marissa, just being with me will put you in the spotlight, but add having connections to Shepard and the media will be foaming at the mouth. Just another way being with me will cause you pain."

I shifted my hands to cup her face, and she immediately covered them with hers. "You really didn't doubt me? Not even for a second?"

I placed a soft kiss on her lips. "I know you better than that, slugger. Remember? Only cowards sneak."

She gripped the hair at my nape and pulled me in for another kiss, this one deeper, more passionate. When we pulled back for air, she whispered. "At least now that I know what he's up to I can call him off. There's no way I'm letting him mess with your company."

I leaned my forehead to hers, smiling at her protectiveness. "Not necessary. Spencer, Brant, and I can handle him just fine. Leave that to us."

She pulled away. "I most certainly will not. Having a personal relationship to him, no matter how inconvenient most of the time, gives me an edge you guys don't have. No one can make a man's life miserable like my mother. If I convince her that the way to earn back my affection is to keep him away from your company, he's as good as gone. So, let me handle it."

"No, Ali. It's our company, and we'll be the ones to get rid of him. I appreciate you wanting to help. If we can't find a way to shake him, we may take you up on your offer, but until that time you have to leave it to us and keep quiet about it to your mother." I could see her gearing up for a fight, the green of her eyes practically glowed when she was angry. "I'm not Keith. This isn't a power play. It's no different than you not wanting Holden to help with the trouble at GFS. Please, Ali. The man who loves you enough to punch out his best friend over you is asking for your understanding in a difficult situation."

Ali's expression softened, and she threw her hands up. "How am I supposed to argue with you now? You don't fight fair!" She turned and stomped past the pier, head thrown back as she let out a frustrated groan. She was headed right for the large mud hole that had been left behind by some of the machinery used to re-stabilize the pier's footings. I tried to warn her. I shouted her name and put my hand out to stop her before she slipped. My fingertips just grazed her shirt, not able to grasp on as she turned toward the sound of her name... and promptly staggered back, falling ass first into the muck.

Her startled expression was priceless. She managed to keep her head from falling back as she landed but damn near every other part of her was covered in thick mud. I tried so hard to contain it but the incredulous look on her face was so goddamn comical, I couldn't help but laugh. Once I started, I couldn't stop even when she glared at me and called me an ass. The madder she got, the funnier it was. Between roars of laughter, I managed to say, "I'd offer to give you a hand, but I know how you hate people trying to help you."

The comment was met with a clump of flying mud, which slammed right into my chest. I looked down at it, surprised, and heard her chuckle. So my girl wanted to play, did she? She obviously didn't realize who she was dealing with. I gave her the most intimidating look I could muster, since I was fighting back a smile, and dove head first into the mud beside her.

She squealed and lunged to the side, trying to escape but I pinned her with one leg over her hips, hugging her to my side and scooping a huge handful of warm sticky mud onto her head. She swatted at me and retaliated by shoving a handful inside the collar of my shirt.

By the time we settled down, calling a wary truce, both of us were covered in the stuff. Our faces were mostly unscathed, but there were a few half-dried specks on her cheeks that resembled large freckles. It was so damn cute I couldn't resist pulling her in for a long, heated kiss.

I pulled back and suggested we head back to the cabin to clean up and then get dirty all over again. Ali nodded toward the lake. "Why don't we go for a dip first, so we don't ruin our interiors?"

I stood and pulled her up, our mud-encrusted hands sticking together. "We can both ride back in my truck, that thing has seen a lot worse than a little mud."

She looked at me like I was crazy. "Why not at least try to eliminate some of the dirt before we smear it all over your truck? It'll make clean-up a lot easier."

I shook my head, resolute. "I want a shower, not a swim. Let's just go." I picked a clump of mud from her chest. "Thankfully, I have your necklace in the truck, so at least it didn't get muddy. I want to get you in that shower and clean you myself, just to make sure everything gets the proper amount of attention." I winked, hoping my flirting would derail her train of thought.

It didn't.

She blushed but kept insisting. "Why won't you swim with me? We're all alone here so we can skinny dip." She squinted up at me as the trees shifted in the breeze, and the sunlight played across her adorably dirty face. "Unless you're worried about lake-dwelling monsters or something, in which case I think we're safe. The only large underwater creature that I'd be worried about is the one currently residing in your muddy jeans." She laughed and started to unbutton my pants.

I gently pulled her hand away, clutching it in my own. "As much as I'd love to skinny dip with you, I can't do it here. Okay? I don't swim here, but if you'd like to try a different venue, I'm all for it." I prayed she wouldn't push this. I couldn't explain right now, probably not ever.

Her expression was a mixture of disappointment and confusion, but she didn't say anything else about it. She just nodded once and nestled herself into my side as I made my way back toward the house, dripping mud in our wake. I felt like an ass for turning her down. No, make that a stupid ass because I had to be dumb as the dirt I was covered in to say no to a proposition like that.

I just couldn't bring myself to go into the lake.

I'd refused to jump in all those years ago out of fear, and I would stay out now out of respect.

CHAPTER THIRTEEN

BY THE TIME WE made it back to the cabin, I was infinitely grateful for seat covers and rubber floor mats. The truck was filthy, but it was just a matter of doing a load or two of laundry and hosing off the mats. Ali hadn't said much for a while after we left the lake, but she eventually warmed up to me again. I worried that she was offended by my vague response and strong reaction to the idea of swimming in the lake. I didn't want her to think I was turning *her* down.

It was the lake I wanted no part of.

I made it crystal clear how much I wanted her when I dragged her into the shower with me and gave her body a thorough cleaning, and an even more meticulous licking. By the time I was done, the water was turning cold, so I shooed her out on wobbly legs while I rushed through my shower.

I emerged a few minutes later, free of dirt and noticeably deflated by the ice cold spray to find her peacefully dozing in my bed under a mountain of covers. I leaned down to kiss her head and, figuring it was as good a time as any, threw on some clean clothes and ran out to acquire the evening's libations, after tossing the soiled seat cover and mat in the driveway to be dealt with later.

The trip into town wasn't long, but it afforded me just enough time to consider the events of the day without distraction. How was it possible that all that shit had happened in the span of just a few hours? There were so many issues in my head, all warring for my attention.

I knew there was no point dwelling on the fight with Spencer, we'd both had our say, and that was the end of it. At least until the image of him sitting on the floor bleeding flashed in my mind and made me feel like shit all over again. He'd accepted my apology, so there was nothing left to say on the matter.

Of course, there was still an entirely separate reason for him to hate me; Marissa and her bullshit litigation against the company. No, against *Spencer*. I couldn't for the life of me figure out what the hell she was thinking. There had been plenty of proof that she and I had been involved, even the damn video could be misconstrued as harassment on my part if she found someone shady enough to alter the footage. So why go after Spencer? Had he pissed her off that badly when he'd driven her home that night? She had to know she'd never make the allegations stick. So what was her angle?

If all that weren't bad enough, I'd blurted to Ali that I was in love with her after I'd promised myself never to saddle her with something as toxic as my affection. I was only capable of bringing pain to those I cared about. One glance at Spencer was enough to remind me of that, not that the awareness was ever far from my mind. I knew what happened when someone tried to love me. I ruined them, hurt them; threw their kindness back in their face. It happened time and time again, so I wasn't sure how I'd ended up with such devoted people in my life. I had put them all through hell, but they'd hung on, even when I deserved them least.

Ali would probably hang on as well, if given the chance, but did she deserve that? To be put through all the hell that lay ahead? Would I be selfish enough to ask that of her? It was another of life's cruel fucking jokes. I'd finally fallen in love and because she had made me want to be a better man, I wanted to save her from myself.

Just fucking perfect.

Not that any of it mattered at that point. I'd told her I was in love with her, twice, in fact, and she hadn't said anything in response. Of course, my revelation about my fight with Spencer had momentarily distracted her but I knew it had crossed her mind once things died down. Maybe even when we were in the shower together, when I was lapping at her sweet pussy, was she hoping I wouldn't say it again? Or was she grinding herself into my mouth and silently professing her love as she fell apart around me, clenching my eager tongue as she came?

Which was it? And, more importantly, which did I want it to be?

ALI WAS STILL sleeping when I returned to the cabin, still burrowed deep in the pile of blankets. I stood in the doorway and smiled at the outline of her slender hand peeking from beneath the covers. I had to assume that a dozen orgasms in less than twenty-four hours would tire a lady out. Pulling the door almost closed, I decided to let her sleep a bit longer while I prepared dinner.

Before making my way to the kitchen, I stepped onto the porch and looked out over the mountains. As I leaned over the railing, I heard a rustling in the trees just beyond the pool. A moment later, a small fawn emerged from the wood line, covered in snow-white spots. She couldn't have weighed more than thirty pounds, obviously very young.

I held my breath as I watched her, wishing Ali were awake to see. She teetered on her impossibly long, thin legs for a moment, scoping out the back yard before nibbling the grass at her feet. Soon, she was joined by a large doe. They walked the perimeter of the yard, the doe ever mindful of her baby, alert to any danger. I watched them, entranced, as the doe followed behind her fawn, a familiar feeling of emptiness settling over me.

I kept silent watch over the pair until they re-entered the woods a few minutes later.

Shaking off the tangled threads of my past before they ensnared me completely, I set off for the kitchen to make Ali and I something to eat. I flipped on the stereo on the way, turning the volume low to avoid waking my girl. I got to work chopping sweet potatoes for the fries and, once they were in the oven, began prepping my signature club sandwiches.

Ali emerged from the bedroom several minutes later, head tilted back as she inhaled the scent of the thick peppered bacon I was frying on the stove. With an adorably sleepy smile, she gave me a quick kiss and slapped my ass as she took a seat at the table, obviously content to watch me make dinner. I poured her a glass of the sweet tea she was so fond of and placed it on the table in front of her, kissing her head as I stepped back to the stove. "Did you rest well, sleeping beauty?"

She yawned into her palm and chuckled. "A little too well, I think. I almost slept the rest of the day away."

"You've had an eventful couple of days, and I kept you up way too late last night, so it's not entirely your fault." I winked as I lay the cooked bacon on a paper-towel covered plate.

"As I recall, I was a willing and active participant in our late-night activities." She grinned.

"That you were, Miss Walker. Willing, active, and surprisingly limber." I thought that one would make her blush, and I was right.

Her cheeks flamed red, and she peeked over at the counter, changing the subject. "What's all that?"

"That is all the components of the best damn sandwich that will ever cross your perfectly pink lips."

"Looks like a lot of meat." She cringed when she realized what she'd said, making me chuckle.

"It's going to be quite a mouthful, but I know you can handle it," I smirked, watching her cheeks flame and impressed that she didn't avert her gaze. "Besides, you need protein if you're going to keep your strength up. I've got big plans for you later."

"I look forward to it, Mr. McGavran. I fell asleep on you earlier, but I assure you it won't happen again." She winked and sipped her tea while I finished making our sandwiches, suddenly hungry for something more than the food.

When our meal was finished and the kitchen straightened, I asked whether Ali wanted dessert or a drink, happy when she opted for the drink first. I'd had a fairly shitty week myself and a drink or ten sounded like a great plan for the evening. I left her lounging on the sofa, still muttering her compliments on the food while I went to prepare our drinks. Remembering her preferred drink from my Sunday dinners with her and Talia, I'd picked up everything necessary during my earlier trip to town. I gave her cocktail a final stir and was making my way back to the living room when her phone rang.

She pulled it from the end table and grimaced at the screen before shooting me a look. "It's my mother." I raised a brow and poised myself to remind her about our discussion, but she stopped me. "Don't worry. I'll keep what I know about Holden to myself. Promise." She slid her thumb across the screen and took in a big breath. "Hi, Mom."

I busied myself making my drink and tried not to eavesdrop on the conversation, knowing full well I'd hear every word.

"Where'd you hear that?" I looked up and could see Ali's

reflection in the glass patio doors. A look of annoyance on her face, she listened a moment then snapped, "I know exactly what you meant by it, Mother, and I'm pretty sure I know who you're getting your information from." The last was a snarl. There was a screechy voice chattering on the other end for a while then, "If you're still talking to that bastard after all he's done, I don't have anything left to say to you." Her voice was calm and surprisingly aloof, as if she'd had this conversation before and was resigned to the outcome.

"No, I'm not talking to Benjamins." I snickered at the use of her nickname for Holden. "He'll just tell me I'm right and then try to convince me I should just excuse your behavior because you're my mother. I didn't buy it last time, and I'm not buying it tonight. I'm nearly thirty years old. I don't allow anyone to dictate my life, especially not you. You can't even run your own." A pause and more screeching on the other end as Ali rolled her eyes and reached for her glass. "I'm not in the mood to argue with you tonight, Mother. I'm in the middle of something." She turned and looked over the back of the couch, eyes flashing to me and making a slow pass over my body that was hungry enough to make my dick twitch.

"Who I spend time with is none of your business, Mother, or Keith's or your husband's or anyone else's. I'm a grown woman, and I will do whatever or whomever I please." A bark of laughter escaped me before I could bite it back, and she winked. "And if you insist on continuing to talk to Keith, please give him a message for me, if you don't mind." Ali rolled her eyes as the screeching resumed briefly. "Let him know the *construction guy* is twice the man he is, and that's when it's soft and folded in half."

She pulled the phone away from her ear and gave it a curious look. "She hung up. I wonder if it was something I said." Setting it on the table with a shrug, she waited for me to rejoin her, raised her glass, and said, "Here's to showing exactly as much respect as you're given."

I tapped her glass with mine, laughing. "And to never having to fold anything in half to prove I'm the better man."

After several hilarious toasts, we needed refills and headed into the kitchen to concoct another round. While watching her artfully pour her drink I asked, "So, I'm 'the construction guy', huh?"

She snorted and added an extra shot to her glass, shaking her head in disgust. "Sorry you had to hear all that. I thought I could rush her off the phone like I normally do, but she started in without giving me a chance to beg off. Apparently she's been told that I assaulted Keith's escort to the gala and the construction worker I attended with threatened Keith with physical violence." She smiled sardonically. "We're also shacking up together, and I have been suspended from work after taking too much time off."

"You mean your mom didn't know about the trouble at GFS?"

"Nope. I had no interest in hearing how Keith would never do such a thing, and he's a great catch, which means any troubles we had were my fault. I learned the hard way that I couldn't count on her. I went to her once for help." Instead of pouring the shot she was holding into her drink, she tossed it back and slammed the shot glass onto the counter. "Never again. It was stupid to ever have thought she would help me. She made it perfectly clear when she walked out on my father and me that I wasn't shit to her. Looks like I'm still not."

There was a lot of pain packed into those last five words and my heart broke for her.

I had no idea what to say to that, so I quietly folded her into my arms and kissed the top of her head. I couldn't decide which was worse; a lifetime with a mother who made you feel unloved or a few short years with one who thought you hung the moon, even if you didn't deserve her. I guessed there was pain with either.

Glancing at the untouched cocktails on the counter, I stroked Ali's hair and spoke in a soft voice, "Why don't we skip the drinks tonight? I'll tuck you into bed and bring you dessert. We can even watch a movie if you want, assuming the television in the bedroom works. I've never turned it on." I laid my cheek on the top of her head. "What do you say, slugger?"

She pulled back, her gaze dancing over my face as she forced a swallow and whispered, "I fell in love too, Clay."

Her words slammed into me so hard I fought for balance, the shock of hearing them stealing my ability to speak. I willed my hands not to tremble as I reached up to cup her cheeks. The look on her face, the pure adoration was staggering. I lowered my mouth to hers, tenderly pressing into her lips, making slow sweeps with my tongue. I wanted to taste the words she'd just spoken, wanted to touch every inch of her body, to fuse my soul with hers so that nothing could ever undo the bond her words had created.

She loved me.

I TUCKED HER INTO bed, handing her the remote while I ran back to the kitchen for the previously promised dessert. I placed all the necessary items on the serving tray and hurried back to the bedroom.

Ali sat up and watched me enter, a soft smile on her face. "Strawberries?"

I placed the tray beside her in the middle of the bed, crawling in behind it with a grin. "They aren't as good as the ones we picked ourselves, but the season is over, and some concessions were made." I plucked one from the bowl. "So, would you like whipped cream? A drizzle of chocolate? Or would you rather have it naked?" I wiggled a brow.

She giggled and pushed herself up, reclining against the pillows. "All of those sound amazing. Why don't you give it to me the way you think I'll like it best?" She smirked, knowing her words hit their mark.

"Don't threaten me with a good time. I'm trying to pace myself so I don't leave you sore again, but teasing me is a good way to get yourself fucked raw." I pushed a berry between her lips, sans topping.

She bit down slowly and moaned in the back of her throat, the sound making my cock strain against my jeans. When she'd finished, she licked her lips and said, "You know exactly how to give it to me, Clay. That was so good." She sighed in satisfaction, both from the berry and seeing the lust in my eyes.

"I'm about to give it to you again, Alison. Are you ready?" I asked with a low growl.

"Yes, please. And don't forget the toppings."

After I'd devoured both Ali and an obscene amount of calories, we lay quietly in each other's arms, drifting but not yet asleep. Her head rested on my chest, her arm draped across my middle as I skimmed my fingers up and down her side. She shifted closer to me, wrapping one leg over mine and a sharp inhale caught in her chest. I stilled and asked, "Ali, you alright?"

Her eyes never opened, but she made a soft satisfied sound and nodded.

"Remember what I said, baby. If I hurt you, you have to tell me. A little sore is one thing, but I don't want you in real pain, okay?"

She nuzzled into my chest and pulled the blankets higher around us. I waited for long minutes for her response, worried that I'd taken things too far. Thinking she'd fallen asleep, I switched off the television and lay there in the darkness listening to her soft breathing. Just as I felt sleep begin to over-take me, she whispered, "There is no pain when I'm with you."

THE WEEKS FLEW by in a blur of activity. I spent all my time in Denson with Ali, foregoing returning to Richmond for meetings, which was fine with Spencer since it helped keep distance between Marissa and me. Marissa hadn't made contact and the court date was a ways off, so there was still time to do some damage control. My investigator had finally gotten his ass to work and had been making some interesting discoveries. They were adding up to a win for our team.

I finally knew the name of Marissa's benefactor and all the pieces were falling into place. If things played out like I planned, we'd be rid of two problems in one fell swoop. She would be running scared before the case even made it to court.

Not that it mattered, either way I wasn't letting Spencer take the fall for my mistake. If she wanted to release the video, so be it. I didn't give a damn. Ali already knew what was going on and swore she wasn't worried about Marissa or the video; she had me now, and that was all that mattered.

And have me she did.

Neither of us had further addressed our feelings, but we both knew where we stood. We'd each admitted being in love with the other. No need for repeated declarations. It was just a given.

We also craved each other constantly. Every chance we got, we would sneak away for some alone time. When Talia was in town, we kept it low-key, not wanting to be inappropriate with our PDA, but it was difficult. The apartment had been cleared and cleaned, but I convinced the girls to stay on at the cabin. It had been difficult to get Talia to agree to stay, her assertion that Ali and I needed our privacy was hard to deny, but Ali wouldn't be comfortable staying with me while Talia went to stay alone in an apartment they both saw as tainted. Eventually, I wore her down, playing on her desire to keep Ali happy.

Reining in the intensity of our relationship was difficult for Ali and I. Talia nearly caught us one night despite our best efforts. We were upstairs on the living room couch, long after Talia had gone to bed for the night, and things got heated. By the time Talia had entered the kitchen behind us, I was face down in Ali's dripping pussy. The high back on the couch blocked me from Talia's view; all that was visible was Ali's head as she lay back against the arm of the sofa.

I could barely contain myself as Ali and Talia had an entire conversation while I flicked my tongue over Ali's clit relentlessly, making her gasp and squirm. She told Talia she'd come upstairs to read. Thankfully, Talia hadn't wanted to see the book. Ali's voice cracked when I trailed my index finger close to her ass, but she didn't pull away. I decided it might be interesting to spend more time gauging her reactions to activity in that particular area. Maybe I'd found a new way to make her come.

By the time Talia had finished her glass of water and descended the stairs, Ali was bucking up into my mouth, clutching my face to her as she came. That hadn't been our only close call, but it had definitely been the most fun. I was starting to think my girl liked the danger of being discovered. Sometime soon, I would take her out and test her limits in that area too but it would have to wait until the holiday weekend was over.

Preparation for the Fourth of July festivities started on July second in Denson and Ali was helping Teach run a large booth at the town festival. I'd volunteered to help set up, having grown fond of the man myself since his return home two weeks prior. He'd been delayed a week longer than initially planned because of some additional tests requested by his doctor. Ali had been disappointed to have to wait, but I managed to keep her occupied, even sinking so low as to allow her and Talia to give me cooking lessons as a means of distraction. They said my cooking skills needed to extend to baking. I tended to disagree, but I was willing to do anything to make Ali happy.

During a lesson Talia referred to as Cheesecake 101, I doused the entire kitchen and my instructors with batter. Since then, they've kept to simpler recipes.

I reached Teach's booth and set up the last of the tables, pressing on the surface to check that it didn't wobble as a pair of familiar arms wrapped around my waist from behind. "Think that thing will hold us both?" Ali purred.

"Gorgeous, it only needs to hold you and be able to take a pounding." I teased, turning and pulling her into my chest. "I'm not sure now's a good time, though. Teach is headed this way."

We both turned to watch his slow approach. He walked without a limp or any assistance, but the look of fierce concentration on his face made it clear that it wasn't as easy as he wanted it to seem. He stood about 5'10" and looked as though a stiff breeze might blow him over. His thick hair still showed some of his original brown color under the heavy peppering of gray. And he had the full smiling face of a Macy's Santa despite his thin body; a sign that the weight loss was a bi-product of his recent illness.

The box in his hands was light, being filled with napkins, so I resisted the urge to step over and offer to help. Nothing hurts a man's pride faster than having to ask another man's help with a simple task.

He saw us watching and nodded. "Haven't I worked you two enough today? There's no reason to hang around here all afternoon. Lauren will be here in a minute to help set up the display cases for the pies."

Lauren had been helping Teach at home during the day and working nights at the diner. Whether coincidence or by design, she and Ali had spent precious little time in each other's company since Teach's return. Even Talia was being spared the misery of dealing with Lauren, given that they now worked opposite shifts. From the way he was trying to run us off, I got the impression that he wanted to keep the two women as far from each other as possible.

Ali looked uncertain as she watched her mentor wiping his brow and reaching into the cooler for a bottle of water. "Are you sure you should be out here this long yourself? You don't want to overdo it. It's hot as hell out here, Teach. Maybe you should go on home and let the rest of us get things squared away here." She didn't flinch as she said it, but I knew the thought of working with Lauren was about as appealing as a root canal.

He looked at me pleadingly. "Clay, please take this woman out and show her a good time. She worries too damn much. She needs a break, and I need her to stop hovering. Okay?"

Ali huffed indignantly. "Listen up old man, I don't need you soliciting a date for me. If you want me out of your hair, fine." She smiled to let him know she was only half serious. "But I'm not going to stop worrying about you. You scared the crap out of everybody with that stroke. Get used to people hovering. We love you, and we want you here with us for a long time, so it's not stopping anytime soon." She rose on her tiptoes and kissed his cheek. "I'll see you in the morning at the diner, okay?"

He nodded, misty-eyed at her words.

I stepped forward and shook his hand. "See you tomorrow, old man." He cocked a brow at me, and I laughed. "Teach, I mean Teach. I figured I'd try it since Ali got away with it."

He gave a lopsided grin. "She gets away with more than most." He glanced at her and leaned closer, his voice dropping so that she couldn't hear. "Take care of her, Clay. She's a keeper."

"She sure is, Teach. She sure is."

CHAPTER FOURTEEN

ALI STOPPED TO chat with a few of the locals at their booths as we made our way to the truck. She'd stammered while introducing me at the first booth, not knowing what title I'd find appropriate. I laughed and offered my hand to the smiling middle-aged woman she'd been talking to, introducing myself first as Ali's boyfriend then mentioning my work in town. Ali had the most charming smile as I claimed the title, taking it as an affirmation of some sort.

It was.

After that, she proudly introduced me as her boyfriend to each new person we spoke to, tucking herself into my side even in the blazing heat. It was fucking adorable and flattering that she would so eagerly embrace the title and its implied commitment. We hadn't discussed what would happen when the job was finished or if she was called back to her position at GFS, but I fervently hoped that we could find a way to remain together. I wanted that more than I cared to admit.

We finally made it to the parking lot a while later, sweat pouring down our backs from standing in the sun for so long. I'd just suggested we go for a dip in the pool when Lauren stepped out from between two cars, on her way to help Teach, I presumed.

Her eyes were already trained on us as she strode over, a smug smile on her face. Something about her demeanor, the way she seemed to be stalking us like prey gave me a chill despite the nearly triple-digit heat. She glared at me with ball-shriveling hatred as she approached.

Ali gave an annoyed sigh and started to go around her. "Teach is waiting for you at the booth."

Lauren came to a halt right in Ali's path, and I saw Ali's back go rigid. I was poised to step in, if only to keep Ali from getting an assault charge, when Lauren smirked at me and asked. "You tell her who you are yet?"

My heart skipped and then galloped in my chest. *No. No, no, no, no, no.* From the look Lauren was giving me, it was clear she knew everything. And she was about to tell Ali.

Fuck!

I glanced around frantically, mind churning, trying to find a way out of this before it was too late. There was no point wasting my breath trying to convince Lauren to keep her mouth shut. She was elated by the fear in my eyes, eager to watch Ali's world come apart in front of her. Ali wouldn't understand. And she'd never forgive me for lying to her all this time, no matter the reason. Panic started to set in as Ali turned and glanced at me, her eyes widening when she noted my expression. "What's she talking about?"

Lauren chuckled, causing Ali to turn back to her and away from me. Something about the motion felt so final, so fitting. "I'll tell you exactly what I'm talking about. Your boy toy here has been lying to you for months. He's not just the designer hired to build that house, stupid. It's his land, his house." She smirked at me. "Guess he was trying to hide his money to avoid being targeted by gold diggers. Jokes on him though, huh, Ali? He managed to pick the daughter of the biggest damn gold digger on the East Coast. Or maybe he knew exactly who you were and decided to fuck you anyway, as long as you never found out he was loaded."

Ali glanced over her shoulder at me but didn't turn. "I don't believe you. Clay wouldn't do that, wouldn't think that of me. You're making things up again, Lauren. Like your trip to Virginia Beach the weekend my apartment got trashed. You lie so often, you're starting to believe the shit you make up your-self. Try peddling your stories somewhere else." Ali reached behind her seeking my hand, which I gave with no hesitation. Lauren had totally misrepresented my intentions. If I could get Ali alone, I could explain everything and make her see that there was never any malicious intent.

I just didn't want to be the focus of town gossip.

Didn't want people talking about how I'd ended up with the land.

We stepped past Lauren, whose delighted smile made me livid. Just as we neared my truck, Lauren called out, "Ask him where he first saw you. See if he'll at least be honest about that."

Son of a bitch! This couldn't be fucking happening. It had to be a dream, a nightmare.

Ali dropped my hand and turned, scrunching her brow in the glare of the afternoon sun. "Why don't you tell me, Lauren? I'm sure whatever you've made up is far more interesting than the truth."

I kept my back to Lauren, Ali standing just inside my peripheral vision as my worst fears came to life. "Oh, it's the truth, Ali, whether you like it or not. Allow me to jog your memory." Her voice got closer with every sentence. She was enjoying this and wanted a fucking front row seat. "You made a little trip to the ER last year, remember? Driving all the way to Fredericksburg to be sure you wouldn't bump into anyone you knew?" Ali stiffened beside me, and my heart fell to my knees.

"Claimed that you'd fallen down some stairs, I believe, but we both know you antagonized your fiancé into a fight and then couldn't handle it when you got what you deserved." My fists clenched so tight that my knuckles cracked, but I said nothing, knowing exactly what was coming. "Do you remember some jackass trying to play the hero in the parking lot, picking up your boyfriend and slamming him against a car while you scurried off into the darkness like a cockroach?"

From the corner of my eye, I saw Ali's slow turn in my direction, felt the accusation in her gaze and the humiliation rolling off of her like ripples of heat on an asphalt road. She ignored Lauren's snickering, focused only on me. I was too ashamed to face her, so I stood there as she whispered, "He kept calling you hero. That night at the gala, Keith called you hero, just like he did that night outside the hospital. He was letting you know he recognized you, wasn't he?" I closed my eyes against the sting caused by the anger in her voice. I'd known better than to think I deserved her, told myself this would happen, that I'd hurt her and lose her because I was too fucking selfish to walk away.

When I didn't answer, she shouted. "Wasn't he? He was enjoying watching you parade around with his broken, discarded toy. It must have been especially fun for him to know I had no goddamn clue who you were." Her tone was accusing and angry but laced with despair. "Did you know from the beginning? That day at the lake, did you recognize me? Was all this about you feeling sorry for the poor little waif who you thought couldn't defend herself? Did you think you needed to play the hero some more? Fix me? Rescue me? Fuck me just to prove you were better than him?"

Lauren chuckled, and Ali was suddenly gone from my side. I turned just in time to see her backhand Lauren with enough force to spin the woman around. The sound was sharp and oddly satisfying. Lauren whipped around, one hand on her cheek and Ali slapped her again, this time on the other side. When I saw Ali draw back her fist to continue her assault, I leaped over and grabbed her arm. "Alison, stop. That's enough."

She wrenched her arm away without acknowledging me as she looked at Lauren and spat, "Your work here is done, bitch. You did what you came to do, now carry your sorry ass over and help your uncle before I clue him in on just what a spiteful piece of trash you really are." Despite being a total bitch, Lauren seemed to genuinely care what Teach thought of her, the one person she had any affection for.

Lauren's venomous glare slipped a fraction as she considered that. "And what do I tell him about my face? My lip is swelling, and I'm sure there's gonna be a bruise. How do I explain that?"

"You could tell him you're a heinous bitch who got what was coming to her," Ali suggested with a snarl, then smirked. "Tell him you fell down some stairs. It's always worked for me. And it worked for Keith that night he broke my ribs." She looked between me and Lauren with equal amounts of loathing.

"Or did neither of you know about that? Oh yeah, I lost the first round because I didn't see it coming but, when he followed me back to our condo, I was ready. No man raises a hand to me. He got away with it once because the coward attacked me from behind but he was stupid enough to confront me head on the second time. When he raised his hand to me that time, I beat the ever loving shit out of him. He fared far worse than I did, I can promise you that. While I was moving my shit out of our apartment, he got to make a trip back to the ER, spitting blood and praying someone would be able to go in and find those puny little raisins he calls balls." She glowered at Lauren and me. "So don't either of you think I can't take care of myself, or you'll live to regret it."

Lauren finally left, not turning her back to Ali until she was nearing the corner sidewalk that led to the booths.

Once she was out of sight, Ali turned to me, devastation in

her eyes as she avoided my gaze. "You should go, too. I'm going back to the apartment. I can walk from here." My heart seized in my chest as she went on in a monotone voice. "Talia will be here this afternoon. I'll have her pick up my things from the cabin." She nodded toward my truck. "If you'll just unlock it so I can get my purse, I'll be on my way."

I wanted to plead with her to listen, to let me explain. I wanted to crush her to my chest and tell her how much I loved her and that I'd never meant to lie.

But I couldn't do any of that.

She'd trusted me, loved me, and I couldn't even find the courage to tell her who I really was, what I'd done. I should have done it from the beginning, but I never expected to get this close to her, to anyone.

By the time I realized that I loved her, it was too late.

Going into this I knew I'd end up hurting her, but some tiny shred of hope still existed deep down, and I risked wondering what it would be like to spend my life with her.

Stupid and reckless. I had to stop holding onto something that was never meant for me. Happiness wasn't in the cards, even if I'd managed to get dealt a hand full of hearts.

I pulled my keys from my pocket and thumbed the fob, the headlights flashing to signal that the truck was unlocked. Without a word, Ali walked over and opened the passenger door, leaning down to retrieve her bag from the floorboard. I turned my back at the sight, knowing it would fucking break me to watch her walk away.

When the door clicked shut a minute later, I closed my eyes and listened to the sound of her footfalls as they grew fainter with each retreating step. I stood there like that long after the sound had gone, feeling the crushing weight of my failure bearing down on me. I'd known from the beginning that this would end badly but goddamn, I never imagined this.

I stood there for a long time trying to figure out what the

hell to do next. Where would I go? What would I do? I was lost, completely and utterly lost.

I couldn't go home without her, couldn't face the emptiness alone.

Home.

I'd never thought of any place as my home until that moment. It wasn't the cabin that the word brought to mind, it was her. The scent of her peaches and cream body wash wafting in from the shower in the morning, silently sharing a cup of coffee on the balcony before work, the feel of her body tucked snugly against me as I slept. All those things I'd stupidly taken for granted, now only a pain-laced memory. I'd lost my heart, my soul, my home.

There was nothing left for me in Denson.

Steeling myself for what came next, I pulled my phone from my pocket and called my business partner. He answered on the third ring. "Hey, brother. How's the Denson job coming? Sick of country living yet?"

I blew out a breath and sighed as I walked to my truck. "Hey, Brant. That's actually why I'm calling. I think I need a change of venue. We're swapping projects."

I FINISHED MY CALL with Brant and booked a room at the dingy little motel on the edge of the Denson town limits. I couldn't go back to the cabin, couldn't bear the thought of being there without her, but I wasn't ready to go back to my house in Richmond, either. I palmed my room key and walked across the street to the ABC store for provisions, where I spent a considerable amount of money. Funny how your whole fucking life could crumble in a matter of seconds like a goddamn wrecking ball came through and wiped it all out in one whack. Returning with my packages, I briefly wondered which came first; the run-down lodging or the conveniently placed liquor store. In my experience, the two often went hand-in-hand.

My phone buzzed incessantly in my pocket, and I knew Brant had called the office. Spencer would probably want to say 'I told you so' before someone else beat him to it. If anyone had earned the right, I supposed it was him. The bruises from the punch he took had lasted for a while, taking a couple weeks to fade from garish to vaguely discolored.

Yeah, I thought as I filled an ice bucket at the dispenser outside my room, *Spencer was right again. She was always out of my league.*

I walked into my temporary refuge and frowned, noting the worn carpet and mid-seventies decor. Shit, even the hastily added wall hangings were probably older than me. The air was stale and muggy, causing me to cast a weary glance at the ancient looking air conditioning unit by the window, partially obscured by the thick, musty-smelling drapes.

I shrugged as I closed the door behind me. Soon, I'd be so hammered I wouldn't care whether this was a ten thousand dollar a night room, or the fucking gutter.

I turned my phone off and tossed it on the tiny dining table in the corner of my crappy efficiency suite, trading it for a plastic-wrapped cup that I promptly filled to the brim with bourbon. My drink of choice burned like hell on the way down, and I clenched my teeth with a satisfied hiss. Good. I wanted it to hurt. It was fitting that I'd chosen to numb the pain with cheap ass whiskey that tasted like battery acid, a new pain to mitigate the old.

Apparently, heartbreak brought out the masochist in me.

I left the television off and had the shades drawn, sitting in the dank room, sipping swill as I watched the room darken with the arrival of evening and lighten again with the new dawn.

I'd never in my life had so much to drink and still remained conscious.

It was like my body burned the shit off as fast as I swallowed it, refusing to allow me to dull the pain. Finally sick of trying, I threw the cup against the wall, the soft splattering sound nowhere near as satisfying as the sound of shattering glass would have been. Maybe I'd feel better if I started breaking the liquor bottles.

It occurred to me that I hadn't craved the destruction in a long time, that feeling of peace that always accompanied the swing of a sledgehammer, shattering, bending, and breaking everything in my path. Until that moment, I hadn't yearned for that sensation at all. Not since Ali. She had been my only craving, she had brought me peace.

Now all I had was pain.

And it was exactly what I deserved.

I replayed the look on her face over and over in my mind, the hurt, the devastation, the shame. God, the shame was the one that really got me. To see her eyes gloss over and fall to the ground as if she'd been the one at fault, had fucking ruined me. The Alison I loved had retreated, the confidence I'd seen blossoming in her whisked away in an instant.

I should have told her the truth long ago, but I was weak and afraid.

Just like before.

Ali wasn't the first person I'd let down, and unless I stayed in this crappy motel room forever, she probably wouldn't be the last. I lay back on the cheap floral bedspread and stared at the uneven ceiling tiles, warding off the past and mourning what was left of my future.

Too tired and heartsick to fight anymore, I let sleep and the memories overtake me.

IT HAD BEEN THE summer before my thirteenth birthday. I'd recently discovered girls, classic cars, and a few phantom chest hairs that no one else claimed to see. I stood on the pier by the lake, staring into the murky water and envisioning all the terrifying creatures concealed in its depths. My father had made me watch a horror movie marathon the year before, specifically featuring man-eating lake creatures, and I couldn't get some of the images out of my head. Gooseflesh covered my thin limbs in the late-July heat as I imagined long slimy tentacles waiting just beneath the surface, poised to pull me under the moment I entered the water.

I'd tried to learn to swim the previous summer, my mother forcing my father to take me to the YMCA for lessons. After the second afternoon of watching the instructor patiently try to coax me into the pool, my dad had gotten angry and tossed my rail-thin body into the deep end shouting, "Sink or swim, you little runt!"

The instructor had pulled me from the water, choking and gasping for air as I puked up chlorinated water. My throat and nose burned with every heave. Once everyone made sure I was alright, my father had been asked to leave, causing an awful scene. My mother had been too mortified to show her face there, so my lessons were put on hold, she said, until we could spend some time at our lake. That's how she always said it, 'our lake' as if it was mine and hers alone.

She and my father didn't get along very well, mostly because of me. They didn't know I could hear them arguing through the vent in my room sometimes. Some nights I sat there trembling as I listened to how much my father hated me. He was angry that my mother hadn't gotten rid of me, said she could have been a star if she hadn't thrown it all away to have some stupid kid.

When she pointed out that I was his son he would always laugh and say I was a casting-couch baby. It had been a long time before I understood what he meant but, once I did, I realized that he didn't want to be my father, and I was surprisingly okay with the idea. I didn't want him either. I paid him only the barest amount of respect necessary to coexist *in the same house. No more. If I weren't worried about my mother, I'd have spit in his ugly face.*

Standing on the pier that day, it dawned on me that she never talked about him being a part of our life here in Denson. She'd showed me the blueprints, pointed out where my room was going to be, and talked about all the fun she and I would have at the lake but she never once mentioned my father. We'd planted the willow there together one weekend. She said she could picture me getting married under its shade, building a life of my own on the land when I grew up and started a family. I groaned my displeasure, rolled my eyes at her sappy ramblings as teenagers are wont to do, but she had lovingly stroked the sapling's thin branches, telling me all the while that we could put up a tire swing so that my kids would someday be able to swing out into the water and swim.

She saw us there, she and I, She even saw me there with a family of my own, but nothing in her visions of the future indicated that my dad would be around. It was such a glorious thought I didn't even mind the sentimental bent to her plans as long as he stayed the hell away.

From the corner of my eye, I caught a flicker of movement and heard a splash just as I turned toward it. The water rippled outward, small ringlets of ever-widening movement. My mother's head broke the surface a moment later, so close to the pier that I nearly jumped out of my skin. "Come on in, the water's nice and cool." Her sweet voice beckoned me to join her as she blinked away the water in her eyes. "I'll hold you up, help you learn to float. I promise I won't let go."

Something about her words made my chest hurt, but I shook my head and backed away. "That's okay. Maybe next time. I didn't bring my trunks."

She watched me for a minute, deflated. "Okay, baby boy. We'll save the lesson for next time." She leaned back and brought her legs up, floating across the surface with a serene smile. "We have all the time in the world, you and me. As soon as the house is finished, we can come here every day. No noise, no arguing, just my baby boy and me."

I'd rolled my eyes at the pet name. I was turning thirteen soon, and

I'd grown to resent being thought of as a baby. I had frigging chest hair, for Christ's sakes.

We left soon afterward, having only come for the day to check on how the house was progressing and I spent the entire ride back home trying to find a way to tell her I wasn't a baby anymore without making her mad.

The following Friday, I was on the phone with Spencer; he'd been my best friend for two whole years, and we were inseparable. Spencer talked excitedly about the race that was happening over the weekend, chattering on about his favorite cars. I wasn't as into it as he was, so I mostly tuned him out, sorting through my cassettes looking for something to listen to.

When he started laughing and telling me how his older sister had gotten grounded for missing curfew, all I could think was that meant she would be around all weekend. I hadn't told my mom yet that Spencer had invited me to stay over, but I was determined to go, even more so after I found out Stephanie would be there too.

Stephanie was fifteen; tall and athletic with a great smile and big boobs. Well, big by my standards anyway. I'd always avoided the pool in Spencer's backyard, but I was thinking that would change over the weekend if Stephanie decided to go for a dip. I'd never actually go in the water, but a well-placed lawn chair and my favorite sunglasses sounded like the perfect recipe for a great weekend.

Convincing my mother, however, had not been as easy as I'd anticipated. She reminded me of the swimming lesson I'd narrowly escaped for the fourth time the previous weekend, saying I had to keep my promises. I'd promised her at the beginning of the summer that I would at least try to learn, but I'd been too afraid to so much as dip one toe in the lake. After letting me slide all summer, she was choosing this weekend to dig in her heels? Really? I groveled, begged, and tried to barter my way to a 'yes', but she wouldn't budge.

"You'll feel so much better once you finally learn to swim, you'll see. The lake won't be so scary then." She promised as she ruffled my hair and started packing our cooler for the trip.

I was so angry at her for ruining my weekend, for treating me like a baby, for making me face my fears when all I wanted to do was be with my friends. She asked me to go get my trunks, sounding excited that she was finally getting me in the water. Instead of doing as she asked, I fumed. "I don't want the trunks. I don't want the lessons. I don't want the stupid lake, and I don't want to go anywhere with you. I just want you to leave me alone. You ruined my whole weekend, and I don't want to even be around you anymore."

I stomped off to my room and threw myself on the bed, anger pulsing through my entire body. Why did she have to smother me so much? Why couldn't she just leave me the hell alone?

A few minutes later, there was a tap on the door, and my mother stood in the doorway. I trained my eyes on the ceiling, refusing to look at her. Sighing in defeat, she said, "I called Spencer's mom. She's coming to pick you up in a few minutes." I sat up and stared at her, open-mouthed and disbelieving. She looked away, wet streaks on her face. "Your father mentioned wanting to see the house, so I'll just have him meet me up there after work. Maybe I'll go by and see your Aunt Vanessa on the way."

She sounded so small, so wounded by what I'd said. I wanted to tell her I was sorry, that I didn't mean what I'd said but I was afraid she'd change her mind about letting me go, so I kept quiet. She stood there for a minute, probably hoping I'd apologize, before nodding and walking back to the kitchen.

When Spencer's mom came to pick me up, I was so excited I could barely contain myself. I barreled out the door and down the steps before remembering to go back and tell my mother goodbye. I gave her a quick hug and muttered a distracted 'love you, too' when she told me goodbye, not looking back as I hopped into the back seat.

The call came in that night while I was out in Spencer's backyard catching lightning bugs with him and Stephanie. I was grinning from ear to ear, having just 'accidentally' brushed against Stephanie's left boob while helping her scoop a wayward firefly into her jar.

When Spencer's dad walked out onto the porch, I thought he'd seen what I did. I swallowed a huge lump in my throat when he called me over, preparing to be fussed at for touching the man's daughter. Instead, he looked down at me with watery eyes and told me to get my shoes on because we had to go to the hospital.

The rest of that night went by in a blur of sideways glances and whispers. I sat in the tattered chair in the hospital waiting room for hours, going mostly unnoticed as I stared at the ground and tried to understand why no one would look at me. The one time someone met my eye, I decided it was better to be invisible. I hated the look of pity I'd been given, so I snuck out of the waiting room and shuffled slowly down the corridor, paying little attention to my surroundings, just wanting to get away.

We're so sorry. There was nothing we could do.

The impact was just too much.

She's gone.

The words played over and over in my mind.

She's gone. She's gone. She's gone.

I kept trying to tell myself that they were wrong. She couldn't be gone. She didn't get to teach me how to swim. I didn't get to keep my promise. We didn't get to move into our house and away from my father. We didn't get to do anything she said we would do.

And she was gone.

I'd been pacing the halls for a while when my father's hushed voice filtered into my awareness. I crept closer to the sound, deciding I was tired of all the whispers, I was almost thirteen years old, dammit, and I deserved to know what happened to my mother. She died, that was all I knew, the empty void in my chest a constant awareness of her absence. I'd heard the doctor when he came out and spoke to the adults, could remember the ragged cry that ripped through my grandmother's throat, saw the look of devastation on her face.

But why? What happened? I reached the end of the corridor and spotted my father off to my right, huddled over the receiver of the payphone. "No, I didn't go after her. She stormed off, and I let her go." Silence while the other person spoke, then, "She had fucking pictures, threw them in my face and called me every name in the book." He twirled the metal phone cord in his fingers nervously. "Why deny it, the pictures showed us together plain as day."

He was quiet for a beat, glancing over his shoulder and nearly catching me snooping. "Look, I need to know whether there was enough time for bruises to show up." He glanced around quickly, dropping his voice further but not so much that I couldn't hear. "No, no. She got in my face, called me trash, and I popped her one. Just one and she stormed out of the house. So, would there have been time for it to show? I don't want these people thinking something shady happened here tonight. Rebecca was upset, and she lost control of the car. It shouldn't matter why she was upset, right?"

I watched the tension leave his shoulders as he rose to his full height. "Good. That's what I thought. Now, listen baby, we need to lay low for a while, Let all this die down and I'll give you a call, okay?"

I spun on my heel and ran back to the waiting room.

I had to find Gran.

CHAPTER FIFTEEN

I WOKE WITH A start, drenched with sweat and reeking of cheap booze. Sunlight crept in from under the drapes and I realized I'd slept an entire day away. My damp skin suddenly chilled in the air-conditioned room as my dream came back to me in a rush. Not a dream, a memory. The one memory I'd carry with me all my life, like a thousand pound leg-iron that I dragged with me through every step of my existence.

I could still hear my mother's voice pleading with me to jump in the water and see the tears streaming down her face when my careless words hurt her. I could still feel her silky hair between my fingers as I'd slumped over her casket and begged her not to leave me, promising that I'd let her teach me to swim if she'd just come back.

I promise I won't let go.

I felt bile rising in my throat, dashing to the outdated bathroom and barely making it to the toilet in time. Once I'd emptied the bitter contents of my stomach, I rinsed my mouth and splashed my face with cool water. The haggard-looking man I saw in the mirror was a startling reminder of just how far I'd fallen. My eyes were red-rimmed and dull, my hair was no longer the carefree kind of messy, it was just a damn mess.

I needed a shave.

And a shower.

Yet, what I ended up doing was falling back into bed to wallow in my misery a while longer. Why did it matter if I looked like shit? At least the outside matched the inside, for once.

Maybe if I walked around like this all the time, people would have the sense to stay the fuck away from me. I was a walking, talking, wrecking ball; a destroyer of lives.

A coward.

I must have dozed off again because I was startled awake some time later by a pounding on my door. Not a tap or a knock, but a fierce, angry pounding. I jumped up from the bed, feeling dizzy, and stumbled over to the door. A look through the peephole revealed the blurry outline of my best friend, who rapped so sharply on the door I jumped. "Open the goddamn door, McGavran, or so help me God, I'll kick it in."

Fuck. I should have parked my truck behind the building.

I reluctantly unlocked the door and cracked it open, mid-afternoon light flooded in to blind me. Tilting my head down to keep it from exploding from the onslaught of light and noise, I told him, "Go home, Spencer. I don't want to hear it right now."

I tried to push the door closed, but he stuck his foot in, blocking me. I glanced down at the tip of his steel-toe boot and knew I was fighting a losing battle. Dropping my hand from the knob, I turned and shuffled over to the kitchenette, looking for one of the crappy packets of coffee that came free with the room. Maybe I'd just chew the shit instead of waiting for it to brew; it would save time.

I heard a derisive snort from behind me as Spencer slammed the door closed. I spun around to face him, hands to my head, praying my eyeballs didn't pop out of my skull from the pressure. "Jesus, Spence!"

He was unmoved by my pain. "Boo-fucking-hoo. Somebody got a headache this morning, or more accurately, this afternoon?" He walked over to the table and examined the empty bottles. "Well, this explains it. It's a wonder you're not permanently blind, drinking that shit." He none-too-gently tossed the empties in the trashcan and glared at me. "You trying to fucking pickle yourself or something?"

I said nothing as I struggled to open my packet of bargain basement coffee, getting more frustrated by the minute.

Spencer blew out an annoyed breath and stepped over to me, snatching the pouch from my hand. "Give me this shit. Go sit down before you fall over." He examined the coffee and snorted. "You fought all that time to open this, and it's fucking decaf. Idiot."

I slid into one of the dining chairs with a groan. "Figures. Decaf coffee and non-alcoholic beer should be outlawed." I groused.

I silently watched as Spencer opened the remaining packet, presumably the leaded variety, and filled the small carafe with water from the tap. I was grateful for the help but aware that it would come at a price. When the machine started hissing and gurgling, he joined me at the table. He tilted his head and studied me. "You really stepped in it this time, didn't you?"

"You sound surprised."

"Maybe I shouldn't be but I am. I saw this playing out several different ways, but I never thought it would end up like this."

I glared at him. "And how did you see it playing out? What did you think would happen when you sent me here? When you practically threw her at me knowing what you do about my track record? What the fuck did you expect?"

"You want the truth?"

"No, Spence, lie to me," I deadpanned.

"The truth is I sent her in there expecting one of two things." He paused for effect, eyeing me. "Either she would be the last thing on earth you wanted, or she would be the only thing on earth you wanted. The bitch of it is, I couldn't decide which one I was rooting for, but I knew from the moment I met her that she was going to change everything. And I think you knew it too."

I couldn't even be pissed off at him. He was right. But there was nothing to be done about it. It was over. And I needed to leave before I made it any worse. I ignored his statement and pressed on, not wanting to think about just how much Ali had changed things for me, or how much I let her down. "Brant call and tell you I want out?"

"Oh, I've been quite popular lately, thanks to you." He folded his arms on top of the table, leaning down into my line of sight. "I got calls from Brant, Blake, Talia, Ali..."

I straightened. "Ali? What did she say? Is she alright?" I had no right to ask, but I needed to know.

"We'll get to that. First let's talk about you ditching the project. Brant is fine with you taking over in Charleston, thinks he's doing you a favor by giving you a way out of here, but I disagree. I think you need to keep your ass right here, fight this out and quit fucking running."

I clenched my jaw, causing pain to shoot through my temples. Dammit. "I'm not running. I'm doing what's best for Ali. Blake said he'd fill in for me until Brant can get here. She shouldn't have to see me anymore. I know her, Spence, she's not going to just walk away from her obligation to the company. She'll stick it out because she's no coward. Just look at all she's put up with from GFS. She should have told them to kiss her ass months ago, but she's fighting to keep her job because she can't stand the thought of backing down." I shook my head and folded my hands together on the table. "She's done nothing wrong, and I won't add to her pain by staying here."

"Brant said you told him she has a connection to Holden Shepard. You sure she's done nothing wrong?" The question wasn't meant as an accusation, there was no malice in his words.

I leaned my head into both hands, holding it up by my forehead as I fought back another wave of nausea. "No way, Spence. She's not that kind of person. If I thought so, I wouldn't be as fucked up over her as I am. Besides, she would have nothing to gain from him taking over our company."

He twirled the cap to one of the empty bottles, looking thoughtful. "I tend to agree. I've come up with a theory that I think may explain the connection, though, because you know I don't put much stock in coincidence."

"Should I be drunk for this? Because there're a couple more bottles in that bag over there." I was only half-joking.

He ignored the feeble attempt at humor. "From what Brant relayed of the conversation you two had, I gathered that Shepard is financially enabling Marissa. You hired an investigator who uncovered this?" I nodded my head feeling like it weighed a hundred pounds. "We know Marissa was in the office around the time the build here in Denson started, and we know she was going through the files, ostensibly to steal her own. But what if she came across Ali's new-hire packet and got curious? After I talked to Brant, I went looking, and Ali's file does reference Shepard in the emergency contacts section. We never noticed it because it was irrelevant at the time, but Marissa probably zeroed in on the name in a heartbeat."

"So, you think Marissa got nosy and stumbled on a way to get back at us by using Ali's connection to Shepard?"

He shook his head. "I think she knew Shepard's reputation and decided to help him get his hands on the company as a way to punish you. The lawsuit was probably dreamed up by Shepard, especially the part about naming me. He hasn't shown any interest in trying to buy your shares, just mine and Brant's. I think he intends to keep you on because you've got the most talent to exploit, and the best way he could think of to get me and Brant to sell is to alienate you from us. No better way of doing that than setting one of us up to take the fall for your mistakes." He thought for a moment, twirling an errant bottle cap. "Ali was just a catalyst to get Marissa in bed with Shepard, at least figuratively if not literally. Marissa saw a familiar name on Ali's contact page when she was nosing around and seized the opportunity. They have no way of knowing about you and Ali unless Ali told her mother or Shepard herself."

Shit. "They know. Ali's mom pissed her off, and she was very blunt about the nature of our relationship."

He cocked a brow. "Blunt? Do I want to know?"

"Nope. Just suffice it to say, Holden is probably aware of our personal connection."

"I'm betting that's why he's redoubled his efforts in the past few weeks. Marissa rummaged through basically every scrap of paper in that office, there's no way she missed the contract. Hell, the file was even labeled with our little nickname for it."

I snorted miserably. "The 'Clay' Clause. Perfect."

"So, we have to assume she shared that with Shepard, too. Meaning, he knew you were breaking the contract, and he was laying the groundwork so that Brant and I would know to call him first, should we decide to sell. Smarmy bastard."

I could only stare off into the distance, I had no words to apologize for what I'd done. Not just to him, but to all of them; Brant, Ali, Gran, even Talia. I'd promised her I would look after her friend, and instead I broke her heart.

Spencer reached across and snapped his fingers in front of my face. "So, what the fuck do we plan to do about it? What are you going to do about Ali? About the project? Are you really going to Charleston?"

I regarded him dryly. "Ali and Brant will finish up the build here, and I'm headed to Charleston as soon as the holiday weekend is over."

He gave me a pointed look. "Then why didn't you go back to Richmond? Why stay in this shithole motel when you have a perfectly nice house back in Richmond?"

He wasn't going to let it fucking drop, so I answered through gritted teeth. "Because it's just a house, not a home. I haven't had a home before, not even when my mom was alive. We shared a house with a heartless bastard who made sure I felt unwelcome every day of my life. Our one shot at a home was here in Denson and look how that turned out. Ali is the only home I've ever known." My voice dropped to a pathetic whisper. "I'm not sure how to walk away from that."

Spencer pounded the table, sending a surge of pain through my skull. "You don't. You don't walk away from it. You fight for it, moron." He pinned me with an intense stare. "You just mentioned your mom for the first time since we were kids, do you realize that? Do you think I don't know what losing her did to you? How the fucking guilt has ruled your life?"

I dropped my gaze and shuffled over to the coffee pot, not wanting to talk about it anymore.

Spencer wasn't done, though. He stayed at the table, his back to me as he said, "Don't you think I felt guilty, too?" I stared at the back of his head, suddenly confused. "You were on the fence about coming to my house that weekend. You wanted to go with your mom but thought you'd sound like a sissy if you admitted it. Why do you think I told you about Stephanie being grounded? I knew you liked her, so I used her as bait because I wanted you to come over." He turned in the chair, watching me. "If I hadn't pushed you so hard, maybe things would have been different. For a long time, I blamed myself, thinking Rebecca would never have died in that crash if I hadn't been so selfish."

My chest tightened as I saw the quiet anguish in his face.

"You can't blame yourself for that. I wanted to spend the weekend with you. I wanted to avoid my mother forcing me to go in the lake."

He shook his head, pressing his lips together in a sad smile. "You're not remembering it right, Clay. I called twice to ask you over, and it was only after I mentioned Stephanie that you decided to come. I know what I'm talking about because I replayed those conversations in my mind a thousand times over the next year."

He stood and walked over to where I was pouring the coffee, accepting the cup I handed him with a nod. "You want to know why I stopped kicking myself over it?" Something in his eyes told me I didn't want to know, wouldn't want to hear it, but I nodded anyway. "About a year later, you were staying the night, and I woke up to the sound of you thrashing in your sleep. You were on the bottom bunk, and I leaned over from up top to see if you were okay." He blinked a few times as if his eyes burned. "You were mumbling apologies to your mother, kicking and whimpering like you were running. You said something in your sleep that night that changed everything for me. Want to know what it was?"

My hand shook as I lifted the foam coffee cup to my lips. Blowing on the steaming contents, I slowly blinked, the closest I could come to an answer.

"You said 'Please take me with you. I should have been with you.'" His voice cracked, and my shoulders began to shake. "That's when it hit me. Maybe what I'd done, pushing you into coming over, had kept you out of that car. Maybe you would have died too if I hadn't manipulated you into staying the weekend." He took a deep, ragged breath. "As horrible as it is, I was relieved. I'd been so focused on what was lost, it never occurred to me to be grateful for what I still had."

He placed a hand on my shoulder and squeezed. "I swore I'd never tell you any of this. I didn't want to add to your misery, but maybe it will be your wake-up call. Hell, maybe you should have heard this years ago." He shoved my shoulder slightly. "Stop blaming yourself for shit that wasn't your fault. Stop walking around focusing on what's missing from your life and start seeing how full it is. We all make decisions every damn day that have the potential to change our lives. Stop punishing yourself for a decision from twenty years ago and take a hard look at the ones you're making right now."

I sat my coffee on the counter and braced myself on my hands, needing a minute to get my shit together before I could speak. I took a few slow, deep breaths and forced down the massive lump in my throat. Turning to Spencer, I said, "What if I decide wrong again, Spence? What if I fight for her and later realize she was better off without me?"

He walked into the bathroom and turned on the shower. When he reentered the room, he leaned against the wall and folded his arms across his chest, his crisp, clean shirt a stark contrast to the faded wallpaper. "Do you remember how obsessed I used to be with cars and racing?" I nodded, not sure where this was going. "I sat in front of the television every damn weekend, watching any and every type of race I could find, but my favorites were always road course races."

I smiled involuntarily at the rush of memories of us drinking glass bottles of root beer in his den, yelling at the television and trying to act like grown-ups. "Yeah, you said they were harder, and that made them more fun."

He snapped his fingers, looking pleased. "Exactly. Not knowing what was around the corner made it more dangerous but doubled the thrill. Sometimes they spun out and ended up in the dirt, but they always ran as hard as they could." He smiled. "Life isn't a drag race, Clay. You don't get to see the finish line before you even start. Life's a road course, blind curves and ending up in the dirt are part of the package. Everyone spins out. The difference between being alive and truly living is having the balls to get back on the track and finish the damn race."

He nodded to the steam-filled bathroom. "Get yourself cleaned up and get back in the fucking race or sit there in the grass sucking dust. It's time to sack up, man." He headed for the door, tossing a small packet onto the dresser as he went. "I'll bring you some clothes from the cabin, then you can either carry your ass back to Richmond or man up and go find out for yourself what Ali has to say."

When the door closed behind him, I ambled over to the dresser and picked up his offering. It was one of those single dose packages of aspirin you can grab at gas stations. I couldn't help laughing. The guy was always looking out for me.

I replayed our conversation while I stood under the uneven spray of the shower. He was right. It was time to get back in the driver's seat.

And I knew just where to start.

A COUPLE OF HOURS later I was back in my truck, behind the wheel again both figuratively and literally. Spencer hadn't said a word when he came back by and dropped off my clothes and travel bag. He'd handed me my stuff, pulled me in for a quick hug, and then disappeared like a damn phantom before I could even thank him. It was the first time I could recall when he hadn't had a thing to say. He must have decided that he'd talked enough. He'd made his point and left the rest up to me.

I'd made a few calls before checking out of the motel, taking back control of my life one facet at a time. When the final call had been made, I turned my phone off and tossed it into the truck's console. I wouldn't be needing it again for a while.

I reached my destination but stayed in the truck for a few minutes, hands wringing the steering wheel in anticipation.

Man-up, fucker. You can do this.

I stepped out of the truck, the gravel crunching beneath my boots as I made my way to the backyard and the trail beyond. When I reached the path that lead to the lake, rather than striding down quickly, I took my time, looking around and really taking it all in. The pale yellow wildflowers that had framed the path were long gone, victims of time and unseasonable heat, but there were new pops of color that I hadn't noticed. The deep burgundies and pale purples of the newly-blooming summer flowers were lost on me until that moment.

It was the first time since I'd come back here that I actually took the time to drink it all in, the smells of honeysuckle and freshly turned earth, the warm sun on my back, the sound of the wind through the trees. If I closed my eyes for a moment, I felt like that twelve-year-old version of myself, dawdling on the path to forestall getting near the water. I still remembered the feel of warm grass beneath my bare feet as I entered the clearing.

I stood there for a while looking at the lake, really looking at it for the first time. I'd spent the previous few months keeping it in the periphery of my vision and pushing back any feelings of familiarity. Not today, not anymore. I watched the surface ripple as the breeze swept through the valley and remembered. I remembered the first time I'd seen the lake, my mother rushing ahead in her excitement while I stood at a wary distance.

It pained me to think of all the times I'd refused her. So many regrets centered around this place. Keeping my gaze on the water, I walked to the freshly restored pier. I'd refused to have it torn down, using my tendency toward reclaimed and salvaged materials as an excuse to hang onto the original wood. The truth was, I couldn't let them take it away. It was one of her favorite places to relax by the water.

Walking down its weathered surface, I could still picture her there, lounging back on her elbows with her head tilted skyward and the sun on her face. She had been beautiful, my mother. She'd had a real chance of making it big in show business. My father had been right about that. And maybe I had been the reason she gave up on her dreams. If so, she never let on, never acted like she resented me. That was my father's domain. He took every opportunity to remind me that I was a mistake, particularly when my mother was out of earshot. He'd wait until I was really happy about something and swoop in to shit all over it.

I still mourned my mother every day, even twenty years later but when I thought of my father I felt nothing. From what I was told, he was diagnosed with cancer a few years after my mother's death and died alone in some hospital with no one there to comfort him. Maybe it was heartless of me but when Gran had told me the news all I'd said was, "Good."

I'd been stunned when I was contacted months later by an attorney who informed me that as next of kin, I was the sole beneficiary of my father's life insurance policy. I was just about to graduate college at that point, and it gave me great pleasure knowing he'd resent me getting the money. It was his money I used to start my company though I'd never touched anything I'd inherited from my mother. Not even the land I was standing on.

I'd been a minor, so all my assets were held in trust and overseen by my grandparents. When I'd come of age, I refused to sign the papers to take possession, so it remained in Gran's name all these years, every damn bit of it.

I didn't want the money or the land. I wanted her back.

I wanted not to hurt anymore, not to feel guilty anymore, not to feel like a goddamn curse to everyone I cared about.

I blamed myself for her dying, for Gran and Papa having to bury their daughter, for Vanessa losing her only sister.

All that pain was because of me.

And I carried that blame my entire life, shackled by it to the point that I couldn't reach out to anyone else.

As I stood there on the pier, the sun dipping behind the mountains and the smell of wildflowers filling my nose, I wondered if I'd ever feel the kind of peace my mother had found in this place. My mind filled with images of her smiling up at me as she floated by the pier on her back. That was the kind of peace I wanted.

Then my mind flashed to that first night in the pool with Ali, the contented feeling that had overcome me as we floated across the water hand-in-hand so we wouldn't drift apart. My chest tightened when I was hit with the irony. We hadn't drifted apart, we'd been blown apart by my deception. She might have been my one chance at the future my mother had wanted for me, the one I'd rolled my eyes at all those years ago but now wanted more than anything.

I desperately wanted to fix what I'd broken between us, I just didn't know if I should. What if I really was a curse?

"Hey, baby boy. Thinking of going for a swim?"

I jumped so damn high I almost fell in the water. When I spun around, Gran stood at the base of the pier, watching me with a sad smile. She wore her usual concert tee and jeans, today's shirt featuring Breaking Benjamin, a Celtic knot design that looked like a series of linked hearts. Her attire was anything but grandmotherly, but the concern in her eyes left no doubt. That's exactly who and what she was.

My grandmother.

Flustered by her sudden appearance, I asked, "Why did you call me that? No one has called me that since I was twelve."

She shrugged and started toward me. "Not sure. You just looked so small standing there, like when you were a little boy."

I blew out a breath, heart still pounding in my ears. "Yeah, I feel pretty damn small too. How'd you find me?"

The corner of her mouth turned down. "I knew you'd end

up here eventually. I didn't expect it to happen this way, though."

"You're the one who forced me to come here." The edge in my voice was undeniable. She had put all this in motion, couldn't leave well enough alone.

Unfazed by the accusation in my tone, she nodded. "I suppose I did. I just wanted to help, Clay. I wanted you to face all this so you could move on. You've been running too long, baby boy."

"Stop calling me that." I snapped.

She looked up at me stonily, hands on her hips. "Watch your tone, Clay McGavran. If you *think* I can't still kick your ass, you've got another think coming." She dropped her arms and smoothed her shirt. "Yes, I badgered you into building the house. And yes, I knew it was going to be hard for you but Clay, I wasn't just doing this for you. I was doing it for myself. I was doing it for your Aunt Vanessa and for Daniel." She shook her head, a sad expression on her face. "I needed to feel like I was doing something to honor Rebecca. There's also the possibility that Vanessa might be on her own soon. She and Nicholas are separating for a while, and I wanted her to have somewhere to go in case the break becomes permanent."

"Shit. I had no idea." I thought of Daniel, how confused and sad he must feel. Nicholas loved his son very much and was everything I'd wished my father had been. "How is the little guy taking it?"

"He's handling it well, I think. Nicholas is staying at a hotel but he picks Daniel up from school every day, and they are making everything as normal as possible. Once Daniel goes to bed, Nicholas goes back to the hotel."

Daniel was a smart kid, their attempts at normalcy were admirable, but there was no doubt in my mind that he knew. "What about Vanessa's job? The commute from here is so far. Would she keep working at the hospital?"

Gran shrugged. "Not sure. I haven't discussed the possibility of moving here with her yet. I'm waiting to see how things go. But, at least she'll have options."

Thinking that my mother had wanted the house for the same reasons, I wrapped my arm around Gran's thin shoulders and squeezed. "You're amazing. Anybody tell you that lately?"

"Just a couple of old coots looking for a sucker." She chuckled. "Oh, and all those nice young men at the biker bar. They love my rendition of 'Get the Party Started'."

I groaned and shook my head, pulling away. She worried me sometimes. Ever since my grandfather passed, she'd been acting like a damn teenager. I sort of resented it. To me, it felt like she was happy he was gone.

She watched me as she said, "You don't like me going to those places, do you? You think I should be home knitting or baking or some ridiculous shit like that."

"I just don't understand where it all comes from, that's all. You were never like this before..." I didn't know how to say it without hurting her, dredging up old pain.

"Before what? Before my husband of over fifty damn years left me here all alone?" She was angry and hurt. Dammit. I just couldn't stop messing up. She looked out over the water, blinking rapidly. "You think I wanted to be here without him? That I don't wake up every day with his face in my mind? What I'm doing, running the roads with my friends, going to rock concerts, getting tattoos, traveling, all that is because of how much I loved him, how much I love him still."

She blew out a breath and smiled, her eyes glistening in the fading light. "When we were growing up, there were certain things you didn't do, rules you had to follow to be considered a good person. It was just how things were. People didn't divorce, or go to bars; they didn't get tattoos or listen to rock music. To do those things was to be subjected to the condemnation of others, so we didn't do them." She slipped an arm around my waist, and I tucked her too-thin frame into my side. "When our girls got older, your grandpa was hard on them. He still held to the old standards of behavior and didn't allow Vanessa and Rebecca much freedom. He thought he was doing what was best for them, and I supported him most of the time, only butting heads with him about the girls a few times over the years. Mostly, over Vanessa. Your mother was always a daddy's girl, hardly gave him any trouble at all."

I warmed at the thought. "I remember how she liked to dress me up before we came over to visit. She said Papa thought I was a perfect little gentleman."

Gran nodded. "She did everything she could to please her daddy. All her life, she was that way. When your Papa got sick, he thought about that a lot. He regretted a lot of things in the end." She pulled back to look at me. "Not long before he died, he told me that he thought he'd made a mistake with our girls. Said he should have let them choose their lives according to what they wanted instead of going by what he expected. He was convinced Rebecca stayed with your father for so long because she thought her daddy wouldn't approve of her leaving. He blamed himself for not letting her know he'd love her no matter what."

"Sounds like we all found a reason to blame ourselves," I told her.

"Yeah, looks like we did." She patted my stomach fondly. "That's why I act the way I do. I promised your grandfather that I'd break the damn rules, that I'd have fun and make mistakes without giving a damn what anyone thinks. I do it for him. And I do it for Rebecca because she never got the chance. And because honoring their memory is so much better than dwelling on their absence."

I kissed the top of her head and smiled. "Did I ever tell you mom's vision of my future?"

"No, but I'd love to hear it."

"She saw me making a life here. Getting married under the willow, watching my children swing out over the lake on a tire swing, growing old here with the love of my life." I sighed, a hollow feeling in my chest. "I'm not sure I'll be able to make all that happen, but it would have been a good way to honor her memory. Better than closing myself off and feeling guilty all my life."

She slapped my stomach, making me cringe. "You better be done with that shit, boy. I'm sick to death of watching you wallow. You can make every damn bit of that happen if you get off your duff and go after it." She stepped in front of me, poking a bony finger in my chest. "Ali loves you, stupid. That's not something that just goes away because of one argument. She may not *want* to love you right now, and you might have to eat a lot of crow, but you can make her remember why loving you is worthwhile. Because it is, Clay. Even when you're being a dumbass, you're worth the trouble. But you'll never make her realize that unless you believe it too."

I cupped her wrinkled cheeks in my hands and smiled down at her. "Thank you, Gran. For taking me in all those years ago, for putting up with me when I was an angry teenage jerk, and most of all for knowing exactly when I need a swift kick in the ass to get me straight. I love you, Grandma."

She kissed my cheek and blinked back tears. "I know you do, baby boy. I've always known. And I love you, too." She threaded her arm through mine, turning us toward the shore. "Now walk an old lady to her vehicle on your way out. There's someone else you need to say those words to tonight, and it's time you got to it."

We made our way to the grass, stopping under the willow to look back at the water, the sunlight almost gone, and the moon already high in the sky. I was guiding her from under the branches, worried she would trip on a root, when she muttered, "Well, I'll be damned. That girl is full of surprises."

I'd been looking down to assure Gran's safe passage, but her words drew my head up. I stopped so abruptly that poor Gran was snatched back a step. She turned to me with a huff and said something I didn't hear. The entirety of my awareness was focused on the figure standing at the edge of the clearing.

Ali.

CHAPTER SIXTEEN

I SQUINTED TO make out the outline of the woman I loved in the fading light. I couldn't believe she was really here, that she was willing to even look at me much less seek me out. My chest tightened at the sight of her, and the bottom fell out of my stomach when I realized she'd heard every word Gran and I had said.

I supposed that made us even for me listening in on her conversation with Keith at the gala.

I was torn between running to her and fucking crawling. I'd do whatever it took to win her back, pride be damned.

More muttering came from beside me and I impatiently shushed Gran, who huffed at me in response but said nothing more as we made our way to where she stood. When we were a few yards away, Gran pulled away from me and held her arms out to Ali saying, "Hey, baby girl. I'm so glad to see you." She wrapped Ali in a tight embrace.

They stood there hugging and rocking side to side in that unfathomable way women often did. Men treat hugs like a trip to the dentist, get in and get the hell out. Women treat them like a day at the spa, drawing it out and taking great pleasure in it like it somehow fed their souls.

Then again, maybe it did.

From the way Gran was squeezing her, it was obvious that she loved Ali too. The thought made me smile through my uneasiness. You had to be something special to win over Gran, but I'd known Ali was special from day one.

Wondering if they'd forgotten I was there, I cleared my throat and gave Ali my best smile. She glanced at Gran and smiled back. It was a tentative smile, but I wasn't splitting hairs. I didn't quite know what to do with my hands. I wanted to hug her to me, pull her in close so I could feel her heartbeat against my chest and smell the sweet scent of her dark hair, but I couldn't do that yet. I fidgeted for a minute, crossing and uncrossing my arms as I debated and then discarded the idea of offering her my hand. Stupid. This wasn't a fucking business meeting. This was my future, my heart.

In the end, I shoved my hands in my pockets and tried not to glare at Gran, who was highly amused by my discomfort. "Hello, Ali. You look beautiful today." Yep, if that was the best I could come up with, I was screwed.

She eyed me warily and nodded. "Thanks. You look like shit."

Gran chuckled and patted my arm. "I can see you two want to be alone so I'll see myself out." She blew Ali a kiss and shuffled off toward the house. When she'd gotten about thirty yards away, she yelled, "Spencer is taking me home tonight, but I'll come back here and kick both your asses if I have to, understand?"

"Yes, ma'am." Ali and I said in unison.

I arched a brow at her and took a shot. "You're scared of a little old lady, aren't you?"

She nodded briskly, fighting a smile. "Hell yeah, I am."

Wait a damn minute.

Pointing in the direction where my rotten, bossy, amazing grandmother had just gone, I frowned. "Hang on, did she say Spencer was taking her back?" Ali's forehead crinkled, and she nodded. "As in, she didn't drive to Denson herself?"

Still not understanding, Ali frowned. "I guess not. Spencer's truck was parked in the driveway beside yours, but I didn't see him anywhere. Why?"

He's gonna fucking kill her!

Ali jumped when I roared with laughter. Damn, I wanted to be a fly on the wall when he got his hands on that old woman. Gasping for air, I finally got out, "She stole his fucking truck! He'd never in a million years let her drive that truck. Right now he's at the cabin cussing her for all he's worth, I'd bet my life on it. She can barely keep her little car between the lines, much less a huge dually like his." I wiped my eyes. "She probably drove all the way over here like Mr. Magoo."

Ali laughed with me, looking shocked and a little impressed.

When we finally got hold of ourselves I reached out my hand, hoping like hell she didn't slap it away. She hesitated, looking uncertain, so I prodded, "It's just a hand. I thought we could go sit under the tree, and I'd try my damnedest to explain myself." I held my breath and let her study me, her eyes wary but her body shifting closer in that unconscious way it always did. I caught her eye and whispered, "Please, Ali."

If someone had told me six months ago that I'd be begging a woman just to take my hand, I'd have laughed in their face. What a difference a few months and your future standing in front of you could make.

Ali haltingly extended her hand and I enveloped it in mine as my heart squeezed in my chest. We walked over to the willow, a spot I'd begun to think of as ours, and sat beneath its cascading limbs. Ali left some space between us but turned toward me so that our knees nearly touched on an angle. I wished she hadn't taken her hand away as we sat, the loss of contact felt like a blow.

Trying not to once again dwell on what I didn't have, I decided to be thankful she was here at all. We both folded our arms around our knees and sat watching each other, neither sure where to begin. Deciding I'd done enough damn listening for one day, I started. "Ali, I'm so sorry for not being honest with you. I'm sorry for being a coward. And I'm really sorry you had to hear it all from Cruella de Bitch."

I didn't know what to address first, didn't know if I could even articulate it all, but I had to try. I had to fight. For Ali, for me, for peace. I cleared my throat, deciding I'd start with me. It all started with me. I pointed out at the water glancing over to be sure she was looking. "When I was twelve, I was convinced there were monsters in that lake. My mother tried and tried to get me to get in the water with her, begged me to let her teach me to swim, but I refused. I was scared. I'd nearly drowned when my father tried to teach me to swim 'the man's way', and just the thought of jumping in made me want to hurl. He took a lot of pleasure in making me afraid of the water. I think it was his way of hurting us both." Memories of his mocking sneer made me tense up, but I kept talking. "The last time I was here with my mom, I could tell it bothered her that I didn't trust her to keep me safe in the water. I think it hurt her feelings, but she didn't pressure me. Instead, she floated on her back and drank in the summer sun with a peaceful smile on her face. I think it was the most peaceful I'd ever seen her."

Ali reached out and touched my knee. "You're Rebecca's son." I bit back the lump in my throat and nodded though it hadn't been a question. "The day I met Gran, while you and Spencer worked things out, she walked me around the property and talked about Rebecca. I think I would have liked her."

"She would have adored you." I drew in a deep breath and sighed. "She left everything to me in her will. I'm pretty sure she was about to leave my father, which was why it all went to me. Gran was trustee and handled everything until I was old enough to take ownership but when the time came, I didn't want it. So technically, it's still in her name but the land is supposed to be mine." I met her gaze and saw the understanding in her eyes. "I didn't ever want to come back here, didn't want to even think about this place and what might have been. If it weren't for Gran pushing the issue, wanting to finish Mom's house, I never would have set foot on this land again." I grasped the hand Ali had laid on my knee and whispered. "I never would have found you."

She squeezed my fingers and asked, "So you weren't keeping it from me because you thought I was like my mother?"

"No, of course not. I didn't have any clue who you were when we first met. How could I? I didn't even look at your resume' or see the names on your emergency contact list. I didn't give a damn about where you came from, I only cared about where you were. Right here in Denson, making my time here so much easier than it would have been without you." I took in a slow breath, watching the fireflies at the edge of the woods across the lake and continued, "I never wanted anyone here to know I was Rebecca's son because small towns have long memories. Her accident was big news here, and I don't like talking about it. Ever. It wasn't a malicious decision, I swear. It was just a matter of privacy."

Her hand trembled slightly in mine, and her voice fell to a whisper. "What about that night at the hospital? Why didn't you tell me it was you?"

God, she sounded so ashamed. A little part of me died every time I thought about her with those bruises, but it wasn't her fault. None of this was her fault. "Baby, I didn't know at first. It wasn't until the gala that I put it all together. By then I was so attached, so dependent on you that I couldn't tell you what I remembered. I was afraid you'd pull away from me. We were only friends then, but I wanted that friendship, I wanted it more than I've ever wanted anything, so I kept quiet."

"So you didn't befriend me because you thought I needed rescuing? Didn't make love to me out of some sick form of pity?" Her voice cracked as she struggled to speak.

"Absolutely not." I shifted closer and put a hand on her chin, forcing her head up so she could see my eyes. "I was already yours when I remembered. You dazzled me, Ali. You made me feel alive and excited and buoyant. I haven't felt like that in so long, I almost didn't recognize myself. You made me whole again." Her emerald eyes shone in the moonlight, beautiful and haunted. "And I don't do pity. I never wanted it from anyone, and I never give it. I hated those damn sympathetic looks I used to get after my mother died. It made me feel broken somehow for people to look at me like that." I nudged her chin higher. "And I'd never look at you that way. You're fucking amazing, Ali. Every part of you, everything about you is extraordinary."

She pulled my hand to her lips, softly kissing the pads of my fingers. "You're not broken, Clay, any more than the tree we're sitting under. The one a hurting little boy took his anger out on because he didn't know how else to deal with losing his mother." My heart skipped in my chest when I realized she's made that connection, though I should have known she would. She saw me, all of me, and still came back for more. That angry boy I'd once been sighed from somewhere deep inside, relieved to find some peace after all this time.

Ali turned and ran her free hand over the rough bark of the willow, smiling softly as she bid me to do the same, but still holding my other hand to her lips. "You stomped it, kicked it, split it in two, and it thrived anyway. It became exactly what it was always supposed to be; strong and steady and beautiful. So will you." She bit down hard on the end of my middle finger, the sharp sting enough to make me jump. Then she smiled sweetly and let go of my hand. "But it'll be your turn to get stomped if you ever lie to me again. I've had all the deception I can take for one lifetime. You want this to work," she pointed back and forth between us. "You have to be straight with me at all times. I want the truth, even when it's unpleasant. Okay?"

"Yes, ma'am."

She nodded, smiling at the sheepish look on my face. "Glad we got that settled. What do we do now?"

I raised one eyebrow and winked, which made her laugh, then stood and held out my hands. "Come with me. There's something I want to show you."

She gave me a smiling smirk as I pulled her up. "I bet."

"Not that, silly. At least, not yet anyway." I chuckled and started back toward the path. "I want to show you the piece I've been working on."

THE HANGING WORK lamp gave off just enough light to illuminate the work area I'd set up in the corner of the barn so I could work on my project while I was on site here in Denson. It was a far cry from my workshop back in Richmond, but I'd managed.

Ali ran her hands over the intricately carved trim that encased the enormous slab of oak that would be the back door to my mother's dream home. "It's beautiful, Clay, absolutely stunning. Is it going in the house?"

I absently brushed some sawdust out of one of the grooves and smiled, excited to share this with her. "It will as soon as I finish. I want the entire piece to be perfect." I nodded to strips of carved wood on the sawhorses off to my left. "Those pieces will be the door casing."

She walked over and examined them. "The wood is antique, isn't it?"

"It's about a hundred years old, give or take." I paused to force a swallow. "It was my mother's antique farm table."

Ali's head jerked up. She looked at me with surprise before returning to her inspection, running her hands over the pieces with reverence. "You held onto it all these years?"

"Gran had it in storage until about ten years ago when my friends and I started our company. Once I had a decent shop to work in, I went and picked it up." I shrugged as I brushed away more sawdust. "I wasn't sure why but I wanted it with me. I never had the heart to break it up and use it for a project, though. It's been sitting in the corner of my shop ever since the day I dug it out of storage."

A flood of fond memories rushed through my mind, and I smiled. "My mom had the table crammed in the little breakfast nook in our kitchen. My father hated it, bitched that it took up too much room, but she refused to give it up. We sat there every night, me and her, working on my homework or having a snack before bed. It was my favorite place in the world when I was little, this table."

"And by turning it into a custom made door, you're putting it in your mom's house in a way that will assure it stays there." She smiled at the idea. "I think it's perfect."

"I even made it to an unusual size so it can't be replaced without rebuilding the entire door frame. It's not coming out once it goes in." I couldn't help smiling at the thought. "Now you know what I've been working on all this time while you were at the lake painting." I stepped over and pulled her into my arms. "Speaking of the lake, I seem to recall you offering to skinny dip with me." I kissed the top of her head, not the least bit apprehensive about going in the lake. Not anymore. "That offer still stand?"

Ali beamed up at me, realizing the implications of my proposal. "Absolutely, Mr. McGavran. Lead the way."

~

AFTER GRABBING A couple of towels and a new cotton drop cloth — originally intended for use when the time came to stain the door — we hurried back to the lake. The moon was nearly full, casting a soft white glow on the valley that was reflected in the still water of the lake. The quiet breeze stirred the tall grass at the edge of the water causing it to sway pleasantly. Ali had been playful, pulling me along and giggling all the way to the lake but once we got there, a quiet thoughtfulness settled over her expression.

She stood aside while I lay out the cloth beneath the willow, covering the soft grass. When I was finished, she handed me the towels, holding my gaze as she stepped back and began to undress. The soft sound of the towels falling to the ground barely registered in my awareness as she lifted her thin t-shirt over her head, revealing a pale pink lace bra that looked amazing next to her sun-kissed skin. With slow, deliberate movements she untied the knot that fastened her Capri pants around the swell of her hips. Once the strings were loosened she paused, the hesitation pulling my attention to her face. The corner of her mouth turned up in a sexy smile and, with a quick wiggle of her hips, the cotton capris pooled at her feet.

Holy hell.

Her matching panties were see-through in all the right places and barely large enough to cover the smooth mound at the juncture of her thighs. With the moon at my back, I was able to see every inch of her lush, voluptuous body glowing in the evening light, the ethereal beauty of her staggering. Still pinning me with her seductive smile, she stepped out of the pants, kicking them aside but retaining the wedge sandals that made her legs look impossibly long and taut. A low growl escaped me when she leaned down to slip off her shoes, those perfect full breasts all but spilling from the confinement of her bra.

Ali removed her shoes slowly and purposefully, taking an occasional glance up at me from under her lashes to see if I was watching. She righted herself, nudging the sandals aside and wiggling her pink-tipped toes against the cotton of the drop cloth. When I swiped my tongue across my suddenly parched lips, her tongue trailed slowly across her plump bottom lip in response.

She reached back with one hand and unhooked her bra, the band loosening around her torso while her other hand held it against her. She slid the straps off of her smooth shoulders one by one, taking her time and enjoying making me squirm. When she pulled the garment free, tossing it onto the ground between us and dropping her arms to her sides, my dick pulsed, throbbing. I was hard as fucking granite, and it took all the self-restraint I had not to throw her down on our makeshift bed and bury myself inside her.

Noticing my heaving chest, she smiled a little wider and raised a hand to her breast. Her slender fingers caressed and cupped for a moment before tweaking the high taut nipple, making us both moan softly. She trailed her hand down her ribcage and across her smooth belly, stopping just at the edge of the tiny lace panties that I would soon be using as fucking dental floss.

My gaze flitted back and forth from her gorgeous face with its sensual expression to her roaming fingers that were teasingly dipping into the edges of her underwear. The way my cock strained against my zipper was becoming painful, so I absently unbuttoned my jeans to relieve the pressure.

Ali smirked knowingly and continued her assault on my senses, going deeper and deeper beneath the waistband of her panties until her entire hand was caressing her undoubtedly slick folds. She threw her head back and moaned, breasts rising and falling with her rapid breaths. My mouth was watering, my cock was twitching, and I was half out of my mind with lust.

She removed her hand, and I watched in awe as she placed two of her slick fingers in her mouth, licking them clean with a groan while my whole body shuddered. Fucking hell, I couldn't take much more.

Seeing my control wavering, she hooked her thumbs into the edge of her underwear and in one swift motion, they were on the ground at her feet. She flipped them across the space between us with her right foot, and I caught them just before they hit my chest, crushing the damp material in my fist. I was so turned on I would probably end up eating the damn things just to get a taste of her.

Before I could consider the adverse digestive consequences of that idea, Ali blew a kiss my way and scampered off toward the pier. I took two long strides to give chase before realizing I was overdressed. By the time I made it to the mouth of the pier, my clothes were scattered in every direction, and I was pretty sure I'd never find half of them. Somewhere, a damn squirrel would be stuffing his nest with my socks by morning. I wasn't particularly concerned at that moment because Ali had already jumped into the water with a splash, and I didn't give a damn if I had to drive back to the cabin in a towel. I had more pressing matters to attend to.

I strode down the pier, fully naked and painfully aroused. I reached the last plank and droplets of water sprayed over my torso as Ali splashed me from where she floated on the surface of the lake, the smooth orbs of her breasts breaking the surface, causing me great distraction. I watched intently as the water lapped at the juncture of her thighs, cooling her heated skin as my entire body burned with desire.

Her hand lifted from her side, and she curled a finger to beckon me closer. "What are you waiting for, swim champ? I'm getting awful lonely out here all by myself." She pouted playfully, but there was a watchful expression on her face, as if she was considering that I might not be ready to do this.

Time to prove her wrong.

I motioned for her to stay back and watched with an amused smile as she used her hands to paddle her floating body further from the pier. Not her arms, just her hands in a small flapping motion that was bird-like but surprisingly effective. So damn adorable.

When I was sure she was out of harm's way, I told her, "Can't have you feeling lonely now, can I? Get ready, love. I'm coming in." *In more ways than one.*

I took a deep breath and dove in headfirst, slicing through the cool water with ease, my usual feeling of freedom was expanded a hundredfold. I kicked and stroked and dove until my lungs were about to burst only surfacing when I absolutely had to. I sucked in a breath and dove again, unable to stop. It was only after I reached the far bank that I stayed on the surface treading water and panting in lungful after lungful of the night air that smelled of honeysuckle.

Ali was treading water too, one hand on the pier as she watched me with a look of pride. I gave her a little wave and started making my way back, alternating between slow crawl strokes and back strokes that afforded me a stunning view of the night sky. As I neared the spot where I'd last spotted her, she floated peacefully on the water staring up at the stars and my desire rekindled, burning white hot even in the cool water.

She watched as I made my way over, positioning myself between her legs and telling her to stay just as she was, floating there on her back like a goddess in the moonlight. I wanted to see if coming would make her sink. The water was shallower here, and I was able to touch the bottom, though barely.

I pushed her legs wider apart, smiling when she remained buoyant. I ran my tongue up her inner thigh and chuckled when her gasp made her torso momentarily drop deeper into the water. She resurfaced, and I reached up to palm one of her breasts, careful not to put the weight of my arm on her. She whimpered but stayed atop the water, so I went in for the kill. I locked my mouth over her mound and held her ass up in the water so I could apply just enough pressure to her swollen clit to set her off.

Soft mewling noises echoed across the lake as I swirled my tongue over her, in her. She was the sweetest thing I'd tasted in my life. Her body tensed as she struggled against the urge to grind into my mouth. The desperate sounds she made in the back of her throat told me she was close, she just needed a little push, and she would come apart. I kept working her with my mouth while I walked us closer to the shore, seeking the shallower water to get the leverage I needed with my legs.

Once I was able to plant both feet firmly on the lake bed, I wrapped both arms around her thighs and pulled her into my face, burying my tongue inside her. Pulling back, I swirled it over her clit while I slipped two fingers into her and pumped them in and out, fucking her hard with my hand.

Ali's hands shot up to squeeze and tug her breasts, and soon she was convulsing, quaking in my mouth. She stayed afloat, but I kept one hand below her back, just in case, while I lapped at her clit and thrust my fingers with incrementally slowing strokes. I kept softly licking, kissing, and sucking at her until her contented sigh announced that she'd recovered.

As soon as I removed my hands her lower half sank into the lake, and she began treading water in front of me. Despite the orgasm that had just ripped through her, there was desire in her eyes. She reached out to me — she was still unable to touch bottom — and I took her in my arms. She locked her legs around my middle and kissed me deeply, running her hands through my dripping hair.

I took hold of her, my thumbs at her hip bones and my fingers grasping her ass as I lifted her up and onto my cock. I lowered her slowly, enjoying the feel of her hot flesh enveloping me an inch at a time. When I slipped all the way in, I thought my legs would give out. She felt so fucking good.

She wrapped her arms around my shoulders and pulled her hips back, my dick slipping almost all the way out before she thrust forward and took me to the hilt. She circled her hips, dipped and swayed on my cock until I had to bite my lip to keep from swearing. I'd never felt anything like this, ever. She was so hot, so tight, so...

Oh, fuck!

I grasped her hips and pulled her all the way onto me, halting her motions. "Wait, baby, we can't do this."

She clenched her muscles, gripping me tight enough to make me growl. "Oh, really? It feels like we can." She nipped at my lip and gripped me again.

One more of those and I was going to go off like a goddamn rocket.

"No. That's not what I mean." I thrust my hips forward almost involuntarily before I stopped myself with a groan. "I wasn't thinking straight, hell, I'm still not but we have to stop. I'm not wearing a condom."

She watched me for a moment, finally stilling. "I guess we were a little distracted." She kissed me softly and pushed my hair back off my forehead. "Do you have one at all? In the truck maybe?"

I shook my head. "No. I never keep them in my vehicles or wallet, too much chance of them being ruined by the heat."

She nodded thoughtfully. "Smart. Inconvenient in our current situation but still smart." She looked at me seriously. "Have you ever...? I mean, without a condom?"

"No. Not once. But before you go thinking I'm some kind of Boy Scout, it wasn't about me being responsible. It was me having convinced myself that no kid deserved a father like me because I was a walking, talking curse."

She gave me a sad smile and pulled my mouth to hers for a brief kiss. "That's not true, you know that right?" I nodded, and she looked relieved that I no longer felt that way about myself. "I don't know how you feel about continuing without a condom, but I want you to know that I'm clean. I was tested for everything known to man after Keith and there's been no one else except you." *And there never will be*, my mind supplied. "I'm also on birth control." She pulled my forehead to hers, looking me in the eye. "We can stop right now and go to the cabin. I'm fine with that, truly I am. But, I want you to know that I trust you, I trust *us* enough not to stop if that's what you want."

Hell no, I didn't want to stop. Nothing in my life had ever felt so good, so right. I'd never had sex without that barrier, but with her I didn't want anything between us. Figuratively, or literally. It was the only 'first' I had left, and I wanted it with her. I wanted to feel her, to fill her, to mark her.

I thrust up sharply and nipped at her lip. "I want this. I want to make love to you, feel your body around me, to come inside you over and over. You're mine, Ali. And I'm yours." I pulled out of her, the cool water a sharp contrast to her heated core before slamming back in, going balls-deep.

She gasped at the invasion and said, "I'm yours, Clay. Don't stop. Please."

I set off with a growl, making my way closer to the bank, struggling for balance with Ali still wrapped around me, inside and out. She squealed and clutched my shoulders, "What are you doing, crazy?"

"I'm taking you back to our spot under the willow where I can do this properly."

CHAPTER SEVENTEEN

MIDNIGHT FOUND US lying beneath the willow in a tangle of trembling limbs, each of us sated and content in each other's arms. We lay on our sides, facing each other, quietly talking between soft caresses. Ali asked if Spencer and I were still on good terms, admitting she'd heard that he'd tracked me down like a dog.

I snorted at the memory. "Yeah, we're good. Probably better than we've been in a long time. Lots of shit had been building up. Now we have a clean slate, provided I don't mess it up again."

"Talia read me the riot act, too. I've never had her that mad at me before." She shook her head, eyes wide. "She's scary as hell when you tick her off." I laughed, smoothing her hair, and asked what Ali could have possibly done wrong. I was the one who lied. "Talia said I was running, again. And that I was acting like a coward, which pissed me off." Sounded familiar. Ali's voice dropped to a near-whisper. "She told me that not everyone was going to turn out to be like Keith. She said your lies were different because there was no ill intent behind them, and I would be letting Keith win if what he did to me stopped me from loving you."

I hugged her closer, pulled her into the crook of my neck and kissed her head. "You had every reason to be angry, to want out. That was because of me, of what I did, not because of Keith." I owed Talia a thank you for giving Ali a push but ultimately, Ali had been right to leave.

She blew out a breath and nodded. "I know I had a good excuse, but she's still right. I was running from my anger, from my doubts, from my insecurities. You're not the only one whose past tends to jump up and bite them in the ass." She rubbed her hand up and down my side, the tender gesture giving me goosebumps. "Most of the time, I find constructive ways to manage my emotional baggage. I paint, I read, I bury myself in my work. It's easy to let it all go on every other level but when it comes to relationships, I'm still floundering."

"I'm the same way. I've built my life around my crutches. I break things to get rid of my anger and build things from the wreckage to regain control." I leaned back and begged, "But please, for fuck's sake, don't tell Spencer I said that. If he knows some of his psycho-babble bullshit got through, he'll never shut up."

Ali laughed happily and made a crossing motion over her heart. The wind picked up, the cool breeze stirring her hair, making wayward tendrils wrap around her face as she tried to push them away. She rolled to her back, running her hand over the strands and tucking them behind her ear. Suddenly, her hand dropped to her side, and she laughed uproariously.

I sat up on my elbow, looking at her in confusion. "What's so funny?"

She tried to speak but couldn't curb her laughter long enough to get out anything coherent. With shaking shoulders and tears running from the corners of her eyes, she raised a hand and pointed up. I tilted my head back, squinting into the moonlight to see what the hell she was howling about. A moment later, I caught sight of it myself and barked out a laugh that rang out across the valley. We lay there hugging our middles and laughed until we cried, gasping and sputtering but unable to speak as we kept looking up at it. It looked like I'd been in a bigger hurry than I thought to join Ali in the water.

There, tangled about ten feet up in the sweeping branches of the willow, was my underwear.

SOMEHOW OUR LAUGHTER turned into kissing that turned into another round of lovemaking, during which the wind somehow disentangled my boxer briefs from the tree. Afterward, we lay close together and continued our conversation with sleepy voices. Ali watched me intently, her fingers swirling in my smattering of chest hair and asked, "Do you think your decision to design houses for a living was something that came from Rebecca not getting her dream home?"

I quirked a brow at her. "You been talking to Spencer?" She laughed and shook her head. She didn't need him to tell her I had issues. She was far too intelligent for that. I blew out a breath. "Yeah, I suppose that was part of it in the beginning. I'd always thought it was Spencer who first talked about going into home design but now that I think about it, I guess it was me. Maybe somewhere in my twisted up mind I thought it would make me feel better. The same way learning to swim and getting good enough at it to compete was supposed to make me feel better."

"I understand perfectly." She sighed, her hand coming to rest over my heart. "I'm not sure I ever really wanted to go into marketing. I just wanted to be independent, no matter what I ended up doing. Keith was the one who convinced me to apply at GFS with him." She snorted derisively. "I was touched that he had that kind of faith in me, but now I think he just wanted us to work together so he could keep me under his thumb."

"I'm sure he never thought I'd be more successful than him. He couldn't stand that I could do things on my own, took it as an insult to his manhood. Jackass. It had nothing to do with him. I made up my mind a long time ago that I wasn't going to be my mother. She valued money over her family, left a man who would have given his life for her to find someone with deep pockets and shallow feelings." She shook her head sadly. "That's not what I want for my life, no matter how much she tries to tell me I'd be better off."

Playing devil's advocate, I said, "If she knew the truth about Keith, maybe she'd see it differently."

She blinked rapidly, eyes shining. "After I sent Keith back to that hospital with injuries of his own, I was hurting worse than ever. Broken ribs are a real bitch. I didn't want to drag Talia into that mess, so I went to my mother's house. I don't know why I did it. I guess somewhere deep down I still want her to be a mom to me, even though she's not capable." She brushed a tear from her cheek and grimaced. "I had a week off work for Keith's and my celebratory vacation, the one that was never going to happen, so I ran to my mother's place to lick my wounds. When I told her what happened, do you know what she said?"

My chest ached at the pain in her eyes as I shook my head.

"She said 'Keith is going places. He'll be a good provider one day if you can just get past his little eccentricities. Being with a powerful man always comes with a price.'" Her voice wavered and cracked. I pulled her tight against me, unable to fathom the callousness of the remarks. Ali trembled in my arms, but her voice sounded stronger as she continued. "You were a stranger to me then but what you did that night was the only caring gesture I received. No one else knew what happened, not even

Talia. So, even though I acted like I resented your help, I'm grateful for what you did."

I kissed the top of her head and gave her a squeeze. "I'm just sorry I didn't do more. You deserved to be comforted, held, supported, and you didn't get any of that. What did you say to your mother after she imparted those timeless words of wisdom?" My voice dripped with sarcasm, and I swore to myself that I'd get the opportunity to tell Ali's mom exactly what I thought of her. One day, one day.

"I told her if she thought so damn much of Keith, she should marry him herself. Let him beat the shit out of her just so she could live in luxury. Holden had no idea what was going on when he walked in. I told him I was in a car accident, the same story everyone else got. When he saw my mother in a tizzy and the tension between us, he stepped in and offered her a week at the spa, which she took without even looking back. He went away on business, leaving me there for the week alone. He knew she wouldn't want me with her at the spa and he knew better than to offer me a trip or a stay in a fancy hotel, so he took off."

"Why didn't you go to your father? You've always been close to him, right?" I hadn't met Jeffrey Walker, but I'd spoken briefly with him on the phone when he called the cabin for Ali. He was polite but cautious, not knowing the extent of my relationship with his daughter but just watching her face light up when she talked to him told me everything I needed to know about the man.

She shook her head vigorously. "No way. If he knew..." She raised her brows in a fearful expression. "Remember me telling you he 'hunts' with a camera? Well, just because he couldn't bring himself to shoot *a deer*..." She trailed off, and I knew exactly what Jeffrey would have done. The same thing I wanted to do every time I thought of her with those marks on her body.

I needed to chase away that image, so I steered the conversation away from that night. "So, if you aren't sure marketing is what you want to do, why are you fighting so hard to keep the job at GFS?"

She cocked a brow, smirking. "Because they don't have the balls to fire me. They're drawing out their 'investigation' in hopes that I'll get pissed off and quit. They don't want to get on Holden's shit list, so they are looking for a way to unload me without repercussions from step-daddy dearest." She tilted her head, the corner of her mouth turning up in a sly smile. "So, when the paid leave ended, I started draining my vacation time. Now that it's gone, I have no reason to keep the job. I know they're not going to take me back, no matter what. Even though I'm innocent, there would be rumors, chatter that would cost them clients. The only reason I haven't told them to go to hell is I like knowing they're squirming in their Italian leather shoes and expensive ergonomic office chairs."

I shook my head softly, chuckling. "And here I thought you were a victim in all this, that you had your heart set on going back there because it was your passion."

"Sorry to disappoint, Mr. McGavran. I'm no one's victim. The only thing my heart is set on is you, which works out great because you've become one of my passions as well." She straightened enough to reach my lips, stirring my arousal with a single lingering kiss. Just as she was pulling back to speak again, her stomach growled loud and long, making her blush in that innocent way that I loved.

"Sounds like we need to find ourselves some dinner." I smiled into her deep green eyes and pulled her body on top of mine. "Right after we finish here."

We made it back to the cabin a couple of hours before dawn and decided breakfast was more appropriate given the time. We ate our food slowly, enjoying each other's company and listening to the soft music coming from the radio. A new song started playing, its cadence soft and passionate, and Ali's fond smile made me suddenly feel like dancing.

I pushed back my chair and stood, holding out my hand. "May I have this dance?"

She dabbed the corners of her mouth with her napkin and tossed it onto her nearly empty plate. "Absolutely. I feel like I haven't been in your arms in ages."

There was no mocking in her tone, no irony. She genuinely missed my touch. And the feeling was most assuredly mutual. I held her close against me as we swayed to the music and, when the next song started, we kept our own tempo so we could hold on a little longer.

We danced so long that the first inklings of the approaching dawn crested the mountaintops in the distance, the blackness of the night being chased away by the first colorful slashes of sunlight. I'd remembered that Ali squealed every time she was dipped, so I did it as often as possible. I'd realized a great deal since I last saw the dawn.

That the people I'd been pushing away all my life were the ones I wanted to hold onto most.

That refusing to decide was a decision in itself.

That no matter how high you build your walls, love will always find a way in.

The sun shone brightly in the sky by the time we made our way to my room. Our room. Ali stepped over to the dresser to steal one of my tee shirts while I got ready for bed. She brushed by me as I was leaving the bathroom, her toothbrush in hand and a sleepy smile on her face. I swatted her behind and went to turn down the covers, leaving her to her bedtime ritual.

When I reentered the bedroom, I noticed a cardboard box by the door and called out, "You officially moving your things in here with me? If so, I can clear out one of the dressers for you." I rather liked the idea of sharing more than just the bed with her.

"Um, no." She hedged, her voice garbled because of the toothbrush she was using. I heard the faucet turn on, and a moment later she stood in the bathroom doorway. "That's not mine, though I have no objections to moving in." She pointed to the box with the toothbrush she still held, looking nervous. "Remember me saying someone told me about Spencer hunting you down?"

I nodded with a confused frown, emptying my pockets, placing everything on the nightstand, and plugging in my phone.

"Well, Gran was the one that told me. She called me to find out if I knew where you were, and we talked for a while." She held up a hand with a raised brow. "Now, don't get mad at her. She didn't tell me anything I didn't already know at that point. Not about you anyway. But she did talk about how worried she's been, how much she wished you and I would work things out, how she thought maybe I could help you deal with some things."

I wanted to be angry, wanted to object to being discussed like an obstinate child but I couldn't. Gran was right, again. Damn, I hated having to admit that, even to myself, but I'd known all along that Ali was destined to be a catalyst in my life. I just never thought it would be to such a staggering degree. Sighing, I tipped my head toward the box. "So, that's a box full of things I need to deal with?" I turned and squinted at it. "Must be the first shipment. No way does that cover it all." I stared at it and wondered if Pandora would have opened her infamous box if she had known in advance the unfathomable pain that awaited her.

I said as much to Ali, a wry comment that was meant to be funny.

When I turned to her though, her expression was anything but amused. She smiled sadly and came over to crouch in front of me as I sat on the bed. She dropped the toothbrush on the nightstand and reached up to touch my face, tears pooling in her eyes. "Do you remember what happened the second time the box was opened?" I shook my head, genuinely not able to recall. Ali swallowed forcefully and whispered. "After all the pain and horror was unleashed, all that was left in the box was hope. And hope healed them."

As I stared into her shining emerald eyes, I knew hope for the first time in my life.

~

THE NEXT FEW weeks were some of the best of my life. I was making things right, little by little, and working toward a real future. After so many years of just coasting through my life, hesitant to make major decisions for fear of choosing wrong, I was stepping up and taking control.

I'd taken control of the Marissa situation, moving carefully and singularly until the problem was resolved. I hadn't told Spencer yet, choosing to wait until the weekend when we would both be at Gran's for a family dinner. He'd be pissed that I didn't let him help, but I wanted to fix my fuck up on my own for once. I was hoping he would be so relieved not to have Marissa's accusations hanging over his head that he would forgive me my subterfuge.

I told Ali about Shepard and Marissa working together and somehow managed to garner her promise to stay out of the situation. She said she trusted me to handle it, and she hoped that Holden got what was coming to him. She was behind me one hundred percent, and I loved her so much for that.

I'd also taken action to neutralize Keith, which initially pissed Ali off, but I eventually managed to persuade her to indulge me. I hoped he was smart enough to back off, but I was fully prepared to deal with him either way. He wouldn't get away with sabotaging Ali's career. My investigator had been building quite a case against him these last few weeks. When the time came, the little bastard wouldn't know what hit him. Ali may not want the job anymore but when she left, she'd leave with a clean slate.

Lauren had been a non-issue since the day she accosted us in the parking lot. We never found out what lie she told her uncle to explain the marks Ali left on her face, but he never mentioned it to either of us, so we assumed he was still in the dark. She continued to work at night and spent days helping her uncle, becoming nothing more than a distasteful afterthought in our otherwise serene existence.

And serene it had been. Ali and I were happier than I ever could have imagined.

My favorite days with her were still Saturdays. That was the day we went together to Gran's property; I still wasn't used to calling it mine. I'd admitted to Ali a week or so ago that bears probably weren't a huge threat with all the construction noise but I told her in my most convincing voice that she should probably still stick close to me, just in case. She'd nodded emphatically and said it was probably best, all the while fighting a grin.

So, every Saturday morning Ali stood by the lake painting while I worked on my project in the barn. By mid-afternoon, we would stop for a bite to eat that usually ended with our bodies entwined — either in the lake or under our willow — before we each decided we'd worked enough for the day.

I still swam laps in the pool every morning and sometimes she sat on the edge, dipping her toes in the cool water while she watched with that slight smile of hers that I knew was an indication of her contentment. Other times, I would enter the cabin afterward to the smells of breakfast cooking and find her with Talia, sitting in the kitchen sipping coffee together. I'd staunchly refused to let Talia move out, and I was glad of it. Seeing them together made me happy and not in a creepy ménage kind of way. I liked that they supported each other, that they made each other better. They were more like sisters than any real sisters I'd ever known, and the feeling of family was comforting.

One morning in particular, I walked in from my swim and they were laughing at something the old guys from the diner had done. Talia had the most hilarious stories of their shenanigans. I stood at the top of the stairs and smiled, ruffling my hair with a towel so it wouldn't drip on the floor. Ali glanced over and spotted me, still chuckling. "Clay, you've got to hear this one. I've never laughed so hard in my life."

I wiggled my brows and smiled. "Never? Not even when we found that unusual ornament in the tree?"

Her face turned red, and she giggled into her hand while Talia looked between us with a frown. "Ornament? Tree? Christmas is a long way off, what the hell am I missing?"

"Nothing!" Ali and I said in unison, laughing.

Turned out, Talia's story was just as funny as Ali said. Apparently, one of the older gentlemen who frequented the diner had taken to trying to scare Lauren whenever she waited his table. Last night, he'd really gotten her when he plunked his false teeth into his water glass and then asked for a refill. To hear Talia tell it, Lauren screamed like a little girl and dropped the glass into his buddy's lap. It was made even more hilarious when she told us the first gentleman had burst out laughing, announcing to the entire diner that the teeth in his friend's lap was probably the most action he'd had since before Pearl Harbor.

I laughed so hard I nearly fell out of my chair.

Whoever that old guy was, I wanted to buy him a damn drink. Pure genius.

I had no remorse for taking pleasure in Lauren's misery. She was just getting a little cosmic justice for deliberately dropping our dinner order in the floor the previous week. I'd watched her smirk at Ali, hold the containers up in front of her and then gleefully let them fall. Yep, karma was a bitch or, in this case, a feisty old man with a damn good sense of humor.

Talia said she had a million more stories like that from the diner and offered to share a few of her favorites.

I asked if she minded giving me a few minutes, then excused myself to shower and change. I was halfway through my routine, head tilted back to rinse the shampoo from my hair when the glass door opened, and Ali stepped in. I peeked at her with one eye and snickered. "I'm not going to be hearing those stories this morning, am I?"

She reached out and took my quickly awakening dick in hand, stroking firmly as she sunk to her knees. "I'll give you the Cliff's Notes version. Later."

THAT AFTERNOON, AFTER the crews left for the day, I installed my project with Ali's help. Even though the ornate oak entry door would have been best suited for the front of the house, I chose to place it as the back door. The rear of the house faced the lake, though it wasn't visible through the dense trees. I was sure my mother would have liked that. The back door also opened into the massive rustic kitchen that I knew my mother would have loved. The table I'd used for the project would have been perfectly suited for the room, but I wanted a permanent placement, one that made it part of the house not just a piece of decoration. A part of my mother would always be there in the house. That was the only thing I could do for her now.

Maybe with this final tribute, I could begin to let her go.

Ali stood a few paces away, watching me run my hands over the door frame, the trim, the antique glass knob that had been in the first box Gran had brought, the one with all the things my mother had collected for the house. I'd managed to go through its contents with just enough forced detachment to make rational decisions about what items could still be of use, leaving the paperwork I'd found at the bottom for another time. It hadn't been easy, but I'd done it.

The other box, the one at the cabin, was a different story.

Ali had offered to go through it with me, and I'd reluctantly agreed but after looking at some of the pictures inside, I'd decided to hold off for a while before tackling the rest. Several of the pictures were taken at the lake, ones she'd taken of me and a few that I'd taken of her. Those were the ones that hit me the hardest. Ali understood my reluctance and didn't push. She knew how hard this was for me and she also knew that it was going to take some time.

I was moving forward, even if it was at a crawl.

I reached out and grasped the glass knob, giving the door a push. It swung smoothly and silently on its heavy hinges, revealing the warm interior of the mostly-finished kitchen. The house itself was coming together nicely. The kitchen was closer to completion than the other rooms, most of which still needed drywall and flooring. The electrician was making some adjustments, and once he was finished, the walls would go up, the flooring would go down, and the final details could be addressed.

It wouldn't be long now.

Although Ali and I were mostly inseparable, neither of us had talked about what would happen once the house was finished. I'd been considering some options that would keep her with me, with the company, but I knew that I had to be mindful of her stubborn streak and aversion to being 'saved' or 'kept'. I hadn't found a tactful way to broach the subject, so I'd kept silent, taking my cues from her.

That wouldn't fly with Gran, though. Whether we wanted to or not, we would be discussing it come the weekend. Gran would no-doubt grill us about our future plans at the family dinner she'd insisted we attend. While the thought of her meddling would usually annoy, this time she might be doing me a favor.

Ali was hardheaded, but Gran had years of experience getting her way by any means necessary.

It would be a battle for the ages.

AS A WAY TO mentally prepare for our trip to Gran's that weekend, I asked Blake to hold down the fort while Ali and I slipped away for a little fun. Just one day where she and I had nothing to focus on but each other.

The fact that I was doing a bit of scheming notwithstanding.

If it worked out, great. If not, I'd still get my way.

My mind was made up.

I woke Ali with soft, slow kisses that morning, leaning close and whispering in her ear. "Wake up, slugger. We've got to get going."

The sky was barely lit by the sun, which still hadn't crested the peaks of the mountains in the distance. It was early, apparently too early for Ali.

She groused and pulled the pillow over her head, muttering incoherently.

"I'll make you coffee..." I kept my pitch quiet as I crawled into bed beside her, pushing my head under the pillow with hers. "I'll cook you breakfast..." More groaning and a sweeping motion with her arm that was meant to shoo me away. "Okay, I'll buy you the good coffee and a big breakfast on the way, but you have to get up..."

Finally, a muffled reply. "On the way where?"

"It's a surprise."

That got her attention.

She tossed the pillow away, her hair covering her sleepy face like cotton candy. "You have to tell me where we're going so I know what to wear."

I slipped my hand over her abdomen, smiling inwardly at the fluttering flesh under my fingers. "Well, for the next few minutes, you're attire is suitable."

"I'm naked."

I pulled the sheet over my head as I descended her body. "As you should be."

~

AFTER I'D FINISHED my breakfast, courtesy of my delicious lady, I instructed her to dress in cool, comfortable clothes with her swimsuit underneath.

She'd looked at me strangely at the request but didn't push for more information. I liked to think the mind-blowing orgasm had left her too relaxed for a stand-off.

After half an hour in the truck, she realized we were pointed away from the coast and asked again where we were headed. I brushed off the question and couldn't help smiling at the pouty face that greeted me every time I glanced her way.

We stopped off for coffee and a quick bite to eat; Ali still annoyed at my secrecy but not annoyed enough to keep her from tucking into my side at every opportunity. She knew I was keeping something from her but this time she trusted me enough to know I'd tell her when I was ready.

I found that thought comforting.

When we were a few miles away from our destination, I asked, "Do you remember me telling you I was offered a contract to build some pieces for an amusement park?"

She perked up a bit and smiled. "Yeah. A post-apocalyptic rise of the machines type of thing, right?"

"Exactly. Well, the time to make a decision is fast approaching, and I haven't even seen the park..." I trailed off, taking a page from Spencer's book to prolong the suspense.

"And?" She urged, dragging the word out.

"And I thought you and I could take a look around, maybe ride a few rides, hit the water park. Just to get a feel for the place." I turned to her and found her grinning. "I'll still have to take a little time to meet with the art director and check out the layout of the location, but I thought that part might interest you, as well."

"Absolutely. I'd love to see things from an artistic point of view." She was bubbling with child-like energy, fidgeting in her seat.

And it was contagious.

I found myself getting more excited the closer we got.

This was going to be fun.

When we got there, she looked at the Closed sign by the entrance and her face fell. "Are we too early?"

I smiled at her and drove up to the entrance, pulling up to the single attended booth. I greeted the attendant, an older woman with a bright smile and thick glasses, as I retrieved what I needed from the console. I passed her a sheet of paper and, after making a quick call to confirm, she handed me two VIP passes and a parking placard before wishing us a good day.

I pulled forward, getting just through the gate's arm before stopping and hanging the parking pass from my rear-view mirror.

Ali shook her head at me. "You're just full of surprises, aren't you, Mr. McGavran?"

I pulled her in for a kiss so deep my toes curled before continuing toward the parking area. "You ain't seen nothin yet, Miss Walker."

We exited the truck, meeting at the front bumper and instinctively clasping our hands together. It was the way we walked everywhere, a habit we each greatly enjoyed. Just the feel of her hand in mine somehow managed to feel familiar, comforting, and erotic all at the same time. I lifted our joined hands to my lips and kissed her fingertips as we walked. "The park doesn't open officially for another two hours. We have the place all to ourselves."

"For business or pleasure?"

I nibbled her fingertip and smiled. "Didn't you know? With us, it's always both. Everything, every moment with you — whether at work or play — is pure pleasure, Alison."

She stilled under my gaze. "You called me Alison. That's the third time you've used my full name without erotic intent. What gives?" She teased.

"When were the other times?"

"When I was about to fall into that mud hole." She chuckled at the memory before sobering. "And when I was about to hit Lauren in that parking lot."

It took me a moment to puzzle it out, going over each situation in my mind, lingering on a few favorites before the answer occurred to me. "Ah. Now I understand. It's not just when I'm turned on. It's when you've got my blood pumping, whether in the bedroom, at the edge of a mud pit, or in the middle of a fight; it's about adrenaline."

She shook her head. "None of that applies right now. No Lauren." She gestured to the parking lot. "No mud pits." She dipped a pointed glance at my crotch. "And I'd know if you were turned on. So, what's the adrenaline factor this time?"

"Possibility." I lifted her hand and placed it palm down over my racing heart, covering it with my own. "Feel that?" She nodded. "That's what you do to me. That's what the idea of a future with you does to me."

"You were thinking about our future?" She pressed her hand firmly over my heart, smiling. "What about it?"

I tipped my head in the direction of the park's large

entrance, filled with turnstiles and ticket scanners, all standing empty before us. "I was thinking that today might just be the springboard that launches us into something great. Together."

She followed my gaze, thoughtful for a moment as she pieced together what I was considering. Then her eyes widened, and she turned back to me. "Wait, do you think...?"

I pressed my lips to hers, the kiss not enough to chase away her grin. "If I have anything to do with it, absolutely."

She giggled happily and pulled her hand away, eagerly rubbing her palms together.

She was coming up with possibilities already.

We spent the day laughing, screaming, and making out in every darkened corner we could find. Our two hour window allowed us time to make it to each and every roller coaster in the park — all manned by bored looking operators — in addition to a very encouraging meeting with both the park director and art director. After the crowds started filing in, a sea of sun visors and strollers, we decided to take a break for an early lunch.

We sat in one of the Italian themed sections of the park, listening to the chatter and noise of the passing throng over the melodic sounds of old world music streaming through the artfully disguised speakers. We talked little over our meal, each of us mentally replaying the morning and its significance as we moved forward.

The meetings had gone well for both of us.

There wasn't a damn thing that could have wiped the grins off our faces that afternoon. We were free, in every possible way. The only thing binding either of us was our entwined fingers.

I drove back to Denson with her head on my shoulder and her hand in mine. Occasionally she would breathe a contented sigh and squeeze my fingers, perfectly happy in the silence as we pondered the future stretching out before us.

CHAPTER EIGHTEEN

THE WEEKEND WAS finally upon us, and Ali's nerves were getting the best of her. It was charming. She'd talked to Gran on the phone, met her in person on more than one occasion, but I think the idea of Gran having the home-field advantage was a bit intimidating. We planned to drive up early that evening and stay the night, spending all of the following day with Gran, Vanessa, and Daniel. I was hoping to see Nicholas, Vanessa's husband, there as well.

I watched Ali sort through her clothes for the fifth time, not sure what to wear for a family dinner with an eighty-year-old hell-raiser. She held up a thin-strapped summer dress, and I gave a nod of approval. She tossed it aside and rummaged through the closet while I watched from my position propped against the headboard of the bed. When she muttered a curse and another garment came sailing out, I laughed out loud.

Her unsmiling face appeared in the doorway, and she smirked. "Keep laughing, McGavran. You just wait until we go to visit my dad in a couple weeks, see how funny this shit is to you then." With a huff, she ducked back into the closet and rummaged some more.

I sat up with a start and frowned at the empty doorway. "What do you mean 'a couple weeks'? I don't remember you saying anything about us going to Asheville any time soon. I thought it was more of a long-range plan." I tried not to sound as panicked as I felt, but Ali's triumphant chuckle told me I'd failed.

"His birthday is in two weeks, and I haven't seen him in months. I'm going no matter what, and I assumed you would be escorting me since we are visiting *your* family as a couple this weekend."

There was a thinly veiled threat behind her words. Basically, I was fucking going home to meet Daddy, or I was going to suffer the consequences.

There was no need for her to be intimidated by Gran. Given the way she'd just handled me, dinner with the family was going to be evenly matched.

Once Ali settled on an outfit, she went for a shower while I checked in with Spencer, who was staying at the cabin with us. He had come into town the day before to go over some changes with the electrician. Brant wasn't working on the project, but he was still sending ideas via email and one of them had taken hold, necessitating a few adjustments. Spencer could have handled the situation from the office or, gasp, left it for me to take care of myself, but he insisted on coming out to meet with the electrician personally.

I was pretty sure the fucker just missed me.

Rather than have him go all the way back to Richmond, I suggested we all go to Gran's together. He'd hesitated at first, but Ali stepped in and told him we wanted him along. She ended up convincing him to stay until Monday, making me suspicious of her motives. Talia was back to staying in D.C. most of the time since Teach was getting back in the swing of things but she still came to Denson on Sundays for our customary dinners. Ali had been very specific when she convinced Spencer to stay the weekend, making sure he knew he was expected for Sunday dinner.

It looked like our girl had plans for Talia and Spencer. As I joked with him about Ali's behavior that afternoon, I thought she might be onto something. Not that I'd ever let her know that. She and Gran could meddle all they wanted, but they were on their own.

Guys don't play matchmaker.

～

ALI EMERGED FROM the bedroom looking good enough to eat and told me, "Shower's all yours." She smiled at the heat in my gaze and shook her head.

"We could have saved water if you would have just let me shower with you."

She glanced at Spencer, cheeks flaming. "No way, buster, you are not going to make us late today." She pointed back to our room. "You get ready, I have a quick errand to run, and we can leave as soon as I get back."

"What kind of errand? Can't it wait until we get back?" I knew she still worried about the diner and checked in periodically to go over the schedule and check deliveries, but Teach was doing well enough to handle those things himself.

"No, I have to go now. There's something I want to bring with us for Gran, and I forgot to get it yesterday."

"What is it?" She had my curiosity peaked.

She smiled and shook her head. "Uh uh. Not telling. There might be something for you as well, so just go get ready and I'll be back in a few."

I shot her a look of annoyance and kissed her on my way to the bedroom. "Fine," I grumbled.

I heard her giggling as I closed the door behind me. Little sneak.

～

NEARLY AN HOUR later, I sat at the kitchen table with Spencer, drumming my fingers and staring at the wall clock. Where the hell was she? Spencer could see I was getting worried and tried to make small talk to distract me, but I didn't bite. I couldn't focus on anything except the odd feeling in the pit of my stomach.

I'd tried to call Ali to see what was taking so long, groaning in frustration when the sound of her phone ringing echoed from the bedroom. I went in and retrieved it, shaking my head as I placed it on the table between me and Spencer. Fuck. I couldn't believe she'd walked out without it

I ran my hands through my hair and blew out a breath. "What the fuck could be taking so long? What did she have to go to Charlottesville to get whatever the hell it is? Did she have to make the shit herself?" I stopped, brows rising as it hit me. She'd been hiding her paintings from me the last few weeks, covering them whenever I came to the lake to check on her. That was what she'd gone to do. She went to get the paintings.

I snatched my keys off the counter as I relayed my theory to Spencer, who kept right on my heels as I shot down the stairs and out the door. Something was off. She should have been back by now.

An icy cold feeling of dread snaked its way up my spine and clenched my galloping heart.

Something was wrong.

Terribly wrong.

Spencer insisted on driving, and I didn't even bother to argue. I tossed him my keys and climbed into the passenger side, mind reeling and wondering what the hell could have happened in such a short amount of time. I snatched my phone out of my pocket and called the diner. When Lauren answered, I glanced at the clock on the dash, realizing just how late it had gotten. "Lauren, this is Clay. Is Ali there?"

"No. Ali doesn't work here anymore. Shouldn't her boyfriend know that?" For once she sounded more confused than snide, which threw me off.

"She went to run an errand, and I haven't seen her since. If she comes in, have her call me, okay? I know you aren't fond of either of us but now isn't the time, so please just tell her to call me."

Lauren sounded genuinely concerned as she said, "Okay, I will. I promise."

We turned onto the road that led to the house, and as soon as the open gate was visible, I knew I'd been right. I tried to relax, knowing that this was our safe place, the place we came when we needed to regroup. Maybe Ali was sitting by the lake gearing up for our trip and lost track of time. Maybe this was all in my head.

All the rationalizations in the world weren't going to untie the knot in my stomach. Only having her in my arms would do that.

We emerged from the tree-lined driveway, and my attention was immediately drawn to the blue Jeep parked beside the house. My eyes darted to the lake path, wondering if I'd find her standing at her easel putting finishing touches on a painting. Would she laugh at my concern?

I glanced over at Spencer and saw him squinting through the windshield as we drew closer to the house. Following his gaze, I tried to decipher what had grabbed his attention. My eyes narrowed when I saw that someone had left the fucking backhoe parked right up against the house, blocking the basement door and sitting on a recently poured slab of concrete. Someone was going to pay for that. The weight of that thing was going to buckle the concrete.

I started to turn to Spencer when a flicker of light caught my attention. I frowned as I searched the front of the house for the source, finally locking in on the living room window. I squinted and stared as Spencer steered the truck off the gravel and onto the grass in front of the house, picking up speed. The flicker came again, faint behind the large cloth the crew had used to block the blinding sun from the room.

Was that candlelight?

Oh, God! No no no! It wasn't the light from any fucking candle. The house was on fire!

I snatched my door open and leaped from the still-rolling truck, Spencer yelling at my back. I didn't slow to see if he was behind me. I raced up the stairs and reached for the knob, twisting it furiously before jerking my hand back with a hiss. Fuck! The knob was too hot to touch.

I looked around in a blind panic for something to throw through the window, as Spencer bounded up the steps and yelled. "The whole room is filled with flames, we have to find another way!" Not waiting for me, he jumped off the porch and ran toward the side of the house. Rounding the corner behind him, I nearly ran into his back. He was stopped just beside the backhoe, cursing as he checked for the keys.

He pulled back, empty-handed and stared at me blankly. I was just about to tell him to check the barn for the keys when I heard it. The faint sound of someone yelling was coming from the other side of the basement door. I went to the egress window, but there was a film of soot that kept me from seeing in. The window, I remembered, was reinforced like all the others. The only way to open it was from the inside. I crouched down and yelled, "Ali! Come over to the window and I'll get you out. If you can get it open, I'll pull you out, baby. Okay?"

I tilted my head to one side, straining to hear. I couldn't make out much of what she said but the words 'my leg' were crystal clear. She couldn't stand, and if she couldn't stand, she couldn't reach the window. Goddamnit!

I pressed as close to the window as I could, telling her, "It's okay, Alison. I'm going to get you out. Cover your mouth and nose with your shirt and I'll find a way to get to you. I swear I will."

I didn't wait for a reply. I sprinted to the back of the house and prayed the fire hadn't spread to the kitchen.

I jumped onto the back deck and leveled my gaze on the monstrous oak door. I tried the knob, cautiously this time and found it cool to the touch but locked tight. My terror doubled when I realized how high on the frame the deadbolt was. No well-placed kick was going to pop that door open. The solid, oak door.

With Ali's muffled cries ringing in my ears, I clenched my jaw and charged the door, throwing all my weight, anger, and fear into the blow. Stepping back, I braced myself and rammed my shoulder into it again. And again. And again. On the fourth strike, I heard a pop and my whole arm felt like it had been thrown into the flames.

Son of a bitch!

Spencer's voice rang out from behind me. "I have the keys but there are ten on the Goddamn ring, and I don't know which one it is or if the backhoe key is even fucking on here."

I took a deep breath, gathering my resolve and ignoring the pain in my arm as I shouted. "Don't you dare give up!" Though, whether I was talking to him, or Ali, or myself was anyone's guess. "I don't care if you have to ram that fucking thing with my truck, you get it out of my way. I may not be able to get back out once I'm down there. Now GO!"

I stepped back to the edge of the porch and charged the door again.

Holy motherfucking shit!

My arm hanging uselessly at my side, I backed up and rammed the door again. This time I was rewarded with the cracking sound of splintering wood. I stepped back and narrowed my gaze on the door, locating the weak spot and refocusing my efforts.

Adjusting my aim a few inches to the left, I hit it again. Crack! I could see the light from the fire through the slim opening.

Again.

Crack!

Again.

Crack!

The whole door split, and a blast of smoky air hit me in the face. Turning my head and taking a deep breath, I kicked my way through and shouted for Alison. I snatched off my shirt, sending buttons flying in my haste. I wadded it up, covering my mouth and nose. Why the hell wasn't the fire alarm going off?

I turned to my left and strode across the kitchen toward the flame-filled hallway that separated the kitchen from the living room. The door to the basement was a few feet down the hall on the left, directly across from the living room, which was also filled with flames. I watched in horror as the fire edged closer to the door, slowly cutting off any possibility of getting to Alison.

I turned back toward the shredded back door, remembering the extinguisher that had been mounted under the sink. Darting over to the cabinet and triumphantly snatching the canister from its bracket, I rushed back to the hallway entrance and wedged it between my knees so I could pull the pin, sweeping the nozzle in a widening arc as best I could with one mostly useless arm.

I managed to clear an area large enough to allow me access

to the basement door before the canister sputtered and died. Tucking it under my injured arm with a grunt of pain, I wrapped my shirt around the knob and turned. The door popped open with a groan, the heat having warped the wood in its frame. I pulled it closed behind me to keep the smoke out and rushed down the stairs into the basement.

Spencer must have turned on the headlights on either the truck or the backhoe because it filtered dimly through the egress window and small glass panels in the door. The smoke was thick at the top of the stairs, stinging my eyes and forcing me to step carefully with tears blinding me. When I reached the bottom, the smoke had thinned somewhat but was still dense. I swept my gaze around the room and froze. Ali lay motionless on the floor below the window, pieces of a broken flashlight scattered all around her. Lungs aching and eyes burning, I blinked several times at her smoky silhouette, brokenly waiting for her to move.

Oh dear God don't let it be too late.

The smoke wasn't as thick down here, but she'd been trapped for so long.

She wasn't moving.

This couldn't be fucking happening.

I couldn't lose her. Not her.

She wasn't breathing.

She couldn't leave me alone.

The crushing weight of grief settled over me as I slumped to my knees, just a few feet from where she lay so small and still. I removed the shirt from my face, no longer caring if the smoke overtook me. I let the extinguisher slip from under my arm, barely registering the sound of the empty canister hitting the concrete floor, the metal ringing out loudly.

Wait!

Did she?

Was that a flinch?

Oh my God, did the sound make her flinch?

I held my breath and stared, staggering to my feet when her fingers flexed. I stumbled over to her, coughing and grinning down at her through the smoke. I crouched down and lifted her into my lap, my right arm screaming out in protest. I stood as slowly as possible, careful not to hurt her but also making sure my injured arm wasn't going to give out and make me drop her.

I stared into her soot-covered face. "Alison, can you hear me? Talk to me, slugger. Let me see those gorgeous green eyes for just a second. Please, baby, look at me." Nothing. I begged again, my voice pitiful and shrill. "Please, Alison, don't you leave me, dammit." I lay my forehead on hers, her faint breath tickling my cheek and giving me the hope words had not.

She stirred a bit in my arms, groaning and coughing softly. "You called me Alison." It was barely a whisper, but it was the most beautiful fucking thing I ever heard. I pulled back to look at her face, and her eyes fluttered open for just a moment before she smiled softly and closed them again. "I guess I was wrong again. I did need you to save me." With that, she went limp, having passed out in my arms.

I pressed a kiss to her lips and whispered, "No, baby. You saved me."

The sound of the backhoe starting drew my attention from her face, and I started making my way to the door. Once I got to the other side of the large basement, I leaned us against the wall for a moment to catch my breath, thankful I'd brought my shirt with me so I could cover Ali's face with it. She needed it more than I did.

A moment later, when I saw the piece of equipment begin to move, I staggered to the door and fumbled with the lock while trying to keep Ali in my arms. It took an excruciatingly long time, but I finally managed it. Spencer stood on the other side with his hand on the knob, jerking the door open as soon as the lock disengaged.

He rushed in and tried to pull Ali from my arms. I all but growled at him, not wanting to let her go but he reminded me that we needed to get her to the hospital as fast as possible, and I was barely able to hold her much less run with her.

I made it out the door before I reluctantly let him take her. I staggered along behind them, the sounds of sirens wailing as an ambulance and firetruck emerged from the tree-lined driveway. The flashing lights irritated the fuck out of my furiously stinging eyes, but I was so glad to see them that the tears running down my face were only partially from the smoke.

Everything started happening in a blur, lots of voices and noise, yells from the firemen as they started to work on battling the flames and clear, concise directions from the EMTs as they began assessing our injuries.

I stayed as close as physically possible to Ali, waving off the attempts of the insistent paramedic trying to get a look at my shoulder. I didn't care about me, didn't even feel my own pain anymore as I watched them place a mask over Ali's face to give her oxygen. They clipped something on her finger and looked concerned when numbers started to appear on the LED screen. Three of them worked on her simultaneously, never pausing as they slid her onto a backboard, another paramedic appearing alongside with a stretcher.

Through all the chaos, I could barely hear a damn thing but when she coughed once and reached a hand out, I was at her side in an instant, clutching her hand to my chest. She looked up at me from behind the clear mask over her nose and mouth, the fear and pain in her eyes dimming as she fought to smile. A cough wracked her body, and she squeezed my hand, flinching in pain.

She was in no position to talk right then, so I spoke for us both. I looked into her red-rimmed eyes, fighting to hold my composure so she wouldn't see how fucking scared I was and told her in a wavering voice, "I love you, Alison. And I'm not ever letting you go. Not this night or any other. So, don't worry. You're going to be just fine because I won't allow it to be any other way."

I followed beside the moving stretcher and climbed into the ambulance with her, refusing to leave her and telling the EMTs they could check me out on the way.

I glanced outside the ambulance doors and saw Spencer coming out of the basement, coughing his fool head off and carrying what looked like two brown paper wrapped canvases toward the truck, a firefighter on his heels bitching him out. He looked up at me at the last second and nodded, indicating he'd be right behind us and climbed behind the wheel while the fireman stormed off in anger.

A moment later, the last of the medics climbed in, pulling the double doors closed behind her. Just like that, we were off, siren screaming into the night.

I kept Ali's hand in mine the whole way, even when I was being examined. A few prodding hands on my shoulder had reawakened the searing pain, but I gritted my teeth and ignored it, not taking my eyes off of her face. If she awakened for even a second, I wanted my face to be the first thing she saw, and for the reassuring pressure of my hand on hers to be the first thing she felt.

I barely blinked when a sling was pulled over my head, and the EMT slid my arm into it, rattling off information to her colleagues that I neither understood nor gave a damn about. If she wasn't talking about Ali, it just didn't fucking matter. They asked to start an IV, saying they could give me something for the pain that way, but I refused. They probably wouldn't have given me anything anyway, unless it was something to knock me out to get me out of the way.

Baiting me with pain meds wouldn't work, though.

The pain was keeping me focused, and I needed that.

I welcomed my pain and wished like fuck I could take on hers too.

AFTER WE ARRIVED at the hospital they whisked Ali away, and Spencer was the only thing that stood between me and a jail cell, not for the first time in our lives.

I paced the length of the waiting room, cursing under my breath and clenching my fists. Every time I did that, a shot of agony ran the length of my damaged arm, causing me to hiss in pain. But I kept doing it, I couldn't help myself.

Spencer sat by the door, at a table that was meant for consults, watching me with weary eyes. "You need to let them look at you, dumbass." He muttered for the tenth time.

I ignored him just as I had every other time. I was angry, not necessarily at him, but at the fact that I'd been refused entry to the section of the hospital where they'd taken Ali. A beefy orderly with a bored expression had stepped out to stop me when I tried to brush past the nurse at the door. I'd been reaching for his throat when Spencer snatched me back and slammed me into the wall so hard my head swam. He'd taken hold of my good arm and dragged me to the waiting room without a word, closing the door behind us.

He knew there was no point trying to talk me down, so he poured himself a cup of coffee that closely resembled burnt motor oil and sat at the table, effectively placing himself between me and the exit.

He was trying to keep me out of trouble, but I still wanted to choke the piss out of him for getting between Ali and me.

I paced a while longer and finally slumped into one of the chairs across from him, exhausted and wired at the same damn time. "We should call someone. I don't know how to get in touch with her father, but I need to call Talia. She'll kill me if I don't." I ran my hands through my hair and pulled out my phone, the smell of smoke heavy on my skin. "I was supposed to take care of our girl..."

"Already done." Spencer offered. "You brought Ali's phone with us to the house, it was still in your truck, so I made some calls on the way here. It's only been an hour, but I'm betting Talia will be here any minute."

My shoulders sagged with relief, another flash of pain ripping through me. "What about Ali's dad? I'm not sure how Ali will feel about it, but her mother probably needs a call too."

Spencer stood and plucked another foam cup from the counter, pouring me a shot of black syrup from the coffee pot. "All taken care of, Clay. I called Talia, she called Ali's mom while I called Jeffrey, Brant, and Gran."

Shit. I forgot about Gran. "Jesus, did she freak?"

"Nah. She cussed like a sailor for a few minutes, and I could hear her slamming the lids on some pots, probably for the dinner she was making us. She's on her way here. I made her promise to have someone else drive." He shook his head, frowning. "Her car is slow as hell, usually a good thing, but I wouldn't put it past her to snag someone else's ride." He paused and added wryly, "Again."

TWENTY MINUTES LATER, there was a commotion out in the hall, and I saw Talia looking up and down the corridor frantically, purse clutched to her chest like a life preserver. I sprang from my seat and snatched the waiting room door open, preparing to call out when she spotted me.

Her eyes widened as she approached, taking in the sling on my arm and my soot stained appearance. She pulled me in for a hug, careful to keep her hand off my injured shoulder. She was still crushing the shit out of my arm by default, but I gritted my teeth and held on tight. She shook and sniffed in my arms, muttering unintelligibly into my shirt.

When we finally broke apart, I stood aside and waited for her to enter the waiting room before pushing the door closed behind us. She walked over to Spencer, introducing herself and thanking him for calling, wrapping him in a brief hug before turning back to me. "What happened? Have you heard anything from the doctors yet? Where did they take her?" A sudden gasp of terror ripped through her and she looked at me with pleading eyes. "Oh, God, was she burned? Did they take her to the burn unit?"

I stepped over to her, and put a hand on her shoulder. "No, she's not burned. We haven't heard anything yet from the doctors, and we're not sure how the fire started." Leaning closer to get her to meet my eye, I told her, "All we can do right now is wait. It's fucking miserable and scary, but it's all we can do. Wait and hope." I walked her over to the table and pulled out a chair for her, grateful when she quietly took a seat. I settled in the chair beside her and said, "I suck at waiting, always have, but I know she's going to be okay. She has to be."

Talia nodded and wept a few silent tears; pulling out the tattered picture I'd last seen when she'd placed it under her pillow all those weeks ago. She stared at it for a moment and held it to her chest, closing her eyes. I wasn't sure if she was praying or remembering or a mixture of the two, but it seemed to calm her.

Damn, I envied her strength. She was a fighter. I'd known it from the start.

The biggest comfort I derived from knowing Talia was a fighter, was how much she and our girl were alike. Ali was a fighter, too.

⁓

AFTER WHAT FELT like a damn eternity, a middle-aged man with kind eyes and wrinkled scrubs came out to talk to us. When he asked who the next of kin was, Talia and I both stood, linking arms as Spencer rose beside us. "We're all her family," I told him. "How is she?"

He pulled the surgical cap from his head and blew out a breath, doing that goddamn hesitation thing I hated so much. I was on the verge of snapping at him when Talia said, "Spit it out, will ya? We're freaking out here." She said it in an exasperated way that somehow still sounded civil. I'd have to get her to teach me that.

He looked up at her and smiled, not offended in the least. "Sorry, lack of sleep." He motioned for us to sit and slipped into the empty chair. "Alison inhaled a lot of smoke. It's taking us a while to get her O2 saturation back up, but she is improving. We've intubated her to get the oxygen to her more efficiently and given her medication for pain. Her throat is inflamed, and she's got a fractured right ankle, as well as a hairline fracture of the foot on the same side." He looked down at the chart in his hands, flipping pages. "Other than a few bumps and bruises, that's it. Treating the smoke inhalation is priority number one right now, everything else is minor."

Talia spoke first. "You said she was intubated, but she's able to breathe on her own, right?"

My heart fucking stopped at the thought that intubation might be the same as being on a ventilator.

He smiled reassuringly, and I pulled in a ragged breath, relieved by his demeanor. "She's breathing on her own but she needs a little help, that's all. She's been sedated for now. We've done everything necessary to get a baseline measurement on her situation and, once her stats improve a bit more, we'll check everything again just to be sure and then the tube can come out." He patted Talia's hand and stood. "We may be able to remove it as soon as the morning, but that's all up to Alison."

I stood, reaching to shake his hand. Thanking him, I asked, "Can I see her?"

"Sure, but only for a minute or two and let's keep it one person at a time, okay?"

We all agreed and, after a nod from Talia, I followed him out.

CHAPTER NINETEEN

I STOOD HELPLESSLY by her bedside, listening to the hiss of the machines as I watched her chest rise and fall. There were tubes and gadgets everywhere, measuring and dripping and beeping out a mournful song. There were no actual rooms in the ICU, just segments of open space arranged in a circle around the nurse's station and partitioned off with curtains. I supposed it was safer that way, making it easy for the staff to look in on the patients, but I would have given anything for a private moment just then.

A shadow crossed the foot of the bed, bringing my head up as I hastily swiped at my damp cheeks. The man was nearly my height with a slightly thinner build and thick head of gray-streaked mahogany hair. He glanced at me and then locked his gaze on the woman in the bed, the woman I loved more than anything else on earth.

His daughter.

He crept closer, eyes never leaving her face as he took silent inventory of her condition. He reached for her hand with one of his, extending the other across the bed toward me. "Since you look like I feel, I'm gonna venture a guess and say you're the boyfriend." His voice was nearly as deep as mine, with a steady strength that I admired.

I gave his hand a firm shake and nodded though I knew he didn't see. "Yes, sir. I am." I looked down at the woman between us, the corners of my mouth curling into a hopeful smile. "That is until she agrees to have me as her husband."

He didn't look up, gave no indication of surprise though I'd shocked the shit out of myself. What was even more shocking was that I meant it. Every damn word. And I wasn't the least bit afraid.

Jeffrey Walker, hopefully my future father-in-law, just nodded and said. "It's nice to finally meet you, son."

Son.

He said it like it was the most natural thing in the world.

WE STEPPED OUT a few minutes later, knowing Talia was anxious for her turn. Walking back to the waiting room, we passed by the nurses station, and I whispered, "I can't believe they let you back here. We had to promise to keep it one at a time."

Jeffrey snorted and didn't bother whispering when he said, "I didn't promise 'em shit. I'd like to see someone try to keep me out."

Yep, there's that family resemblance.

We didn't even make it to the waiting room before Talia scurried past, placing a quick peck on Jeffrey's cheek and heading to the ICU. He just smiled as he turned to watch her leave. "That girl must think a lot of you. I would have bet good money she'd be the first back there to see Ali."

I smiled in her wake, knowing he was right. "Well, I made sure I had permission before I went. I've been roughed up enough for one night without having to take her on."

He chuckled and slapped my good shoulder. "Yeah, best to hang onto that one good arm if you can. I think my little girl might find some comfort in it when this is all over. Let's grab a cup of coffee while you fill me in."

I ducked my head into the waiting room to ask Spencer to join us, but the room was empty. I checked my phone and discovered he'd sent a text. *"Going out front to wait for Gran. She'll be here soon, and I don't want her terrorizing the staff looking for us."*

I shook my head and sent him a reply wishing him luck, then headed to the cafeteria.

~

AFTER FINDING THE cafeteria and procuring a decent cup of coffee from the bored cashier, Jeffrey and I sat at one of the booths and I told him everything the doctor said. After that, he asked about the fire, why Ali was there, how it started. I explained why she'd gone back to the house, but the rest was still a mystery.

He studied me thoughtfully for a while, sipping his coffee. Placing the nearly empty cup on the table between us, he pointed to my shoulder. "How'd that happen?"

"I had to bust through the back door to get to her." I avoided his penetrating stare and attempted to shrug it off with my uninjured arm, pain lighting through the other one though I hadn't moved it.

"Must have been one damn strong door to do that. Or one damn determined man."

I remembered the pop that had accompanied my injury, wincing. "It was a good dose of both. The door was oak, solid and reinforced." I sighed, gingerly touching my shoulder "Built it myself out of an antique farm table, and I built it to last."

He pursed his mouth in a solemn smile. "From the look on your face, I'm guessing that thing meant a lot to you." I nodded.

"How many times did you hit it after you did that to your shoulder?"

I thought back and couldn't recall. "I'm not really sure. I just kept going until it gave way."

"How bad did they say the injury is? Anything broken? Dislocated?"

"No idea, I haven't had it checked yet. I'll let them look at it in the morning."

He narrowed his eyes. "You'll let them look at it right damn now, son, or you and I are going to have a problem."

I bristled, not liking his tone one bit. "I'm not letting them touch me until I know Ali is okay. It'll wait."

"And if waiting causes irreparable damage? Then what? You plan to carry my daughter over the threshold with one arm?"

"Carried her out of a burning house with one arm, didn't I?" I growled.

He sat back and glared at me a minute before breaking into a smile. Chuckling, he said, "Damn if the two of you aren't perfect for each other. She's a stubborn one, too." He held up a finger, sobering, "But I know she'll give me hell if I don't look after you while she can't. So, as soon as she peeks one eye open, you're getting checked out, or you're going to have to fight me one-handed. And, son, I fight dirty."

Much as I tried to resist, the fatherly lecture made me smile.

ALI'S MOTHER CALLED Talia just before midnight to say she and Holden were two hours out. I didn't ask for the particulars, but I gleaned from Talia's side of the conversation that they had been out of town. It was also apparent that Talia wasn't particularly fond of the woman, given the near constant eye rolls and general air of exasperation while they spoke.

I hoped for Ali's sake that the woman would step up and act like the mother she deserved, even if only for one night.

And I'd deal with Holden later.

Ali was my priority, now and always. The rest be damned.

Between Spencer and I, we managed to charm the nurses into letting us all take turns at Ali's bedside. Brant texted to say his flight was delayed, but he'd be there by morning if he had to rent a damn helicopter and figure out how to fly it himself.

Brilliant as he was, there was a good chance he could do it.

Gran showed up mid-way through the night, scowling and blaming Vanessa for her tardiness. Apparently, Vanessa hadn't been able to drop everything to drive her right away, causing her and Gran to have words. From the weary, defeated look on my aunt's face, it had been a long damn ride.

I hugged them both and gave them the run-down on Ali's condition, pausing to introduce them to Jeffrey when he stepped back into the waiting room. He greeted them warmly and signaled to me, letting me know it was my turn to sit with her. Gran still looked distraught despite being told that Ali's oxygen levels were improving, so I told her to go on ahead. She and Vanessa had come a long way, and I wasn't going to make them wait.

When Gran returned a few minutes later, Vanessa silently stood and walked out of the room, Gran pointedly not looking at her. I walked over and put my good arm around Gran, squeezing reassuringly as I steered her toward the table where Spencer and Jeffrey sat quietly talking. I kissed her forehead and told her, "You need to quit snapping at Vanessa. She was probably on duty tonight and had to find a replacement. It's not her fault. Okay?"

Gran huffed indignantly and pouted, saying nothing.

I somehow resisted the urge to strangle her. "I'm not asking, Gran. I'm telling you. I don't need this shit tonight. No one here does. We're here for Ali, and she's what's important. So suck it the hell up or go home. I won't have your dramatic streak upsetting Ali." I stood and walked out of the room, unwilling to put up with her childish behavior a moment longer. It was the first time I could ever recall giving Gran an ultimatum.

I needed to see Ali, needed the calming affect her presence had on me.

I stepped through the doors of the ICU, garnering a pointed stare from the nurse. She didn't say anything, but I knew we were on thin ice as it was and having two visitors in the room was pressing our luck. I smiled my most charming smile and told her we were swapping out not doubling up.

When I closed in on Ali's 'room', I nearly ran into Vanessa as she made her exit, clutching a tear-soaked tissue. She and Ali weren't close, having only met the one time, so I had a hunch that her tears were mostly about Gran. I pulled her into a hug and softly shushed her, telling her everything would be alright. Whether Gran had gotten there five minutes ago or five hours ago, there was nothing she could do to help. None of us could do anything but wait. Ali had to do this on her own, and she was going to come through with flying colors.

I had no doubt in my mind that she'd recover twice as fast as expected, it was just the way Ali was made.

Overachiever to the core.

I CAME AWAKE slowly, feeling disoriented. Faint remnants of my dream lingered at the edge of my awareness, images of flames and smoke, and the sound of Ali's screams. I didn't get to her in time in the dream, the door was too strong, like steel that I battered myself against until I was broken and bloodied. Instead of saving her, I feebly pounded on the oak barrier with bloody hands as I listened to her screams.

The soothing sensation of fingers running through my hair made me want to drift back to sleep. I'd dozed on and off all night, each time fighting flame-filled nightmares as I lay huddled in the waiting room, letting everyone get their turns visiting. But I wasn't in the waiting room as the warm hand stroked my disheveled hair, lulling me back into a warm floating state somewhere between consciousness and oblivion.

When I realized where I was, I sat up with a jolt, surprised when Ali's green eyes greeted me. They'd taken the breathing tube out hours ago, but Ali had remained unconscious. I'd fallen asleep slumped over the edge of her hospital bed, her scraped hand held carefully in mine.

Seeing her shining eyes blinking back at me, I launched myself at her, folding her into a tight hug that had my arm screaming in protest. She gasped and coughed in my arms, and I released her immediately, embarrassed at my impulsive actions. "Sorry, baby." I scanned her face for signs of discomfort. "Are you in pain? Do you need me to call the nurse?"

She tried to speak but only emitted a jagged croaking sound, wincing and putting a hand to her throat.

"It's okay. Don't talk. I'll see about getting you something to drink." I pressed a chaste kiss to her parched lips. "Your parents are here. Talia, Gran, Spence, Vanessa, Teach — the whole gang. Even Brant flew in from Charleston. I need to let them know you're awake. Who do you want to see first?" I paused. "Or would you rather they come back later?"

She shook her head, tears welling in her eyes at the mention of all the people gathered here for her.

I cupped her cheek and smiled. "We love you, Ali. Where else would we all be?" I tipped her chin up and kissed her again. "I'm thinking you either want your dad or Talia first, which is it?"

She mouthed the word 'Dad' and I stood to leave, excited to tell everyone she was awake. Her gaze fell on the sling across my chest, and her hand shot out, stopping me. She raised a brow and pointed at it, expecting an explanation. I shrugged my good shoulder and told her not to worry before setting out to find the others.

As soon as I told the packed waiting room the good news, everyone jumped up at once, vying for the first spot at her side. I chuckled and held up my hand, staving off the stampede. "Whoa, whoa. Not all at once." I surveyed the crowd and pointed. "Jeffrey, you're up first." Everyone seemed to respect the decision, well, everyone except Ali's mom who scoffed indignantly before plopping down on the industrial looking couch in the far corner, the furthest she could get from her ex-husband.

Holden had been noticeably absent, allegedly downstairs taking care of important business all night. Eileen, Ali's mom, went on and on about how inconvenienced they were by the need to return to Virginia, saying her husband was repairing the damage done by their hasty departure.

I didn't buy that for a second, though. He was avoiding my partners and me — and for damn good reason.

He may have also been avoiding Ali's dad. From what I'd gathered, there was no love lost there either.

Jeffrey smiled as he approached. "Good call, son. I was going no matter what, and I'm sure you remember what I said about fighting dirty." He winked and tugged me out the door with him. "I also remember saying something about kicking your ass if you didn't get checked out. She's awake... now go do what I told you." His tone brokered no argument, so I grudgingly left Ali in the capable hands of our family.

Our family.

Odd as it was to think of them all that way, it fit.

~

NOTE TO SELF: Refusing pain medication when someone is forcibly snapping your bone back into place is a bad fucking idea. Especially when it takes multiple tries. If the flash of white light I saw was any indication, the bastards tried to kill me.

The only good news was that the pain was greatly reduced once the bone was back in its proper place. One more round of x-rays to be sure it was seated properly, a fist full of ibuprofen, and I was on my way back to Ali's room.

I'd just exited the elevator on her floor when Spencer rounded the corner and gave me a cautious glance. "You okay, shithead?"

"It's nothing a few weeks in a sling won't cure but next time I'm driving the damn truck through the front of the house. Resetting? Yeah, not fun." I cocked a brow as he fell into step beside me. "Remember those old action movies where the hero would dislocate his shoulder and then reset it by slamming it into the nearest wall?" He gave me a sly smile and nodded. "Yeah, I used to think that was so cool when I was a kid. Know what I think now? Bull. Shit."

He laughed briefly and stopped, putting a hand on my uninjured arm. "I'm glad you're alright, but I kind of wish they would have doped you up."

"What the hell for?"

He glanced down the hall, an unreadable expression on his face. "Because Lauren just showed up asking to see you and Ali."

Well, fuck. Maybe a little Valium or something wouldn't have been a bad idea

Luckily, everyone else had gone down to the cafeteria before Lauren's arrival, so she hadn't had a chance to alienate our family. Spencer headed off to join them, trusting me to handle the situation with tact, if only for Ali's sake. I entered the waiting room and wordlessly motioned for Lauren to follow me.

I resented her showing up here, but Ali insisted on hearing what she had to say. One look at Lauren's subdued expression told me I didn't want to hear a damn thing from her. If she was here to start trouble, she'd fucking regret it. Now wasn't the time for her attention-seeking.

The sound of her footfalls behind me grated on my nerves, and I was on the verge of sending her away despite Ali's wishes when she cleared her throat and said, "Thank you for this. I know you both hate my guts, but I wouldn't be here if it weren't important." Something in her tone gave me pause. She sounded... remorseful.

I turned to look at her, but she dropped her head and stepped into Ali's newly-appointed room ahead of me.

Not liking that she was standing so close to Ali, I circled the bed and took Ali's hand, pinning Lauren with a stoic look. Ali squeezed my hand but otherwise ignored me as she spoke to the woman who had been making her miserable for months. Her voice was hoarse and gravelly when she spoke. "Hello, Lauren. Spencer said you wanted to speak to us." Her tone was cool but civil. "We've had a long night so I'd appreciate it if you could make this quick."

Lauren didn't flinch at the insinuation that she wasn't welcome. Instead, she dropped her head slightly and nodded. "I understand. I just wanted to come here to let you know it wasn't me."

Ali's frown matched my own.

She was really coming here to discuss the break-in now? I narrowed my gaze on her and asked, "Don't you think this could have waited? The shit happened almost two months ago. We already asked you about where you were, and you lied."

She shook her head, looking between Ali and I. "No. I mean the fire. I just wanted to make sure you both were okay and tell you I had nothing to do with it."

Ali grasped my hand tighter, and a flicker of fear crossed her face. "Why would you think anyone would accuse you?" She turned to me. "Wasn't the fire an accident?"

"I haven't heard anything from the fire marshal, but I assumed so." I watched Lauren as she dropped into the chair by the bed, looking apologetic for the first time since I'd met her. "Why would you think otherwise, Lauren?"

She glanced between Ali and me, "Because of Keith."

You could have heard a fucking pin drop as we processed what she was saying. What his name implied.

I leaned forward, jaw clenched as I growled, "What would Keith have to do with the fire? And how the fuck would you know about it?" I had to let go of Ali's hand to keep from crushing it. A white-hot rage was boiling up inside me as the scenario in my head played out.

"Because I've been helping him."

Ali jerked back with an angry gasp, causing another wave of coughs that looked as painful as they sounded. Even Lauren reached up in an attempt to soothe her before I pushed her hand away and barked, "Don't you fucking touch her." Ignoring our uninvited guest for the moment, I picked up the foam cup beside the bed and offered Ali a sip of water. She sipped and coughed, sipped and coughed, until finally the spasms stopped.

When she settled back against the pillows, she looked over at Lauren, a wounded expression on her face. "Do you really hate me that much? I know you were never particularly fond of me, but to team up with him?" Her voice broke in a way that had nothing to do with her injuries. "Why?"

Lauren raised her arm and looked as though she wanted to reach for Ali's hand but thought better of it, dropping it back to her lap. "I don't hate you." She looked Ali in the eye and shrugged. "Okay, maybe I hated you a little. You had everything, and you acted like you didn't want it. Back in college I watched your rich mother climb out of a Bentley and beg you to go celebrate your twenty-first birthday with her. You shot her down and walked away like she was nothing. That's when I started really hating you. Before that, you were just annoying, soaking up all Teach's attention but when I saw you do that, I hated you." She looked up, eyes red as if she was fighting not to cry. "Some people would give anything for the chance to have a mother who cared that much."

Ali's face was unreadable. I wasn't sure whether she was ready to choke the woman or hold her fucking hand. She didn't comment, didn't tell Lauren how wrong she was about her parentage. Instead, she simply asked, "And Keith? How did that happen?"

For the first time since I'd known her, Lauren looked afraid. "He looked me up around the time you came here. He remembered me from college and knew I was Teach's niece. I didn't think much of getting a friend request from him but when he asked for my number, I had to admit that I was curious. Mostly because I knew the two of you had been together for years."

She sighed and gave a thin-lipped smile. "He was charming at first, we talked on the phone a lot, met once or twice for drinks." She raised a brow at Ali. "He liked to talk about how horrible you were to him and how he wanted to get even. Eventually, we decided that undermining you at the diner would be a fun way to make you miserable. He said you hated to admit mistakes, so he suggested I screw with the books, payroll, ordering, whatever you were in charge of so it made you look incompetent."

I leveled a lethal stare in her direction. "But you didn't stick to the diner, did you?"

She wouldn't look at me, knew there was no sympathy to be found with me, so she gave Ali a pleading look. "I didn't want to do that. By then, I didn't have a choice."

Now anger radiated off of Ali in waves. "No choice?" she croaked out. "No choice? Do you have any idea how much damage you've caused? Not just the things you've destroyed, things I can never replace, but what you did to Talia? How can you sleep at night?"

Lauren searched Ali's face, genuinely confused. "Talia? What did I do to Talia?"

Ali sneered, gripping the thin sheet in her fists. "The frame you broke from her bedroom? Did you notice anything other than my face? Did you not see the little girl in the picture with us? The only picture of that little girl in the whole apartment?" Tears streaked down her face as she shook. "The only picture Talia had here of the daughter she buried."

Seeing Ali's pain, and remembering Talia clutching that same picture in the waiting room the night before had my own eyes burning. The look on Lauren's face was one of shame and devastation. For once, I didn't think she was acting. She was genuinely remorseful, if only for Talia's sake.

"Oh, God. I didn't know." Her face crumpled, and tears streaked down her cheeks. "I swear, I didn't know. Keith was blackmailing me, and I only did what I did to keep him quiet." She wrung her hands and stared at the floor, repeating, "I swear, I didn't know. I remember her being pregnant back in college but I assumed the kid didn't live with her, like shared custody or something. I had no idea."

"No, I'm sure you didn't but you still knew what you were doing was wrong." I refused to feel sorry for her. "So, what did Keith have on you? Catch you out stealing puppies?"

She shook her head, wiping away guilty tears and meeting my gaze. "Not to be a bitch, but if I wanted to talk about it, he wouldn't have been able to use it against me now would he?"

"So you set out to destroy innocent people to save your own ass? Why am I not surprised?"

"I never said I was protecting myself. I'm not that narcissistic, despite what you must think of me." She wasn't being snarky, she was serious.

I'd only ever seen her act like she gave a damn about one

other person besides herself, one person to whom she was close enough that she would want to protect them.

Ali reached the same conclusion that I had, whispering, "Teach."

Much as I hated it, I could see the truth in Lauren's eyes when she nodded, swiping at the tears rolling down her face. "I had to choose, and I chose him." Her eyes shifted, and she stared out the window, seeming far away. "I know you think I'm some kind of monster, and I probably deserve that, but I'd never intentionally set out to hurt anyone. I did what I had to do to save my uncle. He's the only person in my life that matters anymore, and I wasn't putting him at risk."

Touching as her impassioned speech was, I needed fucking answers. "So, you think Keith started the fire? Why? How did things go from ransacking the apartment to attempted murder?" I just didn't see him having the balls to do something like that.

"I don't know for sure, but the things he was trying to get me to do were getting scarier and scarier."

"Scary how?"

She looked from my shoulder to Ali's injured leg, and dropped her gaze to the floor. "He wanted me to tamper with vehicles, slash tires and stuff like that. Then he asked if I knew what a brake line looked like..." She trailed off, frowning. "That's when I told him I was done. I refused to do anything that could physically harm anyone. He threatened to use what he knew, but I could tell he wasn't ready to give up his leverage. He thought he could coerce me into it, so he backed off for a while."

"And then?"

"He tried again, telling me that it was just meant to scare you and no one would get hurt. I told him to fuck off. He made a few threats and hung up." She looked me in the eye for the first time since she sat down. "That was three days ago. I haven't heard from him since."

Ali looked up at me, real fear in her eyes. "What if...?"

I ran my hand over my jaw, scraping along the stubble that had accumulated there as I paced the floor beside her bed. Had I pushed Keith too far? Was it possible that he'd wanted to torch the house to get even with me? I certainly couldn't rule it out.

Lauren sat with her back straight, and her eyes downcast, looking resigned to her fate as she picked at the hem of her skirt. I rounded the bed to stand beside her chair then thought better of towering over her like that, so I sat on the edge of Ali's bed. I still needed more information from this woman and intimidation was a good way to assure that I got nothing further. I had to play this very carefully. "Aren't you worried that telling us about this will put Teach in more danger than he already is? Why risk it?"

She looked past me to speak directly to Ali. "Because the fire scared the shit out of me. The thought that you could have died."

"Because you didn't want to be charged as an accessory to murder?" I asked.

"No, because she doesn't deserve to die for leaving an abusive piece of shit." She cast a scathing glance in my direction before refocusing on Ali. "I had no idea what you went through with him until he told me about the night Clay helped you outside the hospital." She swallowed thickly, giving Ali a sympathetic smile. "He told me what he'd done to you, tried to make it out to be your fault. I wasn't in a position to argue the point with him, but it made me physically ill to see the sickening gleam in his eye when he talked about how he hurt you. It was like he got off on remembering it."

An involuntary snarl escaped me, and she jerked in her chair. "Sorry. I guess you didn't need to know that." She timidly looked up at me. "And I'm sorry for what I did to you both that day in the parking lot. I know you think I enjoyed trying to destroy your relationship, but I didn't. And I think what you did, trying to save a stranger from a bad situation, was one of the most heroic things I've ever heard." She sniffed and turned to smile at Ali. "The world needs more people like that. That's why Teach is so important to me. He was my hero when I needed one and I won't let anyone hurt him because of that."

Ali reached out her hand on the bed beside me, and I started to take it in mine before I realized it wasn't my touch she sought. Stunned, I looked down at her slender fingers, an offering I wasn't sure Lauren deserved. Ali's eyes never left Lauren's, didn't waver or show the least hint of hesitation.

I watched from the corner of my eye as Lauren leaned forward and haltingly reached out her hand, obviously as disbelieving as me. Their hands joined together, and Ali placed her other hand over Lauren's in a gesture of comfort. "Lauren, I owe you an apology, too. I should never have slapped you like that."

Lauren shook her head vigorously, black strands flying. "No, you don't owe me anything. I deserved it."

"You're wrong," Ali said in her gravelly voice. "No one deserves to be hit. Not ever. And I of all people should never have forgotten that. I didn't deserve what Keith did to me, and you didn't deserve what I did to you. From the bottom of my heart, I apologize."

How the hell did that woman continually make me fall further in love with her? Just when I thought I couldn't love her more, she opened that amazing heart of hers, and I was falling all over again.

Hating to break up the love fest, I cleared my throat and waited for all eyes to swing my way. "We still have to figure out how to handle this. The police will probably be around sometime today to take statements, and they may have some indication about the fire's origins. I say we wait to see what they have to say before we assume anything was deliberate."

I turned to Lauren, hoping like hell trusting her was the right decision. "Do you have any texts, emails, voicemails, anything from Keith that we can use to prove his intentions?"

She shook her head. "No. He was careful about that. He always called me, always from a blocked number and never with any warning or regularity. It was like he didn't want me to be able to anticipate his calls. He just sort of flared up like a hemorrhoid."

An apt description if I ever heard one.

I looked back at Ali, who was wincing and sipping water from the foam cup left by the nurses. "Did you see or hear anything when you got to the house that was unusual? Was anything out of place or were there any signs that someone had been there?"

The straw between her lips began pulling air as she emptied the cup, and Lauren jumped up to refill it from the pinkish pitcher on the tray table. Watching her thoughtfully, Ali shrugged. "Not really. Someone parked the stupid backhoe right up against the house but other than that..." Her head tilted to one side, a crease in her brow. "Now that I think about it, I thought I heard something when I was around the side of the house, cussing whoever parked it there and blocked the basement door."

"What did it sound like?"

"I don't know. There are so many little noises out there, critters all around, the wind in the trees, all noises that I was used to. Somehow this one noise was different. Maybe like the click of a door or something. I wasn't sure I heard anything, to be honest. It wasn't disturbing enough to keep me from grabbing the flashlight from my glove box and going into the house. Not a scary noise, just something that sounded out of place."

I nodded, filing that away for later. "What about when you got inside?"

She pursed her lips. "Nothing else, just the usual settling noises that houses make. I knew the electrician was making adjustments, so I didn't bother to try to turn on any lights, just followed my flashlight beam to the basement. It was almost dusk, and I knew there wouldn't be much light down there." Her expression darkened as she replayed it in her mind. "I'd hidden my surprise for you and Gran behind a stack of drywall in the far corner of the basement, so I went down to dig the canvases out. It took a few minutes because I was trying to crawl back there without damaging anything and juggling the light while I shifted the heavy drywall sheets out of the way. I stopped twice because I thought I'd cracked one of the sheets."

Ali cleared her throat painfully, and Lauren handed over her newly-refilled cup. She nodded her thanks and took a few sips before continuing. "It only took a few minutes. I got the paintings, slid the drywall back into position, and climbed the stairs. When I got to the top, though, smoke was rolling in under the door. I opened it, and the gust of air that came in made the flames in the living room flare in that direction. I was so startled that I jerked backward and slammed the door. I lost my grip on the knob and tumbled down the stairs." She looked down at the thick boot on her foot and ankle. "I think I must have hit my head or something because I blacked out for a while. When I woke up there was smoke everywhere. I tried to get to the window, knowing the door was blocked, but I couldn't climb up with my foot the way it was."

She was trembling all over with the memory, and I wished like hell I could fold her into my arms. I reached for her hand and found Lauren beat me to it, so I took hold of the other one. "I'm so sorry it took me so long to get to you."

She squeezed my hand and gave me a sad smile. "Stop that.

You're my hero. I just wish I could have gotten the paintings out of there. You would have loved them."

"I forgot to tell you, Spencer went back in for them. The fire chief cussed him like a dog and called him a moron, but he said there was no way he was leaving there without them." I brushed away the tear rolling down her cheek at his thoughtfulness. "He knew they were important to you. And that you are important to *me*."

Ali smiled softly, fresh tears streaming down her face as I turned to Lauren, wanting to get things back on track. "You need to think about getting Teach out of town for a few days, at least until we know what Keith is up to."

Ali squeezed the hell out of my hand, pulling my attention back to her. "Do you think he'd hurt Teach? I thought he was threatening to expose information not physically harm him." Lauren nodded in confirmation but looked afraid.

I glanced between them both. "Yes, but now that Lauren has defied him, he might be looking to do more damage. I don't think it's worth the risk. I'm going to make a few calls and find out where Keith has been the last couple days and, just as importantly, where the hell he is now."

Ali looked at Lauren, panicked. "Get him and Marilee out of here. Make up an excuse, lie, whatever you have to do. And you should probably go with them. Keith might decide to come after you directly."

Lauren started to argue, and I interrupted. "You two hash this out, come up with an excuse to get Teach out of town, I'll be right back." I stood to leave, kissing Ali's hand.

"You trust me alone with her?" Lauren sounded shocked.

I did my best to look at her without glaring, knowing the risk she took by telling the truth. "I guess I do. You didn't have to come forward, so I figure you aren't entirely evil." I softened the statement with a half-smile and left the room as the two of them started rattling off ideas to protect a common interest.

CHAPTER TWENTY

MOST OF THE GANG was in the waiting room when I got there. Noticeably missing were Eileen and Jeffrey. That was one reunion I was glad not to be invited to. Eileen had pointedly ignored me all night and was in a snit about not getting enough time with Ali since she awakened this morning. Drama was a passion for that one. I fleetingly wondered if she was still in contact with Keith but decided I'd pursue other avenues before resorting to conversation with that woman. I had a feeling she would lie anyway.

I told everyone Ali was resting and asked that she be given a little while alone, only Gran raised a doubtful brow at my explanation. She always knew when I was lying. I'd never sneaked one by her, ever, but she didn't call me out on it today and for that I was grateful.

I motioned for Spencer to follow me out and waited until we were in the elevator headed for the lobby to relay Lauren's admission. It was a good thing I had. He let out a string of curse words at a volume that would have gotten us all kicked out if we hadn't been alone in the elevator car.

The doors opened, and I took the lead, needing to get

outside for some fresh air. "I'm calling my PI to have Keith tracked down. I want to know where he is, where he's been, and where the fuck he's headed. And I want to know now. My guy has been digging into his involvement with the shit at GFS for a while, so he should be able to give me some answers." The automatic doors opened as I caught sight of myself in the reflection. Jeez. I looked like shit. I turned to say something to Spencer and saw that he'd stopped just outside the doors, an odd expression on his face. I walked back over and asked what the hell was wrong.

He looked at me with wide eyes and asked, "What if it wasn't Keith? Marissa has been awfully fucking quiet lately. What if it was her?"

Oh, right. I hadn't gotten a chance to tell him. "No. Marissa isn't going to be a problem anymore, for any of us."

He looked at me warily. "What do you mean? Did you do something?"

"Yeah. I fixed my mistake. Trust me, she's going to stay the fuck out of our lives. There's no way she set the fire."

He eyed me with suspicion and tapped his foot, getting pissed off and wanting answers, so I told him. "She said she'd release the video of us at the office, right? She threatened to label you as a letch, too." He nodded impatiently. "Well, I sent her a little counter offer. She backs off, and I don't turn her in to the cops for trying to run me down with her damn car."

"You have no proof of that."

"I have footage from my home security cameras. I held onto it just in case she decided to come calling again." I grinned at the expression on his face. Was that what he looked like impressed? I thought so. "Needless to say, when presented with the possibility of jail time, she wasn't feeling as litigious."

"Why didn't you tell me about the tape before now?"

"Marissa asked the same thing. I told her that since I'd been out of town, I was unaware of the particulars of the lawsuit until recently and, once I was up to speed, I thought it was time to put an end to the bullshit." I shrugged innocently. "As far as telling you, there was nothing to tell. Absolutely nothing."

He studied me for a beat and said, "You mean you bluffed her? There was never a tape?" I couldn't tell if he was pissed, or proud.

"Yeah. I didn't even install my new security system until after she tried to turn me into a speed bump, but she doesn't know that. She was so scared she deleted her copy of the footage from the office and dropped the suit. I had her overnight paperwork verifying that, of course. I guess she figured even Shepard's money couldn't erase that tape."

As if speaking his name had conjured him, Holden Shepard came casually strolling across the parking lot.

He looked totally nonplussed in his tailored suit, the slight sheen of the fabric reminding me of a snake's skin, and he walked with an air of authority that only came from a lifetime of self-importance.

I stared him down as he approached, the set of my jaw letting him know I was less than impressed.

The automatic doors swishing closed at my back barely registered until Brant stepped to my side, his eyes following mine. Shepard's arrival snuffed out any attempt at conversation.

I stood there rigidly as the bastard took his time sizing me up, totally oblivious to Spencer and Brant, who flanked me protectively. His attention never wavered from me as he spoke. "I assume you know who I am, given your recent correspondence." There was an edge to his voice that belied his anger though he gave no outward signs.

Spencer and Brant stood there looking like they knew exactly what was going on though neither was privy to what I'd done. Looking him dead in the eye, I stood my ground, "And I assume you finally realized who you were dealing with when you opened that *correspondence*."

Apparently, he'd decided not to directly acknowledge the contents of the envelope I'd sent. Photos my investigator had obtained for me of Marissa 'paying' Shepard for his help. Most of which occurred with her head in his lap. Luckily for me, his face was much more recognizable than hers.

He huffed softly. "I suppose you think I'm concerned about your little threats? But what would Alison say about you breaking up her mother's marriage?" His cocky smile told me that, like so many others, he didn't know Ali at all.

"Actually, she said it would serve you both right. Eileen would lose her loveless marriage, and you would lose half your shit. No prenup, Holden? Rookie mistake for a man of your standing." Being addressed by his first name obviously rankled, that was exactly why I'd used it. I leaned a little closer, brandishing a cocky smile of my own. "She also saw the pictures and wasn't at all impressed. Guess money can't buy everything, huh?" I was surprised that Ali hadn't wanted to expose the affair to her mother, but she reminded me that Eileen expected certain 'eccentricities' and probably wouldn't leave him anyway. Luckily for us, Shepard didn't know that.

He almost succeeded in hiding his fear, almost.

Spencer cut in, speaking to me but never turning his eyes from Shepard. "Surely you're mistaken about the prenup, Clay. A cutthroat business man such as our friend here would never forget a thing like that."

Shepard spared him a fleeting glance as one might acknowledge a gnat hovering at the edge of their vision, but returned his attention to me without comment.

I nudged Spencer in a conspiratorial way and said, "Oh, I'm sure he thought about it after the fact, but he was in such a hurry to steal Eileen from the man who she was engaged to — Holden's business rival — that once he had her on the hook, he whisked her off to Vegas before common sense had a chance to set in."

There was a flicker of genuine hatred in Shepard's eyes before his mask slipped back into place.

Apparently, Spencer saw it too because he snickered softly. "Maybe he's not the formidable opponent everyone thinks him to be. I mean, hasty decisions don't work out for him as evidenced by his lack of forethought in his marriage, but meticulous planning hasn't worked out well for him lately either. He had quite a few months to work on his little plan to bring us down and look how that turned out. Here we stand, three nobodies who currently have him by the short-and-curlies. That must be a real blow to his pride."

Shepard's fists were clenched at his sides, and I could practically hear his blood pressure skyrocketing.

It was glorious.

Brant cleared his throat, drawing Shepard's attention. "And just so you know, it was never going to happen. Ever. I'd sooner sleep in a viper's nest than do business with you."

Spencer stepped in, nodding. "That contract was never going to be enforced. Ever. No matter how or why it was broken. We'd rather stand shoulder to shoulder with Clay on a sinking ship than cruise away with you on your fancy yacht. We wouldn't leave our company and we damn sure wouldn't walk away from our brother. Not for your money or anything else, you smug bastard. That's what friendship is. And, for all your business savvy, that's something you wouldn't have a fucking clue about."

I wanted to take pleasure from the indignant huff Shepard uttered as he walked away, but all I could do was stand there in awe of my partners. My friends. My brothers.

I was so much luckier than I ever realized.

Brant nudged my shoulder. "Blackmail, huh? I'm impressed."

Spencer chuckled, stepping over to the courtyard vending machines and getting the three of us water. "Why didn't I think of that?"

"You're too damn scrupulous for your own good," I observed, heading for the small garden area to our left. A large flowerbed filled with deep reds and purples sat at the center of the space, a small koi pond in the middle. Tall, boxy shrubs created a circular border, blocking out most of the parking area from view. "Luckily for us, I'm still capable of being an asshole when necessary."

"Good to know falling in love didn't take that from you." He teased, sitting on one of the stone benches that flanked the flowerbed and taking a long drink from his water bottle.

"Yeah. I'm hoping marriage won't either."

Spencer choked and sputtered, spitting water everywhere just as I anticipated.

Brant just laughed and slapped my back.

Yeah, I was still an asshole.

SPENCER AND I stayed outside for a while making phone calls and trying to track down Keith. My investigator was having no luck so far and whoever the hell Spencer was speaking to in a hushed voice was having no luck either. It was like the bastard had fallen off the face of the Earth.

We should be so lucky.

Frustrated, I told Spencer to keep trying while I went to talk to Ali. When I got back to the room, Ali was trying to convince Talia to go home to D.C., knowing she had an event scheduled at her restaurant that night. Thinking that the best thing for everyone would be to leave Denson for a few days, I had to concur. We eventually wore her down, and she grudgingly left with strict instructions that she be provided with regular updates.

Once we were alone, I suggested to Ali that we go spend a few days with Gran after her discharge from the hospital, using the excuse that we had been going there anyway, and now we needed to decide how to proceed with the build. There was still no word from the fire marshal on the cause of the blaze, but I didn't need to know how it started to know that it was a total loss. Ali was hesitant to leave, as I knew she would be, but mentioning the house stopped her objections. She would want to help Gran and I come up with a plan. It was a dirty trick, but I didn't give a damn. She had to get the hell out of town until I could find out how the fire started and where the fuck her psycho ex had disappeared to.

I had just finished telling her that I was stepping out to talk to Gran about our visit when Eileen walked into the room. The scathing glance she tossed my way indicated her displeasure with what she'd heard. Her expensive heels clicked on the tile floor as she sauntered over and took Ali's hand. Her unwrinkled wrap dress and perfectly styled hair seemed out of place; cold somehow given the situation. Maybe I would have respected her more as a mother if she'd looked disheveled and haggard, or at least given some outward sign that nearly losing her daughter had shaken her even a little.

She looked down at Ali, raising a perfectly plucked brow as she surveyed her only daughter. "Why would you go stay with strangers when you can come home with Holden and me? We have your room all ready and an entire staff to look after you. You wouldn't have to lift a finger."

Of course she would assume Ali needed a damn staff. I'd only known her a few months, and even I knew better than that. How did this woman not know her child at all? I watched with thinly veiled distaste as she smoothed Ali's hair back and tried to wipe a smudge of soot that was still on her face. The gesture was awkward and obviously unnatural to her. Was she putting on a show for my sake? Even Ali looked surprised at her behavior. "Mother, why are you acting so oddly?" Ali reached for me, so I walked over and slipped my fingers through hers, locking them together in a show of support. "You haven't even spoken to Clay since you walked in. Isn't it somewhere in your etiquette handbook that it's rude to ignore someone's presence? Have you even bothered to speak to him this whole time while I was being treated?"

She pursed her lips but said nothing, knowing Ali didn't need verification.

Ali blew out a frustrated breath and pulled away from her mother's hand. "Mother, this is Clay McGavran. Clay, this is my mother, Eileen Shepard."

Eileen scowled but offered a manicured hand in my direction, looking less than impressed. "Ah, yes, I remember. The construction worker." She sniffed rudely. "Ali has mentioned you in passing, I believe."

I shook her hand quickly and made a point of wiping my hand on my pants when I answered. "Yes, I believe I was there when she told you about me." I quirked a suggestive brow just to piss her off. "Sorry if my hands are rough. It's the price you pay when wielding a BFH all day."

I could see Ali smirking out of the corner of my eye when Eileen took the bait. "And what exactly is a BFH?" She asked coolly.

I cocked my head to the side, hoping to look confused. "I thought you would have been able to glean that from what Ali told you. A BFH is a big hammer. I'll let you figure out where the 'f' factors in while I go make arrangements for our stay at my grandmother's. If you need help figuring it out, ask your daughter. She knows all about it." I leaned down to kiss Ali briefly, and she nipped my lip playfully, thoroughly entertained by my interactions with her mother. I nodded to Eileen on the way out and told her, "Thanks for the offer to take Ali in, but I think she'll be better cared for by us strangers."

GRAN AND VANESSA were still lingering at the hospital, waiting to find out when Ali would be discharged. I tracked them down to the cafeteria and got myself a cup of coffee before joining them at their table. Vanessa seemed to be faring better this morning, so Gran must have taken my threats seriously.

They inquired about Ali's condition, and I told them what I had in mind, leaving out the part about Keith and the possibility that the fire was intentional. No need to worry them unnecessarily. When I suggested that we stay at Gran's for a few days, the two women eagerly agreed and started planning everything from the dinner menu to what clothes Ali would want to bring, volunteering to pack our things for us so that we could leave immediately. It was nice watching the two of them chat animatedly about all the things we could do while visiting and joke about how Daniel, who was with his father for the weekend, was going to fawn all over Ali when he returned.

Seeing them back on solid ground made me happy.

I gave them the entry code for the cabin, telling them to go get some rest and hash out the details over dinner. There was no way Ali was leaving the hospital at least for one more day so I didn't see the need for everyone to cram themselves into that tiny waiting room another night. I hugged them both and set off to look for Jeffrey, hoping he was more receptive of my plans than his ex-wife had been.

It made no sense to me that the two of them had once been married. They say opposites attract but damn...

On my way up to Ali's room, I ran into Lauren. She had gone back home to work on getting Teach out of town for a few days, and I assumed by her reappearance that she had been successful. She smiled tentatively as she joined me in front of the bank of elevators, and I returned the gesture. It was unsettling to be in this position, to look at her as a possible ally. I couldn't be sure of her intentions, but I could find nothing in her admission that would benefit her in the long run. She had a lot to lose by talking to us. Did she do it just to keep from being implicated in the fire? I had no way of knowing for sure, so I wasn't ready to trust her yet. I'd never be foolish enough to tell her so, though.

Keep your friends close and your enemies closer. Words to live by.

The doors opened and the accompanying ding startled Lauren, who jumped slightly before stepping ahead of me into the elevator car. She turned and waited for me to select Ali's floor before speaking. "I guess I could just tell you what's going on instead of bothering Ali again." She cleared her throat softly, looking nervous.

I stepped back a bit, realizing that the close quarters might make my size and deep voice intimidating. "Whatever you feel comfortable with, though I'm sure Ali will want to see you. She's just as concerned about your uncle as you, so it's not a bother to have you stop by, I assure you."

She nodded lightly and gave a half smile. "While we have a moment alone, I'd like to apologize for the way I've treated you these last few months. Starting with the first time I saw you at the diner. I can't blame any of that on Keith. That was me being a bitch, plain and simple, and I'm sorry. You took great care not to be hurtful when you refused my advances, and I should have appreciated your tact instead of acting like a bitch."

This was one of those conversations that got guys in fucking trouble. I, in no way, wanted to encourage her to think that I was interested in her. A lot of women made statements like that just to flesh out a compliment and, despite my dislike for her, I felt somehow obligated to tell her she wasn't a bitch. Of course, it's even more complicated when I know damn well that's exactly what she'd acted like.

Fuck. Me.

I should have taken the damn stairs.

I decided to go with the less-is-more approach. "Apology accepted." I nearly sighed in relief when she nodded and thanked me, not saying anything more.

We exited the elevator, and I sent her on ahead while I went to talk to Ali's dad. I found him in the waiting room, smiling down at his phone as he typed out a text. I stood silently watching until he hit send and looked up, his expression a mixture of guilt and embarrassment. "How long you been standing there?"

I ignored his question and started telling him about my plans to take Ali away for a few days. He was no fool and immediately asked if there was something going on that he needed to know about. I shook my head and answered as honestly as I could without heaping more worry on the man. "Nothing concrete but I'm not willing to put Ali at risk while I wait for answers." I held his eye and made it clear from my expression that I wasn't going to elaborate further.

He looked ready to argue but seemed to think better of it, saying only, "If I can't trust the guy who carried my daughter out of a burning building to keep her safe, who can I trust?" He stood and shook my hand, reaching across to slap my good shoulder. "You do what you have to do, but I expect to be kept apprised of the situation. Remember what I said about fighting dirty?"

I smiled and nodded. "Yes, sir."

By that evening, most everyone had said their goodbyes and went their respective ways. Only Gran and Vanessa remained, and I had to practically chase them back to the cabin after their early evening visit. Their visit included bringing a large batch of homemade soup for Ali intended to soothe her raw throat. Gran said hospital food was designed to make a person sicker, their way of assuring repeat business according to her theory. She and Vanessa fussed over her like two mother hens, and it warmed my heart to see her glow under their attention.

Strangers, my ass.

Those two had done more to make her feel loved in the span of that one visit than her own mother had in a lifetime. She was family whether she realized it or not. And she would continue to be, whether Eileen liked it or not.

Once we were finally alone and all the noise of the day faded, I carefully crawled into the narrow bed, lying on my undamaged shoulder and mindful of her injuries. I should have stayed in the reclining chair the nurses had brought in, but I needed to be near her. I needed us in the same bed even if the only thing keeping me from falling out on my ass was the cold metal rail pressed against my back.

Maybe if I could feel her next to me, the nightmares would stop.

I held myself up on my elbow, head resting against my palm as I watched her dozing; her labored breathing was a constant reminder of how close I'd been to losing her. I shifted myself as close as possible, wanting to reach her exposed arm with the fingers protruding from my sling. It wasn't the most comfortable position in the world, but I was willing to suffer for the connection.

I kept my touch light and slow, my eyes never leaving her face as I grazed her forearm with my fingertips. After a while she shivered, and gooseflesh spread across her skin. I fumbled with the thin blanket until I managed to cover her up then stretched out beside her and drifted off to the sound of her breathing and the faint smell of smoke in her hair.

THE DOCTORS RELEASED her the next morning, cautioning her that she needed to limit physical exertion for a while since she could be prone to loss of breath while her body healed. That statement had been followed by a pointed look in my direction and a lot of blushing on Ali's part.

We would both have to stop by the police department to make statements before we left for Gran's, but I knew Ali would want to go back to the cabin first to clean up and pack. She'd politely refused Gran and Vanessa when they offered to pack for her though I knew the offer had been appreciated.

I went to pull the truck around while Ali groused at the nurse who was insisting that she be escorted out in a wheelchair, causing her stubborn streak to flare. She would have to get used to needing help, at least for a little while. I was hoping that a few standoffs with Gran would resign her to it and save me a lot of arguments over the next few weeks. We both needed to recover, and we were going to do it together.

I had to bite back a laugh when I drove up to the front doors and saw her sitting in a wheelchair with a sour expression, rolling her eyes at the nurse who stood beside her holding a crutch. Damn, this was going to be fun.

I helped her up into the cab and thanked the nurse before climbing back behind the wheel. "You ready to go, Miss Walker?"

She nodded, breathing heavily as she rolled down the window for fresh air. The breeze blew her hair in all directions, and she looked like it was the best feeling in the world. Pushing the strands from her face, she turned and smiled at the array of flower assortments and gifts in the back seat, presents from our families and her friends at the diner. There was enough to fill the floorboard and the entire seat. "It looks like the get well gifts multiplied since last night." She beamed, looking touched by the display.

"That's because they stopped me on the way out to give me the ones that they hadn't had a chance to bring up to you yet. More flowers and cards and stuffed animals, though I forget where they all came from."

She reached back and plucked an item from the pile, smiling. "I haven't had a teddy bear since I was a little girl." She read the tag and hugged it to her chest. "From my dad."

I couldn't help the chuckle that escaped me as I thought of him trying to sound like a hard-ass one minute, and picking out stuffed animals the next. I liked him already.

When I turned to tell Ali about his lecture, the look on her face gave me pause. She was staring down at the bear with an odd expression. Something crossed her features, a flicker of something I couldn't quite name which in turn morphed into her being suddenly excited. "Are there still wildlife cameras around the property?"

I frowned, not getting the connection at first. When I realized why she was asking, my whole body came alive with a shot of adrenaline. "Shit! Why didn't I think of that?" I changed course and stepped on the accelerator, the truck's diesel engine roaring beneath the hood as we shot forward, the force making me wince as my left shoulder protested. Funny how a random object can make you think of something so important.

Ali rubbed a hand over my bicep, not able to hold my hand since I was using it to drive. "You were a bit distracted. What with pulling me from a burning building, your injury, dealing with our family and friends... Plus, it's not like anyone else remembered the cameras. We've all been busy processing everything. Hell, it's been quite a while since I even checked them. The only reason it occurred to me was because of the teddy bear."

I definitely owed Jeffrey a beer when this was all over. No telling when or even if we would have thought of the cameras without his help.

"There are three cameras that might have gotten useful shots around the perimeter of the house. They're set up to start motion detection an hour before dusk, to avoid all the activity during the day." I glanced around the truck, sighing when I spotted my laptop, which was being used to weigh down the strings on Ali's balloons. I could check the memory cards on the spot, and if the pictures showed that bastard starting the fire, he'd better fucking pray the cops found him first.

∾

IT ONLY TOOK A few minutes to pull all the memory cards from the cameras, though it would have gone faster if I'd had the use of both hands. I hurried back to the truck where Ali sat anxiously waiting. I climbed into the cab and saw that she had already started up the laptop and was patiently holding out her hand for one of the cards.

Rather than try to take over, I handed her one and waited for her to insert it into the slot. After all she'd been through she deserved to be the one to see the images first.

The computer whirred to life, and a few seconds later a window popped up on the screen. From my angle, I wasn't able to make anything out, so I watched Ali's face instead, looking for any signs of recognition. She scrolled for a minute, brow furrowed in concentration before blowing out a sigh and asking for the next card. I handed it over and watched as she scrolled through another stream of pictures, not finding anything.

One card left.

I handed her the final memory card and tossed the others into the console while she waited for the pictures to load. Once again, she scrolled, and I kept my focus on her face. Just when I assumed this was another dead end, her eyes widened. Not in that slight way one does when they receive confirmation of something not altogether unexpected. No, not like that. This was a look of astonishment beyond anything I had ever seen. Incredulity was soon followed by confusion and fear.

"What? Ali, what the hell is it? Is it Keith?" My pulse was roaring in my ears, and the truck seemed suddenly claustrophobic as I watched her head turn toward me, her hand flying to her mouth.

There was something in her eyes right then that was dangerously close to pity, and my own fear was amplified by the thought. She didn't answer, just stared at me with unfathomable sadness as she turned the screen to face me. It was as if everything moved in slow motion, the breath in my chest feeling thick as molasses as I tried to expel it from my body. Inch by inch the computer turned, the glare of the late morning sun momentarily blinding me. I blinked the dark spots from my vision and rubbed my burning eyes, not entirely sure I wanted to reopen them.

When I did, I searched out Ali's face, needing one last moment before whatever was on that screen changed everything. She blinked back devastated tears as she held my gaze and whispered, "We'll get through it, I promise. I love you, Clay." Twin tears rolled down her cheeks. I followed their path with my eyes as they fell one by one onto her chest. The soft pink fabric of her tee shirt darkened as the salty tears soaked in and I kept my gaze moving, down, down, until the image on the screen was all I could see.

Oh, God, no.

No, no, no, no, no...

I closed my eyes to block out the pain and rage that tore through me like a wildfire, burning me alive from the inside out. When I reopened them, hoping against hope that I'd seen it wrong, the picture was unchanged.

Unmoved, unrelenting, undeniable.

Unforgivable.

CHAPTER TWENTY-ONE

I PARKED IN THE driveway at the cabin a while later, hurrying around to help Ali out. It frustrated me that I couldn't simply carry her into the house, but I'd been warned about my shoulder and the risk of it popping out of place again if I tried to overuse it. Anxious as I was to get her inside, I had to allow her to do this in her own time.

Slowing down to focus on her was the best thing I could do, for her and for me.

She wouldn't be running any marathons in her condition, but she made impressive work of that flight of stairs. Only a few minutes from start to finish, though she was definitely winded by the time she reached the second floor landing. I waited for her to clear the doorway and entered behind her, wondering where our visitors were lingering. I didn't have to wonder long.

Gran's voice rang out gleefully, followed a moment later by Vanessa's. They hugged and babied and fussed over Ali for a few minutes while I ran back to the truck for her purse, knowing she needed her medication. I reentered the living room to the sight of Gran propping Ali's booted foot on a pillow. I pulled a bottle of water from the fridge and brought over her pills, thanking Gran for her help and eyeing Ali carefully. "Here, slugger. Take these and I'll see if Gran here will help you get cleaned up while Vanessa and I unload the truck. That sound okay?"

Before Ali could respond, Gran was scurrying off to the master suite to start the shower muttering, "I'll find her some comfy pajamas, too, just give me a minute."

I sat on the coffee table beside Ali's foot and held her eye, saying nothing, aware that we weren't alone and hoping that she would know what I was asking without needing it vocalized. She glanced around, spying Vanessa in the kitchen, her back to us. She watched me intently and gave a slow nod, indicating her cooperation.

I stood and kissed her head, the smell of smoke that still lingered in her dark locks causing a tightening in my chest. Dropping my mouth to her ear, I whispered, "You're it for me, Ali. I love you."

When I lifted my head, Vanessa had walked back over and handed Ali a glass of ice to go with her water, a motherly smile on her face. It was sheer force of will that kept my voice even as I asked my aunt, "You ready to step outside? I've been anxious to talk to you."

I FOLLOWED VANESSA out to the driveway, eyes boring into the back of her head as she yammered on about inconsequential bullshit. When she reached the truck I asked her to start with the front passenger seat and waited for her to open the door, my arm protesting as my hands fisted involuntarily.

The door swung open, and Vanessa stepped in, the sound of her sharp gasp filling the air a moment later, indicating she'd seen the computer screen. My jaw clenched as I waited to see if she would have the guts to turn back and face me. I'd left the laptop on the seat, the picture from the game cam still open and zoomed in to show the detailed image of my aunt running away from the house just minutes before the flames started.

I could almost smell the damn fear wafting off of her. She didn't step back from the truck, choosing to remain obscured from sight by the door as she quietly said, "Clay, honey, I can explain. If you'll let me, I promise I can explain what happened."

Uh uh, not like this she isn't.

I stormed over to the truck and spun her around to face me, my chest heaving as I fought to control my anger. "You want to tell me what happened?" I growled. "I know what fucking happened. I saw what happened. How about I tell you what happened? How about I tell you how Ali fell down the basement stairs, breaking her foot and spraining her ankle as she went, or how it's a miracle she didn't crack her skull on the concrete. How about I tell you how she lay there in the darkness, her flashlight having broken when it hit the floor? How about I tell you what it felt like to see her crumpled there surrounded by smoke, or how I thought she was fucking dead when I found her? The only woman I have ever loved. Want to hear any of that?"

My whole body shook with the force of my rage. "Because that's all I see when I look at that fucking picture. I see her lying there motionless while I begged whatever God's would listen to please not take her from me. I see the moment when I dropped the rag from my face, deciding that letting the smoke overtake me would be infinitely better than having to live the rest of my life without her." The broken look on her face at my admission should have pleased me, but it didn't. Instead, it fueled my anger, making me want to lash out more. "Does your fucking explanation fix any of that? Will whatever bullshit excuse you feed me make the nightmares stop? The ones where

I'm lost in the smoke and I can hear her screaming, but I can't find her? The ones where I have to listen to her burning alive? Will any of that go away once you explain?"

She blinked back tears, hanging her head and not saying a goddamn word. I was just about to launch into another tirade when my phone chirped in my pocket. I recognized the distinct tone as a text from Ali. Ignoring Vanessa's sorrowful expression, I pulled the phone from my pocket and checked the message, my concern for Ali overriding every other emotion.

Getting in the shower soon. Remember, if we could give Lauren the chance to explain herself, Vanessa should get the same consideration. She's still your aunt. I love you.

Dammit! Why must she always be the voice of reason?

I looked up at my aunt, trying hard to keep Ali's reminder at the forefront of my mind. Vanessa turned and closed the laptop, still wincing at the sight of herself in the picture. I decided I would make the effort, if only because Ali asked me to. She'd earned the right to call the shots on this one so I would honor her wishes.

Running my hand over my hair, I stepped back and motioned for Vanessa to follow, turning and setting off for the backyard without waiting to see if she was behind me. When I reached the seating area by the pool, I pulled out a chair and pointed to it, taking the one across from it. "You have five minutes, so make them count. And you owe them to the woman you nearly killed because I wouldn't be listening to you without her prompting."

Vanessa settled into the chair and sat forward, arms on her thighs and hands clasped tightly together. She looked out toward the woods, her face wan and tired. "I went to the house to look for Rebecca's box. The one Gran left there for you." She sighed, looking defeated. "I thought there might be something in there, something Rebecca had with her the last time she was here, and I didn't want you to see it. I was afraid you'd misunderstand."

I narrowed my eyes, not liking where my mind had just gone, but I had to ask just the same. "Pictures. You were looking for the pictures, weren't you?"

She started, looking surprised. "You already saw them?"

"No, I heard my father on the phone the night Mom died. He was talking to his mistress about pictures and how Mom had thrown them in his face." I sat there in stunned silence as I watched her, finally able to choke out the words, "He was talking to you."

She blinked stupidly for a moment before springing from her seat like she'd been hit with a cattle prod. "What? No! Why would... how could you think that?" Her voice was high and alarmed, making me almost believe her. "I'm the one who gave Rebecca the pictures."

Wait, what?

She paced back and forth behind her chair, hands flying as she talked. "Your father was a disgusting pervert. Every time he got two seconds alone with me, he tried to hit on me. Rebecca didn't want to believe it at first, so I set it up to catch him on camera. A friend of mine took the pics. He tried groping me, kissed my neck a few times before I finally had enough. He made my damn skin crawl, but I had the proof I needed. I convinced your mother to let me have him followed, knowing in my gut that he was having an affair and probably more than one."

She stopped pacing and put her hands on the back of the chair, gripping so hard her knuckles were white. "I got the file back the day before the accident. I added the pictures of him coming on to me with the rest and called Rebecca to tell her everything was ready." Her chin quivered slightly, and her voice began to falter. "After you left for Spencer's the next day, she decided to come by and get the envelope so she could confront him that night." She wiped her eyes and came back to sit in the chair, looking exhausted. "No one ever saw the pictures after that, and I assumed your father had taken them. But when your Gran mentioned that box, I was worried that maybe they were in there. I didn't want you to find those pictures and assume the worst, so I went to look for the box while I knew you'd be gone."

Much as I wanted to hold onto my anger, it was starting to dim. Then a thought occurred to me that made it flare anew. "The fire... did you start it with one of your fucking cigarettes? Is that how it happened?"

She shook her head emphatically. "No. What kind of idiot do you take me for, Clay?" I gave her a sarcastic look, unmoved. "I honestly don't know what happened. I went in to look for the box, realized the lights weren't working, tried to turn on the main breaker, and heard a car outside. I hid in the pantry until it was clear and then took off. I never saw who came in, or where they went, and I definitely never saw any smoke or flames. Hell, I never even saw the stupid box."

There was nothing in her voice or body language that made me think she was being deceitful. I considered a moment, going over what she said. "You flipped on the breaker? The main breaker?"

"Yes. I flipped it on, but it kicked right back off. I don't know why." She shrugged helplessly. "I figured it was a safety feature or something, like maybe nothing was wired up to it yet."

A shuffling sound caught my attention, and I turned to see Ali stepping onto the patio, looking winded in the same clothes I'd brought her home in. I jumped from my seat and rushed over to help, not wanting her to take a tumble on the downward slope between the house and the pool. "I thought you were in the shower? How'd you get down here by yourself?"

She huffed indignantly and blew a few strands of hair out of her face, shifting her weight onto the crutch at her side. "I'm capable of getting around, maybe not fast, but I can still make it just fine on my own." She reached up and touched my face, fingers splaying over the stubble of my jaw, placating me. Stubborn ass woman. "And I didn't make it to the shower. Daniel called, and Gran has been on the phone with him for the last few minutes so I told her I was stepping out to check on you." She looked over at Vanessa, not a trace of resentment in her expression. "I thought you might like to talk to Daniel. I think he was asking for you."

Vanessa stood and took Ali's hand in both of hers, looking more sorrowful than I'd ever seen her. "Ali, I'm so sorry for my part in what happened. I shouldn't have been there, but I want you to know that whatever I did to start the fire, it was unintentional." Her tears ran anew as she pleaded. "I hope you know I'd never do anything to hurt Clay or you. I was there trying to protect him from something trivial and nearly cost him the most precious thing in his entire world."

My aunt turned to me, swiping at her tears and fighting for composure. "I'm sorry the door was destroyed, sorrier than I can begin to tell you. It must have been devastating to have to tear it down that way."

Watching Ali's eyes widen, I realized she hadn't known until that moment what I'd had to do to get to her. Her chin quivered slightly, and I cupped her cheek with my hand. "Don't be upset, Ali. I'm not. There's nothing more important to me than you. Hearing that wood splinter and crack gave me hope, urged me forward, toward you. It was the most satisfying thing in the world to be able to break it down, and I haven't regretted it or mourned the loss for even a second." A single tear rolled down her face, lingering at the corner of her mouth. I leaned in and softly pressed my lips to hers, kissing it away. "I told you, Ali. You're it for me. There's nothing in this world strong enough to stand between us. Past present or future."

Vanessa went back inside a few minutes later, and I finally convinced Ali to sit down. We settled on the lower level patio, needing to be shaded from the sun. We sat in silence for a while, just watching the trees sway in the muggy afternoon breeze. More accurately, Ali watched the trees, and I watched Ali.

Without looking my way, she said, "I heard you, you know, about the dreams." I sucked in a breath and closed my eyes, the mere mention of the nightmares sending a jolt of terror through me. I felt her hand on mine and grasped, blindly reaching for her as she said, "I was standing on the balcony upstairs giving Gran some privacy and that deep voice of yours kind of carries. I wasn't trying to eavesdrop, I promise, but I'm glad I heard that." She gave my fingers a squeeze, rubbing her thumb over mine. "Can I ask you a question?"

I opened my eyes and turned, her eyes sparkling like emeralds in the light. "You sure can."

"Did you have any nightmares last night after we were together in the hospital bed?"

I thought for a minute, trying to remember where I'd been when I awoke from each dream. "No, I don't think I did. The first was in the waiting room that first night. I must have dozed off for a few minutes. The others... They all happened either in the waiting room or when I was sleeping by your bed waiting for you to wake up."

She nodded, her soft smile radiant. "Looks like the best way to keep those dreams at bay is to have me sleeping by your side. Lucky for you, that's exactly where I intend to be."

I ENDED UP helping Ali with her shower, much to her relief. She said she liked Gran and everything but felt weird about having to take her clothes off in front of her. I got a playful smack to the back of the head for laughing at that. And several more smacks when I was overeager to help her wash certain areas.

She didn't like the idea of doing that with Gran around either, apparently.

Shit. It was going to be a long week if I couldn't get her over that little aversion. She might not be able to exert herself, but she could damn sure lay back and let me take her over the edge.

When she was all cleaned and dressed, She perched on the edge of the bed while I helped her pack. I wasn't sure where things stood with Vanessa, but I couldn't back out of the trip because of it. I was done running from difficult situations. We'd face it, deal with it, and move on, one way or another.

I sent Gran and Vanessa on ahead while Ali and I headed to the police station to give our statements. On the way there, Ali asked if we could stop by Teach's place to talk to Lauren. She wanted to let her know that Keith hadn't started the fire, hoping to relieve some of the woman's worry, I supposed.

Lauren had come up with a scheme to get her uncle and aunt out of town for a few days, and I gladly footed the bill, for everyone's peace of mind. They were spending the week at a Spa in Charlottesville, none the wiser about our erroneous assumptions.

When we arrived at the house, Ali asked me to stay in the truck, wanting to speak privately with her former nemesis. I wasn't crazy about the idea but thought better of tempting Ali's stubborn streak. I'd be dealing with it enough over the next few weeks while she healed, no need to make things worse.

It took every ounce of willpower I had to watch her struggle out of the truck and hobble up the front steps of Teach's single-story brick home. I had to keep reminding myself that I couldn't follow behind her like she was a child, waiting to catch her should she fall. She would tire of that quickly and, truth be told, I knew she could do it on her own. I just had to fight my natural instinct to protect her. It wasn't going to be easy. Not after the fire.

Lauren opened the door a moment later, looking hesitant to invite Ali in. They spoke for a while, and she opened the door wide, a grudging look on her face. Shit, I really hoped they weren't going back to that again.

Deciding to do something useful while I waited I pulled my laptop from under the passenger seat and opened it, intent on deleting the photos of Vanessa from the memory card. Ali was going to tell the police she was the one who tried the main breaker; we were pretty sure an electrical short caused the fire. She said there was no need to drag Vanessa into it when there was no ill intent, making it easier on everyone.

She was more selfless and forgiving than anyone I'd ever known. And she was mine. Would be mine forever, though she didn't know it yet.

I pulled up the file and started highlighting the pictures, dragging the cursor to the bottom of the screen. Just as I reached up to hit 'delete', the final three frames caught my eye.

Son of a fucking bitch!

I fumbled for a second, removing the highlighting from the pictures, afraid I'd accidentally delete the damn things before I got another look.

I pulled up the pictures, enlarging to full-screen. One by one I clicked through them, a fresh rage welling inside me. We'd never looked any further than the first few pictures, never thought we had a reason to.

I remembered then how Vanessa said she hadn't seen who came in, and she made no mention of seeing Ali's Jeep when she rushed out though it would have been easy to spot. She didn't see Ali's Jeep because it hadn't been Ali who she heard entering the house.

It had been Keith.

CHAPTER TWENTY-TWO

I SLAMMED THE laptop closed, my anger boiling to the surface. No one had seen that son of a bitch for days, my investigator still had nothing new to report, having been focused more on past transgressions than current activities, and I didn't like that one fucking bit. Ali needed to know, sooner rather than later. I couldn't sit still another minute, needed to get to her and get her the hell out of here. I'd give the memory card to the cops and let them have a shot at trying to locate him. God knew I wasn't having any luck.

Lauren needed to know, too. She'd pissed Keith off, and it looked like he was capable of just about anything at this point. I scrambled up the steps and knocked on the door, not waiting to be invited in. I closed the door behind me and called out in the empty foyer. "Ali? Lauren? Where are you?"

Ali's voice was halting, odd when she replied. "Um, we're in here. I'll be out in a minute. Go back to the truck."

Her answer had come from the back of the house. I considered what she'd said, not liking the tremor in her voice. "I need to talk to you, both of you, it's important." I didn't wait for her reply, heading in the direction her voice had come from.

I walked through the empty living room, past antique furniture and an entire wall of expensive bookshelves, neatly lined volumes filling them all. My boots made little sound on the plush carpet, sinking in slightly with each step. Normally, I would have removed them upon entering someone's home but I didn't have the time for such niceties today. There were far more pressing matters with which to contend.

When I turned a corner into the formal dining room, I spied Ali sitting stiffly in a wingback chair in a small seating area by the window. I started to speak as I stepped in her direction, noting Lauren in my peripheral vision. Before I could explain what I'd found on the card, a throat cleared behind me, the tenor distinctly male.

I spun around just as Keith stepped out of the shadows, having been partially obscured by a large china cabinet. His intense stare was hardly impressive but punctuated by the handgun he was holding by his thigh, it was enough to give me pause. "Glad you could join us. It would have been a shame for you to miss this."

There were still several feet of distance separating me from Ali. I risked a glance in her direction, looking for any indication of injury and subtly shifting my weight, hoping to inch my way closer.

"Not a chance, hero," Keith said, pulling Lauren along behind him with his free hand and standing behind Ali's chair. Lauren's whole body was stiff with fear, her eyes wide and pleading, silently begging me not to make him angry. There were faint streaks on both her cheeks, slightly gray from crying through her makeup. From the looks of it, she'd been crying for quite a while.

How long had he been here?

I held up my hands in a show of surrender — technically, the one in the sling just sort of looked like it was waving — unwilling to push him when he had such an advantage. Both of the women were at risk, and I fought to remain calm while my mind whirred with all the possible ways I could handle this. Nothing I came up with would end well. No matter how fast I was, he would have time to pull the trigger before I could get to him.

Not an option when he had more than one target to choose from. If it were just me, I'd risk it but I couldn't risk Lauren and I wouldn't risk Ali.

He held Lauren around the throat with his left hand, the gun held firmly in his right. He wasn't pointing it directly at any of us, but the threat was implied. I watched Ali glancing at the gun from the corner of her eye, heard her take in a shaky breath. "Just let them go, Keith. You've gone through all this trouble to get even with me, well here I sit. You win. You have nothing to gain from harming either one of them." She wouldn't look at me as she spoke, knew that I'd never leave her here.

Not while there's breath left in my body. No fucking way.

Keith snorted. "You're one conceited bitch, you know that? I wasn't even here today looking for you, you frigid cunt. I have a score to settle with Lauren. You showing up was just karma finally catching up with you. I could care less about you really, but I do intend to seize this opportunity since you're here." He lifted the hand holding the gun, stroking her cheek with the cold steel causing her to flinch. I started forward, intent on stopping him, willing to do anything to stop the look of terror on her face.

Keith jerked his head up and leveled the gun at my chest. "What did I tell you, hero? Stay where you are or I'll put just enough bullets in you to keep you subdued while I take your bitch for one last ride." His lip curled in a stomach churning grin. "Yeah, I'm sure you hate knowing I got to fuck her first. Maybe I should treat you to the live show, let you watch me bury my cock in her throat. She liked that, you know, sucking me off. She said it was her favorite way to make me come."

Ali snorted. "Yeah, because it took two seconds and I was in no danger of choking." She looked up at him with hate-filled eyes. "I could have whistled around the damn thing, stupid." His hand shot out, and he caught her across the face with the side of the pistol, her mouth gushing blood almost instantly.

"You son of a bitch!" I lunged forward, torn between reaching for her and ripping his goddamn head off. I made it two steps before the tip of the barrel touched my chest, stopping me cold. I glanced down at it, not giving Keith the satisfaction of eye contact. There were flecks of blood on the barrel, Ali's blood. I looked over at her, watching her cup her face while Lauren tried desperately to snag a cloth napkin from the table.

Keith snatched Lauren closer, cutting off her air. "Get the damn napkin. Slowly. And hand it to Alison. I don't want her bleeding all over me while I fuck her." I met his eye exactly as he'd wanted. He loosened his grip marginally, and Lauren's fingers took hold of the square of cloth, passing it across Keith's body to hand it to Ali. Once she was finished, Keith tightened his grip again, turning slightly to lick her cheek, his steely gaze on mine.

He wasn't putting his hands on them, either of them, even if I had to take a whole clip of bullets to stop him.

Ali had the napkin pressed to her face, coughing slightly. She was probably choking on her own damn blood. Goddamn it! I had to do something.

She dropped the towel to her lap, tilting her head back and testing the corner of her mouth with her fingers. Keith paid her little attention, his focus clearly on me. I held his unblinking stare, waiting him out, hoping he would give me just one brief moment to act. A flicker of light caught my attention, but I didn't look away, didn't want to make Keith aware of it. From the corner of my eye, I watched Ali's hand moving slightly beneath the discarded napkin. The sliver of light peeked out again.

Her phone!

She had her phone in her lap, hiding it from view while she called the police.

God, I wanted to kiss her right then, but I knew that making the call wasn't the same thing as having help. I had to get Keith talking, keep things calm for a while longer.

And I had to make damn sure he didn't spot that phone.

Eyeing Keith curiously, I asked, "How do you see this playing out? I mean, you must have a plan, right?"

That smug grin of his was back. "I've been thinking about that very thing. At first I thought you and your bitch showing up would complicate things. Now, though, I think it's going to work out so much better this way." He pulled Lauren in and kissed her cheek, her face scrunching up distastefully at the contact. "See, I know Lauren here had a thing for you a while back, and we all know how hard it is to turn down a piece of ass like her. So, I'm thinking maybe you didn't turn it down. Especially in favor of a cold fish like Ali. I mean, she doesn't even swallow. It's the least she could do, am I right?" He smirked at me, and it fucking killed me not to rub in the fact that she'd done that for me from the beginning. But I needed to keep him talking not piss him off. "Maybe you've been running around behind Ali's back, and maybe she showed up here today and caught you with your side piece."

Ali still had one hand beneath the napkin while the other edged its way toward her crutch, propped against the wall beside her chair. It was impossible for me to signal her — to tell her not to do anything stupid — not with Keith's eyes boring a hole in my head. So I did my best to keep him talking while readying myself for whatever might happen and praying for the damn police to get here before all hell broke loose.

"So, you see this as, what? A murder-suicide thing?"

"Why not? Everybody knows bitches get crazy over cheating. And from what I've gathered about you, I doubt anyone would jump to your defense. You've got quite a track record with women. I'd be impressed if you hadn't ruined it all by falling for a frigid bitch. I have to call into question what kind of womanizer would waste his time on someone like her." He reached back, not looking as he ran the barrel up the inside of Ali's thigh, pushing the hem of her skirt as he did. "Then again, maybe you really did manage to wake that pussy up. Guess I'll find out soon enough." He sneered and dropped his other hand from Lauren's neck, moving it to fondle her breast.

I gritted my teeth hard enough to make them crack as I bit out, "There aren't enough bullets in that fucking gun to stop me from killing you with my bare hands if you don't get your hands off both of them, especially Alison. Now." Keith started to raise the gun from Ali's lap and I was poised to make a play for it when Ali — who thankfully picked up on my use of her full name — whipped up the crutch, slamming it into his hand on the upswing and into his head on the way down. He flung Lauren away, her thin body slamming into the wall. The gun clattered to the floor, skittering under the table as I lunged forward and tackled Keith, at a serious disadvantage with only one good arm.

We tumbled to the floor, and I slammed my injured shoulder hard into his jaw as we fell. Though the pain was excruciating, the sound of his jaw cracking was fucking worth it. He struggled under me, snarling and swearing but unable to shake me off. I could hear Ali and Lauren yelling back and forth as I reared back and landed another blow across his pathetic face. His left arm crossed in front of me as I tried to lift myself up, and I roared in agony as he connected with my shoulder, the pain traveling across my entire torso.

Fuck!

Before I could recover, another vicious blow hit like a bolt of lightning, accompanied by the distinct feel of the bone unseating from its socket. I clenched my jaw against the urge to cry out. It wasn't easy to bite it back, but I wasn't giving him the satisfaction.

You wanna play motherfucker? How's this?

I rammed my head forward, catching the bridge of his nose with the top of my head, and was rewarded with a satisfying crunch followed by a yelp of pain.

Just getting started.

I braced myself with my right arm, looking down into his blood-soaked face with something akin to glee. Pushing back suddenly, I used the momentum to strike out with a right cross as I fell forward, his blood hitting the wall behind us with a spattering sound. He pushed me off, blinking away the tears and blood in his eyes, trying to scurry away. I landed on my back, fighting for breath as I prepared to give chase.

Keith was half-standing when Lauren spun and leveled the gun on him. "Don't move, asshole. Don't even blink or I swear to God, I'll blow your puny little brain out the back of your head." Her voice shook, but her hold on the gun was surprisingly steady as she stood over him. Despite my reservations about the woman, I was kind of proud of her right then.

With 'Needle Dick' neutralized, Ali pulled herself to her feet and hopped over to where I lay, plopping down beside me with no regard for her injured foot. Her eyes and hands were everywhere, checking for wounds, I presumed. Her voice was high and panicked as she ran her hands over my chest. "Where are you hurt? Where is all the blood coming from?"

I had to glance down to see what she was talking about. The front of my shirt was covered with blood, but not mine. "Shh, Ali." I told her, rubbing my hand over her arm. "It's not my blood, it's his. I'm fine. Well," I winced, sitting up, "I'll be needing to get my shoulder reset but other than that, I'm fine."

She stood and leaned against the chair-back, offering me a

hand up. I slipped my hand in hers and made sure to do the brunt of the work myself, not wanting to pull her down with me. Once I was on my feet, I kissed her hand and stepped over to Lauren. "Are you okay?"

She nodded, never looking away from the pathetic bastard cowering on the floor before her. "I am now. Thank you, both of you. If you hadn't showed up..."

I slid an arm around her shoulders, feeling the need to comfort her. "If we hadn't been here, he still would have gotten his ass kicked. Of that, I have no doubt." I gave her shoulder a squeeze and let go, reaching for the gun. "How about I take this, and you go open the door for the police?"

"The police?" She hadn't seen Ali place the call.

"Yeah, I called while everyone was distracted. They should be here any time. I'd go let them in, but I think I broke my crutch over dumbass's head." She glowered at Keith.

Lauren smirked and handed me the gun, making sure to keep it pointed at Keith at all times. She patted my arm on the way by. "I'll go wait for the cavalry. The second cavalry, that is. You and Ali were the first." She stopped to squeeze Ali's hand on the way out, the women exchanging warm smiles.

When she was gone, I stared down at Keith. "It looks like you'll be trading your tailored suits for prison orange. I wonder what your bosses at GFS are going to think."

His defiant stare was comical given the amount of bruising and blood covering his face. "I'll be out before Christmas. I never fired a shot, and you can't even prove it's my gun. All we have here is a domestic disturbance."

I made a tsking sound and shook my head. "I'm sure the 911 tape of you describing how you intended to kill us will send you away for a while. Plus, arson carries more than a three-month sentence."

"Arson?" He and Ali said in unison.

Not bothering to address his pathetic attempt to sound

innocent, I spoke to Ali. "Oh yeah. I was coming in here to tell you that we missed the last few pictures from the game camera. Turns out Keith paid a little visit to the house right before the fire. He's the one that started it." He paled at the mention of pictures, saying nothing further as the wail of sirens drew closer to the house. "If all that isn't enough to impress your bosses, I could tell them about your little embezzling habit. My investigator has definitely earned his paycheck these past few weeks." Feigning like I was sharing a secret, I held his eye and dropped my voice to a whisper that could still be heard by everyone in the room. "Your little girlfriend from the gala works in accounting, doesn't she? I'm betting she'll toss you right under the bus to save herself some jail time."

He sat there bleeding on the floor and looking for all the world like he was wishing we'd just shot him and gotten it over with.

Not getting off that easy, asshole.

Ali looked over at him contemplatively for a moment before meeting my eye. "What do we do about Lauren and Teach?"

Just as the sound of footsteps echoed through the house, I bent closer to his face and whispered, "I'll see to it that your time behind bars is excruciating if you so much as breathe one damn word of whatever you had on Lauren and her uncle. And you better pray no one else lets it slip either. If it comes out by any means aside from their own admission, I'll assume it was you and start calling in favors. Within twenty-four hours, you'll be the penitentiary's newest social butterfly." I met his widened eyes with an unblinking stare of certainty. "You'll get a taste of what you had planned for Ali and Lauren. Only these guys will be packing way more dick. You understand me, Keith?"

He nodded weakly and looked almost relieved when the police and EMTs stormed in.

I laid the gun on the table and stepped back out of the way. Once the officers verified who needed apprehending, Ali,

Lauren, and I were escorted to the living room to give our statements. Given Keith's connection to the fire, we did a two-for-one and spent the next several hours wrapping things up. Ali's lip didn't require stitches, and I managed to talk one of the paramedics into resetting my injured shoulder so I could avoid a trip to the hospital. Somehow it wasn't as bad the second time around.

But it still hurt like hell.

When it was all over, we stood on the porch with Lauren, having long ago watched Keith be taken out in handcuffs. Ali hesitated, studying Lauren before turning to me. "You know, Teach is going to be gone for a few more days. I don't like the idea of leaving Lauren here alone all that time."

Following her train of thought I nodded, looking at Lauren. "She's right. You don't have to stay here alone. We can wait for you to pack a few things, and you can go with us to Gran's for the week. She has plenty of room and cooks enough to feed an army. She'd be thrilled to have someone else to look after."

Tears welled in her eyes at our unexpected invitation, but she shook her head, smiling. "Thank you. I appreciate the offer, I really do, but I think I'm going to stay here and follow through with my promise. Teach trusted me to run the diner while he's gone this week, and I don't want to let him down. It meant a lot to have him ask me to manage the place, you know?"

Ali smiled warmly, nodding. "It's a big responsibility. And I know you'll do great." She gathered the woman in a friendly hug, doing that side-to-side thing again. Pulling back, she said, "But don't hesitate to call if you change your mind. The invitation stands."

I reached out to take Lauren's hand, this time my smile was entirely genuine. "I just wanted to let you know that I had a little talk with Keith before the cops came in. Your secret, whatever it is, is safe. Keith won't be breathing a word to anyone."

Her bottom lip quivered as she choked out her thanks.

I just shook my head and pointed at Ali. "It was her idea. I was just doing what she wanted. And I may have taken pleasure in making the little maggot squirm one more time before they hauled him out." I leaned down and looked at both women, my expression fierce as I recalled their ordeal. "I want you both to know that as long as there was breath in my body, he never would have touched either of you." I damn well meant that. Every single word.

Neither of them spoke, choosing quiet hugs over further conversation.

A few minutes later Ali and I piled back into the truck, finally on our way out of the tiny town, the mountains in the rearview, and the future sprawling out ahead.

THE WEEK AT Gran's went better than I ever could have hoped — so much so that we ended up staying on for an extra week. Ali and Gran only butted heads once or twice, each time managing to come to a compromise, or what I called a split decision.

Talia called every afternoon, and Ali spoke to Jeffrey regularly, happily relaying the news that her dad was finally seeing someone. Seeing him smiling into his phone at the hospital that day had given me that impression, but it wasn't my place to mention it to Ali. I knew he'd tell her in his own time.

Spencer had come to visit and brought Ali's canvases, earning him a huge hug and teary thanks. He'd blushed with embarrassment and waved off the gratitude, telling her it was what family did for each other.

And we had the best family in the world.

We sat in Gran's living room the afternoon after his visit, Ali and me on the plush floral sofa, and Gran to our left on the matching love seat. It was the same furniture she'd had as long as I could remember, and it still looked brand new. The fact that she had insisted on making Ali a little nest on that sofa spoke volumes about her fondness for my girl. No one had ever slept on that couch. Ever. Gran said it flattened the cushions. But she'd lovingly tucked Ali into a pile of home-made quilts and refused to let her move for the first couple of days.

Ali handed Gran and I each a brown paper covered canvas, an ethereal smile on her face.

Gran opened hers first, slowly tearing the paper away. She nearly dropped it as a startled sob tore from her throat. She looked at it through teary eyes for a moment, one hand clutched tightly to her chest before turning it around for me to see.

The scene Ali had painted stole my breath away. It was the lake, as expected, with the willow and the pier so expertly brushed it looked like a photograph. It was spectacular in its detail, the colors vivid and sharp but what made it truly breathtaking was the expertly rendered image of a woman standing beneath the willow, smiling peacefully as she looked out over the water.

My mother.

I looked from the canvas to Gran, eyes burning as I blinked back tears. She met my eye and smiled, turning the painting back around and reaching a hand out to Ali. "Darling girl, this is the most precious thing I've been given since my grandsons were born. Thank you can't even begin to cover it." She stood and pulled Ali into a hug, kissing her cheek and whispering softly to her before turning to leave the room, blowing me a kiss on the way out.

Ali watched her leave with a fond smile before turning to

me. "Gran said she thought we should be alone for a while. I think maybe she needed a minute herself."

She reclaimed her spot beside me on the couch, slipping the wrapped painting from my lap. "I should probably help you with this. It's not exactly a one-handed job." The endearing blush that crept up her neck would never get old. "Um, I mean... Oh, screw it. You know what I mean." She chuckled, the sound of her laughter somehow breaking the tension that had crept into my limbs.

She turned the canvas over, pulling the thin strips of tape off the thick brown paper. Once the back was open, she turned it right-side-up and placed it back in my lap, slowly sliding the covering away. I'd thought seeing Gran's painting had prepared me for what mine would be.

I was wrong.

The image was an up-close rendering of the lake, its depiction so real I expected to feel water dripping from my fingers as I trailed them over the surface. There in the lake my mother and my twelve-year-old self floated side by side, our fingers entwined to hold us close to one another, matching looks of serenity on our faces. The likeness was absolutely astonishing. Not only did she manage to capture my mother's face, every freckle, every curve, every fleck of gold in her hazel eyes; she also depicted me at twelve in such a way that I felt like I was back there. It felt more and more like a memory the longer I looked at it. I held something real from my past recreated in a tangible way to remind me of the happiest time of my childhood.

"I hope you don't mind that I used some of the pictures from the box Gran left you." She leaned into my shoulder, the warmth of her body blanketing me as I shook my head, too entranced to speak as I trailed my fingers lightly over my mother's cheek.

I'd heard people say that a true artist captures the soul of their subjects and, looking at the incomparable gift I'd just been given, I finally knew what that meant.

~

ONCE EVERYONE'S EMOTIONS leveled off, we settled into a comfortable coexistence. Gran hovered and worried too much, but we loved her for it, and I was quite frankly glad to have her where I could keep an eye on her. Though I had to admit I kind of liked her new ink; a clever depiction of a ball of wadded up paper that was made more realistic by the wrinkled flesh beneath. The caption beneath it read 'Screw the rules'.

Despite understanding the sentiment behind it, I still worried about her insistence on acting like a teenager. I might have even exaggerated my injury a bit to keep her from going to karaoke night. I suspected she was on to me, but she never balked. She stayed right by my side, fussing over me like I was a child. It was nice.

And I'd probably pay dearly for it later.

Mostly, we all talked and ate and rested. Gran and I reminisced a lot, talking openly about my mother for the first time since her death, the paintings having left us somehow freed. It was nice hearing her say my mom's name without hesitating out of fear of upsetting me. I hadn't realized just how much Gran had needed that; to talk about her with me. It was nice, remembering without the pain. So much went off track the summer my mother died — altering the man I would become — but being with Ali and facing my past gave me the feeling that I was somehow finding my way to being who I could have been.

My summer in Denson had affected me in ways I'd never anticipated and, damn, I was glad of it.

We discussed what to do about the house. Rebuild or redesign? Maybe both; maybe neither. Gran still said the house was never the point, so she refused to make a decision, leaving *my* house and *my* land up to me now that I was ready to offi-cially claim my inheritance.

I had a few ideas, but I wasn't sharing just yet.

We talked with Vanessa and played with Daniel when they stopped by to visit, both of them looking especially happy when Daniel shared the news that his daddy was sleeping at home again. Vanessa had been incredibly relieved to know she hadn't been the cause of the fire. She and I were in a good place again, maybe even better than before.

Ali and I still didn't know how we were going to deal with our return to our regular lives, having thought we still had a few weeks left in the build to figure it out. She seemed intrigued by the idea of moving to Richmond but was hesitant to leave Talia.

There was so much still left to figure out, so many possibili-ties. No matter what we decided, we'd be together, on that we were both in agreement. And for now, that was all I needed to know.

Toward the end of the week, Gran left to go out with her friends for bingo night, at least that's where she said she was going. I had my doubts. But her absence meant Ali and I were alone in the house for the first time since our arrival.

Seizing the opportunity, she and I did something we'd been dying to do for two weeks.

We snuggled on the couch and watched old corny comedies, content with the closeness of our bodies. We were unconcerned with going any further until we knew we were both healed enough to do it right. And do it right *we would*, but until then, having her fall asleep with her head on my chest was close enough to ecstasy for me.

It was home.

EPILOGUE

Denson

THE LATE-OCTOBER breeze was cool and crisp, a far cry from the relentless heat I'd grown accustomed to while working here over the summer. The sun was barely peeking over the distant mountains, the first stirrings of crickets announcing the arrival of evening.

I stepped out of my truck and took in the cleared lot where the house once stood, its chance at completion thwarted a second time. Nothing was left but a gaping hole that I once would have seen as a defeat, now viewed as a fresh start.

Everything was falling into place. Ali had agreed to move to Richmond after Talia assured her that she was fine on her own and the distance wasn't enough to keep them from seeing each other often. I'd taken the contract with the amusement park and, after taking one look at Ali's work, they'd commissioned Ali as well. Once we finished this installation, there was the possibility of traveling to their other parks to help with coordinating attractions. The idea of travel excited us both.

After news of Keith's arrest broke, GFS had burned up Ali's phone trying to make amends but she wasn't interested. Her heart was never in it, so it was easy to walk away. And she'd done it with a clean slate and an offer for a glowing recommendation, should she need it.

The contract with the theme park suited her just fine, though. She was already excitedly working on sketches and collaborating with the park owners to set up a special weekend to benefit the Outreach Hospice with a portion of the park's sales going to the charity. I'd never seen anyone smile so much.

And, as always, it was contagious.

Ali came around the front of the truck, threading her arms around me from behind, the warmth of her body as familiar to me as ever and still alluring enough to stir my desire. I covered her hands with my own, pulling them up to my mouth to kiss her palms before releasing them from my grasp.

She moved to my side and leaned in, nudging me playfully. "So? Are you going to tell me your idea or not? You brought me all this way without so much as a hint. I thought we'd be looking at blueprints in your office or something. What's this brilliant idea you have for the rebuild?" She pursed her lips, pouting.

The drive to Denson had been entertaining, at least for me. She tried everything she could think of to get me to talk. I hadn't cracked, though, even when she offered to do something very unsafe at such high speeds. That one had been tempting. We hadn't made love in weeks. Between my shoulder and her still healing lungs, it just hadn't felt right to push things.

Ali had gotten her all-clear from the doctor that morning, and my shoulder was fine as long as I didn't try to heft a sledge-hammer; a mistake that I wouldn't make twice.

She'd looked disappointed when I suggested a trip to Denson, that naughty gleam in her eye making it all too clear what she would have rather spent the evening doing. She finally caved at my insistence and here we were just a couple hours later, her filled with confusion and me filled with excitement.

I laced my fingers through hers and smiled, pulling her along as I walked. "I told you it would be worth the wait, didn't I? Just a couple more minutes, I promise."

"Why are we going to the lake? It's nearly dark out. I thought we were here so you could show me your big idea about the house?"

"Patience, Alison, patience. You'll understand in a minute." I could barely contain my excitement, having to force myself to maintain a leisurely pace when all I wanted to do was barrel down the path and into my future.

"What's that noise? Is there an engine running?"

I grinned. "Maybe."

She huffed indignantly but kept pace beside me, her curiosity outweighing her annoyance.

We came into the clearing, and I slowed, letting her get half a step ahead as the willow tree came into view. She came to a sudden halt gasping loudly and gripping more tightly onto my hand. "Oh, Clay! It's beautiful."

The entire willow glowed with light, from the trunk to the branches to every pendulous limb; every inch was wrapped in soft white light. The branches swayed softly, the golden color of its autumn-kissed leaves amplifying the glow.

The same glow that reflected so dazzlingly in Ali's eyes.

I gave her a minute to take it all in, silently thanking our friends and family for all the work they'd put into this endeavor. Though we could hear the generator, it was tucked far back into the wood line, giving an almost magical feel to the scene before us.

Seeing tears beginning to form in her eyes, I shook my head, tugging her forward. "No, no. You can't start crying on me now. You haven't seen the best part yet."

She looked from me to the willow, an expression of wonder on her beautiful face. Nodding, she gave my hand a squeeze, and we made our way together to the place we thought of as our spot, awash in the glow of thousands of lights.

I parted the lighted limbs and stood aside for her to enter our canopied love nest. I moved in behind her and placed my hand at the small of her back, smiling to myself as I took in the large blanket spread over the ground. Off to one side sat an ice bucket, complete with a chilled bottle of wine and two glasses. I hadn't thought to request that, so someone went above and beyond making this night perfect.

And perfect it would be.

I made my way onto the blanket, motioning for Ali to join me. When she did, I took a seat and then stretched out on my back, holding one arm out for her to nestle in beside me.

She looked down with a radiant smile and lowered herself alongside me, tucking herself close as we looked up into the illuminated canopy above us. "You were right — this is the most beautiful thing I've ever seen." She whispered in wonderment.

"It's definitely impressive, but it can't even begin to compare to the extraordinary beauty I see every time I look at you. Everything about you is stunning, remarkable, exceptional." I spoke softly, reverently. "Right now, you're seeing the glow of thousands of lights... and all I see is you."

She lifted herself on her elbow to see my face, the words she'd intended to say dying on her lips as her eyes locked onto the tiny box sitting on my chest, directly over my heart.

I laid there watching her, the myriad of emotions playing over her features as her gaze lingered on my offering. "Take it, it's yours." I told her. Whether I spoke of the box or the over-flowing heart beneath, either way it belonged to her.

With trembling fingers, she lifted the box and reclaimed her spot snuggled into my side. She tentatively opened the hinged lid, and I heard her breath catch in her throat. The surrounding light glinted in the antique diamond's surface as Ali traced her fingertips over it. "Was it your mother's?"

"No. Much as I loved my mother, as much as I love her still, I wouldn't want the kind of marriage she had with my father. There was no love, no connection between them. I don't have one single memory of them laughing together or holding hands." I reached over and skimmed the band with my fingers. "This is the ring my grandfather gave to Gran. When I told her I intended to ask you to be my wife, she said it would mean a great deal to her to have you wear it."

My heart nearly stopped when Ali sat the open box back onto my chest.

Thinking it was a refusal; I forced a swallow and fought to keep my composure.

Then she lifted her left hand, holding it straight above us so that the lighted branches served as a backdrop. "You're supposed to do the honors, Mr. McGavran." She teased.

The breath I'd been holding whooshed out of my lungs and I laughed with relief. "Shall I present it to you on one knee, Miss Walker?"

I started to sit up, but she put her hand on my arm, pulling me back down. "No. I've never been one for formality, you know that. Just lay here beside me under our beautiful tree, we can improvise the rest."

I settled back down beside her, pulling her left hand to the spot over my heart. "Alison Walker, I will never be able to properly articulate just how much you mean to me. The beating heart under your fingers now has a purpose because of you. Like the rest of me, it was going through the motions; filled with life but barely living. My entire existence was a reaction to the past, never living in the now or thinking of the future."

I slid the ring from the box and held it at the tip of her finger. "These last few months with you changed that, changed me. Now all I can think about is building a future; with you. I want to give you your dream house and fill it with pieces of us. My home is wherever you are, but I very much want to build us a place that will be ours, even if we can't be here all the time. For the first time in my life, I want to build something of my own. A home, a life, a future... And I want to build it all with you." I slipped the band around her finger. "Alison, will you marry me?"

She cupped my jaw raising herself onto her elbow once more, the gold band on her finger cool against my skin. Her soft lips grazed my own as she whispered, "Yes."

I pulled her into my arms, crushing her against my chest as I pulled her mouth to mine. I kissed her breathless, not able to control my desire. I pulled away long enough to roll her to her back and claimed her mouth once more.

After a few intense minutes, I was able to rein it in enough to take my time. It may have been weeks since I'd last felt her beneath me, but tonight was about more than making up for lost time. It was about savoring every single moment with her, from now until I drew my last breath.

I made love to my fiancé slowly, taking my time and pouring every ounce of my love for her into every caress, every taste, every thrust.

When we lay sated in each other's arms sometime later, I whispered. "I have another surprise for you."

I could actually hear her smile as she sighed. "Are you trying to spoil me, Mr. McGavran?"

"It would be my great honor to do so, Mrs. McGavran, but it's nothing as extravagant as the first gifts of the evening." She kissed my chest as I disentangled myself, pulling her to her feet beside me. I slipped on my jeans and pulled my t-shirt over her head to ward off the chill in the air that came with the Autumn. "Come on, it should be right over here."

I parted the hanging lights at the other side of our little nest and breathed a sigh of relief when I saw the large box waiting for us. I pointed it out to Ali, urging her to go over and open it. She tiptoed through the cool grass, her bare backside peeking from beneath the hem of my shirt and looking gorgeous in the light.

She pulled the bow from the top of the box and opened the flaps, leaning in to see into the shadowy depths.

When she realized what lay inside, she looked over at me, eyes shining with quickly forming tears. I joined her beside her engagement present, smiling softly as I looked into the box, my future wife weeping happy tears at my side.

I never would have guessed so much joy could be brought by a length of rope and a shiny new tire.

The End

Keep reading for a sneak peek at the next title in the Broken series… Flawlessly Broken

FLAWLESSLY BROKEN SNEAK PEEK

Spencer

TWO WEEKS.

What the hell was I going to do with two solid weeks?

I sat behind my sleek, cherry desk, looking over the neatly-stacked files in my outbox. My inbox stood empty on the other side. Mocking me. How was it possible that only a few months ago I had more on my proverbial plate than I could handle, and now I had nothing? Absolutely nothing.

Brant—one of my business partners and a close friend for many years—strolled in with a smile on his face, not a care in the world. He took a handful of chocolates from the bowl on my desk before plopping himself into the soft leather chair across from me. "It's just about quitting time isn't it, Spence? You ready to start your vacation?"

I tapped a pen on my blotter and glanced at the clock, not feeling nearly as chipper as my friend. "I wouldn't call it a vacation. A delay, yes. An inconvenience? Absolutely. This 'vacation' is throwing off the entire build schedule."

He let out a soft chuckle and shook his head, crunching on the last of the candy-coated chocolates before leaning forward. "Come on, man. It's not your fault the owner didn't have his shit together in time. It's only two weeks, Spence, and the build will still finish on time despite the delays. We've never missed a deadline." His brows rose a bit as he nodded toward the pen in my hand. "You're too wound up. You need to let loose for a while, enjoy the time away from the office. Go out and do something that would make Clay proud."

Clay—my best friend since I was ten and our other partner —was away working on a solo project for the next couple of months. Well, not entirely solo. His fiancé, Ali, was working on the project with him. They had until the end of spring to get everything done, as the amusement park that had contracted their artistic skills would be opening at the beginning of June.

Before Clay's transformation into a one-woman man, he was quite the party boy and manwhore. Now, he only had eyes for Ali. I was glad that he'd finally found some happiness. He deserved it after all he'd been through.

I shook my head at Brant, laughing for the first time all day. "I don't think it's a good idea for me to assume the recently-vacated role of manwhore. Look what happened to Clay. He had crazies coming out of the woodwork."

"Yeah, but he had a lot of damn fun for a while there and still found Ali despite all that."

"So, you think I'll find the love of my life by first nailing anything in a four-inch heel? I don't think it usually works that way."

The leather creaked as Brant shifted in the chair, placing his elbows on his knees, hands clasped between them. "I'm not saying to sleep around. I'm saying go out and have some damn fun. Have a few drinks, dance with a beautiful stranger, whatever gets your heart pumping. You spend too much time behind this desk." He slapped the desktop for emphasis. "It's like you're chained to it or something. There's more to life than what goes on behind these walls."

I narrowed my gaze, looking him in the eye. "Where the hell did that come from? You just said more in five minutes than you usually do in a week. I thought you were the quiet one around here, so what gives?" His sheepish look confirmed my suspicions. "Fucking Clay put you up to this, didn't he?"

His silence was all the answer I needed.

Tap tap tap. The pen was hitting the blotter in rapid succession now. "So, he asked you to what? Babysit me?"

"No. He just knew you wouldn't want to take the time off, even if you would be the only one in the office. He asked me to help get you out of here for a while. That's all. You've been busting your ass, juggling more than any one person should. He just thought you needed some time to relax."

"And you agree?"

He shrugged. "I think he has a point. You do take on more than you should and that puts a lot of stress on you."

"That's my business, not his and not yours. I'm a grown-ass man." I was trying not to snap at him. Brant was just the middleman in this and getting pissed off at him wouldn't help the situation.

His eyes met mine and he nodded. "I know you don't like what Clay did but just think about it from his point of view."

"How so?" I scowled indignantly.

"He and I spend all of our time in the field, on job sites, getting our hands dirty. At the end of the day, we get to go home and wash all that away. When you go home you're still taking calls from clients, working on scheduling, balancing the books... it never stops for you. You're on the job 24/7 and we both feel like shit because there's nothing we can do to help. I think that's what Clay was trying to do, help. He wanted to make sure you got some down time because, more than anyone else, you deserve it."

I dropped the pen onto the desk with a groan. "How the hell am I supposed to be mad now?"

Brant just smiled.

~

ON THE WAY HOME, with a seemingly endless expanse of free time stretching out before me like blacktop surrounded by barren field, I called Clay.

He picked up before the second ring, as if he'd anticipated the call. "Hey, Spence. I was just about to pick up the phone to call you. You must be clairvoyant."

I harrumphed softly, the last of my annoyance slipping away. I still had to bust his balls, though. "You sure you weren't going to call Brant instead? Maybe get an update on operation 'Spencer needs a life'?"

There was laughter in his voice when he replied. "It was all his idea, I swear."

"Yeah, right."

He tried again. "Okay, it was Ali. You know how women are." Ali's voice rang out in the background but I didn't quite catch what she said. I did, however, hear a thud and Clay's startled 'ouch.' Served him right. "Okay, okay. It was all me. I'm a terrible friend for wanting you to enjoy your vacation. God, what an asshole I am."

"It's okay. I'm well aware that you're an asshole. At least you mean well. Usually."

His voice was finally serious when he said, "So, I'm forgiven?"

"Yeah, fucker, you're forgiven. Now why were you about to

call me? Ali's there with you, so I know you're not in need of bail money."

He blew out a breath and hesitated.

Oh shit.

He never did that pause-for-effect thing. Hated it. This must be bad.

The soft rustling of a hand covering the phone was followed by a moment of quiet discussion, I assumed with Ali. Clay's voice finally came back on the line, softer and unsure. "I kind of need a favor. Well, we both do."

"What kind of favor?"

"You remember Talia, right?"

I remembered Talia. She was Ali's best friend and—before Ali moved in with Clay—roommate. We'd met for the first time in Denson the night of the fire that had nearly killed Ali. Talia had been a wreck and I had done what I could to keep her spirits up between trips to visit Ali in the ICU. "Of course I remember her."

More hesitation, then, "I told you that she owns a restaurant in D.C., right?"

"Yeah."

"Well, there was some sort of issue there a couple days ago, something with a restaurant critic, and she hasn't been into work since. She won't answer her phone, not even for Ali. No one knows where she is or what exactly happened. All we know is that she texted the manager and told her to take over until further notice. She's been totally off the grid ever since."

From what I remembered about Talia, she wasn't the type to shirk her responsibilities. Something serious had to have happened. But I wasn't sure what Clay was asking of me. "Okay, I'm assuming you want my help, right? What do you need me to do? You want me to try and track her credit cards or something?" I knew my way around a computer, had a few tricks up my sleeve that could help locate her.

He sounded relieved. "You can try the cards but your best bet is her phone. Ali says she carries it with her at all times in case of an emergency at the restaurant."

I told him to text me the number and I'd call as soon as I got home and checked it out.

Half an hour later I had him back on the line. "So, I tracked the number you gave me and got a location." I rattled off the street address that coincided with the red dot on my computer screen.

He sighed in apparent relief. "That's the address of her apartment."

I'd thought it sounded familiar. I should have remembered since I'd been there a few months ago helping Ali move her things out.

I heard Ali's voice in the background for a moment before she came on the line. "Spencer?"

"Yeah. Hey, Ali."

Her voice was strained and afraid. "She's at the apartment? You're sure?"

"Yep. I'm looking at the signal right now. If she has the phone with her, she's at the apartment."

"I know you have all these cool tech skills... can you activate the camera on the phone or something? Anything to verify that she's all right?"

I blinked stupidly for a second, not understanding the desperation in her voice. "I'm not quite that skilled, I'm sorry to say." She sniffed. Shit, was she crying? "Ali, I'm sure she's okay. If you're that worried, can you have a neighbor go and check on her? Or maybe a friend from work?"

Another sniff. "There's no one I trust to check on her. The only neighbors we're close with are the elderly couple who share our floor, and they vacation in Florida from November through April. Anyone else would have to be buzzed in and I doubt she would do that if she won't even answer her phone." She paused for a second. "Unless..."

"Unless what?"

"I could call the front desk and have them let someone in. They all know me, and I could convince them that whoever I send is there to water the plants or something. I don't live there anymore, but my name is still on the lease. Plus, the doormen love me because I bring them presents and snacks, especially during winter."

Clay's voice filtered through the line, and although I didn't catch it all, I could have sworn he said... "Wait. Did Clay just say Stony the Sloth? What the hell is he talking about?"

She clicked her tongue and told Clay to shush. "It's nothing. He doesn't like one of the doormen. Swears the guy is high every time he sees him, but that's beside the point." The line went silent for so long I had to check my phone to see that we were still connected. When she finally spoke, it was with quiet pleading in her voice. "If I call ahead and get you cleared, will you go check on her for me? I know it's a long drive, but you're the only one I trust to do it. I'd do it myself but I can't leave here. We won't be able to grab a day away for at least a couple of weeks."

Me?

She wanted me to go check on Talia? I barely knew the woman. I mean, sure, we spent some time together at the hospital and again when we helped with Clay's proposal to Ali at the lake, but that didn't mean it was okay for me to just show up on her doorstep. The doorstep. Aha! I just found my way out. "Let's assume I go. Getting me into the building won't get me in the door. What if she refuses to answer? I can't very well kick the door in."

"Damn." She sounded deflated momentarily but suddenly sucked in a big breath. "Wait, they have a spare key to each apartment in the office. I can just tell them that I forgot to give you my key and ask that they let you have the spare." The hope in her voice was hard to ignore. "Please, Spencer. She never ignores my calls. Ever. The longer I go without hearing from her, the more afraid I get. If you don't go, I'm coming home to check on her myself, my contract be damned."

Clay started protesting loudly in the background, not wanting her to lose her dream job.

Shit.

Looked like I was headed to D.C.

~

Somewhere between Richmond and D.C.

HOW DID I LET myself get talked into this?

Yeah, Ali said she'd cleared the way and that Talia would be too polite to kick me out of the apartment, but I still wasn't convinced my going there was a good idea. Although, given that Clay and Ali were stuck over four hours away, my nearly two hour drive wasn't such a big deal. Growing up in a moderately rural area—forty-five minutes from everywhere—I'd grown accustomed to long drives to get to a decent-sized city. Besides, I make the trip to D.C. all the time. It was fairly routine to meet with prospective clients there, actually, so the distance wasn't a problem.

The issue was that I had no clue what I would be walking in on when I got there.

Despite Ali's assurances to the contrary, I was half-convinced that Talia was holed up at the apartment with a man, maybe enjoying having the place to herself now that Ali had moved in with Clay.

My luck, I'd walk in on something I'd have to spend the

next twenty years trying to erase from my memory.

Images of whips and ropes flashed like lightning through my mind, making me cringe as my grip tightened on the steering wheel. Not that I had any reason to think she was into that, but one never knew. Just because she looked sweet and innocent...

I wasn't sure what was more disturbing, the thought of walking in on something illicit or the idea of having to live with the image for the rest of my life.

I forcibly shook the train of thought from my mind, rolling my shoulders to break the tension and sinking into the plush leather seat of my methodically-restored 1971 Chevelle. It was my most prized possession these days, my favorite place to spend time. Just me and the road, the roar of the engine chasing away everything else. It had an impressive sound system—accurate retro styling with updated technology—but I rarely switched it on. The deep rumble emitted by the exhaust was better than any music I'd ever heard and I respected the hell out of it.

Once I shifted my focus from worrying about what I'd find at my destination, I was able to enjoy the ride. The Chevelle was the main reason I never balked at having to travel for meetings. That car was my sanctuary. My escape.

And, unfortunately, it usually got me from A to B much faster than I wanted.

Before I had time to revisit my earlier misgivings, I was sitting in front of Talia's apartment building and hoping like hell that I wasn't making a mistake by getting involved.

I stepped out of the car and pulled my jacket tighter around myself as I approached the entrance. The chill in the air was a reminder that, although spring was nearly upon us, winter still lingered.

My breath came out in thick plumes as I hurried into the lobby. The place was somewhere between middle and upper class. Expensive flooring polished to a high shine, a reception desk made out of deep cherry, and beautiful artwork tastefully placed throughout. It was impressive, in a cold way.

I stepped over to the desk, catching the eye of the young man seated behind it as he absently set aside his phone. His reddish hair was long and stringy, tucked behind his ears and in need of a good wash. His light eyes were red-rimmed.

I flashed a smile and tipped my head toward him. "Hey. How's it going?"

His expression was tired and a bit distracted. He cast a longing glance at his phone before answering, "Not too bad. How can I help you?"

"My name is Spencer Erickson. I believe Alison Walker called ahead about me."

It was interesting watching the guy scouring his memory for the conversation with Ali. His brow crinkled and he was midway through shaking his head "no" when the fog lifted and he snapped his fingers, seeming momentarily startled by the sound.

He wore no name tag, but I was betting this was Stony the Sloth.

"Oh, yeah. You're the dog walker or plant waterer or something, right?"

Close enough. I smiled to hide my snicker. "Yep. That's me. Ali said you'd have the spare key for me when I got here."

He rummaged around on the desk, twice grazing a hand over his phone to check for messages before finally pulling the key marked 7B and handing it over. "Here you go. You can't take it when you leave but I have it written down that you're authorized to use it so you don't have to get Ali to call each time you come to..." he stumbled to remember for a moment before adding, "do whatever you do. She told me it was okay."

I accepted the key, knowing full well that I wouldn't be needing to come back but not sharing that information with Stony. "Thanks, man. I'll drop it off on the way out."

He nodded, turning his attention back to his phone without further comment as I waited for the elevator.

Yep, I could see why Clay liked him so much.

~

I STEPPED OUT of the elevator on the seventh floor and just stood there for a minute. It was nearing eight o'clock. The relative silence in the hallway was broken by my growling stomach loudly reminding me that I'd skipped lunch, and dinner was long overdue. It would have to wait. Hopefully, I could make quick work of this little mission and grab something on my way back home.

The door to apartment 7B sounded hollow beneath my knuckles when I knocked.

It was a disconcerting sound, one that instantly brought forth images of an injured or ill Talia lying just on the other side of the door, unable to obtain help all this time.

Shit, I was turning into Ali.

My heart was beating a little faster as I raised my hand to knock again, ears acutely attuned to any hint of sound. If there was no answer after a reasonable amount of time, I would go in uninvited.

I may have had a key, but I preferred not to use it unless I had to.

Three more sharp raps followed by silence.

I was midway through an internal debate about my next move when I heard a rustling on the other side of the door. A few seconds later, it came again. I reached out and tapped the door, calling out to her. "Talia?" No response. "Talia? It's Spencer. Ali sent me to check on you, and I'm not supposed to leave until I see you. Open the door, okay? I just need to know that you're all right and then I can go. I promise."

The rustling sound came again, this time directly on the other side of the door. Talia didn't speak, but the door clicked open a moment later. Just an inch. Then the rustling sound began moving away.

I tentatively reached out and pushed the door open, not sure what to make of her lack of response. Her retreating form moved across the living room, her back to me as she sniffed quietly.

Shit. She was crying.

From the looks of the wadded-up Kleenex covering every flat surface, she had been crying for quite a while.

The floorplan was open, expansive even, with high ceilings and large windows. The living room was directly in front of me, spacious and comfortably furnished. There was a large couch against the wall to the left and a matching loveseat facing the windows. The long coffee table was dotted with wadded Kleenex, as was the small end table next to the love seat.

The kitchen lay to my far left, with its shiny stainless appliances and overhanging countertop that served as a bar, complete with cushioned chairs. Past the kitchen was a wide archway leading to the hallway and the bedrooms and bathrooms beyond.

It was a really nice place in a town where square-footage came at a premium. As a homebuilder, I would know.

I stepped fully into the apartment and closed the door, turning back just as she sank gracelessly into the plush love seat, still facing away from me.

Graceless was something Talia just didn't do. Not the few times I had been around her. It was one of the things I remembered most. She was flawless. Absolutely flawless in every movement, like a dancer. Tall and willowy, she seemed to float on air. It was mesmerizing.

But not tonight.

Tonight she moved like the weight of the world was on her shoulders and it was odd to see her trudge across the room that way. Wrong.

With slow measured steps, I approached the living room. I'd only been in the apartment once before to help Ali move. Talia hadn't been there at the time but the place had felt like her just the same. Warm and inviting, like the woman herself. Tonight, though, the place felt different as I made my way over to her. Empty. Hollow.

Just like her.

I tried not to let the tension I was feeling creep into my voice, not wanting to further upset her, but needing to know what was going on. "I hope you're not angry that Ali sent me. She's been worried about you. She said she's been trying to get in touch with you for days and when you didn't answer, she panicked."

Another sniff but nothing else.

I edged my way over to the couch, not wanting to crowd her, and took a seat. Her head was down, long blond locks obscuring my view of her face. She was hiding. Something about the gesture scared me. I needed to see her face; it was suddenly very important though I wasn't sure why. Maybe it was because I knew a little about the abuse Ali had once suffered at the hands of her ex. Was Talia hiding bruises? The thought sent a shot of rage through my system. If someone hurt her...

"Can you look at me, please?" My voice was soft, disarming.

She didn't move, just fidgeted with a scrap of paper that she'd plucked from the cushion beside her. I took a second to look around and realized that there were tiny pieces of paper all over the floor at her feet, scattered across the coffee table and end table, some of what I'd thought was tissue wasn't tissue at all.

"Talia, I came here as a favor to Ali, but frankly, you're

starting to scare me, too. I need you to say something. Please look at me."

If she didn't say or do something soon, I was going to go over there and move that curtain of hair myself.

"I'm sorry."

The words were so soft I wasn't sure I heard anything at all. I leaned forward, forearms on my knees as I studied her, waiting for something more.

"I didn't mean to scare anyone."

She spoke louder that time but her voice was off, her words slurred slightly. I looked around the apartment and spied a bottle of scotch on the kitchen counter, originally hidden from view by the raised bar. I was familiar with the brand. It was expensive and strong, a favorite of mine. From where I sat, it looked to be nearly empty. I turned back to her with a frown, poised to ask her about the bottle when I locked eyes with her for the first time.

Son of a bitch.

She'd swept her hair aside, finally revealing her face, and her expression was like a kick to the gut. Jesus. It was like looking at a stranger, none of Talia's usual spark was there. Her eyes were empty, devoid of any signs of life, flat. Thankfully, a quick scan of her features showed no bruising or obvious injury but that look...

If pain were to take the form of a person, she would be it.

It actually hurt to look at the expression on her face, stole my breath and made my pulse roar in my ears.

I moved without thought, instantly sinking into the cushion beside her and reaching for her hand. She didn't shy away, didn't seem to react at all. Her flesh was cold to the touch and I barely resisted the urge to rub her hand between both of mine, something my mother used to do when I was a boy and had been outside playing in the snow. "Talia, what happened? Did someone hurt you? Did you get bad news? What is it?"

She just shook her head, blinking with slow deliberation. Her light brown eyes remained shuttered long after her lids ascended. She looked right through me.

I had to try a different approach. "It's okay. You don't have to tell me but can you tell Ali? Where's your phone?"

She gestured absently toward the kitchen, unblinking.

It was all I could do to force myself to go retrieve it. I didn't want to leave her sitting there like that, but she needed to talk to someone and Ali was probably the best bet.

I scoured the countertop but didn't see the phone. I checked the entire kitchen without luck, and was just about to turn back to ask her if she was sure it was in the kitchen when a large bowl of dry rice caught my attention. On a hunch, I walked over and stuck a hand in the bowl, swirling it through the rice until I found what I was looking for. Talia's phone.

I tapped the home button as I made my way back to the love seat and found that the ringer was off, the little icon on the lock screen announcing the setting. I flipped the tiny switch on the side of the phone to turn it back on and looked over at Talia. "You got this wet?"

She didn't look at me. "Dropped it in the sink at the restaurant. It wouldn't work after that. Gina said to put it in rice." Her voice was flat and disinterested; monotone. Scary.

I had no idea who Gina was but she was right. The rice had worked. This also explained why she hadn't been answering anyone's calls. Although, one look at her told me that she probably wouldn't have anyway. "You have a bunch of texts and voicemails here, most of them are probably from Ali. Do you want to call her back now?"

She shook her head and reached for the phone. I handed it to her and watched as she flipped the switch on the side to put the phone back on silent, dropping it unceremoniously onto the end table at her side, a few torn bits of paper stirring from the motion and resettling on the floor.

Well, shit. Now what do I do?

"Okay, so you're not feeling chatty. That's fine. You can call Ali later." I cast a glance at the Scotch bottle on the kitchen counter. "How about something to eat? I can have something delivered. Maybe that would make you feel better." With no way of knowing how much she'd had to drink, the best course of action was to get some food into her, maybe some coffee if she was receptive.

"Not hungry," she said on a slow exhale, sounding exhausted. "You can fix us a drink, if you want. I'm not much company, though."

I considered for a minute, wheels turning in my mind. "Tell you what, I'll go make us a drink but you have to sip slow and talk in between. Doesn't have to be anything specific, just talk about whatever pops into your head because, if you're going to sit there in silence, I'll feel like I'm drinking alone and I hate to drink alone."

She looked at me then, her eyes showing their first signs of life since my arrival. "I don't like to drink alone, either." Her gaze traveled over my face, looking for something I couldn't fathom. She nodded absently, apparently finding whatever she sought. "I'll talk but only if it's a two-way street. No putting me on the spot. And no bullshitting me just to keep me talking. I can spot a con from a mile away." She turned away muttering. "Usually."

I was in no position to argue, so I simply nodded and got to my feet, angling toward the kitchen. "Okay, how about we start by you telling me who Gina is. You said she knew what to do to fix your phone. She a friend? Family?" While I verbally tap-danced around the questions I really wanted to ask, I checked the various cabinets looking for glasses.

"She's the manager at my restaurant and also a friend. She's worked for me for a couple years, starting as a bartender and working her way up. Not sure how I ever ran the place without her."

I located two rocks glasses and began pouring the drinks, pausing to take a quick peek in the refrigerator. *Aha.* There was a small vegetable tray on the second shelf that might entice her to eat. I grabbed it along with our glasses, balancing one glass precariously atop the tray on my way back to the living room. "So, Gina is taking care of the restaurant while you... I mean, in your absence? Ali mentioned that you hadn't been in for a couple of days."

She reached up and snagged her glass from the tray, avoiding my gaze. "Yeah. I told her that I needed her to take over. I assume Ali has talked to her by now if she knows how long I've been out."

There was guilt in her posture and her tone. I didn't like that. She was obviously hurting, regardless of the source, and no one was judging her for that. "Ali's just worried about you. She doesn't care how long you've been away from work. She's more concerned with the idea that you're going through something and she can't be here to help."

Talia's shoulders dropped and she took a long swallow of Scotch, saying nothing.

Maybe if she knew just how worried Ali was, she would give in and call her. "You know, she was going to blow off the rest of her contract to come back and check on you."

Her head jerked up and she stared at me, wide-eyed, as she swayed slightly in her seat. "She can't do that. That's a dream job for her. She's wanted a gig like that all her life."

"I'm sure that's true, but she has also been your friend all her life and that takes precedence." I didn't want Talia feeling guilty, but she needed to know that people cared about her and just how much they cared. Especially Ali.

"Do you think she would really do that? I don't want her to lose out on this opportunity because of me." Her expression had shifted from desolate to fearful in the blink of an eye. She'd never do anything to Ali's detriment, that much was clear.

I shook my head, placing a hand on her forearm to soothe her. "She absolutely would have, had I not agreed to come here to look in on you. For now she's staying put, but if she doesn't hear from one of us very soon, I have no doubt that she will be beating down that door." I pointed at it for emphasis.

She let out a relieved breath. "Okay." After taking another sip of her drink, she eyed me warily. "So, you were basically blackmailed into coming here, huh? That sounds like Ali," she scoffed. "I'm sorry you got roped into this. Not the best way to spend a Friday night is it?" Her brow crinkled as she looked around, momentarily confused. "It is Friday, right?"

The lost expression on her face was so cute, I had to chuckle. "Yes, ma'am. It sure is." I reached out and offered her the vegetable tray, thankful when she scooped up a few carrots. "And I didn't have anything planned, so it was really no trouble. Though I would feel better about coming if I thought I had helped you in some way."

"You did. You got me a drink." She smirked as she drained the last of the amber liquid. "And you're about to get me another."

STAY UP TO DATE

Join Anna's mailing list to remain up to date on new releases and be part of subscriber-only giveaways.

ABOUT THE AUTHOR

Anna Paige is the author of the Broken series; Broken Ground, Flawlessly Broken, and All the Broken Pieces, as well as the Thrill of the Chase series, and is currently working on the next installment.

She lives in a rural town in North Carolina where the only activity is the rhythmic color change of the solitary stoplight and a very real threat of being carried away by mosquitoes. The only alternative to terminal boredom is writing, making life interesting if only on the page.

Anna is happily married, with one amazing son and a pair of hilarious pets. When she's not writing, she's trying to make a dent in her TBR pile. Given that she's constantly adding new titles to the list, the chances of her ever finishing are slim.

And she's completely fine with that.

You can find/follow Anna here:

ACKNOWLEDGMENTS

Like most authors, I have been lucky enough not to have to take this journey alone. In the 14+ months since I wrote the first word of Broken Ground, I have found encouragement and support from many places — some of those places completely unexpected. I often struggle to properly express my gratitude, finding that 'thank you' isn't nearly enough. Just know that I appreciate, value, and am truly humbled by the support.

First and foremost, I would like to thank my husband, Shaun. For being my biggest supporter, my favorite sounding board, my safe place amid the chaos. Given that 'thank you' isn't enough after all you've done to help me achieve this dream, you can bet that 'I love you' will never be enough to express the depth of my feelings for you. Even when words fail, you have my unwavering adoration. It's you and me, babe. Always.

Valerie Lea — my person, my alpha/beta reader, my lifelong friend — Your encouragement and support made huge impact on this book, and on me. Long lunches, plotting over (too many) drinks, random messages at all hours of the day and night — you really are my 'person' and I wouldn't have it any other way.

Julie Jaret, without you this book would never have been finished, much less published. I was at a critical point in the writing process — the thin line between dogged pursuit of my dream and deleting every damn word; never to write again — you stepped in and made all the difference. You saved me from doubt and fear and frustration. You're my hero.

Trenda London, my beta reader turned content editor, I will

never be able to thank you enough for the countless hours you spent working with me on this book. I think you may be the only person on Earth who has read it as many times as me. Your feedback has been invaluable but it is your faith in me that made the biggest impact. From the bottom of my heart... thank you, my friend.

Beta readers Amanda Ward, Lisa Fay, Sally Johnson, Sandy Montemayor, Lesley Strausbaugh, Saleena Chamberlin, and Shasta Sonnabend — you ladies are fantastic. Every. Single. One. Of. You. Thank you all for taking the time to read and give me feedback. Your comments (all of them; good and bad) helped to transform my words into an actual story. More than one of you made me cry — you know who you are — and guess what? I still love you. I love you all.

My critique partners, Renee Kennedy and Lucy Lit, you ladies are amazing. Thank you so much for working with me. Whether we swapped a few chapters or entire manuscripts, your insights were honest and extremely helpful. Best wishes for bestsellers!

Kim Black, you amaze me. Between writing successful books and running your own business, you somehow found the time to gather and organize my beta group, design my cover (and teasers), and answer my endless string of questions about self-publishing. I was a stranger to you and you reached out to offer your help, time, and support. You are the type of person I aspire to be. You are a treasure and I am thankful for you every day.

Amy Donnelly, my editor, thank you for finding time to take on this 125k word beast. Not only have you done an awesome job, but — thanks to you — I now have a hilarious file filled with the comments you left throughout the process. I will refer to it whenever I need a reminder that at least one person out there thinks I'm funny.

Cassy Roop, your formatting skills are phenomenal. You

took Broken Ground on short notice and made it absolutely beautiful. Thank you so much. I can't wait to see what you do with my next book.

Claire Allmendinger, thank you for helping me figure out how to get started, for supporting me through my doubts, and for being the type of friend who checks up on me just because. You're the greatest.

Monique Tarver, the BookAddict Mom, thank you for all of your help spreading the word about this book and for your continued encouragement. You're beautiful inside and out, and I'm happy to call you my friend. Book friends are the BEST friends!

Speaking of book friends...

Jennie Simpson, you went from stranger to book friend to one of my best friends in a matter of months. I never expected to find you when I agreed to do a book swap but your friendship and support have meant more to me than I can ever say. You've encouraged and supported me, had my back when things went wrong, and given me a swift kick in the ass when I desperately needed it. I don't know what I'd do without you. I know you read through a lot of acknowledgements to find your name but that's only because I saved the best for last, my friend.

Printed in Great Britain
by Amazon